THE REVELATION OF THE ELDERS

BOOK 1 IN THE ELDERS SERIES

GILBERT S. MANE

National Library of Australia Cataloguing-in-Publication entry

Creator: Mane, G. S., author.

Title: The Revelation of the Elders / by G. S. Mane.

ISBN: 978-0-994-6153-2-9 (Paperback)

Subjects: Good and evil – Fiction. Australian Fiction

Delphian Books

(a division of New Frontier Creative Services Pty Ltd)

6 Merle Street, Epping NSW 2121 Australia

www.delphianbooks.com.au

For my father
Samuel Mane
(1922–2015)
The kindest and most generous of men
(the Yiddish is his fault)

and to my mother
Dawn Mane
(still withus)
Who is very proud of her son,
but found the first draft unreadable

If I am conspiring to control the world I'm making a poor job of it

In Response to the Accusation that I am Part of a Vast Jewish Conspiracy to Control the World

David Adès, 2014

TABLE OF CONTENTS

ACKNOWLEDGEMENTS

In 2009 I completed my first book, *7 Steps to Freedom,* a non-fiction work detailing some practical ways of increasing self-awareness. My wife, Sarah, suggested I try a novel next. So my first acknowledgment is to her. And not just for the suggestion. She has been my greatest support throughout the eight-year odyssey that both brought this story to fruition and resulted in the decision to become a full-time writer. She is truly an ever-present refuge in time of trouble.

I came up with a concept for a story which I thought would work. I took the idea, beloved of all conspiracy theorists, that there is a shadowy cabal of the powerful 'pulling the strings'; manipulating the markets, the politicians, and the wealth of the world, while poor shlubs like you and me toil away to fill their coffers. And I asked myself: What if it were true, but what if this secret group acted to protect the world, rather than exploit it?

I thought this would be a good basis for a story, so I cracked my knuckles, opened my laptop, and started typing. I wrote a couple of pages and the result was wooden, dull, flat, two-dimensional. I could go on.

I realized two things. First, I had no idea how to write a novel with an engaging plot, living characters, realistic dialogue; and second, that I had to find someone to teach me my craft.

So I started asking everyone I met if they knew of a good writer's course I could sign up for. My brother, David, told me of the Writer's Studio in Bronte, Sydney. For that, and for being a great friend and support as well, he gets my second acknowledgment.

But wait, there's more. A few months into the writing process I gave a chapter to a few people to read and got some enthusiastic feedback. When I gave it to David, he hunted around for a pencil, read it in silence all the while crossing through words and scribbling marginal notes. Then he handed it back to me and said: "Yeah, it's pretty good." I had found one of my editors! So double thanks to him for reading the third draft, suggesting changes, and giving it an enthusiastic tick.

And speaking of editors, Luke Carman, author of *An Elegant Young Man,* provided a timely and crucial Reader's Report of the first draft alerting me to some rookie mistakes. The result? Six months of rewriting and, I hope, a much improved story.

Mel Jewell then took the result and passed the finest of fine-tooth combs over the spelling and punctuation, and also pointed out sections where the narrative needed clarification. So Luke and Mel get acknowledgement numbers four and five.

A group acknowledgment goes to the sterling team at Delphian Books, Ron and Kristina Proft who, respectively, readied everything for an eventual e-launch, and did one final read through, just to settle my fears that I'd missed any typos and left in unexplained plot twists. And also to my web redesigner Karl Kaczmarczyk, with his characteristic Polish devotion to the lonely letters at the tail-end of the alphabet.

A very heartfelt acknowledgement is awarded jointly to Roland Fishman and Kathleen Allen of The Writer's Studio, where I did, indeed, learn my craft.

With their first course, 'Unlocking Creativity', I absolutely got what was written on the tin. I persevered, and they did too, for four more years under their expert tutelage.

And I met loads of great people there. Aspiring authors who had the courage to present their work to Roland's scrutiny, and for regular review by their fellow writers. This is a group that started as strangers and ended as intimates.

There are too many to acknowledge all individually but some I need to name for their special love and support: Ingrid, Kim, Wallace, Shereen and Fred; Rodolfo, who doubles as my Spanish teacher, and gets to hear and comment on new chapters as they emerge; and James and Ben, with whom I still meet to read and critique our writing, and eat Anzac biscuits and cake. And my biggest thanks in this elite group of Ninja Writers goes to Clare Gillis, who has the best idea for a novel ever, and who always brings a bit of sunshine and, with her two little girls, makes the best Anzac biscuits for Ben, James and me.

The final huge acknowledgement goes to you, the reader. I had a blast writing this story and getting to know the characters and cheer them on. I hope you do too.

Gilbert S. Mane,
Sydney, 2017

CAST LIST/DRAMATIS PERSONAE

The main characters in the book are listed here with a brief description.

Some characters who are merely mentioned and don't appear, and some who appear but have nothing to say for themselves are also listed, but there were lots of these so I may have overlooked a few.

Stern Family – LA California

Aaron "Ronnie" Stern: 18; High School Senior; go-along-to-get-along type; Katie Liebovitz is his girlfriend; Elder Power – healing

Mishi Stern: 14; Ronnie's sister; Middle School student; brainy, irascible, doesn't suffer fools, sharp-tongued; Best friend: Emma Schwartz; Elder Power – mind control

Reuben Stern: 52; Ronnie and Mishi's dad; Carpet Wholesale and Retail; quiet but smarter than he pretends to be; not an Elder

Doctor Miriam Stern: 46; their mom, Professor of Quantum Physics; eminent in her field; cool and competent, except where her family's safety is concerned; Elder Power – telekinesis, especially electrical devices

Liebovitz Family – LA California

Katie Liebovitz: 18; High School Senior; Aaron's girlfriend; smart, feisty, sharp; Elder Power – psycho-location, she can locate people she feels strongly about

Sam Liebovitz: 16; her brother; High School Junior; tech nerd; not an Elder

Donny Liebovitz: 55; Katie and Sam's dad; Insurance Executive; passive, henpecked

Alice Liebovitz: 49; their mother; sharp-tongued, angry, possessive

Bobbeh Katz: 81; Alice Liebovitz's mother; Elder Power – visions of the past and future

Shnayvise Family – LA California

Melvin Shnayvise: 18, Aaron's best friend, computer genius, all-round brainiac

Sarah Shnayvise: 38, Melvin's mother

Hannah: 15, Melvin's oldest sister, shy, clever

Myron and Mendel Shnayvise: 6, Melvin's twin brothers

Sadie Shnayvise: 2, Melvin's little sister

Calvin Coolidge High Staff – LA California

Hiram X Snell: 56, Social Studies teacher, Organization stooge

Soledad Gutierrez: 63, English teacher, much admired

Millard Fillmore Middle School Students – LA, California

Emma Schwartz, Mishi's friend

Daphne Bernstein, Mishi's enemy

Elders LA

Dr. Amadeus Califario, Leader of the Elders, has several powers

Mordecai Ben Zvi, Israeli, Elder Power – mind control

Wolfgang Holst, German, Elder Power – strength, agility

Dr. Mortimer Jabez Dunkeldorfer, Elders Archivist; Elder Power – can detect items which generate occult energy

Other Elders

Francois Pierrot (Kansas City, MO), Watchmaker, mind reader

Colonel Landon McAllister (Pentagon, VA), Soldier, mind control

Jamalia Brookes (Dallas, TX), Nurse, healer

Elders 'Assignments'

Major-General Susan Cartwright, in line for appointment to Joint Chiefs of Staff, Landon McAllister's assignment

Samuel J Packenham, Kansas City benefactor, Francois Pierrot's assignment

Miss Jones, Samuel J Packenham's Secretary

Alfred Sweeney, Founder and President of Pharmaco Industries International, Jamalia Brookes's assignment

Alison Kochenko, Pharmaco's Chief Research Officer

The Organization

Randolph Lassiter (CT, NY) 38, Canadian, UN Under Secretary for Environmental Sustainability and Climate Change

Kim Park Singh (LA), Korean/Sikh

Craig McInnes (LA) Australian

Sally Portland (Various locations); known as 'The Poisoner'

Nikos Georgiakis (DC)

Waldo Gantz (LA)

Minnelli (LA)

Mulligan (LA)

Emilio Lubrano (Dallas, TX)

Albert Severin, 57, photocopier salesman, Detector, has the ability to detect Adepts, people with psychic powers

Cardozo Research Team

Professor Olaf Svensson: 72, Swedish, Professor of Medieval Studies at Cardozo University, NY, Nobel Peace Prize winner, Organization operative

Mary Blakely: 26, post-grad student of medieval manuscripts, member of Professor Svensson's research team

Sean Singleton: 24, post-grad student of medieval studies, member of Professor Svensson's research team

Jeremy Plensk: 24, post-grad student of medieval studies, member of Professor Svensson's research team

Historical Figures, mainly from Aaron's Visions

In this book there are many historical sections and scenes. They mostly involve fictional characters in semi-fictionalized settings. The characters who have been drawn from actual ancient or historical sources are:

Moses (given the fictional Egyptian name Amun-Tut-Moses)

King David

King Solomon (Shlomo Ben David)

Abishag the Shunnamite

Yohanan Ben Zakkai

Titus Flavius Vespasianus, better known as Emperor Vespasian

George Washington

Benjamin Franklin

Charles de L'Enfant

Haym Solomon

Other (fictional) People from Aaron's Visions

Amun-het-Ma'at – Egyptian Priest, Moses's master

The Seven Patriarchs of the Elder Families in 70AD:

Ovadyah Ben Ahaz

Nadav Ben Amos

Adayah Ben Nathan

Micah Ben Levi

Azariah Ben Yosef

Tzadok Ben Nun

Hosea Ben Elihu

Caius Legatus of Neapolis, sailor

Mynheer Kapitein Van Houten, captain of *The Abigail*, sailing for the Massachusetts Bay settlement

Reuben Ben Solomon, Sarah, his wife, and his family, sailing on *The Abigail*

Characters who have brief walk-on appearances, or are merely mentioned

Carmelita – Sterns' housekeeper

Miss Oligovsky – Aaron and Melvin's kindergarten teacher

The Reverend Cyrus B. Abernathy, of the Second Baptist Church of the Holy Congregation, Chicago

Mrs Clarissa Abernathy, his wife

Cindy Grayson – 15, lives next door to the Sterns, friend of Mishi, has a crush on Aaron.

Calvin Coolidge High School students

Julie Fitzpatrick, has the sniffles, cured by Aaron

Luis

Brady

Deanne Dworski

Ryan Santiago

Fred Johnson, activist, hassles Melvin

Miscellaneous Support Cast

Rabbi Elhanan Elbaz – The Stern family Rabbi. Actually, there is a real Rabbi Elhanan Elbaz who lives in Jerusalem. He was extremely kind and generous when he performed my nephew Jack's Barmitzvah at the Wailing Wall. There are many ways people show their gratitude. Putting him in my book is mine.

Lester Rosenblatt – Melvin's scary lawyer uncle

Caroline Lassiter – Randolph Lassiter's wife

Emily – Randolph Lassiter's daughter

Jake – Randolph Lassiter's son

Rosie – the Lassiter's housekeeper

Manuel – Lassiter's driver

Mrs. Schwartz, Emma's mother – offers Aaron cake and chicken soup when he turns up looking for Mishi

Daphne Bernstein's party guests

Justin (as in Bieber) – guest at Daphne's party, takes a shine to Emma

Calypso

Charmian

Brent

Marcus

Jamalia Brookes' Family

Eugenia Brookes – her mother

Jamal – brother, deceased

Kareem – brother

Josiah – brother

Bernice – sister

Carl – Bernice's husband

GLOSSARY OF YIDDISH WORDS AND TERMS

Note: 'kh' and 'ch' are both pronounced as gutturals as in Scottish 'loch'. Another point, most of the terms for fools, or jerks, are often used affectionately or as light ribbing, rather than as mortal insults. I think, at some time in my life, I have been called all of them, by my father and brother and friends. Hey, wait a minute...

Bissel	A little
Bissel Yiddishkite	A little Jewishness, and a bit of Jewish Culture, and Heritage
Bobbeh	Grandma
Chutzpah	Cheek, gall, bravado, nerve, impudence
Farshtunkeneh	*Literally,* stinking, *figuratively,* contemptible
Gefilte fish	Minced poached fish cakes
Goy	Non-Jew; *plural:* Goyim
Hob rakhmoness	Have mercy
Klutz	Clumsy person
Knaidlach	Matza ball dumplings, usually eaten floating in chicken soup: Matza: unleavened bread eaten during Passover Passover: Jewish Festival celebrating freedom from Egyptian slavery. The general description of this and most other Jewish celebrations: "They tried to kill us, we survived, let's eat!"
Meshugena	*Adjective,* mad, crazy, nuts
Nu?	so?; a general interrogative meaning, among other things, 'go on', 'say more', 'go ahead' e.g. *Sue Me, lyrics from Guys and Dolls: All right, already, so call a policeman*

	All right, already, it's true, so nu? *So sue me, sue me, what can you do me? I love you*
Nudnik	A pest, a jerk (but often used affectionately)
Oy gevalt	General expression of dismay; Good Grief!, Oh my God!
Oy vay	Woe is me; general expression of sorrow or worry
Putz	Fool, ass, jerk (It also has a ruder meaning, relating to the male anatomy)
Shlemiel	Idiot, bungler
Shlub	Oaf, blockhead, yokel
Shmendrick	Fool, jerk, hopeless case
Schnozzola	Nose
Shpilkhes	*Literally,* needles; *figuratively,* agitation, nervousness
Shpilkes in der tuches	Ants in the pants
Shtetl	Town or village in Eastern Europe with Jewish inhabitants
Shtup	To have sex
Shyster	Conman, trickster, cheat; often used of lawyers
Tuches	Buttocks, one's rear end
Tuch	Anglicized version of tuches
Tzatzke	Toy, frippery, cheap showy bauble
Yenta	Gossip, busybody, usually applied to women
Yiddishkite	*Literally,* Jewishness; *more expansively* Jewish feeling, culture, heritage, sensibility

PROLOGUE

Cordoba, Al Andalus

The Almohad Emirate, Spain 541AH (1147AD)

May the Seven Demons of the Seventh Circle of Hell pluck out your liver before your living eyes!"

Heavy mallets smashed at the front door.

All evening the young man, upstairs in his library, had been searching through piles of robes and books. Sweat ran down his forehead and dripped into his eyes. His hands pushed aside scraps of parchment, quills, and inkpots, pulling out drawers and up-ending their contents.

The room was small, its walls hung with patterned rugs, and its windows, covered with shutters let in the breeze to cool the Iberian night. Two lamps threw crazy shadows on the walls and ceiling. The man wracked his brains. The Caliph's men would be here soon.

"Where is it, where is it, where is it," he muttered.

He backed into a stool, knocking a colored glass bowl to the floor. It smashed, scattering green and red shards across the tiles. Water soaked the piles of clothing, and three goldfish flapped in their death throes.

The stool then toppled into a stand and a skull, covered in candlewax, rolled onto the floor putting one of the goldfish out of its misery.

"Ah-iee!" the man cried, scooping up the skull. "Praise be to the God of Israel, the Lord Jesus Christ, and the All-Merciful Almighty."

He opened its jaws and extracted a purple ribbon attached to a tiny key. He let it dangle for a moment from one long elegant finger, then he slipped it into a pocket of his robe.

He turned and tore a hanging carpet down from the wall and threw it onto the floor. He piled clothes, shoes, books, gold plates, a pair of loaded dice and a pack of marked cards, glass vials with various powders, and three dried pomegranates onto the rug. He grabbed a curtain cord and tied the four corners of the rug together. He smiled at his handiwork, made a loop in the cord and shouldered the makeshift sack.

He selected his favorite stiletto and was fastening it to his woven waistband when the thud of approaching boots was carried in on the night air. The ceiling of the room began to dance in geometric patterns from the light of approaching torches.

The smile disappeared from his face; his eyes darted left and right. He spotted a brass astrolabe; he grabbed it, put this final treasure in the sack, and was tying it up again when a booming knock at the front door reverberated through the house.

"Israel ibn Ibrahim!" a voice shouted. "Open the door, in the name of the Caliph, the Servant of God."

A moment later mallets began crashing against the door. The young man, clutching his burden, and checking the key again, tiptoed through the broken glass toward the doorway. His foot caught the fallen stool; he staggered and tripped, and fell through the opening into the arms of his maidservant, Fatima, clad in a sheer cotton chemise. The candle she was carrying clattered to the floor and went out.

"Oh," she said, "Master, a thousand regrets, I..."

"Ah, Fatima," said the young man, disentangling himself, "I was just stepping out for a moment."

He hefted the carpetbag back onto his shoulder. Downstairs the door shook with heavy pounding.

"Israel ibn Ibrahim, whose crimes are more rank than the dung of a hundred elephants, you are required to answer for your misdeeds."

In the half-light the young man saw the color drain from Fatima's face. Her eyes were round with terror.

He gave her a friendly pat on the cheek. Then he held her chin and concentrated. He gazed at her with his dark eyes. He felt her relax, and before she went completely limp he said: "Those men downstairs want a word with me," he said smiling encouragingly, "Let them in would you. I'll wait up here."

"Yes Master..." said Fatima, dreamy and faraway. "... Men downstairs..."

"Open up, Jewish Dog! Filthy Apostate!" The sound of splintering wood echoed up the stairs. "Thief, swindler! A man who would steal the last crumb from a starving mother, the last drop of milk from a baby! False convert! Despoiler of the innocent! A Pretender who deceives with his honeyed words!"

Ibn Ibrahim took Fatima by the shoulders and turned her around to face the stairs.

He gave her a little push.

"May a thousand camels urinate on the graves of your ancestors!" the shouting continued. "May your nose be roasted on the pitchfork of Shaitan! May the iron beaked crows of the Mountains of the Moon tear your belly and feast on your innards for a thousand years!"

"Now that is hardly fair," ibn Ibrahim muttered. He put his attention back on the girl, a smile played on her lips. "Go Fatima, let them in and tell them I'm up here."

The maidservant floated away to the stairs as the front door shook to another heavy blow. She looked back at him, a shadow passing over her face. Israel ibn Ibrahim made a shooing movement with his hand.

Fatima disappeared down the stairs to meet her fate. Ibn Ibrahim scooted the other way down the hallway. He opened a double screen, stepped out onto a balcony and peered out. He saw a crowd at his front door. His neighbors had gathered to enjoy the show. The palace guards, their dark

Nubian skin gleaming in the torchlight, were standing in a loose semi-circle with scimitars drawn.

Standing beside the door, watching two sweating slaves smash at the wood with heavy hammers, was Ras Tariq ibn Abdul, known to all Cordoba as The Flayer, for his favorite punishment. Israel ibn Ibrahim, confidence trickster and charlatan, born a Jew into an eminent family of Rabbis and Scholars, known as Leonardo Da Silva to his Christian acquaintances, a recent convert to Islam, had every intention of keeping his skin where it was.

But he could not leave Cordoba without his greatest treasure.

He dropped to his knees and prized up one of the balcony flagstones revealing a cavity. He pulled out a small casket, its lid decorated with a filigree of interwoven acacia leaves. As the noise below reached a crescendo Ibn Ibrahim took out the key from his pocket, unlocked the casket and lifted the lid.

Lying on red velvet was a scrap of papyrus covered with symbols and writing.

Ibn Ibrahim felt the power throbbing from this ancient scrap. To the sound of the front door finally giving way, he closed and relocked the casket. He tucked it and the key into the folds of his robe and looped his sack over his shoulder. Heavy boots clattered up the stairs.

He moved to the end of the balcony, picked up a coil of rope, and climbed up onto the balustrade.

Before anyone could alert the angry inquisitor Israel ibn Ibrahim threw the rope up into the air and muttered an incantation. The rope turned rigid. He tested it with a tug. Then he shimmied upwards and, with a gentle 'Pop', vanished into the night, and from Cordoba.

FIVE YEARS BEFORE THE PRESENT DAY

ALBERT SEVERIN

At 11:07 am on April 9th, Albert Severin, photocopier salesman, hit pay dirt. He was footloose in LA on a hot spring day. He hitched his shiny brown suit pants over his belly and scratched his scalp. He examined a few damp white flakes caught under his nail and wiped his hand on a sweaty handkerchief.

He had done some business and it had gone better than expected, a rare event in Albert's life, so he'd boarded a bus and gone Detecting.

The bus had taken him along freeways and local streets from an area of boarded up shops, cracked sidewalks and graffiti, up the LA hills to the tonier suburbs.

Following his instincts Albert had rung the bell and got off. He had walked along leafy streets past big houses with green lawns, tall columns flanking their entrances, and European cars parked in the drive. He walked through shopping precincts and glanced into stores at clothes and handbags and electrical tzatzkes with no price tags.

But Albert wasn't window-shopping for high-priced junk.

He kept moving and he found himself walking by tall steel railings surrounding a schoolyard. The school building in the distance was all glass and stone with a flagpole out the front. Old Glory hung limp in the heat.

The schoolyard was full of kids shouting and yelling and running.

Albert was walking by when his wires jangled.

He felt pressure. If he'd been interested in describing the feeling he might have said it was like a strong wind blowing through his mind. And it was coming from the schoolyard.

Because what Albert the Detector detected was people with psychic power, Adepts. And he was sure detecting a whole bunch of it now.

Albert wasn't a total moron. A middle-aged man, bald and perspiring in a cheap suit taking a bit too much interest in kids playing. You don't have to draw a picture here.

So Albert pulled out his cell like he'd received a call. He shot his cuff and pretended to look at his watch. A guy talking on his phone, who just happened to be near some kids.

He turned slowly to the schoolyard to get a better fix, and saw three little girls standing near the fence in a huddle. They were facing five or six bigger kids. Even Albert, to whom children were as mysterious as Amazon jungle tribes, could see this was not a happy meeting.

But his guts were churning with the strong energy flow coming from one of these kids. One of these kids was an Adept, and finding these people, Adepts, was what he got paid a whole lot of moolah for.

Albert was wondering what to do next, when one of the bigger kids, mean looking, his jeans too small and his shirt sticking to him, swaggered toward the three little girls. He was sweaty, with curly brown hair and hard eyes. The girls cowered. He said something and snorted. His pals yucked it up and slapped their thighs.

Was this guy the junior Adept? Albert focused. Nope, not him.

The bully took another step forward, and the little girls shrank back. Albert could sense danger.

Albert was no humanitarian, and could have cared less if three little girls got a schoolyard beating. But he felt the familiar excitement of discovering a new Adept, and his chest tightened when he thought of the cash he'd get. Trouble was he couldn't tell yet which of these brats was the source of the energy.

He was about to change position when he was hit by a wave of energy so strong and laser-like that he swayed and had to take a step backward. He put his hand out and steadied himself on a parked car.

One of the little girls, a skinny one with brown curly hair and freckles, had turned to their tormentor. The energy was pouring off this skinny little kid. To Albert it was like standing in a wind tunnel.

Miss Skinny narrowed her eyes and stepped forward. She got right up close to the bully, and raised her hand. He tried to slap her hand away. But after a fleeting look of surprise, his face went doughy and expressionless.

Then one of Miss Freckles' friends tried to drag her back. "Mishi, don't. Just ignore him."

Albert squirreled the name away and watched as she shook her friend off. Mishi's face changed. One moment she was a little girl, round-eyed in the face of playground persecution, then her features flattened, her eyes flashed and the corners of her mouth curled into a smile. Like the one the Wolf had when Red came through Granny's front door.

Mishi's hand, still resting on Mr. Mean and Nasty's arm, twisted a little. The boy looked confused, he turned, and tried to kiss one of the tough girls in his back up team. A whole lot of Er! Yucking and Ugh! Grossing later and Mr. Bully had fled in humiliation, with his gang scattering in different directions.

The girl called Mishi looked drained, but smug. Her friends surrounded her chattering like monkeys in a zoo.

And Albert, collecting himself before someone did call the cops, moved off. He punched in a number on speed dial.

"Severin here. I'm in LA. You're gonna love this. I found another one. And she's a doozy. A big one in a very little package. What do I mean? I mean she can't be more than nine or ten years old. Yup, you heard me right. And a real bad ass. Name of Mishi..."

PRESENT DAY

CHAPTER ONE

13TH SEPTEMBER

AARON STERN

1.

Are you supposed to have a spooky premonition on the day your life changes forever? I'm only asking because if there's some good fairy who had the job of poking me in the ribs and making me sit up in bed, untwist the blue tugboat and ship's anchor pajamas – Hey, they're comfortable OK? – then she was on her coffee break.

All I got that morning was Mom calling me from the kitchen. Like always. Because I was going to be late for school. Ditto.

I shuffled around my bedroom – large, comfortable, with a view of suburban Brentwood. I searched under the desk, around my computer and behind my electric guitar for socks and jeans and homework.

I stood in the bathroom leaning with both hands on the sink, looking back at myself, skinny, messy dark hair falling into dark brown eyes and olive skin, and treated myself to a glass of water.

Half way down the stairs I could smell the pancakes and maple syrup. I walked along the hallway past the living room, Dad's den and Mom's office toward the sound of cutlery and plates.

In the kitchen Carmelita, our housekeeper, was at the sink washing up. My kid sister Mishi was sitting at the table eating, her curly brown hair falling forward and covering her face. Mom was at the trashcan scraping off her plate ready to hand it to Carmelita.

"Buenos dias, Señor Aaron," said Carmelita in her sing-song voice.

"Buenos dias, Carmelita," using up a hundred per cent of my conversational Spanish.

I stifled a yawn and joined Mishi at the breakfast table, grunting at any attempts at conversation, that'd be Mom, or snide sarcasm, and that would be Mishi, fourteen going on thirty.

Dad was already at work, Stern's Carpets, doing an inventory count.

With the pancakes and eggs safely on board I was drinking a glass of milk.

"Don't forget to take your sister to school," said Mom.

"Take Mishi?" I said, looking at the kitchen clock. "Hey, wait a minute how come it's only seven-fifteen?"

"Because, Mr. Capital L Loser," said Mishi, tossing her hair back and fixing me with a look, "Mom woke you early, because you gotta drop your sister early. You remember your sister? What was her name? Pishie? Mushie? Oh that's it!" she snapped her fingers, "Mishi! And you're supposed to drop me at school today. I've gotta get to Science Club, so the bus is no good, and Dad had to start super early at the warehouse, and Mom is flying out for some stupid conference."

"Mishi, don't talk to your brother that way."

"Why not, Mom? Mr. Brainless here isn't going to remember what I said." At this point my delightful sister began to twirl her index finger against her temple in the universal sign of 'I'm talking to an idiot', sticking her tongue out of the corner of her mouth, and crossing her eyes.

I laughed so hard the milk nearly came out of my nose.

When I'd finished coughing and choking, I said: "OK, I get the privilege of taking the Stern family diplomat to school. Let's get this over with."

2.

Calvin Coolidge High is pretty typical, I guess. A main building accessed by paths that crisscrossed a grass lawn, and then up a flight of brick steps to glass doors. Behind the main building lurked a scattered collection of labs and sports fields.

On the day I left Mishi at Millard Fillmore Middle School there was one last spot under the eucalypts for Mom's silver Lexus. When her conferences were out of town she let me have her car, especially when Mishi needed a chauffeur. Mom's actually Dr. Miriam Stern PhD, and she's all cool scientist, and quantum physics, and particle accelerators and stuff, but when it comes to her kids, she turns into psycho-Mom. You know, 'Wear a scarf, you'll catch a cold. Make sure you drive at zero miles an hour, cause you'll crash.'

If she could she'd line the roads with bubble wrap wherever Mishi was going.

So, bottom line? Aaron Isaac Stern gets to impress the Calvin Coolidge student body with a very acceptable silver Lexus.

Do you hear me complaining?

I pinged the alarm and joined the stream of students walking the fifty yards or so to the front entrance. I was getting my backpack organized when Melvin came up behind me and shouted in my ear.

"Melvin," I said, "You are without doubt..."

"The greatest friend a guy could dream of having."

"Not quite."

"A stalwart pal for all occasions."

"Nope, not it."

"Someone with crib notes for Mrs. Gutierrez's Friday Quiz, eager to share them with anyone who appreciates his greatness."

"Melvin, I think I can say, without fear of contradiction, that no other human being on earth appreciates your greatness like I appreciate your greatness," I said.

"I knew it," said Melvin.

He looked up at me from his five foot-two-inches. He was short, dark, with black curly hair, thick glasses and with a gargantuan schnozzola. He was a genius, funny, and had survived the bullies of elementary, middle and high school with a mixture of great negotiating skills and cowardice.

And he had computing skills that made people suspect he was Bill Gates' and Steve Jobs' love-child. He could fix any electronic device, program any computer, and several times his hacking had skirted the edges of legality.

He was my best friend. On our very first day of school as five year olds we had sat together to eat our snacks. Then, along with twenty-six classmates, we shared a mat to gaze up at Miss Oligovsky.

We loved Miss Oligovsky. No, we LOVED Miss Oligovsky.

With a name like that I guess you're picturing a gray old lady with a Babushka headscarf, but Miss Oligovsky was the exact opposite. She was beautiful.

Every girl wanted to grow up and be like her. Every boy couldn't wait to be old enough to ask her to marry him, Melvin and me included. You only get one teacher like that in your school career, and Miss Oligovsky was ours.

I heard a while back that she did marry, and moved to New Jersey and had a couple of kids. One of my secret fears is that she did turn into that Babushka. I prefer to remember her as the Miss Oligovsky of my dreams.

So, Melvin and I had had lunch together that first day of school, and we still do.

We were heading down the corridor weaving our way through gangs of fellow students, shouting greetings and discussing last night's TV. We were approaching the staircase to the second floor classrooms when we saw a familiar blonde ponytail swinging purposefully ahead of us.

"Ah," Melvin called out, "the fair Miss Liebovitz!" Katie turned at the sound of her name.

"The magnificent Melvin and his faithful sidekick Aaron." She took my hand and kissed my cheek.

For the ten-bazillionth time I couldn't believe that this was my girlfriend. She was smart, beautiful, funny, and scary.

I was tall, dark, gangly, with black hair that never did what it was told. An average student, mostly because study and note taking and revision for tests and, let's be honest, work in general, was stuff that happened to other people.

Katie was at her scariest when she fixed her mind on eradicating one of these shortcomings. When she was on a campaign I found it best to be what they used to call 'simple'.

Mostly this is not a hard act.

I don't get girls. I try. But I found the best way to weather Hurricane Katie was to pull the doors shut on the storm shelter and ride it out.

But don't get me wrong. Katie was sweet and gorgeous, smart as a whip and wise beyond her years. It's just that, when it comes to me, she often feels the need to go into 'improvement mode'.

She put her arm through mine and squeezed. We completed the last few yards to the classroom.

The room was filling up and Katie took a seat in the front row. I grabbed an empty spot a few rows behind her. Melvin squeezed in over near the window.

3.

I slumped in my chair, my chin on my hand, and my elbow slowly sliding out from under me. I was watching the morning sunlight streaming into the classroom, lighting up the specks of dust. I listened to chairs scraping and the pre-class chatter.

My attention was caught by the swing of Katie's ponytail three rows ahead. She arranged her laptop and pens, and tapped her notes into orderly stacks. Then she squared her chair to the table, and sat up straight. Katie Liebovitz, Super Organizer Woman.

My reverie was interrupted by a wad of paper bouncing off my head. I picked it up and threw it back hitting Brady on the ear. Cheers erupted from an appreciative crowd.

The door squeaked open and closed and the last students shuffled in, unslung their backpacks and found the remaining empty chairs.

Last of all Julie Fitzpatrick, short, dark and a little overweight, came in and stood irresolute, looking for somewhere to sit. She coughed and sniffled.

I stiffened. I was picking up a familiar signal. My nerves began to jangle and my gut tightened.

My skin felt a size too small.

Her eyes watering, Julie fished for a tissue and blew her nose. She made her way down the row of desks. The hunched bored boys and gum-chewing girls quickly ducked out of her way, dodging Julie's backpack as she turned this way and that, sniffling and apologizing. Papers were swept to the floor. Students bent to pick up scattered notes.

Julie was closing in on me.

I felt the energy building up.

I'm not sure how a volcano feels before it blows its stack. Must compare notes with one if I get the chance. Because sometimes I get this pressure cooker feeling inside me when someone near me is in pain or sick, and then ...

Well, it was about to happen.

Julie came up level with me in the narrow aisle. I stretched, extended my hand and casually brushed it against hers.

I gasped. I felt the energy flow up from my gut, down my arm and through my fingers and into Julie's hand. She kept walking down the aisle as if nothing had happened, but pain shot up my arm, my vision clouded and a red haze colored the room. The screech of my chair across the linoleum cut through the chatter.

Katie swiveled around.

"What's up?" she looked concerned.

"Nothing." I said, struggling to keep my voice level, natural.

"Really," Katie's eyes narrowed. Katie Liebovitz, the walking, talking lie detector; Katie with the X-ray vision. Her lips tightened, her silence was a brooding, boyfriend-crushing force.

I braced myself. "Nothing ... really."

See, I have this secret. A lot of people know about it now, so I suppose it's OK to tell. I'm a Healer. That's with a capital "H". For as long as I could remember I touch someone who's sick, or troubled, or unhappy, and they get better. Not everyone, I get the energy build up and that's the signal that this girl or that man is the target.

And then I touch them. The energy flows out of me, and in return I get a blast. Sometimes I see red. Literally. I mean like I'm looking through blood. Then it wears off.

Them? They get better, and stay better.

Don't ask how it works. I don't know. It just does.

I can feel sick or sad people coming. I used to hate it when I was a kid, but I learned to live with it.

And people need help. So, I help.

The reaction to Julie was bigger than I'd expected. She must have had more than a sniffle.

"Are you OK Ronnie?" said Katie. 'Aaron' was for when people, mainly of the female persuasion, were mad at me. "Are you still alright for this afternoon?"

"OK, right, yeah." Playing for time. My memory banks temporarily wiped. "This afternoon. Sure, depend on it, I'm there." Then, thank God, a spark of recall. "That's right, Bobbeh Katz, the hospital. Sure, no, really I'm OK. Great, the hospital, yeah, right after class."

Katie's grandmother, Bobbeh Katz, wasn't well, so she'd been checked into Cedars-Sinai Hospital. And Katie wanted me to go with her to visit after morning classes were over. Katie and I had a scheduled study afternoon and, as seniors, we could leave the school grounds. Today 'study' was going to consist of a field trip to Cedars-Sinai.

Bobbeh Katz was nice, I liked her, and if I could do the healing thing, Hey, why not?

The kick in the guts went with the job.

Katie held my gaze for a moment longer, making sure I was OK, I guess, and then she turned back, getting herself ready for the class.

I settled back to lick my wounds. Julie Fitzpatrick, now apparently feeling much better, sat down, her cough and sniffles gone.

Good, I thought, massaging my arm, mission accomplished.

4.

We finished Math and History and filed into the last class before lunch. English with Mrs. Gutierrez.

She came in and unpacked her books and notes. She was a middle-aged Latina, black curly hair with streaks of gray, short and round and a bit, let's be honest here, dumpy. But lively, talkative and sharp.

"Class, why are we here?" she said, with a broad grin.

"To open our minds and expand our horizons," we parroted. It was corny, but everyone liked Gooty so parrot we did.

Except Deanne Dworski, examining her nails, and sighing loud enough so no one could miss it. And Ryan Santiago, sitting next to her, all proprietorial and boyfriendy.

Deanne had her charms. She was a pretty brunette in a get-it-while-it-lasts kind of way. Ryan was the typical high school jock whose future would all be behind him as soon as he graduated. They had a crowd of admirers, who they let into their magic circle.

And Aaron Isaac Stern, and Melvin David Shnayvise were definitely not allowed in.

Just the day before Fred Johnson, one of Deanne and Ryan's cronies, wanted Melvin to sign some pro-something or anti-whatever petition. Fred was the coordinator of the Affirmative Action and Diversity Training Coalition, or was it the Action Committee for Training in Diverse Affirmations? I could never remember.

Anyway Melvin, who never puts his name to anything he hasn't read the fine print of, and then taken to his super scary lawyer uncle Lester Rosenblatt, said no. Uncle Lester appears on a cable TV show called *Lester's Law* so he must know what he's talking about right?

So Fred piled in on Melvin about checking his white privilege and so on. It was a set up of course because even Melvin's standard class-clown shtick doesn't always protect him. His smart mouth, and brilliant grades occasionally draw the attention of the Calvin Coolidge High School patricians.

And Melvin's guard must have been down because he just snorted at Fred's white privilege riff.

"Privilege? Privilege!" rising pitch here, "I'll give you white privilege! My family were dirt poor and persecuted for centuries, being booted out of one village after another every time a Tsar got bored shtupping the help. That's getting over-cozy with the servants for those who need a translation."

That Melvin, what a card. What a diplomat. Winning friends with his witty arguments.

"I'll give you white privilege," says Melvin, warming to his theme and ignoring my frantic hand signals. A crowd was starting gather.

"My great-grandparents came here with exactly nothing, lived ten to a room, and worked eighteen hour days to get enough to send my grandparents to school, and my grandparents did the same to send my parents to college. You know what you can do with your white privilege? You can go wrap your white privilege in your stupid petition, tie a pretty ribbon around it, and stick it up your shiny ..."

At this point I grabbed the protesting Melvin and dragged him away before he said something that got him suspended from school. And kicked out of California.

So Melvin, and by association me, was not on the jocks' or the activists' Christmas list.

I put my attention back on Gooty, and the set text, *Moby Dick*.

"My job is to teach you to think," Gooty was saying, she always said things like this. And then she'd say something like, "Why is a whale like an acorn?" Or, "What does Melville want you to think about the use and abuse of power?" Or, "What would you have done in Ishmael's place?"

All annoying questions which were impossible to answer, until Gooty prodded and cajoled us into coming up with something. Then, on a good day the discussion would start flying around the room. On the best days there was a groan when the bell went and we had to stop.

Mrs. Gutierrez was great.

5.

Forty minutes later, our minds opened and our horizons widened like nobody's business, we crammed out through the classroom door. I rearranged my books and papers waiting for the press of bodies to ease. No sense courting trouble.

"Hurry up Ronnie," said Katie, looking at her watch. "I don't want us to be late."

"OK, on my way." One of my books seemed stuck. "Coming. Give me one minute."

I just couldn't get it into my bag.

"Look. Let me do it." And, a miracle, I was packed and ready to go, and Katie was escorting me into the corridor, down the green linoleum hallway, past pierced, gelled, tattooed students slamming locker doors.

The cafeteria, a cavernous space with a high ceiling, which I think was the gym before the new one got built, announced itself with shouts, loud laughter and the banging of trays and cutlery. All accompanied by the mixed bouquet of lasagna, pizza, french fries and steamed broccoli.

Katie and I moved through the throng. I could feel the envious glances following me. And I could feel a lot more; aches, pains and depression, coming in waves from the crowded room. But I wasn't getting the tell-tale build up which told me I had to cure someone.

This was life for me, Ronnie Stern, human pain sensor. Your feelings detected while you wait, your ills cured by his lightest touch. Step up! Step up!

Katie and I answered a few shouted greetings and parried a few side-splitting suggestions as to where we were going, and what we were going to do when we got there. We pushed open the double glass doors on the other side of the cafeteria, passed into a short hallway and then out through the main school doors.

We emerged into the sunlight. We stood side by side for a moment at the top of the short flight of brick steps.

We held hands and headed down, then turned left along the path to the parking lot, through the stand of tall eucalyptus trees, their gray-green leaves moving slowly in the afternoon breeze. I squinted at the bright sunlight reflected off the silver Lexus.

Enjoy it while it lasts, I thought.

I had to hightail it after the Hospital because I was this evening's designated taxi service, little sisters my specialty. Mom's Quantum Physics Conference was going to last a few days; and Dad was staying back late to finish the inventory – 'Stern's Carpets: Let Us Find A Magic Carpet For You!' The source of the Stern fortune.

Mishi had after-school gym training so I got to do the brat run.

We emerged from the trees and Katie's bag began playing The Eagles' 'Witchy Woman'. Her Mom's ring tone. Very appropriate.

Katie fished in her bag for her cell.

"Hi Mom, we're on our way." Pause. "What?" Katie's voice rose. I felt the hammer blow of her panic. My gut began to heave. My eyes throbbed, and the red haze began to shimmer.

"What! No. No, that can't be right. She was fine yesterday, she was OK. They've made a mistake. No, you're wrong. The doctors are wrong. We're coming right now." She clicked off and turned to me.

"Oh, Ronnie!" her face collapsed, and before I could prepare myself she fell forward into my arms, burying her face in my chest. Her shoulders convulsed.

I felt the waves of her pain course through my body. The whole scene took on the red haze. I held Katie tight.

Then she looked up at me, blinking away her tears, feeling better.

"Come on," she sniffed, "we have to go."

"What did your Mom say?"

Katie looked like she'd cry again, but she shook herself, "Bobbeh's taken a turn. Please, Ronnie, we've got to go."

First Julie, the sniffler, then Katie, and soon the hospital. I was getting a month's quota of knocks in one day.

I had the keys ready as we reached the Lexus. I unlocked and we climbed in. I started the engine, backed out of the parking space, and headed for the hospital.

We drove for a while in silence. Katie was lost in a world of grief. I kept one hand on the wheel and held hers with the other one.

The leafy suburban streets gave way to busier roads. We took San Vincente until it became Federal Avenue, then we turned left onto Santa Monica. The Lexus wove smoothly in and out of gaps in the flowing traffic. We were passing a shopping mall when Katie spoke.

"You hate hospitals. Are you OK with coming to visit Bobbeh?" I hesitated a fraction too long. She pulled her hand away.

"Look, you can let me out here and I'll catch a cab."

"Katie, I'm coming, OK?" I hunted around for something else to cool her down, "I like Bobbeh Katz, and I'm, uh, totally OK with hospitals. Sort of. Mostly. Anyway you're not catching a cab."

I reached out and took her hand again. With one hand on the wheel I eased the car through the building traffic.

And I concentrated my energy.

I felt a familiar warm vibration rise from my gut and flow out through my fingertips. It was part of the healing thing, but I couldn't turn it on and off. I had to concentrate and build up to it. And it left me feeling light headed and weak.

I felt Katie's hand relax, and she seemed to lose her train of thought.

After a moment or two she said, "All right. OK, I guess I'm upset about Bobbeh."

We turned off Santa Monica onto Beverly Drive and the traffic thinned. A gray block of vertical lines and dark windows came into view, framed by acres of black asphalt parking lot. Cedars-Sinai Hospital.

"I'll drop you and park. I'll see you in there."

"OK, she's in room 307, third floor of the Spielberg Wing." Then she leaned over and gave me a kiss on the cheek. She struggled to smile and a tear squeezed past her iron defenses. I turned to her and brushed the drop from her cheek.

"See you soon, Katie."

RANDOLPH LASSITER

Randolph Lassiter's alarm went off at 5:07 am. He turned it off, and swung his legs over the side of the bed. He was wearing dove gray, brushed flannel pajamas. He slotted first his right and then his left foot into soft leather slippers with green tartan lining and quietly walked the eight steps to the bathroom. It was tastefully tiled in marble with subtle gold lattice finishes. The underfloor heating had commenced its work at 4:21 am.

Randolph Lassiter cleaned his teeth, rinsed and flossed. Then he took the customary minute to examine the conventionally handsome face which looked back at him from the bathroom mirror – pale blue eyes, patrician nose and strong chin, a face that was perfectly at home in the Hamptons or Martha's Vineyard.

He slid out of the slippers, leaving them four inches to the left of the glass digital scales. He disrobed and hung the pajamas on hooks placed at the perfect height for that purpose. He stood on the scales. He glanced down at the readout and grunted with satisfaction – one hundred and fifty four pounds.

He took the pen clipped to the calendar hanging on the back door of the bathroom and he wrote down his weight under today's date. Each square up to today was filled in. Every one said: 154 lbs.

Randolph Lassiter stepped into the shower for eleven minutes. Then he toweled off and shaved away his blond stubble. He brushed his hair into a neat side parting.

Another examination, another small grunt of satisfaction.

In the walk in closet, Lassiter dressed in a dark gray Brooks Brothers suit, black John Lobb shoes polished to a mirror shine, a white shirt and, today, a pale yellow tie – the daily choice of the tie was his concession to spontaneity.

He breakfasted on two soft-boiled eggs placed before him by Rosie the black house-maid (lowered into cold water, brought to the boil and extracted after seven minutes and fifty seconds). Copies of the *New York Times,* the *Washington Post,* the *Wall Street Journal,* and, a reminder of home, the *Toronto Globe and Mail,* were placed on a small side table.

Lassiter glanced quickly at the headlines and the opinion pieces as he ate his eggs in the fourteen minutes allotted to breakfast.

He thanked Rosie, stacked the papers neatly – edges parallel, folded just so – and pushed his chair back.

Upstairs again, his wife Caroline stirred as he kissed her forehead. He pocketed his wallet, keys, Mont Blanc fountain pen and slipped his ID lanyard over his head and centered it precisely on the yellow tie.

Down the corridor he looked into Emily's room. She was asleep, tightly hugging her Elmo doll. Next-door Jake, under a Buzz Lightyear coverlet, stirred sleepily as his father quietly closed the door.

He walked to his study and collected his briefcase, which he had packed last night with papers and reports, all thoroughly scanned, with margin notes, and yellow post-its peeping out in soldierly rows. Penciled recommendations were paper-clipped to the front sheet.

At 6:14 his official car, a black Cadillac De Ville touring sedan, glided up to the curb.

Manuel, his regular driver, came around the rear of the car and opened the door for him.

"Good morning Mr. Under-Secretary," he said.

"Good morning, Manuel, all is well with you and your family, I trust."

"Yes Sir, thank you very much for asking," Manuel replied.

Lassiter settled himself for the drive. He placed his briefcase on the seat next to him, clicked open the latches and lifted the lid. The trip from Greenwich, Connecticut down the I95 to Manhattan at this time of the morning gave him time to reread several of the papers.

On arrival Manuel guided the Cadillac expertly into the underground parking area. Lassiter glanced at his new Patek Phillippe Calatrava, an anniversary present from his wife. Today the journey had taken one hour and fourteen minutes. Not bad.

Randolph Lassiter rode up in the elevator to the seventeenth floor, turned left and walked past several identical doors until he reached his own. He glanced at the name-plate: *Mr. Randolph Lassiter: Under Secretary for Environmental Sustainability and Climate Change.*

He unlocked the door and entered, passing through the small reception area and into the inner sanctum, oak-lined with furled Canadian and UN flags in the corner, a photograph of the Queen and, next to it, exactly the same size, the benign face ofBan Ki-Moon, Secretary General of the United Nations.

He opened his briefcase, removed his papers, tapped them into an orderly pile. He separated them by the color-coded paper clips and placed them neatly in the correct trays. He set the brief case down in its place beside the hat stand and took a moment to look out across Turtle Bay and the East River toward Queens.

Then he sat. The diamond button office chair answered with the creak of real leather. He unlocked the third drawer of the desk and took out a secure laptop computer whose presence was heavily and expertly masked from any unwanted surveillance, including that of his employers.

He opened it and saw a message. He waited a moment or two for the decryption.

"Proceed with the Da Silva operation."

Showtime. At last.

AARON STERN

1.

After dropping Katie at the entrance, I drove to the hospital parking lot. I nosed into a space, got out and locked the car, and stopped for a moment, my back to the hospital, feeling its dark malevolence.

I turned and walked past other cars along a path that delivered me to the glass entrance doors of the hospital, toward the death and disease, the pain and misery that crouched in wait like a living thing.

People were coming and going, carrying bunches of flowers wrapped in cellophane, a couple of doctors wearing light-blue scrubs were talking quietly to each other, a nurse was sitting on a low concrete wall smoking, and filling in a Sudoku puzzle.

My body was wracked with tension and increasing pain, the red glow was beginning to color my peripheral vision. It took all of my will to get up the flight of steps, through the sliding glass doors. They opened to let a tired lady push a wheelchair-bound geezer out into the sunshine. I slid past them and walked by the reception desk to the bank of elevators.

When the elevator doors opened I stepped in with three other visitors, and pressed the third floor button, which lit up with a green glow. The stainless steel doors slid shut, my heart was racing and my breathing was shallow.

I was feeling faint when the doors re-opened, but I staggered out and set off toward Bobbeh Katz's room, down the antiseptic corridors, my nose twitching with the smells of disinfectant and decay.

Bobbeh Katz's room was silent except for the slow, steady hum of mysterious medical machinery, and the sobs of Katie and Mrs. Liebovitz.

Katie's brother Sam stood a little apart, his glasses had slipped down his nose. He looked more embarrassed than grief stricken. Mr. Liebovitz, his arm around his wife, had the jowls and drooping eyes of a basset hound at the best of times. Now he looked like someone had fashioned him out of clay and had accidently dropped him.

At the center of the tableau was Bobbeh Katz, her eyes closed, lying on her back, with her arms on top of the starched white sheets, surrounded by machines and tubes and cables. The skin of her delicate veined hand was a pale transparent ivory.

Katie held Bobbeh Katz's other hand. She nodded at me and tried to smile.

I reached for the back of a visitors' chair and waited for my heart rate to settle. My skin didn't fit, and someone was driving hot spikes into the back of my eyes.

2.

I looked at Bobbeh Katz, a gray old lady on the threshold of death.

Her eyes fluttered opened, she turned her head my way, and deep tranquil, bottomless pools focused on me. My heart slowed and my chest relaxed. My grip on the chair eased and the red haze began to fade.

I felt myself sinking into those depthless eyes.

I forgot myself, my surroundings, the grieving Team Liebovitz, the sterile antiseptic room.

Awash just moments before in a private world of hurt, I found an instant of ineffable joy. I began to surrender to its warm embrace…

"Aaron Stern!" said lovely Mrs. Liebovitz. Her face pinched, her beaked nose pointed accusingly at me. She was not, in fact, my favorite person, and nor was I hers. Our dislike for each other was the only thing on which we saw eye to eye.

"Young man!" she said. Her voice could peel paint. "I'm talking to you. You look terrible. If you're sick you shouldn't be here. You shouldn't have come. Katie, why is he here? Why did you bring him? He looks terrible. Honestly, I don't understand you. Look Donny," turning to Katie's father, "he shouldn't be here. He's not family. He's sick. He's ..."

Each word was a hammer blow. The room began to move.

"Mom, please," said Katie. "Please, don't ..."

But Mrs. Liebovitz turned on her. "He shouldn't be here. You shouldn't have brought him."

The querulous whine was like sandpaper. A spinning sensation began in the pit of my stomach. I felt clammy and cold. Sweat began to trickle down my forehead and neck, and soaked my shirt.

Like a drowning man grabbing a life preserver I looked back at Bobbeh

Katz. She held me with her gaze. The crackling brassy edge of Mrs. Liebovitz's voice faded into the background.

I was drawn forward, into a world populated by just Bobbeh Katz and me. I reached out, and she took my hand in hers.

The instant our hands touched my world turned upside down. I felt like someone was gripping my head and my feet, and was twisting me and pulling me apart. I felt nauseous. The ground opened up beneath me, and the hospital disappeared. I plunged into a black void.

3.

The First Vision

Just when I thought I was going to be pulled to breaking point the stretching sensation eased. The blackness slowly retreated and, wherever I was, my vision began to adjust.

I was in a dimly lit tunnel, a corridor, with stone walls, floor and roof. I watched mesmerized. I couldn't move, couldn't react. I wasn't sure if I was really there, or merely a disembodied observer of a dream. But I could feel a dry enveloping heat, and smell the burnt edges of a sun-baked climate.

The silence gave way to the sound of approaching footsteps. It got louder and around a corner came two men. They came toward me down the long stone corridor, each carrying a flickering torch, casting an eerie glow on the pale yellow walls, covered in carved symbols, letters, animals, and sculpted kings, priests and men and women in the side-on Egyptian style.

The two men, their sandals flapping on the stone floor, were dressed identically in loincloths. Their heads were shaved and their bodies glistened in the dancing firelight. Each wore a polished metal armband.

They were heading straight toward me. They had to see me. But, when they were close enough to reach out and touch, they walked silently by without a glance.

The taller and older of the two had a bag slung over his shoulder. He had a sloping forehead and calm oriental eyes. His face was impassive, and serene. His companion less so. More energy, more anger, his face was narrower, a shade darker and his features sharper.

My vantage point shifted, following them as they made their way through a maze of corridors, stone staircases, and in and out of chambers and storerooms, until they reached a patch of wall covered, like all the others, with hieroglyphs and images of Pharaohs in heroic poses. There was a beautiful carving of a cow, chest-deep in wavy water, crying to its calf, who was being carried across a river on the back of a boy.

The older man carefully handed his bag to his companion. He then turned back to the wall and brushed both hands over the carved words and figures. He allowed his fingers to probe the smooth stone.

The tall man's finger found the eye of the calf and pressed. It slid inwards. He pushed against the wall and a section of it swung silently open.

4.

The scene faded, and I was back in the hospital, looking at Bobbeh Katz. I felt disoriented. Katie's mother was still yammering away.

What, in God's name, had just happened?

Bobbeh Katz and I were still holding hands.

And now I felt a sense of urgency flowing from her. Like time was running out. She was looking into my eyes, like she was trying to tell me something. But what?

I shook my head. I didn't understand. I didn't know what she wanted to tell me.

A look of infinite sadness shadowed her face. I felt like I'd failed a test of some kind, like I'd somehow disappointed her.

But my head was full of concrete. I was confused, befuddled by the vision of the two Egyptians, and I was left with a dark foreboding weighing on my heart. The red haze was flickering at the periphery of my vision. If only I could clear my head.

Bobbeh Katz looked at me, and sighed. Her eyes closed and her hand still held in mine went limp.

And then all hell broke loose.

A tidal wave of agony shot through me. It was like a lifetime of Bobbeh Katz's pain and suffering flowed into me through my fingertips, up my arm and into my body. It was an anguish I had never felt before.

I reeled back, catching a small side table, sending metal kidney dishes, paperback thrillers and a small vase with a single wilting purple flower crashing to the floor.

I hit the wall and slid down to the floor. I heard Katie's mother's voice from a long way off: "Aaron Stern, what have you done?"

Clan Liebovitz was closing in on me.

Panic gripped my throat. I had to get out of there.

I rolled over onto my hands and knees, pushed through the forest of Liebovitz legs, stumbled to my feet and ran out into the hallway.

Someone behind me called my name and said something about never speaking to someone else again, but I didn't know who all these people were, and I was way past caring.

I cannoned off one wall then another, dodging startled nurses and dressing-gowned patients. I had to get out of this hospital.

It was that old nightmare, running through molasses trying desperately to get away from some hideous pursuer.

The corridors turned themselves into an impossible maze. I elbowed people aside and moved as fast as I could through a tunnel of anger and abuse.

I had no idea which way to go and I kept turning down one sterile, featureless passageway after another until – blessed relief! – I found a staircase. I half ran, half fell down several flights of stairs. I collapsed against the crash bar of the fire doors, and emerged blinking into the harsh sunlight.

5.

Doubled over, my hands on my knees, gasping in air, I waited for the nausea and light-headedness to pass, putting life on hold until the panic subsided and some semblance of reality returned.

My breathing settled down to a mere asthmatic death wheeze. I straightened and stretched backward, my hands pushing into the small of my back.

And then I jumped out of my skin when I saw a dapper little man in a cream suit and matching panama hat sitting on a bench a few feet away, grinning at me.

He was smoking a black cigarette and had his free arm resting on the back of the bench, his fingers lazily stretched toward the No Smoking sign. He had a pointed chin, a broad forehead and black hair. Laugh creases circled his eyes.

He took a long lazy drag on the cigarette and exhaled. The plume of smoke was whisked away by the light breeze.

Then he looked at me and raised one eyebrow.

"Mr. Stern, so happy to finally make your acquaintance."

I stood there.

"The time appears to have come to take matters up a notch. Is this a phrase?" He spoke with an accent, guttural but pleasant. I knew enough Israelis to recognize it.

"But, I am being too rude. I haven't introduced myself. Mordecai. Mordecai Ben Zvi." He rose catlike and extended his hand. I just looked at it. Then I looked at him. His dark eyes twinkled with amusement.

He withdrew his hand and looked at his nails, and gave his cuff a fastidious flick to remove an invisible speck of dust.

"You are still a little, hmm, under the weather. This is how you say it?"

"Look I don't know who you are or what you want."

"But, Mr. Stern, that is precisely what I would like to clarify. To make all things plain. I am a sheet of glass. Completely transparent."

Big expansive gesture, indicating the bench.

I was still feeling lightheaded and not too steady on my legs, so I followed him back to the bench and slumped down next to him.

He waved a hand taking in the hospital, LA, the world.

"Things are not completely as they seem, Mr. Stern, and I have been sent to explain to you certain matters. Then you will need to make some choices." Still smiling. "Perhaps, hard choices."

"Choices?"

"Yes, choices. Look out at this magnificent sunshine, bathing your beautiful city of Los Angeles. For some, truly, it is the City of the Angels. But not, I fear, for everyone. Some fail to benefit fully from the great opportunities and riches that fall effortlessly into the laps of others. Some bad ones even work to deny those privileges to others. A world of apparent injustices, ever teetering, some might feel, on a knife-edge abyss of chaos and civilizational ruin."

He fixed me with a gimlet gaze. "Too melodramatic Mr. Stern? Is this a state of affairs upon which you have, so far, neglected to ruminate?"

"What? What are you talking about? How do you know my name? Who are you?"

"I told you, I am Mordecai Ben Zvi, at your service." He beamed at me and inclined his head. "And I have been sent to, how do you say, to fill you in."

"By whom? Who sent you to, how do you say, fill me in? Fill me in on what?" I stood up fully intending to leave this crazy man and his fedora and black cigarette and weird accent. Let him screw with the next guy who crashed out of the hospital's emergency exit.

Mordecai Ben Zvi held up a hand and fixed those dark eyes on me. He held my gaze as the seconds crawled by with their fingers on their lips. My jangling nerves began to settle. A feeling of contentment draped itself over me. I felt I could very happily pass the time with this nice man.

Niggling at the back of my mind was the thought that this guy was doing to me what I did to others, what I had just done to Katie in the car. I knew what he was doing, but I didn't resist. Didn't want to resist.

I sat.

6.

"That's better," said Mordecai Ben Zvi, "Now where were we? Ah yes, the injustices of the world, all of us teetering on the brink. It may surprise you to know that much of this roundabout and swings – is this the phrase? – is not as random as it might appear. There are people, good people, who work hard to keep things on a keel that is even. Behind the scenes people. Who look after things. People with certain, ah, gifts, powers you might say. Unusual faculties, who influence things for the better."

"Powers? Influence?" I said, the feeling that I was sitting with a crazy person was doing an encore. Any minute he'd be telling me all about the Illuminati, the Bilderberg Group and, natch, the Jews, running the world in secret. The fact that *I* had one of these powers didn't modify my skepticism.

I folded my arms and crossed my legs.

He narrowed his eyes. "I see that you are not yet buying anything that Mordecai Ben Zvi is selling. But Mr. Stern, I am not selling anything. I merely outline a truth for you. Then, remember? Choices. Yours."

Again the casual wave of the cigarette.

"But, to continue. There are people who work behind the scenes. They have gifts. They influence events. They do it to keep the world humming along, to oppose the forces of darkness. Is that too theatrical?"

When I didn't respond he continued: "And, Aaron Isaac Stern, you are one of these people."

I gaped.

"Think about it. What is it you do? Your little clandestine activity. You see people in need and you position yourself such that you relieve them of their pain and disease. And you pay a price. Oh yes, your secret is not so secret, Mr. Stern. There is a, how can I put it, a transfer of energy. And some of us can feel this. We sensed you a little time ago, and we have been watching you."

"Watching me? How? When? Who has been watching me?"

"Don't mistake my meaning. It has been more of a protective detail. I think that is how they put it on your TV police dramas, is it not? But now, I fear, recent events have shifted things, as I say, up a notch. I like that phrase, so evocative. Your encounter with Mrs. Ruth Katz, Bobbeh Katz, has also changed things. It is lucky for us all that I was nearby, and could be here to greet you as you made your dramatic exit."

"Bobbeh Katz? What has Bobbeh got to do with this? Hold on a minute, you've got me talking crazy as well. There is no 'this' for Bobbeh Katz to have anything to do with it."

"Oh, but that," he said, "is precisely where you are most wrong. The occurrences in that hospital room, as well-intentioned as they were, have the potential to set disruptive events in train. Bobbeh Katz was probably trying to warn you, but she was weak and I assume her effort was ineffective. Either because she couldn't summon the strength, or because you were too, can I say it, obtuse."

"Obtuse?"

"Yes, obtuse. But before we start on an inventory of your shortcomings I have to let you know of the other side of the coin. There are those who work to keep things balanced and healthy, and there are those, who work out of less admirable motives, for power or wealth, or simply because they enjoy doing evil. Yes, that is the word one needs to use. Evil. There are, as I say, those who work just as hard, perhaps harder, to unsettle things, to tear down, where we build up; to destroy where we try to create; to bring darkness where we try to shed light."

I put my head in my hands. I was beginning to ache all over. "Soon it will be time for you Aaron Stern to choose. And be clear my friend, if you choose not to choose, that is itself a choice.

"What are you asking me to choose?"

"To join the forces of light, or not to join and leave the good fight to others, to let others sacrifice themselves to oppose the forces of darkness, without the contribution of your considerable talents."

I stared at him. 'Considerable Talents' were my middle names, of course, but still, I was a high school senior, with average grades, a pretty girlfriend, an annoying kid sister, and zero ambition to fight global evil.

Mordecai Ben Zvi kept talking. "Throughout history we have gone by many names, but at this point in time we call ourselves The Elders."

I jerked upwards, my head lifted by an unseen force. I had no idea what it was like to be poked by a cattle prod, but this must have been close.

"The Elders?"

"Yes, I see the name has an effect."

"Go on."

"The Elders, as I was saying, are a group of Adepts, people blessed with a range of interesting talents, who work to keep the world moving forward harmoniously; and we are pitted against those who would profit from death, disease and destruction. These evil doers are not so coherent. They shift and move and are hard to pin down. We call them The Organization. Ironically I'm afraid, because one of our strongest allies in this fight is their disorganization, their rivalry and even their murderous hatred for each other.

"But there are now signs that something large is in the offing, and the dark forces are gathering. At present we do not know what it is they are planning but the indications are that you, Mr. Stern, whether you like it or not, are going to play a part."

And here he smiled a smile so broad that I nearly joined in.

"Do I get to wear a cape?" I said, "And anyway, while we're at it, what part?"

"Well now, there you have me." A light chuckle. "I was merely sent to persuade you to come along for a small chat with my boss. He is the one with the knack, shall we say, of seeing how things will turn out."

If Mr. Weirdo thought I was going anywhere with him, he was crazier than I thought.

"Go with you, to see a man. Who is some kind of fortune-teller, and who will fill me in on The Organization, which is usually disorganized, but now seems to be getting its act together, to take over the world, or destroy it, either way to get up to no good, and this fellow, your boss, will also tell me about the Elders, who are a secret society of guys with magic powers, who need me because I, for some reason which you can't explain, have a starring role in this Apocalypse. Is that about right?"

Mordecai Ben Zvi slapped his leg and laughed. "You have summarized it beautifully. Shall we go?"

"No, sir, we shall not. This is nuts. I have a splitting headache. My girlfriend will never speak to me again. And despite your fascinating story, I am not going to go anywhere with you."

Mordecai's expression didn't flicker. "Fine. One of our rules is that any choice to join us must be freely made. But, as I said, not to choose, is also to choose. Your decision, it will not be without consequences. Be prepared. Your connection with the late Mrs. Katz – Ah, yes, Mr. Stern I am afraid she has gone to her reward – released such a strong wave of psychic energy that those equipped to detect such things will have been alerted. And not all with such capacity wish you well."

He got up from the bench, brushed a few more invisible specks from his suit, and looked at me. "Be careful Mr. Stern. For yourself and for your loved ones. I do not believe you will have very long to wait before events begin to unfold." He then took from an inner pocket a silver case, which he opened. He took out a rectangle of cream card. "My contact details." I reached for the card and he laughed.

"Oh no, I'm afraid you misunderstand. It would be far too dangerous if the wrong people discovered you to have this card on your person. Please memorize the number, and do not write it down anywhere."

I did and, without another word, he turned and walked away.

RANDOLPH LASSITER

Randolph Lassiter's eyes twinkled with pleasure. He was sitting at his desk in his office on the 17th floor of the UN Headquarters, his back to the view of the East River. On his desk was a report entitled 'Assessment of the Medium and Long Term Effects of Global Warming in the IPCC Moderate Predictive Range in the South Eastern Sector of Amazonas State, Bolivarian Republic of Venezuela'. He used his Mont Blanc fountain pen to make another notation in the margin, turned over the sheet of paper and placed it face down on the pile to his left.

Lassiter focused on the densely written text covered with graphs, columns of figures, and detailed footnotes, each of which he checked. Forty-five silent minutes had gone by when the laptop, secreted in the third drawer, vibrated once. The page in Lassiter's hand quivered microscopically.

He opened the drawer, flipped open the laptop and read the message.

"Severin reports major energy surge in the vicinity of Cedars-Sinai Hospital."

Lassiter sent an acknowledgement of receipt, and another message to his men in the field.

"Investigate energy surge near Cedars-Sinai. Who was there? Any Adepts? Ask Severin. RL"

He closed the laptop, slid the drawer to, and sat with his head bowed. His skin tingled. He loved the moment when he and Caroline were at the opera, and the lights dimmed, and the hum of conversation of the dinner jacketed men and the evening gowned women hushed. Pregnant seconds ticked by, the curtain rose and the darkened stage came to life. He was filled with that same feeling, when the first notes of the overture were trembling on the edge. The opera was about to begin.

The God that he rejected had been kind today, and he allowed himself the smallest of smiles.

Then he turned his attention back to his careful examination of the hundreds of pages, stripped from one forest to report on the perils of another.

AARON STERN

1.

On the drive home from Cedars-Sinai hospital my head was full of dying grandmothers, smooth-talking Israelis, Egyptian visions, Elders with psychic powers, and the small matter of how yours truly fitted into all of this.

I pulled into the drive, got out and walked up the path, my hand lightly brushing the ruler-straight top of the box hedge, toward the stone columns that framed the front door. Potted pencil pines stood guard beside them.

The house was quiet. Even Carmelita was on her night off.

The dull ache in my skull and stabs of pain in my back and chest made it hard to think. I glanced at the hall mirror, and looking back at me was a tall, thin, haggard fellow, the olive skin of his face framed by shaggy unkempt hair, his dark eyes ringed by gray circles. That guy wasn't going to help.

Polished wooden stairs led to the bedrooms and halfway up my cell vibrated in my pocket. It had been doing that all the way home.

Now I got it out and scrolled through all the messages. My heart sank. They were all from Katie.

Whr r u

We hav 2 TLK

TXT ME MED8LY!

There were more.

I tried to summon the energy to reply, but too much had happened that day, so I switched off the phone, and moved Katie down my emotional to-do list.

Mishi's bedroom door beckoned. Inside, the walls were covered with indie band posters, Leonardo's Vitruvian Man, and Einstein poking his tongue out. I sighed. Mishi.

But, in actual fact, no Mishi.

No Mishi lying on the bed reading, or talking for hours on the phone, or writing in her secret diary. What secrets could a fourteen-year-old girl have? Thought I, the gold medal moron.

I had been looking forward to one of our ping-pong conversations that always left me feeling better. Mishi, full of teenage enthusiasms, seasoned with cynicism and spite.

And her fetching mix of hero-worship for her adored older brother (that would be me) together with a knack of slipping in the verbal knife to skewer egotistic stupidities (me again).

Lost in these musings, I stepped toward Mishi's desk, covered with middle school debris. Textbooks, pens, pencils (some with pink fluffy appendages), a laptop (black, with skull and crossbones motif).

And, peeping out from under some loose hand-written sheets of paper was the corner of a book, also pink.

The Diary. It had a lock, and stickers saying "Keep Out, This Means You!" The Diary was definitely out of bounds. No peeking. No thinking about peeking.

I didn't mean to peek, honest, but I watched with interest as a hand, mine, came into view with fingers outstretched. Those fingers slowly closed the gap, and touched the hot pink cover.

A wave of nausea shot through me, and like in the hospital, someone grabbed my head and feet and twisted and stretched me to breaking point. Then everything went dark again.

2.

The Second Vision

This time, when the blackness faded, I was in a room, an office of some sort, with old-fashioned furniture and faded tobacco-brown wallpaper. There was a desk, some plain wooden chairs and a standard lamp.

Not Egypt then.

Behind the desk was a man leaning slightly forward with his hands clasped in front of his mouth in the now-I-lay-me-down-to-sleep kids' prayer position. He was dressed in the tweedy gear detectives wear to solve murders in English country houses. At least according to the TV I've watched.

And he had the kindest face I'd ever seen. Black hair with silver streaks, brushed back from a high forehead, liquid brown eyes and prominent cheekbones, Russia via Madrid.

And Mishi was there. But not fourteen-year-old-today-Mishi. She looked like she was about ten.

She was sitting in a chair opposite the English detective dude. Her legs didn't reach the ground and she was swinging them back and forth, looking at him intently, and admiringly. This was new. There weren't a lot of people that Mishi admired.

Then the scene faded, and I was back in Mishi's room. I staggered backward, the diary fell back to the desk with a thump, and I grabbed the door to steady myself.

This was getting seriously creepy. I felt like I was in two worlds at once.

That man, who was he? The vision had left an ache in my heart, like bittersweet nostalgia for a beautiful world irretrievably lost. I had a burning desire to find that man.

Somehow, I don't know how, I knew he could answer my questions. Questions which, up to that moment I didn't even know I had. Questions about myself, and my healing gift, and about all the mysteries Mordecai had tried to tell me. And which I had refused to hear.

And Mishi knew him.

Then the memory of Mishi waiting at the gym kicked me in the guts. I was standing here in her room in a daze and she was at school waiting. This was not going to end well.

I turned and ran into the corridor.

Constantinople, Eastern Roman Empire 1148AD

In the late autumn of the year of our Lord 1148, when the leaves were beginning to turn red and gold, and the first hint of cool breezes from the mountains of Anatolia had begun to cut through the heat of summer, a young man with dark eyes, smooth olive skin and a proud aquiline nose, his rich brown hair curling out from beneath an ornate green turban, strolled down the gang plank of a Venetian galley. Sailors swarmed up and down rope ladders, furling the sails of the proud vessel which had just arrived at the Golden Horn. This was the busiest of ports, its docks serving Constantinople, the greatest of cities, welcoming ships from foreign lands conveying treasures and spices, gold and jewels, slaves and cloth from the far corners of the earth.

And today, among the many travelers disembarking from dhows, galleys, xebecs and a hundred other forms of water borne transport, this new arrival, his sequined slippers peeping out from beneath a long red robe woven with golden thread, stopped to gaze on the towers and domes, the palaces and pleasure gardens which lined the shore.

He made a minor adjustment to his turquoise silk turban, signifying his status as a Hadji, one who has made the pilgrimage to Mecca. In the cosmopolitan capital of Orthodox Christianity, lying at the meeting point of Europe, Asia and Africa, such a status could take him a long way.

Not, of course, that he had ever been within a thousand miles of Islam's holiest city.

The young man stood on the dock surrounded by shouting merchants, squabbling stevedores, beggars, and mendicant priests. A ragged monk with a stringy beard and filthy robes that could be smelled a hundred yards away called on the throng to repent. The monk stretched out his bony hand, and assured the crowd that they could delay the day of reckoning by sparing a few coins.

Israel Ibn Ibrahim, of Cordoba, now transformed into Hadj Ibrahim ibn Tariq al Andalus, flipped a gold coin into the air and caught it deftly between his finger and thumb.

He also caught the attention of a few nearby porters. He snapped his fingers at one of them, an evil looking fellow with a scar slicing down his face where his left eye used to be. The porter shuffled over, bowing and sniveling.

Ibrahim waved a casual hand toward his bags sitting on the deck of the galley.

"Oh fine Master," said the porter, his scar dancing and wriggling as he bobbed and bowed. The porter revealed two lonely yellow teeth in what Hadj Ibrahim supposed was meant to be a winning smile, "Where would the young Master be wishing to go on this fine day? Oh yes, your servant awaits your lightest word."

The porter began to carry bundles down from the ship, eager to do the bidding of this Musulman Unbeliever. After all, thought the porter, was it not so that the gold of an infidel was the same as that of the holiest monk of Mount Athos? More valuable actually. Those flea-bitten monks would sooner preach a sermon denouncing the greediness of this world, than part with a single copper dhiram.

And this young fellow looked rich and foolish enough to part with a week's wages for a day's work.

"Tell me, my good man," said the young chap to the sweating porter tying the last of the bags to his third mule, "Where might a newcomer to this beautiful city of yours find comfortable lodgings for the night?"

The porter winked his good eye at his friends and said: "Oh Master, the brother-in-law of my sister's nephew owns a very reputable inn in the Fishmongers' Quarter just beside the Holy Cathedral of Sancta Sophia. There the young Master might find comfortable lodgings."

"And might," the young man asked, "a young man, with a few coins to spare, perhaps find some friendly fellows willing to play him in a few harmless games of chance?"

"Oh sir," said the porter nodding eagerly. "Most assuredly, the click of the dice and the shuffling of cards is all that a young man of your taste and breeding will hear until the cock crows to summon the dawn."

"Then lead on my good man," said the newly minted Hadj Ibrahim ibn Tariq Al Andalus. "I begin to love this fine city of yours all the more!"

The Maleficium et MaledictionesArcanum

Secret Crimes and Curses

of

Baphomet, Lord of the Underworld, Prince of Darkness, Bringer of Pestilence and Purveyor of Plagues

As transcribed in a trance by
LeonardoDaSilva,
Magus and Initiate into the Mysteries of Demonic Wisdom

Extract 1: Canto I, Verses 17 and 18

17. ... at the gathering of the Four Signs, even at the coming together of the Four Bringers of the Keys to the Gate ...

18. The City of the Righteous will stand unguarded and there will be a fall so great that the gnashing of teeth and the wail of the afflicted will be heard in the highest Heaven and the deepest Circle of Hell, even, the dwelling place of the Lord Baphomet ...

Extract 2: Canto III, Verses 3 and4

3. ... The First Sign is The Tempus, The Time, when the Great Planets and the Small, will gather in line, when the power of the Heavens will align, when the Sun and the Moon will bow low, yea, when they will bend the knee to the Most High ...
4. ... when the rising sign of the Goat stands opposed to the sign of the Lion and in alignment to the sign of the Fish, and Sirius, the Dog Star shines forth ...

CHAPTER TWO

13TH SEPTEMBER

CONTINUED

PROFESSOR OLAF SVENSSON

1.

Professor Olaf Svensson, tall, ash-blond, and built like a football defensive end, strode up Classon Ave toward Dekalb in Brooklyn. The sidewalk was crowded, the traffic was the usual New York snarl. The varied smells of coffee, bread and subway steam accompanied Svensson to the ornate entrance of the Cardozo School of Graduate Studies, Humanities Department. Six stone steps led up to a gothic arch carved with geometric patterns and the university motto in Latin, Hebrew and English – Supra Omnem Veritatem; M'Al L'Khol, Emet; Above All, Truth. Cardozo, founded in 1946, looked like it had been around for a thousand years and would be around for a thousand more.

The arch framed glass entrance doors, and Svensson joined the graduate students and faculty mounting the steps. He funneled through into the cavernous foyer returning affable greetings. Svensson nodded to the guard at the front desk. He rode the elevator with a dozen others to the third floor, turned right down the gray and white checkerboard-patterned marble hallway and walked to the door of his research rooms in the School of Medieval Studies.

Sean Singleton and Mary Blakely, two of Svensson's three graduate student research assistants, were already at their desks, staring at computer screens, their hands moving across their mouse pads in a synchronized ballet.

The room was small, crammed with three desks cluttered with computers, in-trays, papers and binders pushed against the paneled walls, and a cluster of filing cabinets, cupboards and an assortment of low tables, odd chairs and empty plant pots. The detritus that collects in all University work spaces. The high arched windows let in the noise of a busy Brooklyn morning, but little light. Fluorescent tubes gave the room an incongruous clinical air.

Blakely, tall, thin with straight brown hair and large, black-framed 'smart girl' eyeglasses, was peering at a page of medieval Latin. Singleton, solidly built, his face an earnest mask of concentration, was making notes. His ear buds connected to a phone in his top pocket. He wore a baseball cap with the embroidered words: "I speak Latin, what's your superpower?"

2.

Svensson went to his office and put down his bag. He hung his coat next to the photograph on the wall showing him receiving the Nobel Peace Prize in Oslo, Norway.

He went back into the main room and stood behind Blakely, looking over her shoulder at the Latin manuscript scrolling slowly up the computer screen. Every now and then she took a stylus and highlighted a word or underlined a phrase on the screen.

After a few minutes Singleton at the next desk clasped his hands behind his head and stretched. He looked around and saw Svensson.

"Oh, Morning, Professor," he said, plucking the buds from his ears.

"Good morning, Sean, Mary, your work on the *Maleficium* is proceeding well, is this not so? Our friend, Leonardo Da Silva has yielded some more of his secrets?"

"The usual," said Blakely, turning and looking up at him through her giant glasses. "He wastes a lot of valuable parchment cursing all the people who will feel his wrath when the day of vengeance comes and unquenchable fire rains down from Heaven. Yadda, yadda, yadda."

Singleton swiveled toward them on his chair.

"I've come across another reference to The Four Signs. That makes six or seven times he's mentioned them."

"Jeremy has been looking at the clues in Canto III, particularly the Tempus, the Time," said Blakely.

"Where is Jeremy by the way?"

On cue the door crashed back on its hinges and a tall young man, his hair unkempt, his army issue greatcoat flapping about his thighs, reversed into the room. Jeremy Plensk carried two cardboard file boxes toward the unoccupied third desk. He unloaded his burden and turned with a scowl to the other three.

"Good morning Jeremy," said Svensson. "We were discussing your research into one of Da Silva's signs, the *Tempus.*"

Plensk grunted. "Fat lot of good if we don't know *when* the Time will be. Kind of a crucial piece of the puzzle wouldn't you say?"

"But that is where you might be wrong," said Svensson, "I have been looking into some companion writings of our friend Senore Da Silva, Letter Fragments VII and XI, and he makes reference to an alignment ofplanets."

"Awesome!" said Plensk throwing his hands in the air in a Hallelujah gesture. "And we'll spend another few centuries trying to figure out what it all means."

"Put a cork in it J," said Blakely. "Go on Professor."

"You will be pleased to hear, Jeremy," said Svensson, "There is, in fact, a planetary alignment in the terms Da Silva indicates at midnight on October 3rd to be exact. A little over two weeks from now."

MISHI STERN

I changed positions, pushed my hair back, and looked around for the bazillionth time.

He was late, again. I knew he would be. He was always late.

Charming, friendly, everybody loves Aaron Crapface Stern, Mr. Popular, all the girls dropping dead at his feet hoping he'll notice them. Crap.

Crap, crap, crap. Late.

Again.

I kept looking around for the silver Lexus, or that crappy Nissan he thinks is so cool, hoping that stupid brother of mine would actually finally, just this once, come only a *little* bit late to pick me up.

Crap.

All the talk at home. Mishi this. Mishi that. Mishi, don't walk home on your own.

Who's going to get Mishi?

Blah, blah, crapping blah.

Don't, like, fight over me, or anything.

Mom at some boneheaded conference. Dad at the stupid warehouse. Of course. And Ronnie off with Katie Look at Me I'm Sooo Perfect Lieboshits.

Ronnie's always, like, 'Katie's amazing, Katie's a genius, Katie walked on water. Quick! Let's ring the Pope and get him to make Katie the first Jewish Princess Saint, before some other religion grabs her'.

And I was left sitting on the steps of the school. Looking like the biggest mouth-breather in the entire universe. All the other kids got their rides from their Dads, or boyfriends, or chauffeurs.

While my ass got frostbite.

I wriggled again to get some circulation going. Then I shivered.

What was that? Had I heard something? Was someone out there?

I could hear the distant sound of traffic. It was a long way away. I was alone, sitting in the gathering darkness. And there was something or someone out there.

Ronnie, where are you?

AARON STERN

I ran out of Mishi's room, freewheeled down the stairs three at a time, oblivious to residual aches and pains. I raced out the front door, slamming it behind me and fumbling for my keys.

I was meant to pick her up from Gym practice. Now. Hours ago.

Oh God, I thought, She's going to be so mad. She'll kill me. Worse, she would toss her hair and give me the look, and not speak to me all the way home. She would make me feel lousy without saying a word.

I was mumbling to myself, the car keys jingling in my hand, telling myself to hurry, that it would be OK, that Mishi would be fine.

I got the car door open and jumped into the driver's seat.

Mishi would see the funny side, we'd have a laugh.

Fat chance of that!

Finally the car started.

My heart pounded and the sweat prickled my scalp. I had a picture of those tossing curls, and those blazing eyes.

Leafy streets, houses, stores, pedestrians, other cars flashed by.

I gripped the wheel, willing the traffic to part for me.

A century later the car screeched around the last corner and fishtailed to a halt in front of the school. It had barely finished rocking on its springs when I was out and slamming the driver's side door behind me.

And there was my worst nightmare. Mishi.

I could tell she was mad from a hundred yards away. The set of her body and the unnatural stillness were eloquence itself. Mount Mishi-suvius about to erupt.

"Hi, Mishi, sorry I'm a bit late." Puffing and blowing.

Silence. She gathered up her backpack.

"Hope you weren't waiting too long." I was aiming for cool contrition, but what I hit was a pathetic whine.

More silence. Standing up, tossing curls (gulp), shouldering backpack.

"Oh well, no harm done, eh?"

Very loud silence. Walking past me toward the car without a glance in my direction.

I tagged along, the picture of obsequious brotherhood.

At the car door she waited. I grabbed the handle and opened it for her like I was Jeeves and she was Her Ladyship Michelle Stern, of the Brentwood Sterns.

We stood like that for a frozen moment while she breathed loudly through her nose. She looked like her temperature gauge was rising to Sahara Desert levels. She was about to say something.

Then she got a grip and the Ice Queen was back.

She slid into the car, backpack on lap, seatbelt clipped, lips pressed together, staring straight ahead.

I raced around and got in, started the engine and pulled away from the curb. I was just joining the flow of homeward traffic when she couldn't control herself any longer.

"Aaron, you are without doubt the stupidest ..."

False start.

"Do you know how humiliating it is to ..."

Not quite good enough.

She gathered her forces, then ...

"When I tell Mom that you left me there in the dark for hours to freeze my butt off while every other girl in the entire world was picked up by someone who actually cared about her and I had to sit there while they all must have had a good old laugh at poor old Mishi, Look at her, left behind again, and they're like, Hi Mishi, would you like a ride, and Hey Mishi, can we drop you somewhere, and Gee Mishi, we've filled in the adoption papers so you can come and live with us and never have to see your complete moron stupid dumbass brainless idiot brother who spends all his time walking into power poles and drooling his soup down his front because he can't find his ass with both hands."

She wound to a halt. She sat still again.

I waited for more but this was a different kind of still. A small still.

Then she started to cry. I almost swerved off the road.

I hadn't heard her do that for I couldn't remember how long. According to the rulebooks little girls are meant to cry when they see puppies and kittens. Or watch Bambi's mother meet the hunter. Mishi had skipped that phase. Tough as boot leather, and twice as cynical.

I pulled over and switched off the engine.

She was struggling to get control, hating herself, I supposed, for this sign of weakness.

I reached out and touched her shoulder. A small stab of pain spread up my arm. She angrily shrugged my hand away.

"Oh stop it," she said, "Now you're going to be the big brother who pretends he actually cares. Wait, I have to get the Actors Guild on the line, so they can start polishing your Oscar."

"You're wrong, you know."

"Wrong? About what?" Looking over at me, her face wet with tears.

"I'm not pretending," I said, and I unclipped my seatbelt and reached over and, ignoring the sting shooting up my arms, I hugged her to me tightly. She stiffened, but then relaxed. When the next round of tears subsided I leaned back and looked down at her.

"Tell me what's the real problem here. I've always been a goofball, I'm often running late – OK, OK," seeing her expression. "I'm *always* running late. So what happened this time that was different?"

"Oh Ronnie, I was scared. I felt something. Something bad. Really bad. I can't describe it. And I can't tell you how I knew. But there was something or someone out there that wanted to hurt me. And it wanted to hurt you as well."

DR. AMADEUS CALIFARIO

There was a quiet knock at the study door. Dr. Amadeus Califario opened his eyes, uncrossed his legs and floated up from the meditation cushion in one move. The soft light of the single standard lamp in the corner illuminated the drawn yellow curtains, the tidy mahogany desk, his office chair, which looked like a prop from a Gary Cooper western, two upright wooden chairs which faced the desk, and, in one corner, a low sofa and armchair upholstered in a pattern of large swirling red and pink flowers. A couch that any great-grandmother would be proud to call her own.

"Come in," he said.

"Dottore," said Wolfgang Holst, the Italian title sounded strange in the thick German accent.

"Good day Wolfgang," said Dr. Amadeus Califario. "Please sit, I wanted to update yourself and Mordecai. He will be here presently."

Holst, a big man with broad shoulders and short blond hair, seated himself in the armchair in the corner of the office. He was dressed in white martial arts trousers and robe, tied with a black belt. He crossed his legs, propped his elbow on the arm of the chair and rested his chin on his hand.

"It appears," said Dr. Califario, "That events are accelerating. And our friends in The Organization are upping the ante. They have Detectors, of course, who can find our people, they probably have the location of all of them in North America. At least we should assume they do."

"So what has changed?" said Holst.

"Now our people are reporting the presence of Watchers. They are being observed."

"Do we know why?" said Holst.

"Not yet," said Dr. Califario, "But I wonder if perhaps we can turn this to our advantage, by watching the Watchers and finding out a little more about them."

There was another knock at the door, and Mordecai Ben Zvi entered.

"Good evening Mordecai. Mrs. Katz?"

"Yes, Amadeus, she has passed to her reward, as you predicted. She went out with the bang. A real energy surge."

"Not surprising," Holst chimed in. "The passing of a truly great soul."

"Yes, Mrs. Katz was indeed that," said Mordecai. They sat silently, each lost for a moment in their own memories.

"And how did your encounter with young Mr. Stern go?" asked Dr. Califario, rounding the desk and settling back in his chair.

"An interesting young man," said Mordecai.

"So", said Dr. Califario, "It didn't go as well as we hoped."

"But about as well as we expected."

"He did not fall for your Israeli charm?" Holst was smiling.

"My dear Wolfgang, he's proof against my most winning arguments. I rather liked him."

"But it means," Dr. Califario was all business, "that when he does come around he will be all the more solid for us."

"And you believe he will succumb?" asked Wolfgang skeptically.

"Oh yes, my dear Wolfgang. I have no doubt. But before that happens, I fear that Mr. Stern will be in for a challenging time. Some of the dangers might have been averted had he come to us immediately. Now? Who knows, but I think we should discuss how best to ensure the maximum number of Sterns survive what is coming."

AARON STERN

1.

Carmelita was home, I could see the light on in her room, but it was her night off, so, with Mom at the conference and Dad stocktaking, Mishi and I had the place to ourselves.

I slowed the car and we waited for the garage door to roll up. I slid the car into its space. We got out, Mishi quiet and thoughtful, me just glad to be home. We went through the connecting door to the house, which was a typical home for the area. Big, two stories, looked a bit like the White House. It was, you know, white. With columns and balconies and a flat top. Except not crawling with security guards to guard the President. Come to think of it, how handy would that have been!

My shoes clacked across the polished floorboards, Mishi's runners padded softly, past the furniture, the hall mirror and the framed paintings and sketches. The Picasso was a line drawing, on a napkin, of a dove with an olive branch in its mouth. Apparently he used to pay his bar tab that way when he was up and coming. It was a twentieth wedding anniversary surprise for Mom. Dad never said how much it cost but I googled it and let's just say that we could put a down payment on an NFL franchise, or a Caribbean island, one of the nice ones.

Growing up, Mom and Dad had never made a major deal of the money thing. Mishi and I were expected to do stuff for our allowance. Not, like, start up a software company, or like that. But if I wanted cash I had to mow the lawn, or wash the car. And we had to keep our rooms tidy as well.

Some of this tidying was because Mom and Dad were fanatical about treating the help properly. Always 'Please' and 'Thank you', and Christmas bonuses, and remembering their families.

The maddest Dad ever got with me was when I was about seven and I spoke to one of our housekeepers, Jacinta, rudely. I don't think I meant to, but I must have sounded bossy and I certainly didn't say please when I asked whatever it was I asked.

Anyway, Dad blew his stack. Which was rare, but eruptions of Mount St Helens are too, and look how that turned out.

I certainly got the point.

And Mom and Dad always made absolutely sure to hire legals. This is not, to be completely truthful, a strong suit amongst our friends and cohabitants in the lovelier areas of LA. But Mom and Dad won't hire anyone without the correct papers.

They keep telling Mishi and me that our great-great-grandparents stood for hours at Ellis Island in New York with the imprint of Cossack boots on their tushes, and got their US papers all nice and legal. And don't you ever forget it!

Anyway this is taking the long way round to saying I wasn't going to disturb Carmelita on her night off, simply because we were a bit starvational.

Mishi and I got ourselves something to eat, and we sat down at the kitchen table.

"So, Lummox, how'd your day go?" Mishi asked. Fully recovered you'll note.

Mishi's question brought everything flooding back. You'd think I would've remembered Katie, the hospital, and Mordecai and all, but, like picking up Mishi, my memory banks were blinking on and off.

So I performed the comic ritual of dropping my half eaten sandwich, and rummaging in my pocket for my cell.

I saw all those messages, and more since last I looked. I mean there were a lot. All from Katie. Text after text. All pretty much the same, but with more and more capital letters and exclamation points as they went on.

The last one said: "ring now or yr a dead man" No capitals, no exclamation marks. Ominous.

I eye-browed a "Sorry" to Mishi, and headed for the hallway.

2.

"Hi, Katie. Look, I..."

"Aaron!"

"Yeah, look I just..."

"Listen to me, Aaron Stern. What were you thinking? What was that at the hospital? What did you do to Bobbeh?'

"Me? To Bobbeh Katz? I don't know. She held out her hand and..."

"And you took it and now she's, she's..." Katie started crying and I waited feeling like a beached whale.

There was a break in the sobbing. I said: "Look Katie, I'm sorry. I have no idea what I did. I just took her hand. And then, I dunno, then all sorts of insane stuff began to happen."

"And then you ran away. Big brave Aaron Stern. And Bobbeh died right there in front of us after you 'held her hand'."

An unfamiliar feeling of impatience began to worm its way up my substitute for a spine. Unfamiliar because the Stern Philosophy on Women was wait until the storm is over and things get back to normal. Say sorry a gajillion times. Then carry on as if nothing had happened.

Now I felt, like, exasperated.

"Look Katie," I interrupted, "I'm genuinely sorry about Bobbeh. I liked her. Everyone did and I feel bad for you and your Mom and Dad and Sam and all. But I didn't kill her. I held her hand and then something kooky happened. Then I sort of panicked and ran. I can't go back and change any of that."

I stopped, amazed. I was addressing Katie Deborah Liebovitz in what was almost a peremptory, one might go so far as to say brusque, manner. French noblemen had been guillotined for a lot less.

"OK," she said softly.

"OK?" I repeated.

"Yes, OK, I have to think. And Mom and Dad need me. I'll see you tomorrow at school." Click, or whatever the cell equivalent is.

Stunned, I went back to join Mishi and my half sandwich.

FRANCOIS PIERROT

1.

The day of Francois Pierrot's death began like any other.

The bell that tinkled when the door opened and closed was an old world affectation, entirely in keeping with the rest of the shop, its low wattage bulbs and wooden shelving covered with timepieces in various states of repair.

Several grandfather clocks lurked in the twilight gloom.

On the hour, the noise was tremendous. Bells rang, whistles blew, chimes sounded, cuckoos chirped, and various knights, dragons, steam trains, and milkmaids appeared from their hiding places and moved jerkily along their tracks to announce the passage of another sixty minutes.

The customer, an elderly lady, one of the many who had used the watchmaker's services for decades, walked to the back of the shop and sat on the wooden chair opposite Francois. She chatted with him about this and that, put down the delicate timepiece with the cracked glass cover, and then she left for tea with friends.

Her driver held the shop door for her.

2.

The old man returned to his work. He leaned over his workbench, framed in a pool of lamplight. Electrical tape held the metal lamp cover in place. With his green eyeshade and half-moon spectacles he was the living stereotype of the old Swiss watchmaker.

As it happened Francois Pierrot was French, but only just. A few miles to the east from his hometown of Gex, across the Swiss border, and he would indeed have completed the cliché.

His workshop was a long way from Gex. Kansas City, Missouri to be exact. He'd been driven to America by war and hunger, and a childhood memory of dashing heroes racing down village streets in open jeeps.

Young Francois, holding his mother's hand and waving a tiny French flag, had been awestruck by the sight of these tough warriors in their faded and stained uniforms, chewing gum and smoking cigarettes, and laughing as they drove the mighty legions of the Thousand Year Reich before them.

One day, some of these strange visitors had stopped in the village to look at maps, and confer in their incomprehensible tongue. One man, with tired eyes, black hair, and dark bristles, had detached himself from the discussion around the jeep, and seeing Francois had come right up to him. He had spoken to Francois in French. Not the French they spoke in Gex, but close enough.

Francois, spellbound, had especially understood the chocolate bar the man held in his hand. If Christ himself had descended in glory with a host of angels Francois could not have felt it to be a greater marvel than when this wonderful man held out the chocolate and gave it to him. Francois was hypnotized by the blue and white paper wrapping, and the thin strip of silver foil peeping out from each end.

He looked up at last as the man repeated his question.

"Ou se trouve la Mairie, et le Maire?" Where is the Town Hall and the Mayor? Francois had pointed speechlessly up the hill.

And the man gave Francois a broad grin and said, with mock formality in his strange French, "Merci, Les Etats-Unis tu remercient." The United States of America thanks you.

His next words changed Francois' life forever. In that blissful state of chocolaty wonderment Francois Pierrot heard the man say, "Kansas City, Missouri thanks you, young fella."

Only, the man's lips hadn't moved, no sound had come from his mouth. But Francois had heard and understood the words as clear as a bell. And they were in English, a language he didn't speak.

The man smiled at Francois and turned and walked back to his comrades. They folded the maps and climbed back into the jeep. The engine roared to life and the man gave Francois a small wave. Francois waved back. The spell broken, he carried his chocolate treasure into the house and shared it with Maman.

From that day, and with increasing clarity, Francois found, if he concentrated in just the right way, he could hear and understand people's thoughts. He called it 'Going to his Reading Room'.

The quiet, lonely boy never told anyone about his Reading Room.

3.

Peace came to Gex and no more American soldiers raced through the village in their jeeps. The quiet boy grew into a reserved young man. He completed his apprenticeship with the finest clockmaker and watch repairer in the local area. And he supported his mother until the day she died in the summer of 1959.

The day after the funeral, he packed up his tools and a few keepsakes, including a carefully smoothed foil and paper chocolate wrapper pressed lovingly between the pages of a tattered copy of *Babar the Elephant,* and moved to Kansas City, Missouri.

He found work and made a down-payment on a little shop with living accommodation upstairs on the corner of West 40th and Pennsylvania, in the Westport area, long before it transformed itself from a seedy backwater into a precinct of wine bars, fashionable eateries and yoga centers.

In the spring of 1974 he had been sitting in a café when a dark young man in a tweed suit sat down at the next table.

They had exchanged a few pleasantries after which the man, like the Chocolate God, had switched to French. This had been the first of many surprises that Dr. Amadeus Califario sprang on Francois Pierrot.

The second surprise was that Dr. Califario knew that Francois could read minds. Francois had been 'detected' by another person with hidden powers and that person had passed it up the line until, eventually, it reached the vigilant ear of Dr. Amadeus Califario.

Dr. Califario had introduced Francois to a secret world. A world peopled by men, women and, yes, even children, with unique gifts: mind-reading and healing, psychokinesis and prophecy. Dr. Califario explained that these gifted ones, known collectively as the Elders, worked behind the scenes, using their powers to keep the world on an even keel. Sometimes winning the never-ending battle against dark forces, sometimes retreating in the face of a determined attack, but always chipping away quietly to protect, to support, to encourage, to commiserate. Each of the Elders had an 'Assignment', a man or woman in the public eye whom they influenced.

And now it was time for Francois to take up the responsibilities, which his power conferred on him. Francois was warned to be on the alert for the Adversaries. Because, yes it was so, there were those whose plans and schemes had been thwarted, delayed, knocked off track by the Elders. They had their own methods of sniffing out people like Francois. And they did not play nice.

"In fact," said Dr. Califario, "You've been a bit lucky, mon ami. It is probably because you chose this rather charming city, in what our opponents would doubtless think of as 'fly-over country', that you have escaped their notice. Long may it last!"

Francois had received training, deepening his clairvoyant gift. They had even tried to teach him how to defend himself. At this the shy Frenchman was not so successful. So Francois did a little research, bought a few chemicals, made a few clever modifications to the watch he wore on his left wrist, and prepared himself for the day that the forces of evil found his quiet corner of Kansas City Missouri.

And he had waited for his 'Assignment'. Dr. Califario had been vague about this last bit. "You'll know it when it appears. Be patient, Francois. Your Assignment will find you."

4.

One day, about a year after Francois' fateful meeting with Dr. Califario, a big, red-faced man, with a shock of jet black hair, wearing a charcoal-gray pinstripe three-piece suit with a gold watch chain dancing and jingling from his waistcoat pocket had walked into his shop. A harried assistant trailed after him, her notebook and pen at the ready, hitching up the leather satchel that kept sliding off her shoulder.

"Miss Jones," the man had barked. In all the years that followed Francois never found out her first name. "The clock. The clock!" The man snapped his finger and pointed toward Francois' worktable.

Miss Jones juggled her notebook and pen, put the satchel down on the worktable. Then she reverently pulled out a cloth-wrapped object. She carefully placed it in front of Francois.

"Can you fix it?" The man's tone implied that it was Francois' fault that it was broken.

"Until I discover what it is that is wrong I can not tell you, Monsieur...?"

"Packenham, Samuel J. Packenham."

"Ah, Packenham. I have heard this name."

He had already used his 'reading' gift on his visitors. Eager to please, terrified of failure, supernaturally efficient (Miss Jones); commanding, brilliant, his bark much worse than a surprisingly gentle and kindly bite (Samuel J. Packenham).

Francois gently unwrapped the parcel.

"Half of Kansas City is named after my family, so I should very much hope you had heard of me."

But Francois was only half listening. The last folds of cloth revealed an exquisite gold-inlaid 1758 George Clark of London carriage clock with Turkish numerals.

Francois sat back in awe. It was glorious, magnificent. Francois felt privileged just to sit in its presence and gaze, let alone touch it, or, Heaven! Work on it.

"Can you fix it?" Packenham repeated. "They tell me you're the best." Francois took a few minutes to examine the clock.

"Yes," he said, "I believe I can."

And François had indeed fixed it, and had thereby gained entry into Packenham's circle.

5.

Over the years an unlikely friendship grew between the shy watchmaker and the blustering tycoon. Packenham came to trust Francois's instincts. In that time Francois, with a word, or sometimes merely a gesture, had been able to influence Packenham and, through him, others.

When Packenham had been appointed Assistant Secretary of Agriculture in the second Reagan Administration, Francois had been a regular guest. Under Francois' quiet guidance several important policies had been subtly pushed forward, and one or two significant missteps had been avoided.

Dr. Califario had been pleased.

Francois admired both Dr. Califario and Samuel J. Packenham, and Miss Jones for that matter. But he had always harbored the secret hope that he would one day encounter the greatest hero of them all, the dark-haired chocolate-bringer.

He never did.

Perhaps the man never came home from the war. Perhaps he had simply moved away, or died. After all, everyone did.

And today it would be Francois' turn.

ALBERT SEVERIN

1.

Albert Severin, ace Detector, was nervous. He liked things predictable, and this situation was unprecedented.

It was 10 pm and he was in Brentwood, sitting in the front passenger seat of a black Ford Escalade parked in the shadows under a tree, between two streetlights. He was looking straight at a house about fifty yards away on the other side of the street. He had been there for over two hours.

He risked a glance at the man next to him behind the wheel, sitting as still as a statue, staring straight ahead. The guy hadn't spoken a single word since Albert had been hustled off the sidewalk into the car in Studio City earlier that evening.

But the other fella, a big Asian hombre sitting in the back was the one who really worried Albert. What little talking there was, that dude did it all. And all he had said at Studio City, with the driver blocking Albert's path holding the front passenger door open, was, "Good evening, Mr. Severin, would you be kind enough to join us."

Refusal did not appear to be on the list of options. When they had driven to Brentwood and parked, the same guy had said, "You detect anything. You tell us."

Since then not a word, nothing, zilch, nada.

In all his days as a Detector, Albert had never met the people he worked for. He realized now that he had been just fine with that arrangement.

He definitely did not like sitting at night with these two guys behind darkened windows in a black SUV.

The only excitement had been an hour or so before when a young man, with dark, unkempt hair, had driven up to the house with a teenage girl.

He'd told the guys in the car that he recognized the girl from five years ago. Miss Freckle-face from the playground. Mishi. She'd made that sort of impression on him. They'd just grunted at him.

He'd detected some tell-tale signs as the boy had flashed by in the car. But it had been too quick, and he hadn't mentioned it. Now he was beginning to sweat. Should he have said something? Could he say something now, or would they think he had been holding out on them?

I mean, he thought, who were these guys, what did they want? Were they going to do something to the people in that house? Albert definitely wanted no part of that. Just let him do his Detection thing, and Albert would be gone, vamoosed, oudahere.

Then he had a worse idea. Would they do something to *him*? Was he safe? As soon as this cheerful thought kicked off its shoes and took up residence in Albert's brain it refused to leave.

And then things got even worse.

He felt a traitorous prompting in his loins.

'Oh crap', he thought, 'I need to piss. Can I hold it? How long are we going to be here? I really gotta go. Even if we leave now I'll be half way to somewhere and I'll piss in my pants.'

The humiliation colored his cheeks in the dark. Would he have to raise his hand like a kid? This was getting ridiculous. He was a grown man. If he had to go, he had to go. And that was that. He'd just open the door and go in the shadows over there up against that tree. Albert looked around furtively.

"What are you looking at, Mr. Severin?" The voice from the back seat was crisp and precise with the hint of an Asian accent. It made Albert's blood run cold. Like a snake had learned to speak. A polite snake, with perfect manners. But, a snake.

And if this guy was the snake, Albert was the hamster.

He tried to calm himself. His powers of detection were being affected by fear (and the need to urinate). He would get small bursts of energy and then nothing.

Albert realized the man was waiting for an answer.

"Nothing," said Albert. "Nothing at all. Just moving my neck."

"Hm," came the calm voice from the back.

Albert remained frozen in his seat.

"Smartarse," The man next to him, behind the wheel, spoke for the first time. In an Australian accent. The UN of bad guys, thought Albert bitterly.

Albert's bladder chose that moment to make another plea for attention. How had he gotten himself into this?

2.

Twelve years ago he had been trying to fix a light in the kitchen. He'd fallen off the ladder, and had cracked his head on the dining room table. He had woken up on the kitchen floor. As a precaution he had gone to an outpatients' service. In the waiting room, sitting in a plastic chair leafing through women's magazines with pictures of some English princess and the latest Hollywood starlets, an intern had walked by reading from a clipboard. The guy had lit up like a searchlight and Albert had been pressed back into his seat by a force field of energy.

When he had been able to breathe normally again Albert had looked around at the other patients. Surely they must have felt it. But they just sat dull-eyed and bored. This was Albert's first clue that something funny had happened to him.

He got a clean bill of health, a few weeks passed, and Albert shelved the experience as an after effect of the fall. Then one day, a month or so later, Albert was in the local supermarket looking at the frozen pizzas and a mother, pushing a shopping cart and keeping an eye on her kids, had lit up just like the intern. Albert's fingers left dents in the frozen pizza box.

After that it happened fairly regularly, a month, six weeks would go by and Albert would feel the pressure of the energy flowing from someone.

He occasionally wondered what it was about these people, but Albert was not really built for curiosity. It just settled in as part of his life. He had to be on his guard because it was pretty powerful and he could, almost literally, be bowled over, but with a bit of practice he got good at hiding the initial shock.

3.

Then, one day out of the blue he received a phone call. A stranger with a mellow voice: "Mr. Severin, you don't know me. I have a generous offer which you would be foolish to refuse."

Albert was about to hang up, but something stayed his hand.

"You have a talent which we could use, and for which we are willing to pay handsomely."

"Talent?" said Albert.

"Yes, Mr. Severin," said Mr. Smooth, "You do indeed have a talent. And a rare one I might add. Your talent is to detect."

"Detect? I ain't no detective."

"But you are, Mr. Severin, you are. Of a highly specialized nature. You detect people with energy. Do you not?"

This trick had been his little secret; and it had made Albert, an ordinary shmo, feel important. Like he had one over the rest of the world. Now this asshole, whoever he was, seemed to know all about it. And he knew Albert's name and phone number.

"Say, who are you anyway? What's your name?"

"My name is unimportant, and believe me, you don't want to go there. Let's just say I, and my associates, will pay generously for the use of this, ah, talent of yours."

"Go on." It was the money. Who couldn't do with a little more?

"Good, Mr. Severin, very good," Mr. Suave, "I will give you a cell phone number and bank account details. A new account, in your name. When you detect anyone you will ring the number as soon as possible taking care that the, um, detectee, does not, ah, grasp they have been detected. You will state your name, your location, and as full a description of the person as possible. If you somehow get a name, that will result in a monetary bonus, but you must not delay the call to do any (and here there was merry laughter) detective work."

"And then?"

"And then, five days later you will find a sum of money in that bank account. Your bank account Mr. Severin. It's all quite legitimate. No late night calls from law enforcement officers. Think of it as doing work on the side, as a consultant."

"But..."

"Now, now Mr. Severin, no buts. You will do this or you will find that I, and my associates, will be unhappy. And I assure you Mr. Severin you really don't want that. What I suggest is this. Do nothing until the next time you detect an energy source. Then try it. Ring the number, wait a few days and see if you like being a little better off. Ta ta."

Ta ta? Who was this guy, Liberace?

But Albert had essentially fallen into line. He had known he would. And the guy had been right. It was easy work, and he did like having a little extra dough. Actually a lot. Quite a lot over the twelve years.

But tonight was the first time he had ever met anyone face to face.

4.

All this was driven from Albert's mind as he felt his bladder clamoring for attention. Oh God, I'm going to piss my pants!

"I gotta go!" Albert blurted out as he fumbled for the door handle. Before either of the men in the car could say anything he tripped and staggered toward the trees. His fingers felt clammy and awkward as he fought the zip.

And then he was at the tree, one hand guiding operations and the other resting on the rough bark steadying himself. He stood in the shadows, his head tilted back as he sucked in air, feeling the happy release and listening with pleasure to the tiny, comforting sound of a tinkling stream hitting the ground in front of him.

Albert was rezipping when he was hit by such a wave of energy that he was thrown off his feet. It was unlike anything he had felt before. With pinpoint accuracy he knew it had come from the upper window of the house they were watching. And he knew it had come from the tousled young man.

And he could sense that Mishi girl as well. It was like a binary solar system with two incandescent suns orbiting each other. Two linked souls.

Albert struggled to hold himself together. Then the wave began to fade, leaving Albert's ears ringing.

He clambered to his feet and staggered back to the car. He leaned on the car door. The window hummed downward.

"What's up? Where did you go? Get back in," said the driver.

"I had to pee," said Albert testily, recovering a tiny spark of courage. "I had to pee." He said again, as he resumed his place in the car. "And..."

"And?" said the silky voice from the back of the car.

"And I felt something."

"Mr. Severin, my reserves of patience are not limitless, and believe me when I tell you, if they run out, you will regret it."

"I felt one of those energy waves. A biggie. Coming from the house. From that young guy. And the girl as well."

Albert was hoping his job was done and he could go. He was about to speak when the driver held up a quelling finger, pulled his cell from his pocket and speed dialed. Albert sat still, mesmerized by the finger. The driver handed the cell to the man in the back seat.

"Singh here," said the man in the back, "We're outside the Stern house and Severin reports an energy surge. He says it's both the brother and the sister."

RANDOLPH LASSITER

Lassiter cut the connection on his cell, and sat back in his chair. He was at home in Connecticut, in his den. It was 2 am eastern time.

In contrast to the wood paneled old-world charm of the UN office, this was sleek and modern with floor to ceiling windows overlooking a wooded park. His desk was a single sheet of glass artfully suspended on slender steel legs. The walls were white with a single Mondrian on one wall and a reproduction Calder mobile, its delicate bright red and yellow triangles dangling from thin wires, hanging in one corner. The furniture that looked comfortable wasn't, and those pieces that looked forbidding, like the Barcelona Chair, two studded cushions on curved metal legs, were.

His wife Caroline and his children were sleeping peacefully.

Most interesting, he thought. The brother as well. What an intriguing family these Sterns were turning out to be.

AARON STERN

After we'd eaten, Mishi went up to her room and closed the door.

I was ready for bed. I put the plates and glasses in the dishwasher and headed out into the hall to follow Mishi upstairs. Then I heard a voice. I'd have jumped into Mishi's arms and squealed like a little girl, if she'd been around to protect me, but I was alone. I looked around to see who had crept into the house. No one in sight.

I couldn't tell where the voice was coming from. It seemed to be inside my head. Was I going mad?

Then I caught a few more words.

"We are outside the Stern house..."

My heart raced. I stood still and kept listening, "...detected an energy surge..." It was like a radio with poor reception, fading in and out.

"...he says it's the brother..."

Was this guy talking about me?

My feet started moving toward the window despite the pleas of my mind, which kept telling them to stop. I slid crabwise along the wall and slowly moved the drapes so I could peek outside without anyone seeing in. There was no one in the street. All I could see was a big black SUV a few houses down. Were the words coming from there? From that distance?

But the voice faded out. I was alone inside my head. I couldn't think of anything to do other than go around the whole house and double-check that every door and window was locked. And the outside alarm was engaged. And the outside lights were set on motion detection.

And when I got to my room I rummaged through my closet for my Louisville slugger.

I slept with it that night.

Before I drifted off I remembered that loony Mordecai and his final words: "Be careful Mr. Stern. I do not believe you will have very long to wait before events begin to unfold."

CHAPTER THREE

14TH SEPTEMBER

AARON STERN

1.

The next day I drove to school, parked and caught Melvin again. It was like Groundhog Day.

"How's Shmendrick Man, the greatest klutz mankind has ever seen?" he asked. Shmendrick is Yiddish and is as complimentary as it sounds. As is klutz. I believe both words are googleable.

One of the things Melvin and I have in common is our families' quaint efforts to preserve some of our tribal culture. Most other Jewish kids I know have very little of this. They eat what they like – the more bacon the better – and except for the technical fact of ancestry don't give much indication of being Jewish at all.

But the Shnayvises and Sterns? Our parents have tried to instill a bissel yiddishkeit, a little Jewish culture, into us. And because we both like being the square peg in a sea of round holes we've adopted this difference as a badge of honor.

"Greetings, Captain Nudnik, strange visitor from the planet Shlemiel," I replied. We shot the breeze for the few minutes it took to cross the parking lot and take the path to the main school entrance, joining the river of fellow students.

I was only paying attention with half an ear though. I kept looking around for that familiar swinging ponytail and curvaceous rear end. I had serious fences to mend. I really cared about Katie, and if anything, these latest bizarre events had showed me how much.

But I couldn't see her in the press of bodies so, weaving through knots of students and dodging locker doors, I made my way down the hall and up a flight of stairs to my first class, with...

Now how can I describe this guy?

Suffice it to say that Mr. Hiram X. Snell, Social Studies teacher at Coolidge, was a doofus of galactic proportions.

If evil scientists in a secret mountain lab had been given the job of creating the archenemy of real education, and Snell had emerged from the vat of gooey green liquid, then a cake with candles and back slapping all around would have been the evil scientist order of the day.

Mr. Smell (school kid humor, don't you love it?), was short, fat and bald, with annoying flyaway tendrils of left-over hair like someone had cleaned up after a molting cat and offered him the result halfprice.

His eyebrows and nose and ears, on the other hand! They were a different story. The luxurious hirsute growth from every cranial orifice was a wonder to behold. Pygmy tribes, or so we whispered behind our hands, could have wandered lost for years in Smell's eyebrows. Rare and endangered species might be lurking in his nose jungle.

And, to cap all this off, he had the winning personality of a rectal itch.

2.

I took my place in the class, opened my books and got ready to write.

When the room was mostly full, and the background hum of teen mating rituals was at its liveliest, Mr. Snell bustled in on his miniature legs, and fussed over his notes and overhead transparencies.

He began, as he always did, in a monotone, without calling the class to order; so the first few minutes were lost in the general rustling of papers and scraping of chairs as the awareness that things had begun slowly flowed back from the front row. Luis and Brad in the back corner were always the last to figure it out, keeping up their jock banter until the last moment.

Snell was droning on about global warming, or climate change, or wild atmospheric patterns or whatever the latest euphemisms for "weather" were.

Tell the truth, on that day I was not wholly in the zone.

Snello was boring on and on and on, and I was in a fog when I began to hear something else. And it was crystal clear. It was Snell's voice, but the words were different from those trickling out of his mouth.

"These idiots. I'll show them. One day they'll beg me for mercy. Then they'll be sorry. And they'll whine for my pity. Well they can whine all they like but they'll be fresh out of luck. Soon, we'll show them. Then the whining will really begin."

This went on and on. I stared at him. Was I actually reading his thoughts? Could he be thinking all this crazy stuff?

Then he looked right at me.

"And as for that Stern kid and that smartass friend of his... Wait he's looking at me. Why is he doing that? Can he tell what I'm thinking? Why is he looking at me like that? Oh God, can he hear? Must try to..."

And then the words got scrambled. And my 'hearing' faded, until I was only picking up the normal sounds of the class.

Snell and I kept glancing at each other for the rest of the lesson, and when the bell went he bundled his papers up and practically ran out of the room.

3.

In all the quality movies the hero knows he's got a bad guy on his hands, and he pursues the villain and confronts him. But I had had a very rough, and unnerving, and confusing twenty-four hours.

And it wasn't like I knew what was happening. Later I did, but right then chasing Smell and getting him to tell me what the heck was going on would have been very helpful, but it didn't occur to me.

I walked into the lunchroom with everything that had happened the previous day swirling in my head. And nearly knocked Katie over. She had been waiting for me.

"Ronnie!" she said. Steadying herself with her hands on my shoulders.

"Huh? Oh sorry, Dreamboat. I didn't see you there. I was thinking about things." This did not seem to be a good start to our reconciliation.

But Katie looked at me with round, blue eyes, slipped her hand into mine and led me to a seat.

Then we did that simultaneous speaking thing. "I'm sorry..." We both stopped.

"No you speak..."

"I was just going to..."

And then we were laughing and holding hands, and neither of us had to say anything.

"If I could intrude on this touching scene," said Melvin, from behind me, "Some of us feel the need for, you know, lunch. At lunchtime. Which this is."

Jostling me over, he set his tray down and started in on his food.

"So you two seem to have made up. That's of course if you had anything to make up for. Which I of course wouldn't know anything about. But that handholding and dreamy gazing are the text book signs."

I punched him in the arm and we all had another laugh.

Katie and I weren't hungry so we decided to catch a bit of California sunshine. We went outside and sat on the front steps of the school, holding hands, her head on my shoulder.

After a while Katie kissed me, then she got up and went to her next class.

I had a free period so I sat there, leaned back, my elbows on the steps behind me, soaking up the rays.

And it was then that I saw Snell way over in the teachers' parking lot talking to a big Asian man with coffee-colored skin in a gray suit.

And the voices in my head started up again.

"That Stern kid... think he's in my head... can he do that?"

The big guy's lips moved and in my head I heard: "Calm down Snell... take care of everything... don't panic..."

I sat up. That was the voice I'd heard last night at home, talking about me. What was my wacko teacher doing talking to some big guy who knew my name and had been staking out my house?

It was like a bucket of cold water.

Decision time.

I got out my cell. I scrambled around in my memory for the number, and punched it in.

"Mordecai Ben Zvi at your service, Mr. Stern."

"Look I need to speak to someone."

"Someone?"

"OK, I need to speak to you, and your people."

"Excellent, but no more over the phone. A car will arrive at the school in fifteen minutes. And the school office will receive the sad news of your sudden gastric attack. Go to the students' parking lot and stand beside your mother's car. We will find you."

4.

Mordecai turned up behind the wheel of a Lincoln Town Car, like my chauffeur, grinning broadly and gesturing at me with a wave of his hand. I got in.

"Well Mr. Stern, it is beyond my command of English to tell you how pleased I am, we are, that you called." He winked and leaned toward me. "We were, I can now share with you, beginning to get worried that you would leave it too late."

"Too late?" I said, "What do you mean?" Conversations with this little Israeli clotheshorse made my head spin.

"But Mr. Stern! Surely you remember my dire warnings that you and your family's safety were in the balance, and that delay could tip the scales. In the wrong direction."

I didn't say anything.

"So, the phone call was welcome, very welcome." Mordecai continued, "And now we go to meet my superior, and after that..." a shrug of those perfectly tailored shoulders, "Who knows? But what I do know is that a great adventure awaits you, my friend!"

The car glided into the flow of traffic.

The route took us through the upscale parts of LA. We skirted downtown toward a warehouse district, and then south in the direction of Longbeach. I'd lived in LA all my life but I'd never been to the places we were driving through. This is not very unusual though. LA is a collection of separate villages and, as they say, never the twain shall meet. I don't suppose any kids from South LA do much of their Christmas shopping in Bel Air either.

"Mr. Stern," said Mordecai. "May I call you Aaron?"

"Sure, knock yourself out. Ronnie's fine too," I said, sounding more casual than I felt. I had been truly spooked by Snell and that big Asian dude. And I was just about to ask Mordecai about them, but before I got the words organized he said, "We are going to meet someone who can answer all of your questions." Was this guy psychic?

"What do you mean? Where is this place?"

"Ah, that would be telling," said Mordecai, a mischievous grin danced across his lips. "We believe in hiding in plain sight. But we still believe in hiding. No secret underground lairs, or mountain top castles for us," he trilled. "But nevertheless, we are not in a place where anyone would think of looking. LA is so wonderful for misplacing things."

It sure worked on me. I couldn't have re-driven that route if it had been paved with yellow bricks.

There were very few people about. But that again is LA. It's a city where cars are king, and the sun-baked pavements are not designed for strolling.

We finally came to an area of low rent car yards and vacant lots. There were day-loan stores, five and dimes, and boarded-up shop fronts.

We slowed down as we passed a thrift with racks of cheap, colorful polyester clothing. A few locals were flicking back and forth through the fashion offerings. Next to it, on the corner, was a two-story office building that had definitely seen better days. There were a couple of first floor office spaces. One had "O'Connor, Juarez and Blumenthal – Attorneys at Law" in faded lettering on the window, but the only occupants I could see were some peeling wallpaper and an old filing cabinet.

We turned the corner and behind the building was a vacant lot marked off from the sidewalk by a rusty chain link fence. We passed through a gate and drove over a few yards of cracked concrete, with a profusion of weeds trying to find their place in the hot LA sunshine.

Mordecai pointed the car at a graffiti covered roller shutter door set into the back wall of the office block. He pressed a button on the car's dash. The door clanked and rattled up revealing a dark opening.

We drove in and I was temporarily blinded by the move from bright sunshine to gloom. We were in a tunnel which immediately dipped down. And down. And down. And down.

"I thought you said no secret underground lairs."

"I may have overstated the case," said Mordecai with a laugh, "This does go down quite a way. A lucky find for us, a World War Two research facility abandoned by the military in 1947. Ah, here we are."

We leveled out into a cavernous space. Bare concrete floor, brick walls, some cans and jars on a timber shelves. Lit by a few bare bulbs. Mordecai guided the car nose-in toward a wall of excavated stone.

No large lurid neon sign with flashing lights saying: "Elders HQ – Prepare to have your Mind Blown!"

We got out of the car and Mordecai said: "Welcome to The Migdal."

"Migdal?" I said.

"Yes," he said, "You must work on your Hebrew. It means 'Tower', a fortified place, a secure location. It is what we call this place."

Our footsteps echoed across the concrete, as we walked to an old fashioned wooden door. Mordecai used a remote attached to his key ring, and machinery began to hum, followed by the customary 'I'm here!' ding of an arriving elevator.

"No elevator buttons you notice," he shrugged. "We can never be too careful."

Mordecai slid the wooden door aside, and then did the same to a metal concertina grill. I stepped into a tiny wood paneled space that made a phone booth look like Carnegie Hall.

Mordecai squeezed in after me.

"Snug, is it not?" he said.

"Snug would be an improvement," I said. "This is a coffin built for one." The ride up took forever.

At last there was a judder and a bump, and Mordecai turned awkwardly and slid the metal concertina back and then the wooden door, and we stepped into a dimly lit pale green hallway, last painted before those military guys left for good.

Mordecai ushered me down one corridor after another, and past about a thousand unmarked wooden doors. There was no chance of me retracing my steps on my own. This cheery thought was just beginning to trouble me when we arrived at our destination.

Mordecai stopped at yet another plain wooden door, its veneer beginning to lift and peel, and knocked. There was an electronic buzz, followed by the click you hear when the guard lets you into somewhere with heavy security.

The door swung in an inch or two. Mordecai pushed it open and ushered me in.

5.

"Whoa!" I thought.

I looked around the dingy room and here I was, livin' the dream! But not the 'where should I park-my-Ferrari' dream. More the, 'What the Hell? I saw this in an actual dream' kind of dream.

I was standing in a dingy study with tobacco brown wallpaper looking at an old-fashioned desk. And behind the desk was that English detective guy I'd seen with Mishi. Looking at me unblinkingly.

His hands rested on the desk, fingers spread. It was an odd position but with him more or less everything he did, no matter how odd, seemed the most natural thing in the world while you were there and he was doing it. It was only later that you shook your head and smacked yourself around and thought, what the hell was that all about!

Where was I? Oh yeah. The study. Exactly like I'd seen it in my vision. Mishi had been sitting opposite him, now that chair was empty. Waiting for me, I supposed. Stern-wise, was he collecting the whole set?

These thoughts drifted away under his stare. In fact I was beginning to feel downright calm. A nice change from the nervous dance my heart had been doing up until now.

"Sit down, please, Mr. Stern," he said.

I sat. The chair was an old-fashioned wooden number, with curling shaped pieces making the base, legs, and back. The kind that looks a bit uncomfortable, but fits your tush a lot better than you'd think.

I looked around, taking in the lamp stand, the hat rack and other bits and pieces that really did look like the set for a TV English detective show.

"My name is Amadeus Califario, Doctor Amadeus Califario, and I am very pleased to finally make your acquaintance."

6.

Dr. Amadeus Califario was intimidating in a way I hadn't encountered before. It was a bit hard to tell how big he was, what with him sitting behind a desk and all, but he looked to me to be a very large man. Maybe not physically, but, you know, large. He filled the room. The room wasn't big, but I got the impression he'd fill Yankee Stadium.

Dark hair, brushed straight back, dark eyes in deep sockets, and swarthy skin. Sort of Italian or Greek or Arab looking. Later I found out he was a bit of all of those, with some Armenian, Russian aristocrat and Jewish thrown in as well. And he could get by in all of those languages, and a few more besides.

What can I say? Even before I knew all of this I was impressed.

We sat doing that staring competition thing, the one where nobody wants to speak first.

"Welcome to The Migdal, Mr. Stern," he said, but I totally didn't think it was because I'd won the contest. "I suppose you deserve some form of explanation." His accent had that mix of things, but English, from the snooty part of England, won. Like he'd been to one of those universities that look like a whole lot of left-over gothic cathedrals had been dumped in one spot because no knew what else to do with them.

Again, I found out later that he had been to Oxford, along with a few other places around the world. Are you getting the picture here?

"It would take too long to fill you in completely, so let's just start from where Mr. Ben Zvi left off. The Elders, us, look after the world. The Organization, them, tries to destroy it. There is much more to it, of course, including the involvement of your esteemed Mr. Snell and his Asian contact, but that will suffice for now. It appears that the low level tit for tat, which usually marks our interactions with The Organization, may be giving way to something more lively. They are, in short, up to something. We have a few clues but not enough as yet."

"And this involves Yours Truly exactly how?" I asked.

Dr. Califario settled back and, rested his elbows on the arms of his chair and steepled his fingers. It was, I came to learn, another characteristic gesture. When he was thinking or amused.

"Ah well, Mr. Stern, there you have me. We have a very strong suspicion that you are going to be needed soon. But we don't know how, or when. What we do know is that The Organization has stepped up its endeavors to identify any Adepts. We also know that they are keeping as many as possible under surveillance. And the third thing we know is that you and your family are definitely on their radar."

Now he had my attention.

"What do mean, we're on their radar?" I said, but I already knew what he was talking about. The Asian guy, Snell, Mishi's premonition. It all began to paint a picture.

"Just what I said, Mr. Stern, don't pretend to be simple-minded." His voice was hard. "There is no time to indulge your otherwise charming act."

"Act?"

"Yes, Mr. Stern," a sigh of impatience, "You are a young man of rare talent. You are intelligent, insightful, perceptive. You have a gift for healing, and you are developing other powers as well, almost despite yourself. You can see that The Organization is not the only one who has kept a watchful eye on you."

"Now look..."

"Stop this!" It wasn't a shout but the force of his anger rocked me back in my chair. "There is a time factor here. And you are going to have to slough off the California boy act, and grow up. And you will be required to do it pretty quickly."

I was taken aback. "OK, go on," was all I managed.

"Good, that's better. We don't know how much time we've got to divine The Organization's plans, and implement steps to stop them. And we are working on the assumption that we have very little time indeed."

"And me?"

"And you." Laser eyes bored into me. "We need to get you ready. Here is the offer. You will live as normal a life as possible except you will take up a few extra hobbies."

"Hobbies?" Incisive, no?

"Yes, hobbies. You will meet some new friends. Mordecai will be one of them. A chap named Wolfgang Holst will be another. From them you will undergo training."

I couldn't help myself. "Training?"

"Yes, Mr. Stern training. Mordecai will train you in the nature and scope of some of your unusual endowments. Wolfgang will be your martial arts instructor. And a third teacher is already known to you."

At this point he pressed a concealed button. The door buzzed and clicked and opened.

I turned my head and Katie walked in.

"Hi Ronnie," she said, with a little finger wave.

COLONEL LANDON MCALLISTER

The Pentagon is enormous. The central open space, bounded by the five sections that make up that most iconic of office buildings, is over five acres of open parkland. It has three times the floor space of the Empire State Building. The entire Capitol, the home of the House of Representatives and the Senate of the United States of America, could fit into one of the five segments. And 23,000 people – military and civilian – work there every day.

One of those people was Colonel Landon McAllister of the 54th Quartermaster Company, Mortuary Division. Each day he toiled away in his small corner of the Pentagon's labyrinthine corridors. His unit was actually stationed at Dover Air Force Base in Delaware, but in this man's Army there was always a need for liaison with other branches, and the Pentagon was the place par excellence for military liaison.

Colonel Landon McAllister's specialty was the recovery, identification and repatriation of the remains of dead American soldiers. At one point in his career his duties had taken him and his team to Afghanistan and Iraq, where they had often come under heavy fire. Sometimes, when the bullets were flying, he had fantasized about his Mortuary Unit colleagues picking over skull fragments and tissue samples, only to discover it was Good Ol' Landy.

But such a hilarious moment in the life of the Graves Registration Service, as it used to be called, had never happened. Colonel Landon McAllister, all six feet two inches, buzz cut hair and ramrod back, had come back in more or less onepiece.

His work with the 54th had eventually brought him to the small office in the Pentagon, where, in addition to filling in paperwork and tracking down DNA samples, he could use his mind-reading skills, and channel information to and receive directions from The Migdal inLA.

His posting at the Pentagon allowed regular contact with his 'Assignment' Major-General Susan Wright, aide de camp to the Joint Chiefs, and rumored to be on the fast track to becoming the first female member thereof.

Wright had a special place in her heart for Landy.

On a routine recovery assignment – if 'routine' was ever the right word for operations in Iraq, the land of the IED, and of women in burkas who blew themselves and your friends up right after you'd given her child a polio shot – a marine patrol had come under heavy fire. Landy and his unit had also been pinned down.

The way Landy and his boys saw it, they could join in, or leave their own bodies for a back up recovery unit. So they'd joined the fight and in the process Lieutenant (as he then was) Landon McAllister had run forward and shouldered a badly wounded marine. He had carried the marine back to safety, running all the way under fire. He had a Silver Star, and a bullet fragment in his left hip, to show for it. And he had earned the undying friendship of Major-General Susan Wright who, in her spare time, turned out to be the marine's mother.

Landy, and via him Dr. Califario, had been able to exercise useful influence on the Joint Chiefs via Major-General Susan Wright.

Now McAllister sat at his desk working through a pile of papers, and occasionally turning to his computer screen to answer emails or work on the reports he was obliged to file with the many other Army departments.

On this particular morning there was a precision knock at his door.

"Enter," he said.

"Good morning Sir," a crisply uniformed Sergeant snapped off a regulation salute and stood at attention with a folder under his left arm.

"At ease, Sergeant," said McAllister returning the salute. "How can I help you?"

"I have a report for you, Sir!" The sergeant had his eyes fixed at the unofficial regulation height of six inches above McAllister's head. This gaze signified that all officers, until proven otherwise, were either (1) assholes, or (2) dangerous lunatics, or (3) both; and were to be treated with outward respect, and inner contempt, until such time as real respect was earned.

McAllister knew he was guilty until proven innocent.

But McAllister had an ace up his sleeve. The Sergeant put the report down on the desk. McAllister, with a smooth movement born of years of practice, made sure their hands brushed together.

Pictures filled McAllister's head, feelings washed through his heart and, in a dozen other ways, this man's life was laid bare to him. The Sergeant was dutiful, courageous to a fault, loyal to those who had earned his trust (this did not yet include McAllister). And he loved his country with a passion that McAllister shared.

McAllister's gift was to read others' thoughts and feelings and personality. His ex-wife was still mystified how he had found out about the affair so soon.

He had to be in physical contact, which sometimes took a bit of doing.

McAllister was especially vigilant at the moment because yesterday he had found the Watcher. LA had alerted him and since then he had been unusually affable, shaking hands and clapping people on the shoulder right up to the limit of what was deemed acceptable in a military establishment.

Even so, he had found the Watcher almost by accident.

The Organization's man in the Pentagon was a janitor, wheeling his trolley along the miles of Pentagon corridors, invisible, able to go anywhere untroubled, and unsuspected. The tip-off was the squeaky wheel. McAllister had noticed the squeak go past his office a shade more frequently that normal. A sidestep in the corridor, the brush of a hand and McAllister knew everything he needed to know.

Now, Colonel Landon McAllister, of the 54th Quartermaster Company, Mortuary Division, was watching his Watcher.

AARON STERN

1.

"What? Katie?" I stammered.

Katie hesitated and looked embarrassed.

My suspicions, already dancing a fandango, were immediately set ablaze.

For those of you who haven't met Katie Deborah Liebovitz, or the many Katie Deborah Liebovitz's who dot the universe, the words 'Katie Deborah Liebovitz' and 'embarrassment' or 'hesitate' are like oil and water, chalk and cheese, Red Sox fans in New York City.

They just don't occupy the same quantum space. This is a scientific fact. Go ahead, look it up, I'll wait.

So when 'Katie' walked into Dr. Califario's Study and looked abashed and sounded hesitant, my world kinked out of alignment.

"What are you doing here?" I said.

"Perhaps I might be allowed to explain," said Dr. Califario, all smooth charm.

"Go ahead, I wish someone would," I said. My initial surprise was giving way to thin wisps of anger. The kind you feel when everyone is in on the joke except you. And you're beginning to suspect the joke *is* you.

I'd just stepped through the Looking Glass into the parallel universe of these Elder guys and The Organization, all these dudes who wanted to rule the world or save it or whatever, and me being some kind of super kid with magic powers and all. And now to top it all here was Katie. An explanation seemed to me, on the whole, like a grand idea.

"Go on," I said. "I hope it's good."

"Yes, well, I believe Mordecai told you that we were keeping a watchful eye on your family. Because we knew The Organization was beginning to take an interest."

"Uh huh." I said.

"It was for you own good," Katie blurted. This, by the way, was the first time I had ever heard Katie blurt.

"Doing what exactly," I said, turning in my chair. The anger and humiliation were building up a head of steam. I had an inkling of the answer but I wanted to hear it from her. "For the past eighteen months Miss Liebovitz has been tasked with looking out for you."

"Spying on me."

"No! Well, yes, sort of. But it wasn't like that Ronnie."

"Well you two seem like smart people," I said, hearing the words come out of my mouth, too late to stop them. "Why don't you try explaining to the world's greatest moron exactly what it was, if it wasn't spying. Cause right now, it sure seems a lot like spying. From the point of view of the spyee. If *his* opinion counts for anything, that is."

"We wanted to make sure you were safe," said Dr. Califario.

"Safe? And so you get the hottest girl on the west coast to pretend to like me so she can keep tabs on me? Is that how you guys work? Cause that does not strike me as a very honest way of going about things."

"Oh. Ronnie," said Katie in a small voice, which made my heart break, "I wasn't pretending."

You know how it is. You're about to say something stupid. Which is going to hurt people you love, and you can see it coming, and you just can't stop.

"Well," I plowed on, "so you say, but from where I'm standing it looks a lot like pretending. You're probably pretending now when you say you're not pretending. Is everything a lie? Is Bobbeh Katz about to walk through that door?"

I knew this was hitting her where it hurt but I couldn't help myself.

"Ronnie I..."

"Just stop," I said, "I've heard enough. Give me a moment to get my head around the fact that my girlfriend, who I thought really cared about me, has turned out to be a fraud. Just let me out of here, and I'll go back to fighting my sister for the last pancake at breakfast. That's about the level of conflict I'm up for at the moment."

Katie's clear blue eyes swam with tears. If my heart wasn't shattered before, it sure was after that. But I'd painted myself into a corner, I couldn't stop the train wreck, so I returned her look with cold hard eyes.

She held my gaze for another moment and turned away.

At the door she turned back to Dr. Califario. "I'll help if you still need me, but as you can see, my usefulness is probably over."

The door closed quietly behind her.

2.

"So," said Dr. Califario. "Where were we?"

"Hold it, hold it." I said, my mind reeling. "What do you mean 'we'? 'We' are nowhere. 'We' just found out our girlfriend is a secret agent, a honey-trap for naïve idiots. The whole idea of 'we' holds very little appeal for me right at this moment!"

"Mr. Stern, I'm not going to spend valuable time placating your ego and smoothing your ruffled feathers. You will undertake training, and your issues with Miss Liebovitz will not interfere with it. Now get over yourself, sit down and listen."

He hadn't raised his voice, and whether he was using Adept skill, or he was just a super authoritative fellow, I wasn't sure, but one thing I did know was that my training was about to get underway.

He sat looking at me until I realized I was supposed to say something.

"OK. I get it. Or at least I think I do. This business with you and The Organization is serious, and you think I'm in danger and my family is and I need to be trained up to protect myself and them. And so I can give this

Organization hoozie one in the eye. Is that about it?"

"Excellent summary. Yes."

More waiting. "OK. I'm in."

"Good choice. So where were we?"

He had efficiently re-established what passed for normality, given that we were in a secret hide out, plotting to foil world-destroying evil-doers, and my relationship with my girlfriend was a figment of my imagination. That kind of normality.

"Your training begins at once, but you still have to live the life of a high school senior. This will place extra strain on you. And you must let us help you – with school assignments and so on."

"Like cheating?" I said, the sourness still seeping though the cracks.

"No," said Dr. Califario, equably, "not *like* cheating. Since you appear to be in a refreshing spade-calling mode. It is *actual* cheating. You have work to do, and a lot of catching up to undertake. So, yes, we have people who can complete your assignments, and then brief you on them, so you can appear to know what you have handed in."

"Well," I said, "if you put it that way..."

"I do," he said. "Now, can we move on?"

Without waiting he continued. "As I was saying earlier you will have trainers. One to give you greater control of your powers. Another to teach you mind control techniques. A third to show you how to defend yourself, and the fourth to introduce you to the archives and artifacts we have accumulated over the millennia."

"Millennia?" I said, cleverly repeating his last word to show that I was following.

"Yes, Mr. Stern, millennia. The origin of the Elders has been lost in the mists of time, but as best we can ascertain, and there are many of us who have done extensive research on this question, the first real indication of a group of Adepts concerned with guiding and protecting society appears in Ancient Egypt. And there are some who feel that Solomon's Temple is another fruitful area of enquiry.

"In any case the past is a fascinating study on its own account, but its true utility is that the lessons of history can inform decisions and actions in the present. And, I'm afraid, Mr. Stern, the endeavors of a few venomous, power-hungry, gold-enamored fanatics who wish to tear down all that is fine and beautiful and replace it with a society carved in their own image, is a leitmotif of the ages."

"Leitmotif?"

"Theme. Repetitive phenomenon. Something that happens a lot." He raised an eyebrow to see if I was following.

"Got it," I said.

"The Organization is a slick twenty-first century rebadging of any number of historical precursors. These people always think they reinvented the wheel, but their aims and techniques have been chronicled in the most ancient texts known to mankind. These cabals of villains generally kept themselves secret because they know that sunlight really is the best disinfectant. Shine a light on their activities and even the mass of people, blissfully ignorant of the struggle that goes on behind the scenes, would revolt against their ideas and plans and schemes. Generally speaking we play a very long game with The Organization. Which is why, Mr. Stern, this recent acceleration of their activities is most interesting, and not a little disconcerting."

"And me?" I said, bringing the conversation around to, well, me.

"Ah yes, you," he said doing the chair rocking, fingers steepling thing again, "you, Mr. Stern, are of special interest for a number of reasons. First, you have some remarkable gifts. You are an Adept and, without the training we usually give, you have developed at least one gift, healing, to a high level of sophistication. That's fascinating. Second, you appear by all reports to be developing other powers. The visions, the hearing of thoughts. This is most unusual. Third, because of this The Organization will tumble to you, if they haven't already done so. They will be especially interested because up until now you were apparently unknown to them, despite the fact that you were unaware of the need to mask your talent from them. You are a Hidden Adept. I did not believe I would meet one in my lifetime."

"Cool," I said, "I understood about half of what you said."

"And fourth," Dr. Califario, ignoring my witty interjection, "the Organization will now begin to pay close attention to your family."

"My family?" a cold stone appeared in my gut.

"Yes, Mr. Stern, your family. This is another thing that makes you especially interesting. Adept abilities are passed down from parent to child. Initially through seven families of guardians of the Holy of Holies of the Temple in Jerusalem, but the vagaries of history caused their descendants to be dispersed, like the Jewish people as a whole, around the globe. These powers are not now restricted to Jews. Adept power can turn up anywhere, in anyone, but we assume that somewhere lost in history is an ancestor from one of the seven families. Sometimes the power skips a generation or two. There is no gender inequity here. Mother to son, father to daughter, grandfather to grandson."

"Whoa, hold up there," I said, "parent to child. So you're saying..."

"Yes, Mr. Stern, your mother Miriam Stern is an Adept, an Elder of high degree, and, may I say, a dear friend of mine."

I sat there, practicing for my audition as a ventriloquist's dummy. Dr. Califario looked at me, and when it was clear that I wasn't going to say anything he continued.

"But there is one almost universal rule. Just one per generation. Only one sibling gets the power."

"Almost?" I was getting good at these one-word responses. Dr. Califario squinted at me.

"I see, Mr. Stern that I shall have to be on my guard with you. You are not, as they say, as dumb as you look, or pretend to be. Yes, 'almost' is the key word here. For more than one sibling in a family to carry Adept faculties is exceedingly rare. Mr. Stern, your mother is one of us, and, more to the point, your sister Mishi is also an Adept of very advanced power indeed."

3.

Before I could break in with a million questions he clapped his hands together and said: "But I fear we have spent too long delighting in this little chat." He was all business and bustle, "Your training must begin immediately."

He did the buzz and click thing again, and this time Mordecai and a tall, built hombre came in. Mordecai's pal was blond, with close-cropped hair, and pale blue eyes. He was a real stiff. Lay him flat and you could iron your shirt on him.

"Mordecai, you already know of course. And this is Wolfgang."

"Wolfgang," I said. "Of course he is."

He flashed a set of perfect teeth, all very jovial.

I got out of my chair and took Wolfgang's extended hand. It was like having iron wrap itself around my hand.

"As I said, Mr. Stern, you will need training in a range of areas and Wolfgang will look after you in martial arts and self defense."

"Perfect," I said wriggling my fingers to get the circulation back.

"You will meet your other trainers soon, but for now, Mordecai will show you around before we begin in earnest."

4.

Mordecai led me out of Dr. Califario's office, turned left and took me a few yards down the hallway to a door marked Sitting Room. They had a special room for that? Did they have Standing Rooms, and Jumping Rooms, and a Handstand Room?

Mordecai opened the door and gestured me through.

This room was large and comfortably furnished with armchairs and low side tables. It was carpeted in a soft green and pink floral pattern. There was a glass-fronted bookcase with a vase of fresh flowers perched on top. The windows at the far end were covered with a drawn blind, and framed by gray and pink drapes. I could hear faint traffic noises.

In one corner was a sink and some cupboards and a shelf with coffee and tea bags. There was a small fridge next to it. It was like the teachers' faculty lounge at my high school.

I could smell coffee.

There was a little man sitting in one of the armchairs holding the *LA Times* in one hand. His feet didn't touch the floor. He was sipping from a proper cup. There was a matching saucer on a low side table. No Starbucks takeout here.

The man lowered his paper and looked up at us. "Good afternoon Mordecai," he said.

Then he looked at me over half-moon glasses. He had a bald dome, with a neatly barbered fringe of hair. Kind of what I imagine Elmer Fudd might have looked like when he was relaxing after a long day hunting wascally wabbits.

I got all my culture from the finest daytime TV reruns that money could buy. My mother was in despair about this. I did try to get in a bit of reading of actual, you know, books between episodes of *Gilligan's Island, Rocky and Bullwinkle* and *The Munsters*.

But I digress.

Elmer folded his newspaper and got up. He looked shorter standing than he did sitting down.

"Allow me to introduce you to Doctor Mortimer J. Dunkeldorfer," said Mordecai with a flourish. Where did they get these names? It sounded like the scriptwriters from daytime comedy had been moonlighting. The 'J', I found out later, stood for Jabez, for Pete's sake.

Doctor Mortimer J. Dunkeldorfer looked up at me and extended a short arm.

Was this guy an actual midget? Should I be all, you know, diversity sensitive, and not use words like small, or little, or tiny, or wee, or minute? I was always getting into trouble at school when I forgot the euphemism 'du jour' for the identity groups everyone was busy slotting themselves into. It made my head hurt. I missed Melvin, who couldn't have cared less for any of this hogwash. And was able to say anything and get away with it.

I shook myself out of these thoughts, and took Mortimer J. Dunkeldorfer's hand.

"I will be seeing you later, Mr. Stern," he said as he settled back to his paper and picked up his cup. "We will be looking at the archives together. I promise you a scintillating time of it."

Scintillating? That word and 'archives' didn't seem to fit in the same sentence. But Mordecai was already heading for the door.

Constantinople, Eastern Roman Empire 1148AD

Three days after the arrival of the elegant Hadji on the dock of the Golden Horn a ragged monk with dark eyes and mud-streaked face, staring wildly, strode through the back alleys of the workingman's district of Constantinople. His black filth-encrusted robe flapped about his sandaled feet.

"Repent! Repent!" he shouted. "Oh ye sinners! Whoremongers and moneylenders! Winebibbers and fornicators! The hour is at hand. Come to the Lord and beg his mercy or burn forever in an everlasting lake of hell fire!"

He carried a large brass bell, which he rang constantly. Women threw themselves down at his feet and touched his grimy hem as he passed by. Men crossed themselves and muttered prayers of absolution for their sins. Babies cried, and children whimpered and hid behind their mothers' skirts.

"Repent, Sons of darkness. Come to the Lord, who yearns to forgive. Although your sins be black as pitch, yet you will be washed as white as snow in the blood of the lamb!"

The coins held out by eager hands disappeared as if by miracle into the folds of his black robe.

The monk, turning a corner into Jewry Lane, was immediately confronted with a narrow winding alley of goldsmiths, tinkers and traders, all plying their trade. Every third doorway echoed to the sounds of Hebrew prayers. Men in black kaftans and yellow turbans, women with their hair covered, and dark-eyed children averted their gaze from the crazy Christian.

The monk halted in mid-cry and was just turning to find more lucrative fields for his preaching when an old man with olive skin and full black beard spoke to him in Spanish.

"Israel?" he said, "Israel ibn Ibrahim? Is that you? It's me, your uncle Shabtai ibn Shaprut, brother to your mother's sister-in-law."

"No, no, Jew," the monk spat, looking around nervously. "You have mistaken me for one of your accursed tribe."

"It is you!" said the old man leaning forward and squinting at the monk, "I thought I recognized you. The news of your escape from Cordoba, from the clutches of the Inquisitors of the Prophet has become a legend."

The monk flapped a hand urgently toward the old man. "Uncle, lower your voice, I am in disguise."

"This much I can see for myself," said Ibn Shaprut. "The blind beggars of Isfahan, on a moonless night, in a sandstorm, could see that you, a faithful Jew, son of Rabbi Ibrahim ibn Yosef of Cordoba, have chosen to conceal yourself in this strange garb."

"Filthy son of a Jewish dog! How dare you address me in this way," shouted the monk, then, conspiratorially, "I am on a secret mission from the Caliph himself, sent to spy on the, on the... um, the Christian King here in Constantinople."

"Oh, Israel, my boy," Shaprut put a friendly arm around the monk's shoulders. "You and your stories. They got you into a lot a trouble in Cordoba. And the magic tricks, and the alchemy, and the card games, and your special dice. Oh, and the girls, of course. What was the name of that pretty one? The girl from the Grand Vizier's own harem? That was a big mistake." Shaprut laughed, "And drawing scandalous pictures of the Caliph on the walls of the mosque? That was not, I think, such a good idea either."

Shaprut chuckled at the memory, while Israel Ibn Ibrahim looked left and right from under his monk's cowl.

He saw a Christian tavern-worker glance up Jewry Lane toward them and stop in his tracks.

"Silence, Old Jew, Unbelieving Dog!" Ibn Ibrahim called out loudly. "Unhand me."

Hush now," said Ibn Shaprut, failing to take the hint, and failing to see that a coachman with a leather whip had joined the tavern worker. A blacksmith with tree-trunk arms hefting an iron bar also joined the group. "Keep your voice down. The Christians do not take kindly to their monks being insulted. They also," Ibn Shaprut said meaningfully, "don't like renegade Jews impersonating their holy men either. Your father and mother are worried about you. You must return home to them."

"Um, Jewish Idolater!" Ibrahim shouted. Then in an urgent whisper, "Run Uncle, run."

Shaprut just looked at him blankly, the smile frozen on his lips.

"Take your infidel hands off me!" Israel shouted, then he hissed, "Uncle, go, now, get out of here!" He turned to the gathering crowd at the mouth of the alley. "I say, Unbelieving Cur! Return to your ill-starred tribe!"

Shaprut's temper snapped. "Whence this insolence?" he shouted. He slapped the 'monk' across the face. "How dare you speak to your uncle thus?" And turning to passers by and pointing he said, "This man is no monk. He is my neph..."

"Help! Help!" cried the monk, grabbing Shaprut's hands. "Help me, this Jew is attacking me!" He then pushed Shaprut into the arms of the Jews who had stopped to see what the commotion was all about.

"Take him!" Israel said to them. "Get him out of here, can't you see the mob?"

The crowd of Christians at the opening of the alley began to murmur and growl like a living beast. Men began to roll their sleeves up. Some hefted wooden staves and others felt for their knives.

Israel turned to look at the gathering mob, and said in a low voice over his shoulder: "Give mother and father my best."

But when he turned back he only just caught a glimpse of rough hands hauling a red-faced and protesting Ibn Shaprut through a nearby doorway, which immediately slammed shut, just as the mob stirred itself and began shouting: "Destroy Jerusalem! Burn the Christ Killers! Kill the Moneylenders!"

As if by magic the stalls, the shopkeepers, the crowds of men, women and children, all the Jews who moments before had been crying their wares and bargaining over food and cloth and spices, had vanished, and the last heavy oak doors crashed shut, the last iron grills were locked over windows.

Rough sandals slapped against smooth cobblestones, and the shouts and cries of the mob surged around the corner and funneled up the narrow alley.

The monk, still rubbing his burning cheek, danced and gibbered and pointed. He joined in the shouting, and raced down the alley at the head of the throng until he spotted a narrow passageway between two houses. He ducked into the gap leaving the crowd to vent itself impotently on the impregnable walls, doors and ironbound windows of the Jewish quarter, and to meet the Imperial Guard which had been dispatched to restore order.

Three hours later peace had been re-established and the Guards, questioning a few ringleaders, heard a story of a mad monk inciting the crowd. Someone found a filthy robe and a pair of worn sandals stuffed behind a water barrel in a narrow lane.

They called off the search for the crazy monk, and concentrated on ferreting out a smooth-tongued confidence trickster, a Muslim dandy, who had cheated the Chief of the Emperor's Palace Guard and the Head Deacon of Santa Sophia out of a total of one hundred and forty two gold dhirams in a dice game which had lasted for two and a half days. The cheat had also made off with the Chief Guard's golden wand of office, and the Deacon's ruby ring. He had even won one of the Palace retainers, whom he had taken as a manservant and bodyguard.

That evening the 'monk', now smooth-shaven and dressed in the close-fitting hose and homespun cloak of an Italian merchant slipped aboard a galley an hour before it weighed anchor.

"Leonardo Da Silva is my name," he said in answer to the Shipmaster's enquiry. "My family originates from Portugal and I now call the pleasant hills of Tuscany my home. But, my friend, I think I hear the riches and excitements of the fabled kingdoms of the East calling."

He tossed a coin to the head porter who signaled his men to start loading up the merchant's bundles.

"Your business seems to have been very profitable."

"Yes, indeed," said Da Silva, signaling to a muscular young man who hefted a sturdy stave. "Geminio, make sure the parcels are tied down securely."

Da Silva then looked back at the dock, teeming with traders, sailors and porters. He rolled the weighted dice in his pocket, and felt the hard beveled-edges of a ruby ring. "Yes, very much so. And now I wish to journey to mysterious lands beyond the knowledge of civilized men."

His darting eyes, dark pools above an aquiline nose, relaxed only when the ship rounded the headland and entered the Hellespont, and Constantinople slowly disappeared from view.

The Maleficium et MaledictionesArcanum

Secret Crimes and Curses

of

Baphomet, Lord of the Underworld, Prince of Darkness, Bringer of Pestilence and Purveyor of Plagues

As transcribed in a trance by
LeonardoDaSilva,
Magus and Initiate into the Mysteries of Demonic Wisdom

Extract 3: Canto III, Verses 12, 13, and 23

12. ... will find the Locus, The Place of Destiny, where the Sun and the Moon meet.

13. Oh Ye of little faith, hear the word of The Lord of Misrule, Baphomet the Thrice Great, King Under the Earth, Master of the Boiling Pools of Everlasting Hell Fire, know the location to be in an undiscovered land where the Sun finds its rest, where the Great Ocean ends, where a westward journey of a thousand times a thousand leagues comes to its final harbor...

23. ... the Finger of God points to the Heavens, there you will find The Place, even the Place of Destiny. The Finger of God is the Second Sign... And will not the measure of the Finger of God be the Number of the Beast?

CHAPTER FOUR

15TH & 16TH SEPTEMBER

PROFESSOR OLAF SVENSSON

I think I've got it Professor," said Jeremy Plensk, hunched over his workspace, his skin green from the glow of the computer.

"What is it Jeremy?" said Svensson, "What have you found?"

"The Sun and the Moon."

"I think someone might have got there before you," said Singleton.

"Yeah," said Blakely, "They're a little hard to miss."

"Hush now children," said Olaf Svensson indulgently. "Let Jeremy tell us what it is that he has discovered."

"OK, wise guys," said Jeremy, "you know that we've been looking everywhere for this 'Place'?"

"Yes," said Singleton, "And you've been particularly annoying about Da Silva's 'La La Land'."

"Yes, well," Jeremy sounded uncomfortable, "all that occult hooey, you know. OK, so, I thought I'd look around myself. Scientifically, of course."

"Of course," said Blakely.

"And..." said Svensson.

"And, I asked myself, what if Da Silva had somehow discovered a way of foretelling future events. Hypothetically I mean. So I began to link up a few of his inexplicable pronouncements. References to the 'Great Ocean', 'A land in the West', 'A journey of a thousand leagues' and, here's the relevant bit, he refers a few times to a place where the Sun and the Moon meet, and he gives a few numerical references."

He pointed to the page of the *Maleficium* he had up on his screen. He drew the mouse down and then zoomed in on a marginal note, which showed two small circles, the sun and the moon, with a series of numbers next to them.

"They all seem to be referring to a specific longitude and latitude, based on the rising and setting of the Sun, in relation to the phases of the Moon."

"And could you ascertain where this longitude and latitude meet?" said Svensson.

"Yeah, well it's screwy, you know, because it turned out to be a place none of them could have known about. Right off the charts, literally in their case."

"Explain."

"OK, so, those sun and moon co-ordinates indicate somewhere on the east coast of North America."

"Go on," said Svensson.

"We know Da Silva was into the occult, and I started wondering about the same kind of stuff in America. What if there was a link? So I looked into some of those early Masonic Founding Fathers."

"As in US Founding Fathers?" said Singleton.

"You mean the dead white male slave owners," said Blakely acidly.

"Yeah," said Singleton. "No Founding Mothers, and no Founding Persons of Color," Singleton said with contempt.

"Let him speak," said Svensson.

"Thanks Prof," said Jeremy. "So, yeah, I started looking into some of Mary's dead white guys. Some of them were into some pretty heavy hoodoo. And they put a lot of time and effort into planning Washington DC. Like they had this clean canvas to work on, and they went all out. You know Benjamin Franklin, that French guy, L'Enfant, the architect.

"And there was a guy who I'd never heard of. Haym Solomon, a Jew. He was originally from Europe but he came over here in 1775. Made a fortune."

"Typical," said Mary.

"Yep, so, he funded a lot of the revolutionary campaigns. Like, at Yorktown, when the British were cornered and had to surrender, Washington's army wouldn't move cause he hadn't paid them for like, ever. And Haym Solomon just wrote a check. And the rest was history."

"Yeah, this is all riveting stuff, Jer," said Singleton. "But how exactly does this connect any of our dots?"

"OK, so," said Jeremy, "Like there were all these legends about Haym Solomon. Same as Da Silva. You know, levitating, mind-reading, curing people by touch. And I found a few references to an ancient manuscript with mystic powers."

"References? Where?" said Svensson.

Jeremy's face flushed. "On websites, you know."

"Like, mysticmysteriesforlamebrains.com?" said Singleton.

"Look," said Jeremy, "I found references OK? Let's leave it at that."

"OK, OK," said Singleton, his hands up in surrender.

"OK," Jeremy continued. "They had this plan to found a new capital of their new country in a place of high occult energy. And they wrapped this capital up with symbols, and sculptures, and architecture, and even the street layout. For protection I mean. From," he made scare quotes with his fingers, "'The Forces of Darkness', there's a pile of stuff out there," shooting Singleton a look. "On websites."

"So this place is where, exactly, Oh Mighty One," said Singleton. "You're saying Da Silva's Place, the Locus, where the Sun meets the Moon, is in DC?"

"Well," said Jeremy, reluctant now that it had come to the crunch. "Actually, yes, I think it is. On the North American Continent. In the USA. Specifically in Washington DC. I mean, if you assume Da Silva knew what he was talking about, and I guess we must, cause we're like spending hours trying to decipher his mumbo jumbo, and you compare all those other voodoo Dudes, and add in Ben Franklin, and this Haym Solomon guy. Then the *Locus* is basically in Washington DC."

"Well, it has got a 'Finger of God'," said Singleton thoughtfully. "The Washington Monument. But that was only built a hundred years ago. Long after Franklin."

"I wouldn't dismiss it just on that ground," said Svensson. "Sometimes the plans of these people are very long term. And sometimes there is serendipity."

"Serendipity?" said Singleton.

"Yes," said Svensson thoughtfully, "occasionally you just have to trust the evidence of your eyes. Jeremy has uncovered certain apparently compelling evidence, and there it is, the Finger of God, just where that evidence says it would be."

"Wait, there's more," said Mary, who had been clicking and scrolling at her own computer for the past few minutes. "I remembered something. We had a school field trip. The Washington Monument, its base is fifty-five feet six inches. That makes exactly..." She grabbed a notepad and pencil and a calculator. She punched a few buttons, and scribbled a few figures. "...Six hundred and sixty-six inches. 666."

RANDOLPH LASSITER

Randolph Lassiter stared out of the window of his office in the UN building. He looked over the East River. Then he swiveled his chair round to face his desk and dialed Singh.

"We need to up the pressure. Get one of those Adepts to talk. We need more information on Da Silva's signs. There are four of them apparently. And we need to know about them in the next few days."

"We have several Adepts under surveillance." Singh replied.

"Go for as many as you can without alerting the authorities. Just get the information we need."

AARON STERN

1.

I was flying through the air, arms flailing. I crashed into the padded wall, and thumped to the floor, but before I could gather my thoughts, like 'where's the nearest exit', Wolfgang was on me.

Our little get together had started fifteen minutes earlier with him showing me a few defensive moves. I'd only half listened. He'd shown me again. My attention had been on other things. He'd obviously decided to encourage a higher level of student engagement by giving me a practical demonstration of where inattention would lead.

And it led at high speed toward the walls and floor of the practice room.

The aches, the pains, and bruises weren't the worst bit. It wasn't even the humiliation.

It was that merry grin on his big stupid German face.

The guy was having the best time.

He picked me up from my 'don't hit me again' fetal position, and placed me upright on wobbly legs.

"Now zen, Herr Shterrn," he said in his comical accent. A bit too much Colonel Klink for my taste. What can I say, I have high standards. "You fill hef to do bedder zen zis."

"What, can't take the pressure?" That's me, a laugh a minute.

"Your rather weak jokes (he pronounced it 'chokes') will not help you in this room."

"Ouch. Now that really hurt."

"Come, Herr Stern, enough of cracking wise."

"Kreckingk vize?" I said. Softening him up you see. Putting him off his guard. If he could do Colonel Klink, I could pull rank, go all General Buchhalter on him. By the time this session finished I intended to run through the entire cast of Hogan's Heroes.

"Oh Herr Stern, you and your little..." he picked me up half way through the sentence. I had to hand it to him. I was totally not ready for it. He did a little spin thing with me, and again I was flying through the air.

This time I knew what was coming and, as the floor came up to give me a cheery greeting, I went into a curl and managed to somersault to a standing position. The most amazed person in the room was me.

"Not bad, Herr Stern," said Wolfgang, giving me a slow ironic clap. "Perhaps there is some hope for you yet."

"Haa Yah!" I screamed jumping into a fake karate pose. Fake because I wouldn't have known a real karate pose if it leapt out of the toaster with my breakfast pop tart and introduced itself to the whole family.

Wolfgang easily batted away my raised hands and floored me again with a leg sweep. His grin was still there, but I thought I detected a bit of boredom as well. If I kept this up I might sneak out while he slept.

"Ready to give in?" I panted. "I don't want to hurt you, you know."

"You are the soul of generosity. But I fear you will have to give me my comeuppance next time. Our session is over. You were quite abysmal."

"Well thanks, coming from you that means a lot."

We shook hands and he gestured me toward the door. As I turned he scissor-gripped my legs with his, rolled, and again I found myself lying nose down on the floor. He was on his feet in a flash.

"Never let your guard down." Beaming down at me. "Yeah, that bit I'm beginning to get."

2.

I kept eyes on Wolfgang until I was safely behind Mordecai. Still dressed in his dapper threads, and with a broad smile on his swarthy face, he led me down the hallway.

What was with these guys? Grinning like idiots while a horde of crazed loons was on the warpath. To say nothing of me getting the bejesus beaten out of me. How come that was funny, huh?

"Come Aaron," he said taking my arm. I winced. I was going to find a lot of bruises when I took my next shower. "Time for your briefing on your talents."

"But," I said, "I just had a hands on briefing from Wolfgang the Psycho, and I think we established to our mutual satisfaction that I have zero talents. At least in the fighting department." Still cracking wise, you see.

"I believe," he chuckled, "that you will begin quite soon to surprise even yourself. Wolfgang's methods are a little, so to speak, direct. How shall I say, Teutonic. But they are effective. Place you in an extreme position and your powers are triggered, and developed. Ah, here we are."

We were at the Sitting Room door. Mordecai looked in.

"Good," he said. "We have the room to ourselves and we have an hour. My part in your training is to delve into your gifts and to help you gain greater control of them."

He indicated one of the armchairs and made me a cup of coffee, and tea for himself. We even got a cookie. Things were looking up.

"Now," he said settling back, holding his teacup in one hand and the saucer under it with the other. "Tell me about anything unusual."

"Let's see. You mean apart from needing to hurl when someone sick walks by, and, oh yes, meeting kooky Israelis, that'd be you, mysterious Doctors, deranged Germans, and, who was that Dr. Dinglewoofer guy, one of the Seven Dwarves? And then, of course, finding my girlfriend is not my girlfriend but an informant and babysitter for poor little Ronnie." I was letting the resentment trickle out again but I couldn't help it; didn't want to 'help it'.

Mordecai's teacup clinked on the saucer after each sip.

"Have I left anything out? Oh yeah, when I got thrown across the room by Bobbeh Katz I found myself watching two ancient Egyptian Joe Shmoes walking down a corridor. Like, what was that all about? And another time I saw Dr. Califario's study and my little sister Mishi was there. And, how could I forget! I now know that some guys who call themselves The Elders and some other dudes called The Organization have been duking it out for like ever. Let me think, is that the complete list? No! How about some sinister Asian guy staking out my house, and my creepy Social Studies teacher Mr. Smell meeting up with him? And that was right after I seemed to be able to read their minds. Is *that* enough for a start?"

"Well, yes, I should say so," Mordecai looked impressed. "That is quite a lot to be getting on with. Let's start with the mind reading."

And for an hour Mordecai asked me questions about overhearing the Asian dude outside my house, and Mr. Snell during the lesson. No detail was too small or apparently insignificant. And he kept asking about the same bits in different ways over and over again, so I remembered a lot more than I thought.

"That is enough for one day," Mordecai announced. "Now you go to Dr. Dunkeldorfer. And later I will take you back to your mother's car in the school parking lot."

3.

Dr. Mortimer Jabez Dunkeldorfer turned out to be a big surprise in that little package. Basically MJD knew everything. And if he didn't know he knew how to find out.

After our session Mordecai had directed me through a door marked 'Emergency Exit: Do not open', which revealed a metal staircase that was made of that honeycomb mesh that lets you see all the way down. Heights are not my favorite thing so I tried not to think about it, and clattered down as quickly as I could.

So quickly that I didn't wake up to the fact that the bottom was a long, long way down until I reached it. Where was that coffin-elevator when you needed it?

When I ran out of stairs I was in a small dimly lit area, about twelve feet by twelve, with a raw concrete floor and damp brick walls. And no door. I thought I must have passed the door on one of the landings. I was just turning to retrace my steps when the wall in front of me began to scrape and groan and slide sideways. It didn't sound happy about it.

The wall moved on metal runners, revealing MJD cranking an enormous metal wheel.

"Good evening Mr. Stern," he said cheerfully, puffing as he cranked. "Come in, come in!"

In I came.

"Do you mind?" he said, pointing at the wheel.

"Oh, no. No, of course not," I said. I gripped that sticking-out handle that some wheels have which lets you turn them quickly and easily. This one needed to go back to class because 'quickly' and 'easily' were two lessons it skipped at handle school. Too busy chasing girl handles I guess.

After several embarrassing and strenuous minutes, I managed to get the wall back into place.

"Lovely!" he cried. "Now follow me. I have lots and lots to show you. We're going to have a wonderful time!"

We were in a short corridor, the walls were brick, the floor and ceiling were water-stained concrete. We walked about thirty yards and MJD used a huge key to unlock a green painted metal door. The door swung toward us with an ear splitting squeal. Hadn't anyone here heard of oil?

He pulled the door closed, relocked it, and led me down a narrow passageway between shelves stacked high with old cardboard boxes, dusty metal and wooden objects and other detritus from a bygone age. I wondered if any or all of this was leftover from the World War II time, but MJD kept up a brisk pace and there was no time to look at anything.

After a few minutes of this we came to an open area about twenty feet square. The walls were covered in shelving with padlocked mesh doors blocking access to whatever they held.

The air smelled dusty and dry, and metallic. Like someone had been using one of those electric zap producers beloved of generations of science teachers.

There was a small wooden desk and the same curly wood chairs that Dr. Califario favored.

"Welcome to my lair!" MJD spread his arms wide and beamed at me.

"I love what you've done to the place," I said. "Very cozy. I see you've added some touches. The metal cabinets, the dust, the unspoiled brickwork."

"Oh Mr. Stern," said MJD, waggling a finger at me, "you joke now, but wait till I show you what we have in store."

"Yeah, I saw some of the treasures as we walked here. You could open a Dust and Rust shop right now. You'd clean up. Or not."

He bustled back and forth, pulling out a chair for me, and one for himself. "Sit, sit, Mr. Stern."

I took one of the wooden chairs. He perched on the other and put his hands on his knees as if trying to contain his delight.

"I am going to show you a few of our artifacts, tell you a bit about our history, and explore these visions you have been having. So let's start with that last topic first, these visions. Do you mind telling me everything you can about them?"

So I did. I told him about the hospital and Bobbeh Katz and the two Egyptian dudes, and being in Mishi's bedroom and her diary and seeing her and Dr. Califario.

MJD didn't interrupt or move, or blink. He listened, like he was hearing the most wonderful story, and every word was pure gold.

When I finished he said: "Excellent, that is very clear. And most interesting. To be completely honest with you Aaron, may I call you Aaron?"

"Ronnie is good."

"Ronnie. Thank you. Ronnie." Like he was getting used to the taste. "The truth, Ronnie, is this is a bit of a new one for us. These visions. There are, of course, lots of people in literature and history and scripture who have visions, but this ability appears to have waned. At least until, ha ha, you came along. Now we might have to revise our thinking. Find out how, as it were, this power works."

"How it works?"

"Yes, Mr. Stern, Ronnie," he said. "What triggers it. What you see, how accurate it is. In both instances you were in physical contact with someone – Bobbeh Katz; or something – the diary of your sister. Then you experienced nausea, and a stretching sensation, and then you blacked out, and then poof, there you were. Watching, with the participants unaware of you, nor did you interact with them. You cannot, it seems, ah, influence things. You are a silent witness."

"I hadn't thought about it like that," I said.

"May I ask, Ronnie, was it like a dream? You know, internally realistic and logical, but when you wake up, the fact that a live tiger wearing a tutu served you scrambled eggs, or some such, is immediately known to be not a reality which we, thank goodness, generally experience. Was it like that? Like a dream?"

I thought for a moment. "No, not like that at all. I was there. And the 'there' was real. Like I was eavesdropping on a real scene, from the past of course, but at the time it was like it was happening in front of me. And it seemed just as real after I woke up. If some Egyptologist discovered that passageway I wouldn't be surprised. If Mishi told me about a meeting with Dr. Califario I'd already know what she was going to say. I mean, I could have described his office in detail before I'd actually been there."

"Yes, yes, that is a very telling and convincing detail. Almost as if someone or something is trying to get the message across to us to trust this knack of yours."

"I hadn't thought of that." I said this a lot when I was with MJD.

"Let's leave these visions for the time being and move on to some of our treasures." He gave me a broad grin, slapped both hands on his legs, and jumped off his chair. "Follow me!"

4.

He led me to a dark corner where he produced another large metal key. He unlocked the grate and swung it open. It also squealed like a stuck pig. Inside was shelving, each shelf packed with old cardboard boxes.

He dragged a wooden ladder over and climbed up to the top rung. Then he pulled a pair of cotton gloves from his back pocket, slipped them on and reached up to the top shelf. I stood at the foot of the ladder steadying it.

"Ah, here it is," he grunted, as he stretched to the full length of his arm. "Come here, my beauty."

He came down one-handed, clutching his prize.

"Have a look at this," Aladdin in the magic cave couldn't have sounded more entranced. He held up a dark brown stick about eight inches long.

"It's a stick," I said, considerably underwhelmed.

"Oh Mr. Stern," he said with a mischievous grin. "This is so much more than a stick. This 'stick' is probably, no, certainly, the most significant stick you are ever likely to see."

Now he had my attention.

"This stick is in fact a stylus." He looked at me expectantly. I knew what a stylus was, of course, who doesn't. You use it to move things on a computer screen. This was the kinkiest stylus I'd ever seen.

I said so.

"Not that sort of stylus, Ronnie. This is a real stylus. A writing instrument used in the ancient past, before the invention of the quill or pen. This one is from Ancient Egypt."

I took a closer look at the stick.

"Aha," he said, holding the stylus up by one tapered end, "that has sparked your curiosity. The legend is that this is the stylus Moses used to write the Bible. And, I believe, Mr. Stern, Ronnie, that if what you saw in your vision is true then you will see Moses writing with this very stylus. Are you willing to conduct a small experiment?"

"How small?" I asked.

"Actually quite big. If it works. Non-existent, if it doesn't."

"Can I buy a vowel?" I said, perplexed.

"Well, you go into these visions if you touch someone or something significant. How much more significant than Moses' stylus could we get?"

"It's a good point, theoretically. How sure are you that this will work? And when we say 'work' I assume we mean me feeling nauseous, and being stretched like chewing gum, while having my head twisted off, blacking out, and potentially ending up in some kind of strange place for an unspecified time. Is that about it?"

"Well, when you put it like that, yes." More head bobbing. "You have a well-developed gift for capturing the essence of a situation." He clapped me on the shoulder, or as close to my shoulder as he could reach. "Shall we?" he said, waggling the stylus at me, eyebrows raised persuasively.

I was not happy with all of this, but at the time I couldn't see a way out. I was committed to the process, and this is where it had led me.

"OK, let's do this before I change my mind."

"Perfect!"

He ushered me back to the chairs. We sat. There was no ceremony. He just handed me the stylus.

I took it and everything went dark. The same nausea shot through me, I felt stretched to breaking point. Then, again, just as the stretching was getting too much to bear I snapped back into shape.

5.

The Third Vision

When last we saw our Egyptian heroes, the older guy was pushing the stone eye of a calf, and a part of the wall had opened up. Now we all went through the gap into a small stone chamber. The light of their torches threw shadows on the walls. They fitted the torches into metal brackets, and then they each unrolled a small reed mat and they sat cross-legged, opposite each other.

The older man sat with his eyes closed, his hands resting palms upwards on his knees, and I heard a name in my mind: Amun-het-Ma'at.

He started chanting some kind of prayer, to some God he called Je Hooty. (I looked it up later, and they actually spell it Djehuti, at least the guys at Wikipedia do.)

He went on praying for some time, Hail to the All-Wise, All-Knowing Ruler of the Hearts of Men. You get the idea. Even in my vision state my mind began to wander. I mean I say my prayers, occasionally, but I don't take a thousand years over them.

Then this guy, Amun-het-Ma'at, stopped. He sat still. This too seemed to go on, like, forever. Look, I admit I've got a short attention span, but I mean Mr. Patience, the Mayor of Patientville, would've snuck a look at his watch.

Then a funny thing happened. I kinda got into the rhythm of the thing. I found the waiting was not really like waiting. Not like we were anxious for something to turn up. Time was just now. I know, I know, this sounds like someone from one of those hippy dippy communes. But that's how I felt.

The two guys sat as if this was the only thing that was ever going to happen. Hard to explain, but it was kind of nice, relaxing and peaceful. And, for me, unusual. I'm more of a 'What's next?' kind of guy.

After a long time Amun-het-Ma'at opened his eyes.

I looked at the other guy and his name also popped into my head: Amun-Tut-Moses. He was looking at Amun-het-Ma'at. Then he bowed low, his forehead touching the floor.

Amun-het-Ma'at started chanting: "The Great Lord, Thrice Blessed Thrice Great and Thrice Merciful Djehuti, has spoken to me," he intoned, "The world grows dark. A new Pharaoh will arise, a Pharaoh unskilled in resisting the Evil One. Seth, the Lord of Evil, will arise from his prison, throw off his bindings, with which the Noble God Osiris, the Lord of the Nile, has bound him. The brotherhood of the servants of the Most High will no longer be able to hold the Dark Lord in thrall. The Evil One will stretch forth his hand, and he, Seth, the Weaver of Lies, will stalk the Land of the Great River accompanied by his handmaidens, Fear and Greed.

"This will be the triumph of Sekhmet, the Lioness, the Goddess of Destruction, and of Seth, the Black Desert Lord, God of Chaos."

Amun-Tut-Moses piped up. "Oh my Lord, for countless generations the priests of your religion, of the Two Kingdoms of Upper and Lower Egypt, the Center of the World, have chanted prayers, have sung the sacred hymns, lit incense which has risen to heaven. They have propitiated the Gods with sweet sacrifices. What has happened to unleash the wrath of the Lord of Disease?"

"It is as you say, My Son," said Amun-het-Ma'at, still using that chant voice. "The priests have prayed and performed their rituals. We of the Inner Circle of Protectors have guided the world of men, as advisors and counselors to the rulers and great men of the earth. But the web of protection grows weak. Men have ceased to fear an Evil which has been pent up these many years. Seth and Sekhmet look with fire in their eyes to find a crack in their prison walls. And just such a crack will soon appear.

"Standing against the Hell Spawn are the Protectors and their followers. This Protection is woven in an intricate web, stretching across rivers, deserts and oceans to the farthest reaches of the earth, linking the Guardians of different lands."

"Even among the barbarians, the unblessed, who live beyond the Great Nile?" asked Amun-Tut-Moses.

Amun-het Ma'at smiled. "Yes, My Son, even there you will find a depth of wisdom in those strange lands. The land of the forefathers of your own people, in fact, holds the greatest secret of all."

"My people, the Habiru?"

"Yes, the Habiru hold the secret of the One God, and His Law. He awaits you, Amum-Tut-Moses, in the desert. I foresee in the days ahead an encounter between you and your God. Now you live in the palaces of the mighty, soon you will dwell in the tents of the humble. There, in the desert far from the Land of the Nile, you will learn the ways of your forefathers, and the pathways of the One Lord of All. This is a path closed to me, a priest of the Egyptians, but it is the path you, a Son of the Habiru, have been chosen to fulfil. This is your destiny."

"And will I ever see Egypt again?" asked Amun-Tut-Moses.

"Yes, my son," replied the old man. "You will return a conqueror, in Clouds of Glory. But you will not conquer Egypt with an army, or by the sword. You will defeat the forces of Seth and Sekhmet with the Word of your God. And you will take your people, the Habiru, a people bound in servitude, and you will lead them out of the Land of Egypt, out of the House of Bondage unto the Land Promised to your forefathers.

"And now my Son, my chief disciple, Amun-Tut-Moses, highest delight of my eyes. Another task lies before us. We must write down the sacred lore, the wisdom of ages, the secret of secrets, in order to preserve it for Mankind in the dark days ahead.

"You, Amun-Tut-Moses must take up your ink and stylus and papyrus and you must write down all that I shall say. And, when we are finished you must protect this holy writing and preserve it and, when the number of your days shall have reached their end, you will pass it into the hands of a trustworthy successor.

"Your path will be a hard one, but you are ready."

Then Amun-Tut Moses picked up his stylus, a plain wooden stick about eight inches long with a tapering end, and dipped it in ink and smoothed out a sheet of papyrus on the writing board resting on his knees.

And then I felt the wave of nausea and the stretch and the scene disappeared.

6.

"What did you do to him?"

"Nothing, I did nothing. He just..."

"Nothing? Look at him, he's unconscious, he's in a coma, he may never..."

I was lying on something soft and comfortable, a bed I guess, and my hand was being held and stroked. That was nice. The not nice bit was my head, which had turned into an anvil, and someone was using it to get in a bit of hammering practice.

"We were trying to..."

"You were trying to kill him, that's what you were trying to do."

"Katie, that is not..."

At this point I groaned and moved.

"Look, Miss Liebovitz," it was MJD speaking. "He's coming around."

"Yes, Katie," Mordecai, this time. "He's going to recover. He'll be good as new."

"And where," said Katie, "might I ask did you two get your medical degrees, that give you such confidence in your joint diagnosis, *Doctor Ben* Zvi and *Nurse* Dunkeldorfer?"

The air was full of menace. A beautiful, smart, curvaceous menace. The worst kind.

That's my Katie, I thought. Then I remembered, she wasn't my Katie any more. So who was stroking my hand? Time to get the eye opening underway.

"Aaron," said Mordecai. "Are you OK? Are you awake?"

"Awake, Yes. OK? Can I get back to you on that one?"

"Oh Ronnie!" Katie let go of my hand and threw her arms around me and began squeezing. It felt good, except for not being able to breathe. She had my right arm pinned, so I patted her back and stroked her hair with my left.

Then she let me go and I managed to sit up. The headache was fading.

"Aaron Stern," she said. "What exactly do you think you were doing down there?" she turned to Dr. Dunkeldorfer. "What exactly happened?"

"What happened?" said MJD, he was standing at the foot of the bed next to Mordecai, looking worried. If he'd been holding a sombrero in front of his stomach he'd have been turning it clockwise in the regulation 'A thousand apologies, Senor Stern' mode. MJD looked at Katie. "We chatted in the Archive Room. He sat down, touched the stylus of Moses, and blanked out." He turned to me. "After a few minutes I tried to revive you and couldn't, so I called Mordecai and Katie, and we got you here to this room to lie down."

"How long have I been out? How long was I out in the Archive Room?"

"Just a few minutes in the Archive Room, and about half an hour here."

The events in the vision had taken a lot longer than a few minutes. Time was obviously a bit elastic here. And these visions packed a punch, that last one had knocked me out of the ballpark.

I started to tell them what I had seen and heard in the vision.

As I was getting to the end my eyelids started to droop and my words began to slur. Katie took my hand again. She gave MJD and Mordecai hard eyes. "He needs to sleep. Leave him here with me to recover. I'll take him home. Ronnie do you need anything, water, a blanket?"

She was stroking my hair and my cheek. This I could get used to.

"No, I'm fine, just a little sleepy. Can I..." That's the last thing I remembered saying.

Just before I drifted off, I heard Mordecai say, "Amadeus will know what to do."

7.

Katie dropped me at home. It was about four o'clock, the time I'd be getting home from school anyway. She wanted to come in but I had fully recovered, and her Mom needed her to go shopping or bake a cake, or something. So I kissed her goodbye and thanked her for saving my life. She laughed and said not to make a habit of it cause she might not be around the next time.

I got out and I was passing the Grayson's house. They're our next-door neighbors.

"Hi Ronnie," Cindy Grayson, looking a bit flushed, came walking down the drive, all casual, smoothing down her dress.

"Hi Cindy, how's it going?"

"Oh you know, just hanging."

"Great. Your folks OK, haven't seen your Dad and Mom for a while."

"Oh, they're fine, on a cruise, I think, Caribbean, or Alaska, or somewhere. I think I got a postcard. You know, they're always somewhere."

"Yeah, that's where most people end up. Somewhere."

She flushed some more and looked down at her shoes. High heels, oddly out of place for a casual encounter between neighbors. I immediately regretted my tone. All that 'wise-assery' was fine for Melvin and Katie and Mishi. But Cindy was fifteen and, according to Mishi, had a thing for me.

I hadn't been aware of it, but one day a while back Mishi had told me I was being stupid. And I'd asked what exact form my stupidity was taking on this particular occasion. And she'd said I had to be more careful around Cindy, because I had to get my tone right or else I'd be leading her on. And I'd felt bad that I'd been, well, stupid. Because I liked Cindy and I didn't want to hurt her.

And Mishi had narrowed her eyes and given me a look, and she'd said, "listen Ronnie, we need to talk."

Uh oh, I thought, even though she's my sister, she's still a, you know, girl, and it is never, and I mean *never*, a good thing to hear a girl say those words: 'We need to talk'. This is a scientific fact.

"OK," I said, cautiously, "I would like nothing better than to clear my schedule, and accommodate you. I just have one or two things..."

"Cut it out, Moron," she said. That Mishi, what a laugh. "It's happening now. Upstairs. My room."

Can you believe that? That is actually how my sister spoke to me.

She was like that Hadron Collider thingummy that Mom was always flying off to see colliding things. Powerful and focused, and irresistible.

We went into her room and she sat crossed legged on the bed. I pulled her wheelie office chair from under her desk and spun it so I could sit with my elbows resting on the back and my head resting on my hands.

"So, Dumbass, here's the thing. You're my brother and I actually love you. You're not going to hear that often, so stick it somewhere safe. And you may not be as completely ugly and socially repellent as I perhaps sometimes hint at."

"Hint!" I said. "A sledge hammer does more hinting. The Chicago Fire was more roundabout. The Mongol Invasions of Genghis Khan..."

"Ok, enough already. I get it. So, like I was saying, girls, other than me of course, on the whole find you attractive."

"Attractive? Me? Really?" she had my attention now.

"Yes, Idiot, they do. And stop pretending you don't know. Half the girls at school dream of nothing else."

So Mishi had proceeded to tell me the facts of life. The genetic code of centuries of *yentas* pulsed in her veins. Like she was living in a *shtetl,* and wearing a headscarf. Any minute she'd break into crowd-pleasing favorites from Fiddler on the Roof.

Slowly, carefully, and mostly patiently, she explained that women did not want a 'conversation' or a 'discussion' or an 'explanation' or, and here she shuddered, a solution to their problems.

She laboriously explained that girls wanted something she referred to as 'their feelings validated'. My head began to ache. What did *that* mean?

When I asked she rolled her eyes and told me I didn't need to know what it meant. No man could, so don't bother trying.

Forget that, she had said, with an airy wave of her hand. "There are three things you need to remember without fail, Grasshopper."

I leaned in close, even I realized I was about to be handed the keys to the kingdom. I wasn't sure what those keys were, or where the door was that they opened, or even what kingdom they would give me access to; but I knew enough to sit and listen.

"Ready?" she said.

"Ready".

"OK, here goes. These are the three things you have to do when any girl is angry with you."

I waited.

"First, you have to listen to her. Got that?"

"Got it. Listen to her."

"I mean really listen to her, don't pretend."

"Got it. Really listen. Don't pretend. Right. Next."

Mishi narrowed her eyes. "Second, you have to *look* like you're listening. Turn off the TV, put down the paper, hang up the phone, put down the

PlayStation. And look at her."

I nodded.

"Got it. Turn off TV. Look like I'm listening."

"OK," said Mishi. "The third step is the greatest secret of all. Aaron Stern, you have to say this magic formula, and you have to say it exactly as I teach it to you. Are you ready?" Eyebrows raised, a gimlet gaze.

"Ready," I said.

"OK, here goes. You have to say: 'I'm really sorry.' And" – pause for effect – "you have to sound like you mean it."

Silence. "Now say it."

I snapped out of my trance. "Say it? Now? This is a bit silly Mishi. Girls can't actually fall for this."

"You, Aaron," Mishi interrupted, "are my big brother but you are also a doofus, which is to say, you are a male human being. The terms are synonymous. Here I am, betraying the entire female race by telling you this, our greatest secret in the unending war between the sexes. And you, Aaron Stern, are quibbling."

"Quibbling?"

"Yes, Imbecile," she said. "Quibbling. Now. Repeat after me and make it sound sincere: 'I'm *really* sorry'."

I gave in. Mishi did the annoying little sister thing to perfection, and I had four years on her, but when she wanted anything, well, 'wrapping me around her little finger' was the phrase that came to mind.

"OK," I said, "here goes... I'm really sorry." I looked at her expectantly.

"Hopeless. You have to convince her that you mean it. That sounded fake and shallow and insincere and ..."

"All right, OK I get it. Wait a sec," Some throat clearing and a neck-loosening roll of the head. I looked her in the eyes, and said: "Mishi, I'm *really* sorry."

"Better," said Mishi softening. "Actually, better than better. Almost good. Despite myself I felt a warm glow. Good. Well done. Have you got it? One, you have to listen; two, look like you're listening; and three, the *piece de resistance*, say 'I'm *really* sorry'."

"Got it."

"And one last thing. I wasn't going to say this because I wanted to take pity on the women in your life but I can't help myself. You don't know this because you are inside spaceship Ronnie Stern but you do this thing with your eyes, and you have a kind of head tilt thingy. That's it, that's it. You're doing it now. No woman on earth can resist that look."

Apparently, Mishi explained, my eyes had widened, and I looked like a puzzled puppy, with its head tilted.

"I still can't believe this will work," I said.

"Oh ye of little faith" she intoned, standing up with her hands raised over me like an Old Testament prophet. "Try it, and see, and you will believe!"

Then I got up from the chair and grabbed her and wrestled her to the floor and tickled her. She started giggling and squealing, a little kid again.

I remembered all this, or least some of it, the bit about listening, and the sub-text of having pity on these girls, and particularly on Cindy, who was a nice kid.

Mishi was not, you'll have gathered, a girly-girl. While other girls went through a Princess phase, Mishi had set the corner of the garage on fire with one of her chemistry experiments. Mishi was part of a chat-room for Physics Geeks – *nilsbohrfan* was her handle.

Cindy? Not so much.

But Mishi was always there for Cindy who was a little lonely and, according to Mishi, found the whole friend-making thing a bit of a challenge.

So it was often, "I'm going over to see Cindy." Or, "Cindy and I are going to the Mall." Or something.

So Cindy and I talked some more, and I really, really listened, and then I extricated myself, and went inside. I had had a long day.

8.

I walked in the front door, and was surprised to hear my Dad. I knew he was in the living room, sitting in his favorite armchair reading the paper, because I could hear the running commentary on the events of the day.

"Oy, what is this? Russia? How can they do that? If I had a nickel for every time that Nudnik said..."

"Hi, Dad." I stuck my head around the door.

"Oh, Hi Ronnie, I was reading the paper." The *LA Times* held in his hands was another hot tip.

"How're things?" he said folding the paper and putting it down on a side table.

"Oh, you know, fine."

"Good to hear. Yet again the twenty-first century teen has everything under control.

Bu-ut." He made it two syllables.

"But?"

"Yeah, 'but'. But, you don't look so hot. You look a bit worried. Anything on your mind?"

Hmm, I thought, anything on my mind. Aside from a dead grandmother, weird visions, eavesdropping on bizarre head conversations, a mysterious group of X-men wannabe's fighting the forces of darkness, and, Oh Yes, those forces of darkness wanting to take over the world. Aside from all that? "No, nothing much, Dad. Just a long day at school."

"And Katie?"

How did he do that? He was Mr. Normal. According to Dr. C he was not an Adept. He just went off to work everyday – *Stern's Carpets: Let us take you on a Magic Ride to Carpet Heaven!* – came home, read the paper, had dinner, watched TV. And left Mom to arrange his social life, fuss over his clothes, and interrupt him at the dinner table.

But every now and again he'd zero in on Mishi or me, and show he was totally on the ball. Why did he have to pick now to do that?

"You're home early," I said, Deflector Man, able to avoid difficult conversations in a single bound!

"This is true. We finished early. The new guy, James Taylor, you know, like the singer, only he doesn't sing so good. Can't even whistle. But at inventory and management, he's pretty good. So I left him to it. And here I am. Not often I get off early, bu-ut... Now that we've cleared up my problems, let's see if we can get some answers from the first born fruit of my loins, and the heir to my fortune."

He sat looking at me with those deep brown eyes set into a sagging face. He was not part of the California Facelift Brigade, staving off old age by stretching the skin up from their ass to their hairline. Mom neither. A graceful slide into their sunset years as God intended was the plan. 'Acting their age' was the phrase they used whenever the topic came up.

"So, nu?" Dad prompted.

"So... I went to the hospital to see Katie's Bobbeh. She passed away while I was there."

"Yes, I was sorry to hear about that, may she rest in peace. Mrs. Katz was a real nice lady. I liked her. Were they expecting it?"

"No, not at all, it was a bit of a shock for everyone. Katie took it pretty hard."

"I'll bet. And this is what you're worried about?"

"Yeah," I said, "I guess."

"Death is part of life. Everyone moves on eventually. And there's nothing else? I mean nothing else that you want to tell your old man at this point in time?"

"No, Dad, I guess not," I said.

"So you want to eat something? Carmelita has a casserole on the stove. I can smell it from here. And it smells good. You want some?"

If a nuclear blast went off on Rodeo Drive, and Al Qaeda was parachuting in over the Hollywood sign, the first response from Stern HQ would be 'Eat, you gotta keep up your strength.' Followed by 'I felt a draft. You sure you don't need a scarf?'

"I'm OK Dad, I'm not hungry. But can I get you some?"

"That would be nice. Your mother only gets home at ten o'clock. I'll eat now."

"Where's Mishi?"

"She's at Kimberley Horowitz's place with the girls from the gym squad. Working on their verbal communication skills no doubt."

That I could believe. Once I had the misfortune of giving Mishi and three other girls from gym a lift somewhere. The noise had been tremendous. Unending prattle punctuated by laughter and expressions of dismay, all in a high-pitched squeal that only dogs can hear.

I remember marveling how my skeptical brainiac sister could turn into a total tweenie-bopper. Camouflage, and survival instinct I assumed.

"I'll tell your mother about Mrs. Katz. She'll want to send flowers or a card or something. She was a close friend of hers. Always on the phone, you know."

I actually didn't know. Mom? Always on the phone to Bobbeh Katz? The nice old lady, who, somehow, sent me back to Ancient Egypt? This had to be part of the whole 'Mom the Elder' thingy. Clearly I had some catching up to do.

JAMALIA BROOKES

1.

"Clear!" the nurses and interns took the regulation step back from the gurney. The lead surgeon rubbed the metal plates together and planted them on the patient's chest.

There was a loud snap, the body convulsed, and the medical team moved in to monitor, administer, check and tend. The whiter than white lighting shone down on a scene of clinical efficiency, at the heart of which lay the now lifeless body of a young black man, another casualty in the ongoing war of the Dallas-Fort Worth streets.

"Clear!"

The medical team in an array of green, blue and purple scrubs, all in masked anonymity, stood back. More monitoring for signs of life followed the snap and the convulsion.

To no avail.

The knife wounds and head injuries had won this night's life and death battle.

A nurse covered the young man's battered face, and the activity level in the operating theater dropped. Everyone began checking clipboards, snapping off latex gloves, and untying their facemasks.

Jamalia Brookes moved quietly to the gurney and let the warmth build up in her body. She reached under the sheet and took hold of the boy's wrist and forearm. She felt the warmth flow out of her, through her arms and hands. Time slowed down, seconds passed at a crawl.

The fingers of ice that crept up from the pit of her stomach replaced the warmth and began to wrap around her heart. Her head began to swim.

Come on, she thought, I can't keep this up forever.

Then she heard the ping of the heart monitor, and the boy sucked in air.

"He's alive! I got a pulse," she shouted.

Clipboards were cast aside, new gloves were snapped on, masks were replaced.

Lethargy gave way to organized bedlam.

Jamalia took a step back to steady herself against the stainless steel sink. The icy fingers subsided. A few more minutes and *she* would have needed the defibrillator.

An hour later the boy was wheeled out. The last casualty for the night team to patch up, or send to the morgue. The room now buzzed with muted conversations, punctuated by the metal-on-metal of bloody instruments placed on trolleys ready for the autoclave.

The early morning holocaust was already filling up the other ER rooms of the Dallas-Fort Worth Central Hospital.

Jamalia Brookes had seen it countless times. She was not even close to getting used to it.

It was the end of her shift, an all-nighter in ER. Despite the easier options that her seniority opened to her, she couldn't leave the young black men in the late night emergency rooms to struggle for life without her.

Jamalia knew that God had bestowed the gift of healing on her to be used every chance she could get. Tonight had been close, the boy was too far-gone for comfort, the effort had drained her.

2.

For as long as she could remember she had had the gift. She was actually surprised on her fourth birthday when she first realized that others couldn't heal.

Jimmy Considine had fallen from a tree in the park and several mothers, including her own, had gathered around the moaning boy. They cooed and fussed and touched him gently but he didn't get better.

So Jamalia had slid between the chattering women, and knelt by Jimmy. She had laid her hands on the rapidly swelling ankle. She closed her eyes and let the warmth build inside her, then, with an inner release, had let it flow into the boy.

A few minutes later Jimmy was up that same tree again.

After that everyone started talking about the 'Miracle Girl'.

Growing up on the South side of Chicago Jamalia had gone with her Momma and her sister and her brothers to the Second Baptist Church of the Holy Congregation. She had listened to the Reverend Cyrus B. Abernathy call on sinners to repent. She had swayed back and forth and shouted "Amen!" along with all those other folks in church. The Reverend Cyrus B. Abernathy had promised eternal rewards for those that turned away from sin, and a lake of ever burning hell-fire for those that did not.

So Jamalia knew she had to use God's healing gift whenever she could. She certainly didn't want to join all those sinners who boiled and burned for the rest of time, no sir! She didn't like the sound of that glowing lake of molten lava one little bit.

Word of the miracle girl reached the ears of the Reverend Cyrus B. Abernathy by way of the mysterious and speedy ghetto grapevine and, after praising the everlasting King of Heaven, he rolled up his sleeves and got busy doing the Lord's work.

Jamalia Brookes was an instrument of divine grace and all who wanted to be healed could come to the Second Baptist Church of the Holy Congregation (the Rev Cyrus B. Abernathy presiding) on the corner of Martin Luther King and Vine every Sunday at 11 am sharp to be cured of whatever it was that ailed them by 'Our Little Wonder Girl'.

And came they did.

When the word really got out they came in their hundreds. In the end Jamalia was healing an unending line of supplicants all day Saturday and half of Sunday, and on Tuesday and Wednesday evenings from four in the afternoon until ten at night.

The wooden pews of the Second Baptist Church of the Holy Congregation got soft cushions, and work started on a nice new roof. The Reverend Cyrus B. Abernathy was now chauffer-driven around town in a shiny Cadillac De Ville. His home seemed to always have contractors working on something. And didn't Mrs. Clarissa Abernathy look fine in those new clothes and that fancy jewelry?

Jamalia began falling asleep every time she sat down, and could barely string two words together on the way home from the healings.

Jamalia's Momma had a sister who lived in the Dallas-Fort Worth area. Five months from the day Jimmy Considine fell out of that tree Mrs. Brookes folded the children's clothes, the underwear, shirts, the thin cotton dresses and patched jeans, gathered two pairs of shoes each, one winter, one summer, and packed all of it into one old suitcase. She folded her own clothes, and carefully wrapped the plate with the painted songbirds her grandmother had given her in pages from an old copy of the *Chicago Times.*

All Momma's things went into a second suitcase. Including the wooden spoon that Jamalia's brother Jamal had painted when he was six as a birthday present for her. That was on the day before he'd been gunned down by a stray bullet walking home from school.

Momma picked up the two suitcases and took her four surviving children, each one carrying their own carefully handed down Wal-Mart puffcoat, to the bus station and bought five tickets to Texas with the money her sister had sent.

How the Reverend Cyrus B. Abernathy and the uncompleted roof of the Second Baptist Church of the Holy Congregation fared after the sudden departure of their miracle girl were not matters to which Momma Brookes gave a moment's thought.

Ponte a Moriano, Tuscany, 1156

In the village of Palmata, in the hills above the river Serchio in the Province of Lucca, just over a mile from the town of Ponte a Moriano, the sound of the explosion sent a heavily pregnant woman, leading her donkey loaded high with loaves made fresh that morning in her husband's bakery, into labor. The baby, her third child, was born in the dusty Palmata street with the aid of three women who happened to be nearby and who had rushed into the street to find out what the commotion was all about.

The baker and his wife named their son after Saint Emygdius of Ascoli whom the pious invoked as a protection against earthquakes. The boy Emygdius grew up to have a distinguished career as an advisor to Pope Alexander III.

But this is not his story.

The explosion, which heralded the birth of the future Cardinal Emygdius, destroyed a large part of the alchemical laboratory down the hill, on the other side of the Serchio, near the village of Ponte a Moriano. The smoking ruin, which had started life as a barn, had been transformed some years before into a place of dark experiments, mystical research, and strange investigations. And, on occasion, it was a place for Leonardo Da Silva to relax in the warm summer afternoons in which this part of Tuscany gloried.

Two figures staggered out of the clouds of black smoke billowing around the blocks of stone, oak beams and lengths of splintered wood.

Leonardo Da Silva brushed a few glowing splinters from his cloak and stood, his face blackened, his head bare, and his clothes smoldering. His eyebrows would take weeks to grow back. He surveyed the damage and turned to his assistant, Geminio.

"Well, my boy, I feel it fair to say that that could have gone better."

Geminio, when he had finished coughing and spitting, bobbed and grinned. "Yes, Master, perhaps a little less naphtha in the Greek Fire."

"You may be right my lad," said Da Silva waving his hand to clear the smoky air. "But for now we must enlist the aid of our friends in the village to get this place rebuilt."

"They may want to be paid this time, Master."

"Yes, yes, a detail Geminio," said Da Silva patting his pocket for his pair of loaded dice. "Perhaps I will visit Lucca to discuss matters with my financial advisors."

"Oh Master," said Geminio, shuffling from foot to foot and clutching the surviving half of his hat, "perhaps a bit further afield? I believe all the, uh, advisors in Lucca are aware of your, ahem, luck at the tables, I mean, financial negotiations."

"Hmmm" said Da Silva thoughtfully, "Firenze?" Geminio shook his head.

"Pisa? Livorno? Siena?"

"Perhaps, if I might be so bold, somewhere beyond the borders of Tuscany.

Your reputation for skill and intelligence and, er, luck in, um, raising funds from, hmmm, investors, has spread far and wide."

Da Silva grinned broadly and gave Geminio another slap on the back. "Geminio, summon the workmen, I will set off this very hour for Bologna. I wish to see their fine University." He put a friendly arm around Geminio's shoulders, and waved his free hand in the air as if conjuring a vision. "Students, Geminio, ideas in their young heads, fine words on their lips, and gold in their pockets. I feel sure they will prove themselves eager to invest in my enterprises."

Geminio grinned and capered. "Yes, Master, Bologna. Perfetto!"

CHAPTER FIVE

17TH TO 24TH SEPTEMBER

AARON STERN

1.

I was ready for him this time.

Wolfgang circled to my left in a crouch. The blue crash mats deadened his footsteps. The padded walls stood ready to greet me. I arranged my face in that 'Oh no, don't hurt me!' look. Which was not so hard. I'd been getting a lot of practice lately.

Then a picture of Wolfgang flying through the air formed itself in my head.

I faked to my left and Wolfgang smirked. I moved to my right and he came forward hands at the ready, but it was his legs, muscles bunching for a kick to my head, that I focused on.

He made his move. I dropped like a stone under the kick and rolled toward him, feeling the brush of air on my face. I pushed up from the floor, taking his ankle in both hands over my head, and I kept going straight up. The momentum of his kick, with some help from me, lifted him off the ground. He crashed onto his back.

He looked stunned.

"Well, well, well," he said after a moment or two, holding out his hand for a lift up. "You appear to have finally learned something, my friend."

I reached down, feeling pretty pleased with myself.

He took my hand, then leapt up, and with a deft flick had me pinned with his elbow across my throat. "But not, I fear, enough."

OK, I thought, no trusting German martial arts instructors when they pretend to be down for the count. What a shock.

2.

The Fourth Vision

MJD placed a small wooden box on the table. He flipped the latch, lifted the lid, and turned the box so I could see inside. We were back in his underground lair, sitting at his desk on the plain hard chairs.

Inside the box was a lump of marble about the size of my fist, a pyramid with three smooth and polished faces that came to a point. The fourth side, the base, was rough where it had been broken off.

"We were indeed fortunate to acquire this," said MJD looking into the box. "It is a fragment of the ancient palace of King David. At least we hope it is. Would you be so kind, Mr. Stern?"

Here we go again, I thought.

I reached out with my finger and, as soon as I touched it, the stretching and twisting started.

I was in a small room with stone walls hung with tapestries. Three fires in open baskets lit and warmed the room. Out of a square, stone window I could see a night sky studded with stars.

Against one wall was a bed, and lying on that bed under a pile of covers was an old man with wispy white hair and a long straggly beard. His eyes were gummed up and his cheeks were sunken. His skin looked yellow and, despite the heat of the fires, he was shivering.

Sitting next to him on a low stool was a girl. She was dressed in a blue floor-length gown. She was wearing a scarf over her head and her hair, what I could see of it, was black and shiny and tied in a long plait. Long lashes framed dark eyes, and her skin was a rich glowing amber, her nose was straight and perfectly proportioned, her mouth small, and her tongue darted around her full lips as she concentrated on looking after the old guy.

Did I say she was beautiful? She had a face that an artist would love to paint, that launches ships, that would make a priest start wondering about all that celibacy stuff.

Where was I?

Oh yeah. The girl was wiping the old man's eyes and mouth with a damp cloth, which she dipped into a bowl and squeezed out.

This went on for a while, and then a door opened behind me and a young man walked in.

He was tall and handsome. Not handsome like the girl was beautiful. Not in the same league. But he had strong features, a full beard and clear glittering eyes. He was dressed in a white robe, with patterns and animals and birds woven into it. It looked pretty expensive.

The girl put down the bowl and rose to her feet. She kept her head down and her eyes lowered, and she backed away from the bed.

"Leave us, Abishag," said the young man. His voice was rich and deep, quiet and confident. He sounded like a guy who didn't hear the word 'No' much. The girl left, and I heard her footsteps whisper away along the stone flags of the corridor.

"My Lord, Father," said the young guy, "you sent for me?"

"Yes, my son." The old man's voice was a surprise. I'd expected something quavery and old to go with the skin and the eyes. But the voice made me feel like I should check if my hair was combed and my shirt was tucked in.

"Come hither," said the old man.

The young man approached the bed, knelt and took the old fellow's hand, and held it to his forehead.

"Shlomo Ben David, listen to me, and hear my words. Let my words be for you a guide and a comfort. Be strong in the Lord, for He is our God, the God of Israel. Remember my words regarding Joab Ben Zeruyah, and Shimai Ben Gera, do not let their heads go down to the grave in peace."

"I will remember, Father, and will heed your words, even your words of wisdom. Indeed those two Sons of Death will meet their fathers before the setting of tomorrow's sun."

My blood ran cold. They couldn't see me, but, overhearing their plans for these two dudes, that was somehow no comfort.

"My son," the old guy went on, "all that has been said between us thus far, has it not been recorded by the royal chroniclers? But what I say now will be only for your ears, and for the ears of those who come after you on the throne of Israel and Judah, and for the ears of the High Priest of Israel."

"Yes, Father, I listen, and my ears are open, to your words, even to your words only."

They spoke like that. I felt like I was back in Sunday School listening to our local Rabbi, Elhanan Elbaz, reading out stories from the Bible.

"Go my son," said the old man lifting his hand and pointing to the wall, "go to that tapestry, the tapestry with the woven pattern of acacia leaves. Draw it back and reveal the wall."

Shlomo Ben David went to the tapestry and pulled it aside.

"Now count the bricks from the floor, count them until you have numbered twelve bricks from the floor. Even one brick for each of the tribes of Israel."

The young man got busy over by the tapestry. And my point of view shifted so I was looking over his shoulder.

"I have done so, Father."

"Press on the right side of that twelfth brick."

There was stone on stone scraping, and the twelfth brick swung on a central hinge, half went in and half came out, revealing a cavity.

"Reach into the hole my son, I, even I, the Servant of the Lord Most High, command you to do so. Reach in and take the gloves that you will find there, the gloves made of the hide of a pure white heifer, and clothe your hands in those gloves, up to the elbows clothe your hands and arms."

Shlomo Ben David took out a pair of long white leather gloves and put them on.

"Now reach in and take out the scroll which you will find there, wrapped in a lordly cloth, a cloth of purple, woven with threads of gold. And bring it to me."

The young man drew out a purple and gold parcel about eighteen inches long and four inches in diameter. He crossed the room to his father carrying his prize in both gloved hands.

He knelt by the bed, and held it out to his father.

"No my son, no man may touch this holy thing with his bare hands, even though it be covered by the sacred cloth, it is too mighty for mortal man. Only the High Priest, and the Lord's anointed King of Israel may touch the scroll and remain whole. It is the Word of the Lord written by the very hand of Moshe Rabbenu, Moses our Teacher. But now you, my son Shlomo Ben David, son of my favorite Bathsheva, are you not the Lord's anointed? Uncover the scroll and remove the glove from your right hand. Touch the scroll with the index finger of your right hand. If God has been pleased to grant the wish of his servant David, you will walk from this room whole and unharmed. If He, the Lord God of Israel, withholds his favour, then you will be carried from this room on a funeral bier."

Well, give the guy credit. He didn't hesitate. Still kneeling he put the scroll down on the bed, whipped off its cover and slipped off the glove.

Decisive dude, thinks I. The scroll was like a mini-Torah, with a long roll of yellow brown papyrus wrapped around and around two lengths of wood so it could be unrolled and read.

"Oh Lord, show favour to your servant this day," said Shlomo Ben David. "Grant that I may live, and that I may rule Israel with strength and wisdom."

He reached out and touched the scroll.

Light flashed, and a crackle of ozone filled the room. The young man flinched but he held his finger firmly against the scroll. There were a few more crackles and flashes of light, and then, after a few moments, he withdrew his hand.

He replaced the glove and rewrapped the scroll in the purple cloth.

Then he stood up. If a ghostly presence (me) could have taken a step back, I would have. It was like the guy had grown several feet and spread out wide.

Hard to describe it, but he filled the room. He seemed to be in another dimension, beyond the mere confines of the stone walls and floor of this chamber. His eyes were bright and he was looking at things no one else could see.

The old man looked up at his son and nodded.

And me?

I blacked out and came to, with Katie stroking my face and calling my name, and yelling at MJD and Mordecai. Again.

MIRIAM STERN

The Watcher was good. She was seated quietly in the back corner of the crowded lecture hall wearing a red Iowa State University sweatshirt and fashionably torn jeans, her dark curly hair half-obscuring a pudgy face.

Miriam Stern, standing at the lectern, turned another page of her presentation and clicked to the next slide. It showed several scratchy lines of white dots against a dark background, all radiating out from a central point.

She gave an account of the years of detective work, detailing the search for, and recent discovery of, the Higgs boson, the "God Particle", at the Hadron Collider in Cern, Switzerland.

Miriam surveyed the audience, which looked down at her from the tiered seating, some with their heads down scribbling notes or tapping on keyboards, others just listening.

Her lecture wound up to sustained applause. She was eminent and well-regarded in her chosen field, her presentation had been cutting-edge and, unusual in the world of quantum physics, entertaining.

She patted her papers together, disconnected her thumb drive and placed everything neatly in her soft leather brief case. She responded politely to several congratulatory interchanges, and made her way toward the exit. She had to time this exactly.

She risked a glance up toward the back row of seats and saw the Watcher reach for her cell.

Miriam put her hand to her brow and rubbed her right temple. She closed her eyes briefly and tensed her diaphragm.

The Watcher looked annoyed. Miriam saw her going through the 'Hello, Hello! Are you there?' routine, then trying to redial.

Miriam slipped out of the hall unmolested, heading for the car that would take her to the airport. Her Adept gift, the ability to manipulate electricity and machinery, was not just handy when the waffle maker broke down.

What she failed to notice, however, was Craig McInnes. The Australian thug imported by The Organization from its Southern Hemisphere operation.

Michelangelo could see the completed statue in the block of marble, and was able to set it free with his hand and chisel. Craig McInnes was the pre-freed figure; a solid brick of a man, a slab of stone with tiny cold eyes.

And those eyes now watched Professor Miriam Stern's car drive away.

The disrupted phone call had indeed put a kink in McInnes' plans.

He flipped open his cell, which was now working.

"Missed her," no apologies, no excuses.

"Then we will institute the back up plan," said Kim Park Singh.

"The Watchmaker?"

"Yes," said Singh. "And the daughter. The Watchmaker certainly. But let us, by all means, mix business with pleasure, and take the daughter as well."

FRANCOIS PIERROT

The tinkle of the doorbell faded. Francois Pierrot looked up from his work on a particularly fine Panerai wristwatch. Light footsteps announced the approaching visitor.

He got ready to move his mind into the 'Reading Room'. But before he could do so a voice came from the darkness: "Hello Francois. May I call you Francois? My name is Sally. Sally Portland, and I have a few questions for you."

Francois found himself looking up into green eyes set in a round face, with a flawless complexion. The whole picture framed by straight black hair cut in an artless shoulder-length pageboy style. He was impressed. Francois knew how much 'artless' cost.

Sally unslung her Givenchy knock-off tote from her shoulder and placed it on the table in front of him. Her clothing was perfectly coordinated to show off her curves, with just enough data to hint at hidden pleasures.

Francois, elderly, single, but still a Frenchman, noticed all of this, his 'reading' of Sally's mind fatally delayed.

"And you *will* tell me what I want to know, Francois. So no heroics now. Be a good boy, and we'll get along fine."

Alarm bells were going in Francois's head. He roused himself, and concentrated.

Beneath the pretty porcelain exterior he could feel this girl's cold empty heart. How she had learnt a long time ago that an attractive girl could get away with murder.

He felt her thrill at bending others to her will. Her delight at the friendships she had destroyed. An image flashed across his mind, of a broken teacher, Sally looking on smiling, as the police led him away. Francois felt her deep throb of pleasure.

"Now we can pretend or we can get down to business," she said. "I know who you are, and you know who I work for. And," she leaned on the worktable, revealing her impressive cleavage, "I just love my work."

"Mademoiselle, but I do not know what you are saying..."

He started to rise, but Sally, catlike, rounded the table and shoved him back into the chair.

He sat, shocked by the sudden violence. He tried to quell the panic, to calm himself.

Sally produced a roll of duct tape, grabbed his hands and wrapped several lengths around his wrists.

Then she slapped him hard across the face sending his glasses flying.

She smiled brightly, turned back to the tote and brought out a black case, about the size of a hardback book. She placed it on the table, slid its latches sideways and flipped the lid up, revealing a hypodermic and a dozen small ampoules of various liquids.

With one last regretful look at the Panerai, Francois Pierrot arranged his face into a rictus of terror.

"No, no!" he gasped. "No, you do not have to do this. I will tell you what it is you want to know!"

"I know," said Sally, silky, warm and understanding. "I know I don't have to, Francois. But, you see, I want to." A light giggle, her fingers playing over the ampoules.

"I have a natural flair with these you know," she said proudly. "The Poisoner. That's what my friends call me. Now let me see... which one shall we use...? Truth serum? Too easy. Or how about this one?" Her fingers lingered on a pink vial. "It burns your skin off from the inside. I think the Chinese developed it, or the Iranians. I'm such a silly, I forget." She laughed brightly.

"No, please," said Francois, injecting a note of desperation.

"Now, now, don't be a big baby," said Sally. "Mommy's only going to hurt you a little. Actually, (big smile), that's not true. This is going to hurt a lot. And the nice thing is you're going to tell me what we want to know anyway."

Her floral dress twirled as she turned back to the desk.

"No, no, please, I'm an old man I'll..." his voice tailed off into a sob.

Francois slumped forward, thankful that the duct tape allowed his right hand fingers to reach the watch on his left wrist.

He gave the modified bezel a quarter turn, and pressed the extra dial. He felt the sharp sting as the needle punctured his wrist. He quickened his breathing to increase his heart rate.

Sally took out blue latex gloves and snapped one on each hand. Then she picked up the syringe. She fussed over her ampoules and selected one filled with an iridescent green liquid.

Francois took a final deep breath. Then his body convulsed and he fell to the floor. His mouth began to froth white and his legs drummed against the floorboards.

Sally turned from the desk and rushed to his side.

He smiled up at her as his eyes clouded over.

Sally's face contorted with rage. She screamed and began kicking Francois' lifeless body. Then, shrieking abuse, she picked up an old wooden chair and smashed it into the nearest cabinet. Priceless antique clocks crashed to the floor.

She dropped the broken pieces of chair and gave Francois's lifeless body a final kick.

She propped herself against the desk breathing heavily.

Sally knew what she had to do now. No point putting it off. She fished in the tote for her cell.

"Yes?"

"Problem. He had a suicide plan. I should've known."

"Yes, you should have. I take it you failed to find out what we wanted to know?"

"No, I mean yes. I failed."

"Clean up. Dispose of the body. Then report in."

Bud and Charlene Katzenberger's visit to Kansas City was ruined when, the next day, they were taking an early morning stroll along the Brush Creek pathway past the Country Club district.

They were in town for the 42nd Annual Seed Plow Manufacturers Convention, which still had two days to run. They were country music aficionados, and they had tickets that evening to hear Mary Chapin Carpenter at the Kauffmann Center. They sure felt lucky today.

Mary Chapin Carpenter sang that night to an appreciative audience. The house was packed, except for two empty seats in the middle of the third row.

What on their morning walk had at first looked to Charlene like a bundle of old clothes and leaves and driftwood washed down the Creek in the previous night's downpour, turned out to be the body of an old man.

When Bud and Charlene hurried over to investigate, the 'body' opened its eyes and asked, "Where am I?" in a heavy French accent.

Quite a few of the wealthier citizens of Kansas City, and many of that charming metropolis' visitors, staying in the many comfortable hotels which lined Brush Creek, found their morning routines disrupted by Charlene's piercing screams.

AARON STERN

1.

"Well, Ronnie, my boy," Mortimer J. Dunkeldorfer clapped his hands together and rubbed them vigorously. We were down in his burrow again, seated on the same wooden chairs next to his cluttered desk.

"I must say I envy you," MJD was leaning in, a beagle focused on a doggie treat. "You appear to have witnessed Moses writing the Scroll of Destiny, the original of the Revelation of the Elders itself, and you heard him being tasked with carrying it – and the timeless wisdom it contained – out of Egypt with the freed Hebrews, for an encounter with their God in the desert. And," he laughed, "we have another, more famous document which tells us how that turned out."

I nodded. My input didn't seem necessary.

"And King David and King Solomon!" He hugged himself with delight. I thought he'd give himself a kiss. "Let's see if we can continue this record of achievement shall we? Today I am going to ask you to touch a small fragment of golden thread. Legend has it that this thread is from a cloth used by Rabbi Yohanan Ben Zakkai to cover the Torah in the synagogue at Yavneh. You will be aware, no doubt, of Ben Zakkai's famous meeting, during the final siege of Jerusalem, with the General Vespasian, soon to become Emperor of Rome. This fateful encounter led to the preservation and transformation of Judaism. The substitution of prayer for animal sacrifice, and the formulation of many new interpretations of Biblical laws in the absence of a functioning Temple."

If you say so, I thought. I'd never heard of Ben Zakkai, and I didn't know Yavneh from a hole in the ground. Heck, after all this time it might just be a hole in the ground – must remember to Google it.

But I was getting a bit better at this vision thing. Dr. Califario and I had had a few follow up sessions. We had talked about the visions and especially about how I went in and came out. Going from here to there and back again still made me feel like dough being made into a pretzel, but he showed me how I could get some distance on it.

MJD was holding up a slender filament of gold with a pair of tweezers. "Okay," I said, "here goes nothing."

2.

The Fifth Vision

My ears rang with shouts and the clang of weapons, and the roaring crackle of a raging inferno. The sun struggled to light the scene through clouds of haze and smoke. I was watching siege engines, solid mountains of wood and stitched animal hides, creak and groan as they wheeled forward, toward high stone walls. Defenders, tiny dark shapes lining the battlements, threw rocks and tipped steaming vats of oil down onto the attackers. Arrows, spears, stones and acrid smoke filled the air.

I saw rank upon rank of Roman soldiers march forward with plumed helmets and eagle-topped banners, drums pounding and long curled trumpets blaring. Invisible though I was, I was shaking. I mean who could stand in the face of such awesome power?

Even to my untrained eye the advantage was with the attackers. Clouds of missiles flew from their disciplined ranks. The crumbling fortifications shook as rocks the size of small cars smashed into the walls. The defenders were thinly spread, and the return volleys even thinner.

This was not going to be story with a happy ending. For the defenders, at least.

Then my view shifted.

Now it was night and I was in a large tent, more a marquee really. There were half a dozen tall poles holding it up. Spears and shields and swords and furled banners were arranged in orderly stacks around the draped walls. There were several iron baskets on three legs with fires burning in them. A bunch of Roman soldiers were standing around talking quietly to each other. Others were coming and going, a few were pulling parchment rolls out of large iron-bound wooden chests.

A long table was set up in the middle of the tent covered in a jumble of maps and diagrams and other unrolled squares of parchment, their corners weighted down with daggers, pots of ink, small stones and anything else that had come to hand.

A Roman officer was sitting on a plain wooden stool looking over one of the maps. He was old and tired, his round face was craggy with a flat boxer's nose. But it was set and determined. His eyes were clear, and he exuded rock-like certainty, and menace. He didn't look like a guy with a sense of humor. Maybe this was General Vanadium (what had MJD called him?).

Then the tent flap opened and two hefty soldiers came in half carrying, half dragging an old man in a dusty robe. The man was hollow-cheeked, like he hadn't eaten for a while. He had a long gray beard, swarthy skin, and a prominent nose. But, if his eyes were all you noticed, he and the Roman general could have been twins. It was like a second implacable force of nature had entered the room. That tent wasn't big enough to hold these two dudes. Heck, this hemisphere wasn't big enough!

The soldiers gave the old man a last shove and he staggered forward, finally steadying himself with two hands on the table. He was looking the Roman officer straight in the eyes.

"Sir," said one of the guards, standing stiffly before his general, "this one came out of the city in a coffin. We caught him in the Valley of Kidron. He kept saying he needed to speak to the General. You said you wanted important deserters brought to you, Sir."

The General and the old man sized each other up for a few moments.

The General, still seated, spoke first: "Well, Jew. What news do you bring from Jerusalem? What can you tell me?"

"Oh King, Oh Emperor of the Romans," said the old man, "I come as a supplicant to beg mercy of you."

If this was his version of a supplication, I'd never heard a less convincing one. The old man was addressing an equal, an inferior perhaps.

General Vegetation seemed to think so too. His mouth twisted into a sneer. "You ask in a very strange way, Jew. And as for 'King' and 'Emperor', flattery is a poor tool in the mouth of a rebel. A pitiable trick, I say, especially on me. I am a simple soldier, nothing more. The Emperor lives in Rome. If you wish to speak with him I suggest you get back in your coffin and we will arrange passage."

The soldiers around the table laughed in that way subordinates do when the boss cracks a joke.

"Nevertheless," said the old Jew, unfazed, "I still address you as Emperor."

A messenger, bursting into the tent, interrupted them. He half collapsed to the ground, holding out a scroll of parchment.

"My Lord..." was all he could manage.

The General glanced at one of his aides who took the parchment, unfurled it, and handed it to him. The General read the message. His eyes widened briefly. It was like a crack appeared in a stone monument, which immediately repaired itself.

He turned to his aides and began a rapid series of orders. The old man stood impassive throughout this.

The General rose and speaking to the assembled group as a whole he said: "The Emperor Otho is dead and the usurper Vitellius has claimed the throne. The Egyptian legions have proclaimed me, Titus Flavius Vespasianus, as the rightful Emperor."

The room erupted in shouts: "Titus Flavius Vespasianus, Romanorum Imperatorem, Emperor of the Romans!"

When the cheering died down Vespasian turned to the old man. "What is your name, Jew?"

"Yohanan Ben Zakkai," he replied.

"Well, Yohanan Ben Zakkai, it appears that your God has favored you with the gift of prophecy. It has won you the gratitude of an old soldier. And I am a man who pays his debts. Say what it is that you want."

If Ben Zakkai felt intimidated he was good at hiding it. "I want three things," he said. "There is a town to the west overlooking the sea. It is called

Yavneh and is the home of the surviving wise men of Israel. I ask as my first gift your protection for this town and its inhabitants."

"Done," said Vespasian. "Go on."

"I wish for the family of Rabbi Gamliel, descendant of the line of David, to be similarly protected."

"Agreed," said Vespasian. "What more?"

"I wish medical attention for Rabbi Tzadok, who has been fasting for forty years to delay the destruction of the Temple in Jerusalem. The moment of destruction has now arrived, it is time for his fast to end."

"Agreed," said Vespasian.

The tent vanished, and now I was watching Ben Zakkai outside among a bunch of pack animals. It was daylight and I could still hear the sounds of a raging battle. I could smell the smoke drifting across the Roman encampment. Ben Zakkai was packing various things into a leather saddlebag slung over a donkey. The last thing he put into it was a scroll wrapped in purple cloth and tied with a golden cord. He held it reverently, his hands were protected by thick gloves, and he placed it in the satchel like he was laying a baby down in a cot.

Then I blacked out.

The Maleficium et MaledictionesArcanum

Secret Crimes and Curses

of

Baphomet, Lord of the Underworld, Prince of Darkness, Bringer of Pestilence and Purveyor of Plagues

As transcribed in a trance by LeonardoDaSilva, Magus and Initiate into the Mysteries of Demonic Wisdom

Extract 4: Canto IX, Verses 10, 11, and 12

IX:10. Moses the Accursed, the Enemy of Me, Baphomet, gave to the Children of Israel on the Mountain of Sinai in the Wilderness, a Written Word that is now known to all peoples.

IX:11. But there is another Word, a secret Word, hidden from the world. This Word has the power to create and destroy, to protect and to attack, to lock and to unlock. It is the Word of Destiny, written by the hand of Moses the Cursed, when he was yet in Egypt, in the House of Bondage, in Mitzrayim, the Land of the Great River.

X:12. Did he, Moses, not hear the Word of the All-Knowing and inscribe the mystery in a secret tongue? The Word of Power, the Scroll of Destiny, the Revelation of Moses...

Extract 5: Canto IX, Verses 14, and 23; Canto X verse 2; Canto XVI Verse 3 and 8

IX:14. Let us now speak of the Guardians of the Scroll

IX:23. The Secret Order of the Protectors of the Sacred Word of Power are themselves full of the same Power. I Baphomet, say beware of the Guardians of Power, they will smite with an outstretched hand and [words obscure] of Might...

X:2. The Old Ones are from time before time; they are the ones who remember when all others forget; they are the Elders of the Tribe who Guard the Sacred Word...

XVI:3. Protect yourself from the Elders for have not I, Baphomet, spoken unto you that they are the powerful ones who can raise the dead, read minds, heal the sick...

XVI:8. The Guardians are for all eternity. They, even they, the Guardians of the Scroll of Destiny, the Word of Power, hand the secret knowledge down from generation to generation...

PROFESSOR OLAF SVENSSON

1.

"Professor, have you heard of something called 'The Moses Revelation'?" said Sean Singleton. He was scrolling down his computer screen, slowly turning the wheel on the mouse.

"No," Svensson, the Dean of Cardozo College's School of Medieval Studies replied, "is it significant?"

They were in the cramped research room, with its high arched windows set into stone walls, surrounded by desks and computers and filing cabinets.

"I'm not sure. I think so," said Singleton. "I just translated some fresh verses. And I ran a computer search for similar words and phrases. He refers to it a lot."

"And you think it is significant?" Svensson asked.

"Yeah, well, that's why I asked, cause you know his third sign is the *Verbum*, the Word and Da Silva refers over and over again to a sacred writing, a scroll, a parchment, letters of fire and, again and again, to something he calls the Moses Revelation. And he keeps using 'Word' in the description. He says it's powerful and that it can create and destroy, that it can heal and afflict, lock and unlock. He goes on and on like that."

"Fascinating," said Svensson. "Anything else?"

"He says this Revelation is in the hands of some kind of secret order of Protectors or Guardians. He refers to them once or twice as the Old Ones or the Elders," he turned to Mary Blakely and Jeremy Plensk. "Anyone else come across these guys?"

Neither of them had.

"This is a most fruitful line of enquiry. Well done Sean."

"There is one other thing," he said.

"Yes?"

"Well, whenever he talks about these Elders he refers to them as very powerful, as having some kind of magic powers. First I thought, well, here we go again, Da Silva on the same old hobbyhorse, but I looked at some of these powers and he's pretty specific, like mind reading, healing, clairvoyance. Do you know anything about this kind of thing?" he said looking at Svensson.

"No," said Svensson. "No, I haven't. Well done everyone. This is good progress. Keep going with this Sean."

2.

Olaf Svensson closed the door to his office sat back in his chair and thought for a few moments. He pulled out the laptop from the locked drawer and composed an email, encrypted it and pressed 'send'. A few minutes later he was initialing the last page of his copy of the minutes of a procurement committee meeting of the Humanities Department when his phone buzzed.

He glanced at the screen and opened the laptop to read the reply:

Re the Four Signs, excellent news. We know the Time and Place, and now, it seems, we have a lead on the Word; Re these 'Guardians/Old Ones' with powers. Yes, we have heard of people like this, our Detectors have identified many of them and we have them under surveillance. If they turn out to be the Guardians of this 'Moses Revelation' then we can use them to lead us to it. Time to escalate matters. Keep up the good work and find the last of the Signs.

MISHI STERN

"Hi Mishi, wanna hang?"

I spun around and saw Emma, pretty, tall, sporty and easygoing, smiling broadly at me.

We were in the schoolyard on break from another round of cretinous classes devised by dumbass curriculum writers, delivered by cynical time-servers, to zoned out students.

Welcome to my world.

I looked at my best friend, and silently cursed myself. I hadn't even noticed her coming across the yard toward me. That gym thing had spooked me.

"You OK?" Emma's smile faded under my stare.

"Me? Oh yeah, neato, just scoping the ground for enemies."

"Yeah right! Like Mishi Stern's gotta get into her Lycra tights and save the world from the monsters trampling the city."

"Yeah," I said laughing. "That's totally it. Super curly-haired girl off to save the planet from straight-haired blondes with perfect teeth."

"Like the evil Daphne," said Emma, pointing at just such a monster with a gaggle of acolytes hanging on every word and giggling at every laugh line.

"Yeah, like Daphne the Wicked, my arch nemesis!"

With the ESP of the playground princess, Daphne chose that moment to turn toward us. She looked at me then turned to her cabal of BFFs and whispered something. It must have been good because the crowd roared with laughter.

Then Daphne walked over to us.

This was new.

"Hi Emma, Hi Mishi," she said with her perfect, orthodontist's ad smile.

"Ah, Hi Daphne," I was fresh out of brilliant comebacks.

Emma could only manage a finger wave, and what looked to me like a curtsey. Daphne was definitely the queen of the schoolyard, but, really?

"Want to come to my party this Saturday?" said Daphne.

I stood open mouthed. This was the Mayor of Tokyo inviting Godzilla to a cook out, this was Superman chowing down on a Kryptonite sandwich, this was Paris Hilton rummaging through bookstores for their last copy of Kant's *Critique of Pure Reason.*

"Well?" Daphne's eyes twinkled.

"Uh, sure, OK," I said.

"Emma?" said Daphne, the perfect hostess-to-be.

"Yeah, I guess," said Emma, emerging from her own trance. "Yeah sure, thanks, that's very nice of you."

"Terrif, I'll text you the details."

"Terrif," I said.

"Terrif," said Emma.

We looked at each other as Daphne returned to her entourage. "What just happened?" said Emma.

"I dunno," I said. "Maybe Daphne will turn out to be a secretly nice person, who's only pretending to be a mean-spirited, petty, superficial, totally vindictive bitch."

"Yeah, maybe," said Emma. "Anything's possible."

"But, on the off chance that Daphne isn't a Mother Teresa Mini-Me, what do you think she's up to?"

"I dunno, invite the geeky nerds to humiliate them in front of all her coolissimo friends?"

"Sounds plausible," I said. "OK, pact, girlfriend," I extended my little finger. "Pact," said Emma hooking hers around mine.

"We'll enter the goblin's lair, and be on our guard against dark deeds."

"You betcha!"

We shook pinkies.

AARON STERN

1.

The next few days were a bit of a blur. I was being trained to the nth degree by all and sundry.

I got Wolfgang to the floor more often. And I could stop him from getting me into some kind of fancy headlock or arm twist. Sometimes.

MJD gave me more of the history of the Elders down the centuries. According to him the Elders were apparently responsible for everything good that ever happened.

The Italian Renaissance? Check. Cathedral building? One or two Elders cooked that up. Shakespeare's plays? Greek Philosophy? You got it.

I was not totally buying this, I must tell you. What about all the things that went wrong? Did the Elders go to sleep at the wheel? I mean if they were responsible for all the good stuff, were they washing their hair when the plague hit Europe, or some war wiped out, like, half a continent? And what about Hitler? Would it have killed them to get him to stick to painting? Or to, like, kill him?

So, MJD told me it didn't quite work like that. There were energetic waves in human history and at times, when things were flowing positively the Elders could nudge things along. Then it was everyone totally lying around on the grass writing poetry, or composing the Mass in C minor, or like, whatever.

When the flow was negative then the Elders could only try to catch the ear of the few sturdy fellows willing to take a stand. Kind of stiffen the sinews stuff.

MJD also told me about the guys with the black hats. Plotters of Evil who are always trying to get their hands on wealth and power. And how part of the Elders' job is to hinder them at every turn. The Organization was their latest disguise.

Since Moses's stylus Dr. Califario often had me into his study and we'd explore the vision thing. He seemed pretty intrigued. That is, for a guy who didn't have a huge repertoire in facial expressions. He kept noodling around, asking me how it was, what it felt like, was I really there, could I speak to the people in the vision, did they know they were being watched, what exactly did they say?

And we did some mind exercises as well. You know, like concentrating on a flame, or a picture. Or remembering long strings of letters and numbers. That kind ofthing.

I got pretty good at it. I felt sharper, more alive, more, I don't know, 'here'. A lot of the New Agey California Dreaming types talk about the 'Now' or the Present moment, and, well, before all this began to happen to me I thought these guys could stick to saving whales, and eating brown food, and wearing off-cuts.

But, with Dr. Califario I think I began to understand a bit of what they were talking about.

2.

And then there was Katie.

After the bedside revivals the whole 'boohoo-you've-been-spying-on-me' thing got shelved, and we were the perfect couple again. I was crazy about the girl and felt bad about the things I'd said, but I guess she felt equally bad at deceiving me, cause neither of us brought it up.

So, we were cool. And soon we were back to normal.

If normal included sneaking off after school to a hidden location, for cloak-and-dagger training, then life was back to normal. And if normal also meant meeting strange but interesting people, and getting beaten up by one of them, being taught about my spooky powers by another, and getting asked about my travels in Ancient Egypt by a third, then we were 'Leave It To Beaver' in the flesh.

And how about this? Katie turned out to be one of my trainers. Go figure.

Her training happened in a room that smelled of incense and had pictures of the Buddha and other holy dudes on the walls.

If you're wondering where all your missing candles got to, wonder no more, cause they all ended up in this room. It was floor to ceiling with them, in little niches and on shelves.

The first time we had a session together she led me in by the hand and then pointed at a couple of mats on the floor. We sat down cross-legged, knee to knee, similar to the set up in the Egyptian Temple of my Vision. Spooky.

Except we leaned in and held hands. Nice.

"Close your eyes," Katie said. So I did. And she went into a kind of trance. (I know this, cause after about a century, I peeked.)

"Imagine yourself, standing in a field, the sun is shining and it's beautiful..." Katie went on and on like this, and I thought, Oh God, under that gorgeous, cool exterior, she's just another brown rice and sandals girl.

But after an eternity of this stuff I kind of got into it.

Maybe I should try brown rice. Kidding!

But, I found myself entering the spirit of the thing, and after a while I went into a deep state of rest and stillness and peace.

"Now let the face of someone you love appear gently in your mind," said Katie.

Mishi jumped into my head like she'd been hiding behind the door waiting to say Boo!

"Look at the face, with no other thought," Katie continued.

I did and for a while I felt good and peaceful and warm about this annoying, brilliant, creative, annoying, hilarious (did I mention annoying?) little sister.

Then another funny thing happened. I could see her. Mishi I mean, and not only in my mind's eye, but like for real, walking down the hallway at home, standing at the top of the stairs and shouting down at Mom. She was asking about a shirt or pants or something. It was like I was eavesdropping.

"Tell me all about what you experienced," said Katie, when I came to.

So I did. I described what I saw, what I heard, and my feelings. Under her questioning all the little details came out.

She looked impressed. Now, don't get me wrong. I love this girl. And from all indications her feelings for me are not entirely negative either. And we'd been together for, like, a year or more. And the number of times I could count, without fear of contradiction, that I did something that impressed Katie Liebovitz. Well, put it this way, I could be a Saudi thief, and I'd still have a few fingers left over.

So it was nice, and at the same time kind of weird, that this knocked her socks off.

She didn't say much though.

Later I found out that Katie's power – to visualize loved ones, and to know where they are – was similar, and, boy, did it ever come in handy.

Ponte a Moriano, January, 1159

Leonardo Da Silva put down the quill, and resealed the lid of the inkpot. He carefully dried the ink on the last sheet of parchment and added it to the stack on the desk.

He rose from his chair, stretched his arms above his head and moved toward a cupboard that stood against one of the stone walls of his study. He was careful not to brush his feet on the chalk pentacle drawn in the center of the room.

Outside the evening light was fading into twilight over the Tuscan hills that rolled down to the River Serchio to the bridge, from which the village of Ponte a Moriano derived its name.

He should hurry, they would be here soon.

He rang a bell and Geminio shuffled in.

"My robe," said Da Silva. Geminio opened the cupboard and took out a black robe woven with occult symbols. He held it behind Da Silva who inserted his arms into the sleeves and slipped it on. Geminio picked a mask out of the cupboard. It was painted gold, its sightless eyes above a hooked nose and downturned mouth framed by prominent cheeks. Da Silva held it against his face while Geminio tied its ribbons from behind, then he lifted the cowl of the gown over Da Silva's head.

There was a knock at the small side door, the one shrouded in darkness by artfully planted sycamore trees.

"Leave us Geminio," he said. Geminio disappeared closing the main door behind him. Da Silva opened the side door and three black-robed figures, all masked, slipped in. No words were spoken.

The three visitors took up positions at three points of the chalk pentacle and knelt. In the five-sided center of the pentacle was the face of a goat with curly horns and golden eyes with slits for pupils. Those animal eyes looked out on the world through narrowed lids. A silver bowl incised with runes and hieroglyphs rested between the goat's horns.

A few minutes passed in silence, then there was a tentative tap at the side door and another figure slipped furtively in and took up his kneeling position at a fourth point of the pentacle.

Da Silva walked slowly to the fifth point at the apex and stood with his arms raised.

He began to intone in a deep voice. The stone walls reverberated with the rhythm of the chant. The others, shrouded in their black robes, their heads bowed, chanted the responses from their kneeling positions. The incantation grew louder and louder and Da Silva's voice rose to a fever pitch.

As the chanting reached its climax he raised his left hand. It lit up with a bright purple light. He threw his hand down, pointing his glowing fingers at the center of the pentacle. A stream of light shot from his fingers toward the silver bowl, which rattled and shook and danced on the spot. It filled with smoke, which began to bubble and twist and writhe. The smoke rose out of the bowl and wound itself into the shape of a hooded figure with the horned face of the goat and the body of a man. The figure threw back its head and roared and laughed.

"You have summoned me from the depths," the voice of the Goat-man was deep and rough. It smelled of untold ages, it stank of corruption, it held the sinister threat of dark deeds.

Da Silva dropped to his knees, his arms outstretched, his faced turned up toward the Goat-man.

"Master Baphomet," he said. "We praise you and sing of your glories, and abase ourselves in gratitude. You have appeared to us, grant us our wish and give us that which we seek."

Da Silva pressed his face to the floor.

"And what is it that you seek? Why have you called me here?" said the Goat-Man. "Speak, or your lives are mine."

"O Great One, we seek wisdom, we seek knowledge, we seek power," said Da Silva, his voice muffled by the cowl.

"Do you really?" Baphomet sounded amused. "And when you get this wisdom, this knowledge, and this power that you say you want, how will you stop it from eating you up, sucking your flesh, and spitting out your bones?"

Da Silva remained silent.

"I thought so," said the Goat-Man. "You are like all those who play with fire. You forget that the burning flesh that you smell is your own."

"Nevertheless," Da Silva squeaked, "grant us our wish."

"Oh, do not fear, I intend to. Watching the tragedy unfold is how I amuse myself." Baphomet's arms spread wide and the room began to fill with cloying purple smoke. The five kneeling figures coughed and choked, their eyes streamed behind their masks, their bodies shivered.

Then the fourth man, the one who had come late, let out a terrified scream. His body began to rise into the air, his legs and arms flailing and pin wheeling. The other three visitors, frozen in place, hid their faces. Da Silva, however, couldn't help himself. From under his cowl he squinted with one eye and watched in horror as the man, his robe flapping around him, rotated in the air like a pig being turned on a spit.

The man shrieked and screamed and clawed at unseen attackers. Then with one last cry he went limp, six feet above the center of the pentacle. His limbs and head hung lifeless, like he was suspended from an invisible hook driven through his stomach, his body now turning slowly in the air.

Then, as if a cord had been cut, his body dropped to the floor with a sickening thud.

He lay spreadeagled, unmoving in the center of the pentacle.

The purple smoke reformed itself into the image of the Goat-man.

"What?" it said. "You think this wisdom you seek comes without a price? Call this a first payment. There will be others."

CHAPTER SIX

26TH & 27TH SEPTEMBER

JAMALIA BROOKES

1.

Jamalia Brookes walked through the dark streets to the bus stop, tired after her long shift. Her head was down and she let out the occasional sigh. She had that young boy's face, from ten days ago, in her head and she couldn't get him out. He was somebody's son, probably somebody's friend, maybe somebody's brother.

She thought of her own brothers and sisters. Kareem was working as a contractor in the Houston area, his business flourishing. Josiah was in a half-way house, again. Her sister Bernice, with three kids of her own, supported her husband, Carl, who was going to Law School at night.

The boy's face came back to her.

Her other brother Jamal, the brother she was named after, the one she had never met, must have looked just like that boy on the gurney, when he lay in the street around the corner from the Second Baptist Church of the Holy Congregation, with a stray gang bullet in his chest.

No one had been there to save her brother.

The Reverend Cyrus B. Abernathy was not the only thing in Chicago Momma Brookes had wanted to get her children away from.

Jamalia turned a corner. She could see the bus stop a few hundred yards ahead illuminated by a streetlight.

Then she heard the footsteps.

She kept up her pace and began searching in her carryall. A fussy black woman looking for her eyeglasses, or a bus timetable. She stopped fussing when her fingers found the gun.

The Organization was on the move. Watchers were out. She had been warned to be vigilant.

Well, in her carryall she had a loaded Glock 9mm with a spare seventeen round clip's worth of vigilance.

The face of Dr. Califario swam into her mind. She had first met him fourteen years ago at this same bus stop. He had been waiting for her. They had ridden the bus home together, and he had explained that her internet searches for someone with similar healing powers had alerted him to her existence. He had told her about the Elders and The Organization as well. She had stopped surfing the web.

Since then she had received training in the use of her powers, and how to conserve her energy. And other things, including weapons.

Her 'Assignment' had turned out to be Alfred Sweeney of Pharmaco Industries International.

She had met some of Sweeney's subordinates through her work at the hospital. She sat on various committees related to drug trials. Her clarity, common sense and good humor had caught the attention of Alison Kochenko, Pharmaco's Chief Research Officer. Kochenko had reported back to Sweeney.

After a personal meeting, and with the permission of the hospital's Ethics and Conflicts Committee, Jamalia found part of her time was now spent with Sweeney at Pharmaco's steel and glass headquarters in downtown Dallas.

A word here, or a shake of the head there from Jamalia, and certain important lines of development had been initiated, others curtailed.

"Stop there please." The voice behind her was pleasant and polite, and insistent.

"What?" said Jamalia, turning around. "Who are you? What do you want?"

A light chuckle. "Oh please, Jamalia. May I call you Jamalia?"

A young man in a light overcoat stood a few yards away. His dark hair was oiled and shiny and combed straight back from his forehead. He had soft features, a pudding nose, pale eyes and a weak chin. They were in a dark patch where repair crews hadn't replaced the shot away street lamps. The man had picked the place and the time well, dimly lit, no onlookers, no traffic.

"You most certainly may not, young man. And where do you get off stopping old ladies on the street. You get on home to yo' Momma so she can box yo' ears, or how would you like me to do that fo' her, so as she don't have the bother of doin' it hersel'?"

More laughter. "You're good. You should audition for Porgy and Bess. Head of Nursing at the largest hospital in Texas, and now you've gone all Hattie McDaniel on me. And all I want to do is talk."

"About what? I don't know nothin'. Suppose I don' wanna have no talk wich y'all."

"Have it your own way, but my people, you know who they are, need some information which, we believe, you have. And you are going to give it to us, one way or the other. Don't make this more unpleasant than it has to be." He drew a gun, flipped the safety, and pointed it at her face. "Please step this way. My car is around the corner."

There was a muffled shot. The jumbled contents of Jamalia's carryall were as effective as a silencer. The man fell backward, his arms splayed, blood spreading from the chest wound.

Damn, now I've gone and put a great big hole in my favorite carryall, thought Jamalia.

She went through the man's pockets and grabbed papers and possessions, shoving them into the ruined bag.

This man, threatening to gun down a lone black woman, no doubt also someone's son or friend or brother, did not earn a second's thought from her. She was truly her mother's daughter.

Jamalia turned and made her way to the bus stop.

2.

Jamalia Brookes called 911 anonymously from a pay phone near the bus stop. Then she caught the bus, got off at her stop and walked the three hundred yards to her front door.

She sat at her kitchen table and sifted through the fruits of the quick search of her assailant's pockets. There were scraps of paper, a packet of gum, three old bus tickets, and a wallet containing twenty-eight dollars in cash and a Texas driver's licence in the name of Emilio Lubrano.

None of Lubrano's things gave any lead to his Organization paymasters. Jamalia was turning his wallet over and over in her hands, opening each flap and compartment, thinking about the message she would send to LA, when a fold in the inner money compartment gave a little. She experimented and found that the lining slid aside, and underneath it was a piece of paper. She extracted it carefully and unfolded it:

Tail, nurse, Dallas-Forth Worth General

Brookes, Jamalia

Ask about – Moses Revelation

WORD, PLACE, TIME, TWINS???

Use force ☺

MOSES REVELATION!!!!

Jamalia was puzzled, but she knew who would be able to figure it out.

She put everything liberated from Lubrano's pockets, including the note, into an envelope and sealed it.

The next day it was on its way, Express Mail, to California.

The Maleficium et MaledictionesArcanum

Secret Crimes and Curses

of

Baphomet, Lord of the Underworld, Prince of Darkness, Bringer of Pestilence and Purveyor of Plagues

As transcribed in a trance by LeonardoDaSilva, Magus and Initiate into the Mysteries of Demonic Wisdom

Extract 6: Canto XII, Verses 7, 14, and 15

7. Is it not written in the foul words of Moses the Accursed: "So God created man in his own image, in the image of God created he him; male and female created he them"?

14. The Third Sign will be the manifestation of the Gemini, the Twins. In time of War, in time of Trouble, in time of Destruction, yea, is it not so that I Baphomet tell you, this is the sign. The coming of the Two that are One. The Time calls them, and they appear.

15. A branched Soul, divided but unified, two but one, Isis and Osiris, Marduk and Astarte, Adam and Eve, Male and Female, Brother and Sister, the Sun and the Moon, the Rod and the Staff.

PROFESSOR OLAF SVENSSON

"Any clues as to the nature of these Gemini, these Twins?" asked Svensson.

The team was sitting knee to knee in the cramped workspace on the third floor of Cardozo College. Svensson jotted notes onto a pad on his lap. One or other of the students would turn occasionally to their computer to point to a page of the manuscript, or their translation, or to make a note.

"We are pretty sure," said Mary Blakely, "that they will turn out to be male and female, Da Silva is quite clear on that."

"And probably brother and sister," said Singleton. "Maybe not actual biological twins. The term seems to refer to a binary soul system rather than literal twins."

"Da Silva makes some references to Genesis 1:27," said Plensk. "'*So God created man in his own image, in the image of God created he him; male and female created he them*'. We are concentrating on an actual brother and sister. There were a few intriguing references to a rare confluence of great power through a new union of Osiris and Isis. No firm leads yet, certainly not in the present day."

"But," said Blakely, "if there was a brother/sister combination, both of whom have savant or adept powers, then they could be Da Silva's Twins."

"Your work has been excellent my friends," said Svensson. "You are to be congratulated. But, remember, speed is of the essence."

"Got it," said Plensk.

They returned to their computers.

COLONEL MCALLISTER

1.

Colonel Landon McAllister rested his elbows on his desk and watched his cell. The blue dot on Google maps moved slowly. It was tracking a transparent adhesive device about the diameter of a dime and the thickness of a piece of paper. The disc was stuck to a Pentagon cleaning cart making its appointed rounds.

McAllister had been keeping his Watcher under surveillance for the past week. He checked his cell regularly and logged the movements of the cart. He wanted to see who else the Watcher was spending time with.

Dr. Califario had told him of the attacks on other Adepts around the country. So far McAllister had been left alone. Perhaps the Pentagon was not the best place for an ambush. Perhaps attacking a ranking officer in the US Army needed special preparation. McAllister didn't care. He would be ready for whatever they tried, and he would hit back twice as hard.

In the meantime he was not going to sit around and wait for someone to try to put a black bag over his head and spirit him away. He was going to turn the tables on these bastards.

Up to yesterday the route of the cart had been kosher, with the exception of the extra time spent around McAllister's office.

So this morning, when the cart went off its usual path, McAllister sat up and took notice.

He'd kept an eye on its progress all morning, where and when it stopped, and for how long. He'd already made a careful note of the time it should take to do the things a cleaner should do, and he noted the anomalies with this guy.

When he'd seen enough McAllister took up some files and headed down the corridor. Walking by one office he put his head in, saw a thick set, red-faced female lieutenant sitting at her desk.

"Oh, sorry, Lieutenant," after the exchange of salutes, "I was looking for Marine Inventory."

"Down the hall, second on the left, Sir," she said crisply.

McAllister thanked her, snapped off another salute and brushed his hand on the doorframe as he turned, leaving behind a transparent listening device.

Colonel McAllister returned to his own office.

He sat back at his desk and, in between perusing files concerning returned bodies of US servicemen and women from the far-flung reaches of America's overseas postings, he listened to the lieutenant.

Later that afternoon he struck gold, and after a few phone calls and some internet searching, he was ready to report.

He went to a vacant office some distance from his own, let himself in with a pass key, of which he had the only copy, and dialed The Migdal.

2.

"Your man in Washington," said McAllister.

"Good to hear from you," said Dr. Califario. "Any progress?"

"Yes," said McAllister. "I picked up the Watcher pretty quickly. His movements eventually gave me a line on his contact in the Pentagon."

"And?"

"The Washington Monument."

"What about it?" said Dr. Califario.

"Mention of visiting it to see if it was suitable."

"Any idea what that meant?"

"None. They mentioned an address too. Sixteenth and Sumner Row in DC."

"Ah, the Pentangle. That is very helpful."

"I'm glad you've got something out of this. Didn't mean anything to me."

"Well, be assured, you have provided a useful piece of information. But I'm afraid we don't have much time. The enemy is definitely raising the stakes. I would like you to be ready to move at a moment's notice."

"Will do," said McAllister.

DR. AMADEUS CALIFARIO

1.

"He is certainly a fount of information this Ronnie Stern," said Mordecai.

"Yes, yes, indeed," said Mortimer J. Dunkeldorfer, pacing back and forth in front of Dr. Califario's desk. Wolfgang was sitting, his legs crossed, one arm resting on the back of the couch. Mordecai stood leaning against an armchair, smoking a cigarette and depositing the ash in an ornate brass ashtray held in his left hand. "I have never experienced anything like this. It is, it is like, like," MJD waved his arms looking for inspiration, "like interrogating an actual participant, an eyewitness to these amazing historical events."

Dr. Califario had called a meeting to discuss Aaron's progress. After reports from Mordecai, Wolfgang and Dr. Dunkeldorfer, the discussion had turned to Aaron's visions.

"Mortimer please," said Wolfgang, "sit, relax. You are making me dizzy."

"Oh? Oh yes, of course. My apologies Wolfgang."

Dunkeldorfer sat, ready to leap up again at a moment's notice.

"I assume," said Mordecai, "that we have not yet found a way of, how shall I put it, 'aiming' him at a specific target?"

"Not yet, not yet," said Dunkeldorfer. "He goes to a place and a time significant in the, ah, life of the artifact he touches."

"And he is an unobserved witness to events," said Dr. Califario.

"Quite, that is it exactly. One unforeseen problem is the Scroll. He has seen it being written and has given us unparalleled insight into its subsequent journeys."

"Gentlemen," said Dr. Califario, "we are moving into uncharted waters. The location of our copy of the Scroll is a closely guarded secret. For its protection, and yours, only a very few know its hiding place. It would not be good for one unruly high school student to increase that number by one."

"Agreed," said Mordecai. "But, if he is having these semi-uncontrollable visions, who's to say he will not stumble on its present whereabouts. Or that of one of the other six scrolls."

"Simple," said Wolfgang. "No more artifacts. No more visions."

"The counsel of caution, certainly," said Dr. Califario, "but we are receiving, as Mortimer points out, invaluable insight into the background and history of our Order."

"Yes, absolutely. Invaluable," said Dunkeldorfer.

"But," said Mordecai, "is this trade off worth it? Curiosity, historical interest, versus very real present danger."

"Well," said Dr. Califario, "with some reservations, I say we proceed. We haven't had an opportunity like this before and I have a feeling that we may learn something important for our present situation."

"I agree," said Dunkeldorfer.

"With reservations, I also agree," said Mordecai.

"Well, that's it gentlemen. Mortimer, would you stay for a moment?"

2.

"I believe we have another problem," said Dr. Califario, without preamble.

Dunkeldorfer took a step toward Dr. Califario's desk and waited.

Dr. Califario placed a piece of notepaper on the desk in front of him, and looked up at Dunkeldorfer.

"Our friends around the country are being watched, in some cases attacked. We have, in turn, watched the Watchers to see if they would lead anywhere enlightening."

"And?"

Dr. Califario pushed Emilio Lubrano's note across the table.

"Intriguing," said MJD after a moment. "Do you have any insights to share?"

"Regarding the four items: the Word, Place, Time and Twins, none except the obvious. That they think that Ms. Brookes, and others like her have information. But the mention of the Moses Revelation raises the stakes considerably."

"It certainly does," said Dunkeldorfer.

"And our friend at the Pentagon has reported that they have been taking an interest in the Washington Monument."

"Oy vay," said Dunkeldorfer, resuming his seat.

"Yes," Dr. Califario continued. "Oy vay indeed."

"All that clutter that we placed on the internet about the occult elements in Washington DC," said Dunkeldorfer, knitting his brows and allowing his hands to play across each other in his lap. "It muddied the waters as to its true significance. Do you think they have seen past all that and are zeroing in on the real thing?"

"I think the prudent approach is to assume they have, and act accordingly."

"Any activity at 16th and Sumner Row?"

"Yes," said Dr. Califario. "The White House Pentangle seems to be on their radar as well. Which, of course, adds to our concerns."

"Oy gevalt," muttered Dunkeldorfer, "that presents, as you say, concerns."

"Yes, for years conspiracy theorists have accurately identified the broken pentangle pointing at the White House, but draw the exact opposite conclusions as to its significance."

"Yes," said Dunkeldorfer, "they believe it is a sinister attempt to undermine the Presidency, when in fact it is the greatest protection any

President can have. God forbid they should discover its real purpose, and find a way to unlock the key."

"Then we will have to put in some overtime," said Dr. Califario, "work weekends!"

"Hob rakhmoness, have mercy," said Dunkeldorfer. "What are our plans?"

"This is the hard part," said Dr. Califario, "we know something big is going to happen, we have a good idea who some of the perpetrators are, and we know where they are sniffing about. They have tipped their hand somewhat by attacking our people. But until they make a more distinct move, I'm afraid we have to wait. If we go off half-cocked we could force them to do something rash, or worse, send them underground.

"And in the meantime?"

"In the meantime," said Dr. Califario, pointing at Lubrano's note, "I was rather hoping you could do some research into the Word, Time, Place and Twins. Perhaps young Mr. Stern could be persuaded to help?"

"Good plan," said Dunkeldorfer, rising to go. "I will have to give him some of the background."

"As you see fit," said Dr. Califario.

AARON STERN

1.

MJD was making me nervous. I mean he was a wired up kind of guy at the best of times, jumping off his chair and running to look up something in a book, or riffling through sheaves of papers. He was never still.

He wasn't still now, but less in a 'Boy, have I got a surprise for you', and more in an 'I'm afraid it's bad news' kind of way.

We were back down in his hideout again seated at his desk. I braced myself.

"We have something for you to touch," he said, rubbing his shiny dome. "It is not, as it were, the usual thing. Not an artifact. Quite current."

"Current? Like from this century?" I said.

"Well, yes, actually. From this week." His eyes darted to his desk.

"You look a little worried Doctor," I said, perfect grasp of the obvious, that's me. "Should *I* be? Worried, that is."

"Oh no," he said quickly. "No, no, no, no, no."

He might have gone on saying 'no' forever if I hadn't interrupted.

"Well," I said. "That's good. Isn't it?"

"Yes," he said, "that is good." He did his hand clapping and rubbing thing again and picked up a small piece of notepaper with handwriting on it.

"I had better give you some background. One of our friends elsewhere in America, Dallas, actually, um, acquired this from, how shall I put it, an opponent."

"Opponent?"

"Ah yes, one of those who work for The Organization."

"Acquired it? How?"

"I'm not sure that is exactly germane, but she, as I say, acquired it, and sent it to Dr. Califario. And he would like, that is, if you agree... He was wondering if you would..."

"Touch it and go wherever it takes me?"

"Precisely."

"OK."

"You are willing to do this?"

"It's what you pay me for."

"Pay you?" He looked quizzical, then he rocked back on his chair and hooted. "Oh, I see, a joke. Pay you. Very droll Mr. Stern, very droll."

"The note?" I prompted, holding out my hand.

"Yes, yes, of course," he said.

I touched it.

2.

The Sixth Vision

After the twisting and the darkness I was watching a young guy with black slicked-back hair and weak chin, wearing a light coat on a park bench somewhere hot and sunny. He had his cell clamped between his ear and his raised left shoulder, and he was trying to write in a notebook.

"Yeah, yeah,' he said, "I get it, I get it. A nurse, Brookes. Spell that, J-A-M-A-L-I-A, got it. Jamalia Brookes. Yeah I've written it down. OK, OK say that again slowly, Time, Place, Word..."

The park and the bench faded away and now I was in a swanky office, all wood panels and brass fittings. There were pictures on the wall of people in red coats, riding horses with a pack of dogs running along next to them.

There were two flags standing on poles in the corner. One red and white one, Canadian, and a blue and white UN flag.

I could see a neat dude behind a big wooden desk. Dressed in a gray suit with a green tie.

"Yes," he was saying, "that's correct, Time, Place, Word and Twins. And you must ask her about a document called the Moses Revelation." He spelled out all the hard words.

Mr. Slick hung up the phone and immediately redialed.

"Svensson," he said, "I have briefed several of our operatives. They will ask about this Moses document. Yes, the Time, Place and Twins as well."

He waited for a reply.

"You're sure that document is the Word?"

He nodded.

"Good," he said, "I believe we have enough to get started. The third of October is only a little over a week away. We have the Place, and we should get a line on the Word shortly. If you could press your team to move forward with the Twins."

The office, wood paneling, the hunting pictures all faded away.

KIM PARK SINGH

"We are in position," Singh said. He was seated in the black SUV again, holding his cell to his ear and looking through a set of binoculars. McInnes sat in the driver's seat, a stone carving.

"The girl is at home."

"Good," said Lassiter. "Time to increase the pressure. Take her at the first opportunity. Miss Portland flew in to LA yesterday and is rested and eager to harness her talents. She is setting things up at the warehouse. Take the girl there when you have her."

Singh grunted. "We'll keep tabs and get her when we can."

"Excellent," said Lassiter.

Singh snapped the cell shut. And concentrated on the binoculars.

AARON STERN

"A party?" said Mom, trying to keep the surprise out of her voice.

"Yeah, Mom, a party. You know, like with other girls my age, and Daphne might even try to sneak in some of those dorky idiot boys she knows from her oh so cool tennis club or badminton team or whatever. And they tell me that sometimes – you might like to sit down for this bit – they have music playing, and then people, you know young people kind of like oh I don't know, like me, might move around sort of in time to this stuff called music, you might remember it from when you and Dad were young like when dinosaurs roamed the earth, and it's got a name, let me think, oh yeah, I remember, dancing! That's it, that's what it's called, dancing."

We were all laughing hard.

"This is very nice, Mishi," said Dad, "that your friends have invited you to this party. And do you really want to go?"

"Yes," said Mom, "I thought you didn't like the Bernstein girl."

"I do not like the Bernstein girl," said Mishi emphatically. "She is a conniving, selfish, look-at-me-I'm-gonna-be-Prom-Queen, Witch with a capital 'B'. But, what can I say, we were caught off guard. We agreed to go."

"We?" I said, feeling I should join in where I could."

"Yeah, dumbass, we."

"Michelle Stern!"

"Sorry, Mom," said Mishi. "But he *is* a du…"

Mom glared.

Mom was like that. One minute she'd be all particle accelerators and quantum gravity and phone calls from the Cern Hadron Collider in Switzerland wanting her opinion, like where was the 'on' switch or something. And the next minute it was all have you got a sweater, and have you brushed your teeth. And sometimes, like now, she'd be super harsh, when one of her lines was crossed, and bad language in the house, or anywhere else, from anyone, but especially one of her children, was strictly verboten!

"So who is we?" asked Dad.

"Daphne asked Emma as well."

"Ah," said Dad, "that will be nice. You and Emma going to this girl Daphne's party on Saturday night."

The intricacies of fourteen-year-old female social life did not hold Dad's attention for too long. I could feel him itching to escape this scene of domestic bliss, and head for the armchair in the living room, with his paper and a glass of hot tea.

"And Ronnie can take you and pick you up," said Mom.

"What!?!" we said together. It was impossible. I'd made plans with Katie. Arriving with her doofus brother? She'd look like the biggest dweeb on the planet! Michelle Stern! Well, he is a doof...

But Mom was no longer listening.

"Mishi, it's lovely that you are going to a party. But Ronnie will drop you, and Ronnie will pick you up. And that," she said, her hand quelled further protest, "is final."

Ponte a Moriano, Tuscany,

Midnight July 21st, 1161

Leonardo Da Silva carried the silver casket, decorated with filigreed acacia leaves, in both hands. The casket vibrated and was warm to his touch. He placed it carefully on the desk next to an inkpot, a freshly cut quill and several squares of blank vellum. He lifted the lid. Inside lay a scrap of parchment. The lines, diagrams and hieroglyphs which covered it glowed fiery red for an instant, then subsided.

Outside a racing cloud hid the full moon, plunging the Tuscan countryside into darkness. An owl hooted. A dormouse scrabbled through the undergrowth. The owl silently dropped from its branch and snatched up its terrified prey.

Leonardo Da Silva lit two candles and a bowl of incense gum. The room filled with the heady smell of the exotic East. He took up a golden wand. It had come all the way from Constantinople, the reluctant gift of the Chief of the Emperor's palace guard. He struck a brass gong.

The sound reverberated and Da Silva closed his eyes and began intoning a prayer in a tongue unheard for the last thousand years. The candles flickered, the incense smoke began to form itself into shapes and images, faces, animals, writhing bodies crying out in silent torment.

For nearly an hour he chanted and prayed and begged and pleaded, then his voice rose to a crescendo. He cried out and gave the gong a final clamorous blow.

He slumped forward, sweat poured from his brow.

Then his head rose from his chest and he opened his eyes. His irises were bright gold and the pupil of his left eye had turned to a vertical slit.

His hand jerked mechanically toward his quill. The fingers closed around it, dipped it in ink, and began to write.

CHAPTER SEVEN

28TH SEPTEMBER

AARON STERN

"**Ah**, the international man of mystery!"

"Hi Melvin," I said. Katie and I were holding hands, approaching the ice-cream stand on Santa Monica Pier.

It was a sunny fall Saturday and the entire population of Greater Los Angeles appeared to have had the same idea as us. We made our way through the throng of families, little kids, rappers performing for cash, and a juggler dressed as a clown who was snapping back and forward on a unicycle.

The carousel was pumping out hurdy gurdy music, just to give the rappers some-thing to work against I guess. The whole world had converged on this wooden pier stretching out into the eye-watering blue of the Pacific Ocean.

Melvin, against all the laws of probability, had found us roughly in the designated place and more or less at the appointed time.

We got our ice-creams and moved slowly toward the end of the pier. I yawned.

"Is baby Wonnie all tired and wanna sweep?" said Melvin. "Now don't wet me keep you up, widdle man." He batted his big brown eyes with motherly concern.

"Katie," he called above the noise, "take this guy somewhere and put him to bed." Katie gave him hard eyes. "No, not in that way. My brilliant repartee is obviously not sufficiently captivating to keep him awake."

"I yawned once," I said, "and I get this from you? I got a few things going on, OK?"

"A few things," said Melvin.

We did the how-many-holiday-makers-can-squeeze-through-a-narrow-passageway-at-once trick, and spilled into the open space at the end of the pier. We rested our elbows on the rail looking down at some seals flapping their fins at an appreciative crowd.

"A few things that I wot not of," he said.

"Wot not what?" I said.

"It's like a Shakespeare quote, Einstein, from that Comedy of Errors play: 'I wot not by what strong escape, he broke from those that had the guard of him'. Which you would know if you had been awake in Gooty's class. Which you weren't."

"Oh yeah, that's right, Shakespeare," I said. Melvin could have been quoting the Stay Puft Marshmallow Man for all I cared.

"Give him to me, Melvin," said Katie looping her arm through mine. "I'll look after him."

This I didn't mind.

"Oh no," said Melvin, holding on to my other arm. "You owe me an explanation. I claim it by the right of Best Friendhood. It's like they've kidnapped the real Aaron Stern and have him bound and gagged in a cellar. And they have left us with this cheap imitation."

Melvin walked around me, looking me up and down like an art professor examining a statue.

"Why, just look at him Katie," he said, "lackluster eyes, lank hair, stooped shoulders, wrinkled clothing – well, that is normal, I'll grant you. But his nose is dry and cold, his coat has lost its glossy sheen, his tail hardly wags at all. Does he need to be put down? I wonder..."

"He's got a lot on," said Katie. "He's got to take Mishi to a party tonight, and I may have gotten a little tetchy with him about that."

"A little!" I snorted.

"Ah," said Melvin. "It speaks. What Katie describes as 'a little tetchy', was mea-sured on Japanese seismographs?"

"Japan?' I snorted. "Martians are building bomb shelters as we speak."

"That's not fair, Ronnie," said Katie. "I was looking forward to going out with you."

"And, as I've explained, we will. I just have to get Mishi to Daphne Bernstein's house in Bel Air, then I'll come and get you and we can go somewhere, then later we'll pick her up, take her home, and we'll go out somewhere else. Simple."

MISHI STERN

1.

I was disgusted with myself, and I hadn't even made it all the way up the path to Daphne's front door. Against every molecule of my personal credo, I had spent the day worrying about dresses, pants, how my hair looked, and what shoes went with what.

I had pulled clothing out of my cupboard like I was preparing to evacuate LA. The pile on my bed was up to eye-level before I sat on the floor of my room, my elbows on my knees and my chin cupped in my hands. My self-loathing was reaching critical mass.

Then Mom had walked in.

Mom and I were not the classic LA mother and daughter. Mom was not on her third facelift and umpteenth liposuction, living vicariously through her tweenie daughter's love life. As if.

We were more likely to discuss the atomic weight of a quantum particle, than the spaghetti strapped top and the skinny jeans with the spangly high-heels.

But, to my immense wonder, Mom proceeded to sift through the mountain of clothing. She asked me a few questions about the party – who would be there, what were Daphne's parents like – and she held up a few tops and bottoms for the once-over, clicked her tongue at some, put others aside and arranged and rearranged the result.

"There," she said, holding out a couple of garments. "Try these. I think they'll work."

I sat there goggle-eyed.

"Well come on madam," she said, smiling. "What do you think?"

I put on a pale blue T-shirt with red pants, and a navy-blue jacket with pink lining.

Mom held out a pair of gold slip-on shoes.

The result was amazing. I turned this way and that with my head twisting to see myself in the mirror from every angle. My heart was singing.

Then my face fell.

"Don't," said Mom.

"Don't what?" I said.

"Don't remember that you're not supposed to care about what you look like."

"I'm not..." was all I managed.

"Michelle Stern, your best quality, by several miles, is your unflinching honesty. Don't disappoint me now."

"I guess," I said grudgingly. "It's just that..."

"I know," said Mom, "you don't *want* to care about your appearance because it's lame, and superficial, and you think it will make you like all the other girls in school who, from your lofty height, you consider to be loser LA trust fund brats."

"I guess."

"Well, Mishi, let me tell you something. All girls worry about their appearance. Even the grungy ones go to a lot of trouble. How you appear to others is your gift to them, and your signal to the world about who you are. Dress the way you like by all means, but that's the point. It's how *you* like, and it tells the world who you think you are. So, my advice? Get it right. Show them who you are. Like now, dressed like that, you know what I see?"

"What?" I said in a small voice, my eyes down.

Mom put her hand under my chin and lifted my head until I was looking straight into her eyes.

"I see a beautiful, confident, interesting girl, who looks after those who need it, who can think for herself, and has the courage to speak up and do the right thing, even when everyone else is doing the opposite." Mom laughed. "Especially when everyone else is doing the opposite."

I was running the conversation over in my head as I walked up the long path to Daphne's mansion. I could hear the sound of music, laughter and loud conversation. That confident, interesting girl would have turned tail and run, but she had stupidly insisted that her brother drive off after dropping her.

No escape.

2.

The front door of Daphne's house was mock oak made up of fake planks held together by pretend iron nails and metal strips cut to look like spears. It had little windows covered by a tic-tac-toe pattern of twisted iron bars. In case the Mongols or Vikings or whatever attacked, and Daphne needed precious time to pick out a 'what to wear when you're being invaded' outfit.

I lifted the heavy iron doorknocker to announce my arrival, but the door swung open by itself. The party noise got louder. And I could see into a dimly lit hall full of boys and girls about my age talking and grinning.

No one looked my way as I slipped in and stood surveying the scene, with my hands clasped in front of me.

"Mishi!"

I turned to see Emma weaving her way through the throng. I felt a huge wave of relief.

"Hi, Mishi, boy am I glad to see you." She gave me a big hug.

"How's the party going?" I now had a confederate.

"Well I haven't seen many people we know, except for Rasheed and Kimberlee, you know the cheer leader, not Rasheed of course, Kimberlee. And I think I saw Tray, the guy who sits behind Francie in Biology."

Great, I thought, a cheerleader and a guy from biology. And Rasheed, of course, whoever he was.

"Mishi! Emma!" Daphne made her way through the crowd, the perfect hostess. She even air-kissed us! "Come in and meet some people."

Daphne took my hand and Emma followed in our wake. I wasn't buying this. Daphne always had some scheme going and it was never good.

"This is Calypso, and this is Charmian, and this is Brent, and this is Marcus, and this..."

Each new name pushed the earlier ones out of my head. I felt rising panic.

All these wannabes looked at us like we were something they'd scrape off their shoes. They gave our clothes, hair, and everything the once over. They gave each other the 'not our kind of people' look. Daphne was the worst. Like she'd invited Emmy and me just to show her friends she could lure the school dorks out of hiding.

With the introductions over they all turned their backs on us. I was blushing and furious and was trying without success to think of something to say.

I just stood there listening to their prattle. My fists clenched. Emma shifted from foot to foot next to me.

"Ah, Mishi. Mishi?"

"What?" I snapped.

"Can we get out of here?"

I saw a boy on the other side of Emma. He was our age and he had long hair with, No, it couldn't be, an actual Indian headband. He was wearing a tuxedo jacket with peace signs sewn on the upper arms. He was six inches shorter than Emma. He was standing close and smiling up at her, trying to take her hand. Emmy kept snatching it back.

"Mishi?" said Emma plaintively.

"Hey, what's your name?" this from the boy, gazing like a sick puppy, and shouting over the noise. "Mine's Justin, like as in Bieber. You're beautiful. You're my new goddess."

We stared at him.

"Come on," he coaxed. "Let me hold your hand. I'm a nice guy. We could be great together."

"Leave her alone," I finally found my voice.

"Hey," said the boy noticing me for the first time, "butt out, Loser, I wasn'ttalking to you. I was talking to her."

"Well, I'm with her," I said.

"Let go of my hand," said Emma. "Mishi, can we go?"

"Go?" said Justin. "You're leaving Daphne's party? No one leaves one of Daphne's parties!"

"Loser? Who exactly is a strange visitor from the Planet Dweeb calling a loser?"

"You, Freckles. I'm calling you a loser. Her," pointing at Emma with his free hand, "her I'm calling an angel."

My face flushed and I felt the power begin to surge in my gut. I was about to give this infuriating craphead the treatment when a picture of Dr. Califario appeared in my mind. I held myself steady for a moment and then let the energy subside.

You know those mysterious moments at large noisy gatherings when everyone stops talking at once and the music is between tracks?

Daphne's party decided now would be a grand time to go silent. Into this sudden hush I shouted, "I am not a loser and could care less about stupid Daphne Bernstein and her dumbass friends and her idiot party."

There was a shocked moment when everyone's eyes were on me. The gales of laughter were just getting going as Emma and I fled.

3.

We stormed down the drive together.

I rifled through my shoulder bag for my cell. I flipped it open and speed dialed Ronnie. It went to voice mail. "Listen Asshole! It's me. Come and get me now!" I hung up and shoved the cell back into my bag.

By now I was through the ornate iron gates and out on the sidewalk. I folded my arms and lent against the stone wall which marked the outer line of the Bernstein's defenses.

I was alone. Where was Emma?

I went back to the gate, and looked up the drive.

Emma had only made it a few yards from the front door. She was arguing with someone, but she was too far away for me to hear what she was saying. I squinted to see who was holding Emmy up.

Surely that wasn't Justin, like as in Bieber, the hippy-dippy headband boy. But a swirl of oversized tuxedo coat gave it away.

I was about to go back up the drive to rescue Emmy, when I froze dead in my tracks. My body began to vibrate and I shivered. That same feeling from the gym.

Someone was out there, watching. And coming for me.

AARON STERN

I dropped Mishi and headed to Katie's place. I had planned a movie and dinner.

Mr. Imagination, that's me. Señor Suave.

Saturday night LA traffic is not completely terrible. It moves slowly, but at least it moves, mostly. You have to know where to avoid, but sometimes even native Angelinos, trained in the fine automotive arts, can find themselves in a parking lot on the freeway, or on the backstreet short cuts. I was in one now.

The car was inching along. I was drumming my fingers on the steering wheel with shpilkhes in my tuches, ants in my pants. This was our first date since all the spooky Elders stuff had started.

And I was late.

Like Katie had said I would be, and like I had hotly denied. Not a great start to the evening.

Then my cell chimed with a snippet of Elvis singing *Little Sister.* Mishi's ring tone.

What now? I thought.

The metallic green Pontiac ahead of me chose that moment to brake. I took evasive action, and my cell stopped ringing. I waited for the message alert, and tapped the voice mail icon.

"Listen Asshole..." Mishi sounded hugely pissed. I inferred that the party was not going with a swing. Nothing gets by me.

Mishi's peacekeeping talents had probably worked their magic and it was time for Good Ol' Ronnie to ride to the rescue.

In my defense, for a millisecond I did think about going back for her, but I was stuck in traffic, I was over half way to Katie's, and, well, Mishi could be a bit exaggerational.

And, OK, also I was annoyed with her, with the traffic, with lots of stuff. How was I meant to know what was about to happen?

MISHI STERN

1.

The warning signs dropped over me like a gossamer cloth. Another shiver ran through me.

I leaned back against the wall and slid down, until I was sitting on the sidewalk, my arms resting on my knees. I let my head drop forward and I closed my eyes. This was always the hardest part. Not being able to see. The feeling of vulnerability and exposure.

But it was important. Dr. Califario had said so. And I had found out the hard way that he was right. To harness my powers I needed to be defenseless; to fill with energy I had to stay calm; to be strong, he had told me, I had to become weak.

So, eyes closed. Relax. Concentrate.

Something, or someone was out there. I could feel it. They were coming closer. And they were coming for me.

No time to waste wishing my idiot brother was here.

The gathering darkness began to swallow me up, a girl in party clothes sitting on the sidewalk, with her head bowed, and eyes closed.

Now I felt a new enemy closing in. Fear. Curling up from my gut and telling me to freeze, to run, to give in, to fight.

This was not entirely helpful.

I fought down the panic and sent out feelers. The danger signals came back, loud and clear.

Crap.

I had to get a grip.

That flight instinct, to get away from whatever was approaching, was getting stronger. And now I felt hot anger elbowing its way through the gut-churning terror.

A tiny crunch of gravel. A puff of wind on my face.

I opened my eyes and looked up. Staring back at me from three feet away were flat empty eyes. They were on the face of a tall Asian guy, his black hair brushed straight back from his forehead, dressed in a gray suit with a plain navy tie. His mouth smiled at me, but those eyes didn't join in. He held a switchblade close to his chest. The light glinted as he moved it snakelike back and forth.

I pushed down the panic. The man kept smiling.

"Miss Stern," a pleasant, lightly accented voice, formal, polite, dangerous. "My name is Kim Park Singh, and I insist that you come with me. Now."

I couldn't move. I was transfixed.

"If you refuse..." he said, still smiling, still playing with the blade. "Is that young lady I see up there a friend? With that young man. I will cut their throats. And you will be coming with me anyway."

I wanted to edge my way into his steel-cold mind, but I couldn't.

For as long as I could remember I could angle my mind, and slip sideways into someone else's head. I could read their thoughts and their feelings, like I was in a museum.

But at first, when I was a kid, I couldn't do anything with those thoughts and feelings. I couldn't manipulate them, to make people do what I wanted.

Then one day, when I was five, and Ronnie was nine, it became a whole new ballgame.

Team Stern was in New York City. I think Dad was there on a business trip, or Mom was at a science conference. And Ronnie and I were along for the ride.

We had a family day at the Frick Museum and we were looking at a million paintings. I was bored out of my skull. So I pretended I needed another bathroom break, and it was Ronnie's turn to take me.

He made it clear to me that he was not enjoying the job.

I got angry. I slipped away from him and hid behind a large Chinese vase.

It felt great, watching him look this way and that. At first he was pissed. Then he started to get worried. I could 'see' this happening inside him.

I was still inside his mind when terror suddenly swept through him. It hit me like a hammer and, I guess in self-defense, I moved his mental furniture around.

He calmed down.

I organized my face and blinking up at him, I emerged from behind the vase. I was surprised when he scooped me up and bear-hugged me nearly to death. What a freak.

But it was also kind of nice.

Anyway it was clear he didn't know I'd been messing with him.

Since then? I could read him like he's made a movie of his thoughts and projected it in 3D on a giant screen. I could get him to do stuff, pretty much. But I always suspected there was another level to him that I could never penetrate. Like he showed the world one part of himself but there was another part that was hidden from everyone. And the really weird part was that I think it was hidden from him as well.

But from that time on I had mind-bending skills. I discovered their limits – basically my victim had to be pretty close by and some people were definitely easier to get into than others. If fear or nerves distracted me it didn't work. I had hours of fun at the expense of anyone who crossed me, and lots who didn't.

"Come, Miss Stern," said Singh, not smiling now. "Time to go."

The terror was back, gripping my throat, clouding my mind, wrecking my efforts to read him.

"Miss Stern," his voice was cold. "The young lady and her young friend will not be the only victims. Believe me when I say that nothing would give me greater pleasure than to kill every person in that house. Your friends I presume."

Friends? I thought. Usually nothing pleased me more than picturing all those spoiled airheads dying together in a fiery car wreck on the Santa Monica Freeway.

But now that their deaths were a distinct reality, a razor-edged knife's width away, I hoped against hope that none of the other girls and boys, chatting to friends, discussing the competing wonders of Gucci and Prada, would come out and raise the alarm.

And especially not Emma.

Even blocked from his mind, I could feel the dull pleasure he would get from cutting someone's throat.

So I got myself looking all cool and calm, in case anyone glanced my way. I stood and Singh ushered me to a white van parked a few yards down the street. I could still hear the sounds of the party over my left shoulder.

I walked to the van with Mr. Psycho as if it were as natural as anything. Look at me, out for a stroll with my new best friend.

"Mishi, wait up, where are you going?" Emma shouted.

"It's OK, See ya!" I called back. The side door of the van slid open as we approached. I accelerated and stepped quickly up into the van before she could follow. The door slammed shut behind me.

Sitting in the front, her arm resting along the back of the seat, her face turned to me, was a woman with raven-black hair in a severe page boy cut. The internal light of the van showed her clear skin and sparkling green eyes.

"Hi Mishi," she said. "So nice of you to join us. Your cell please."

She held out her hand and I gave it to her. She opened the back and took out the battery. Then she took out the SIM card and broke it in two.

Singh climbed into the driver's seat and fired up the engine.

"McInnes." The woman said, and she nodded at a squat, neckless goon who was in the back with me. He grabbed my wrists and before I could say or do anything he cable-tied my hands and feet, slipped a hood over my head, and threw me down on some sacking.

2.

I'm not going to lie to you. Now I was really scared.

I didn't understand how much I had come to depend on mind-reading. Now it had deserted me.

The van headed off through the LA evening traffic.

At first I bounced and jounced along on the floor of the van, the fear paralyzing me. I was only vaguely aware of the twists and turns of the traffic.

None of the others in the van spoke during the whole journey.

I knew fear was not going to help me, but I couldn't do anything about it. I tried to use my breathing exercises to get control, but I might as well have been bailing water with a sieve.

The picture of Dr. Califario formed itself in my mind again, steepling those long slender fingers of his.

This helped. A little.

At least I figured if I ever got out of this, and it was one of life's bigger 'ifs', I had to be able to report as much as possible to him. I must get as much information on these guys as I could.

I lay on the rough sacking, unable to focus, trying to calm myself.

After about an hour or so we made a sharp left and came to a halt. I heard what sounded like a heavy door being rolled aside and the van eased its way forward.

We had arrived.

AARON STERN

1.

I sat in the stalled traffic forcing down my irritation. When did Mishi go to parties? Never! Except when Katie and I have our first date in, like, a century.

And Mom was all, 'someone's got to take Mishi to the party, and let's vote and, hey, Ronnie you're elected'.

So there I was squeezing the steering wheel, stuck in vintage LA Saturday night traffic. My bratty sister a few miles behind me. But instead of bopping away at the party, she rings me and issues orders to go back and pick her up. Well, she could just wait for a while. Or go back into the party and drink lemonade and eat s'mors, or whatever. I had more important things on my mind. Like my girlfriend up ahead looking at her watch and tapping her foot.

My cell buzzed again. I dug in my pocket for a second too long and the ringing stopped. Mishi again, or so I supposed.

That shiver up my spine warning me that something bad was about to happen? I didn't get one. Fat lot of good it would've done me if I had, stuck in traffic inching my way along Wilshire toward the One Ten.

I picked up the cell and looked at the message. It was from Katie. I assume she was getting impatient for her adoring swain to arrive and whisk her off to paradise.

Coming! I thought.

Then the text signal pinged. Also from Katie. 'Ring me. Now. Urgent!!!'

Oops, I thought, she's mad.

There's that Greek guy, you know the one, Odysseus, trying to get home from Troy, and his ship has to sail through a narrow place with a monster on either side, and one of them is going to get him no matter what.

I knew how he felt.

For a nanosecond I considered disobeying Katie's orders. Then I speed dialed her number.

"Hi, Gorgeous."

"Ronnie, turn around now and go get Mishi."

"?", I said. Then I continued with: "Huh? What...? How did you know she...?"

"Ronnie," she had slowed down now. I could feel the effort she was making. Trying

to get something important through an extra thick skull.

"Turn around now. Go and get your sister. Get Mishi. She's in trouble. Go now."

I finally got it.

"On my way."

I looked in my mirrors, backed and forwarded the car, nosing through irate traffic. I tried to get Katie to tell me more.

"What kind of trouble? How do you know?"

"I don't know how I know, I just know. I can't discuss it over a cell phone, it's my thing, like you've got yours."

I had Healing, and Katie obviously had some kind of Warn-O-Meter. I accelerated down a clear side street.

"OK," I said. "I'm on my way back to Bel Air."

"Hurry, Ronnie, something bad is happening."

She was getting to me now and, boy, did it pack a punch.

I concentrated on the road, which, thank God, remained pretty clear. I couldn't bear to think about Mishi in trouble.

I called Mishi's cell.

"Hi, this is Mishi, um, Mishi Stern, not here now, or I don't want to talk. Leave a message, or better, text me."

I left a plaintive, "it's Ronnie, I'm on my way", and signed off with, "ring me when you get this."

2.

I was doing sixty when I got to the Bernstein's palace. I turned into the drive, sped past the 'No Entry' sign, and scattered gravel as I skidded to a halt in front of the imposing entranceway.

I left the engine running and sprinted to the open front door.

I walked into a world of flashing colored lights, music and screaming teens. Kids were everywhere and I had to push my way through gyrating bodies.

I grabbed a boy with gelled hair, glitter sparkling on his shiny cheeks, and a leather Fonzie jacket.

"Hey, quit it," he said as I spun him around.

"Where's Mishi Stern?"

"Who?" We were shouting at each other over the noise.

"Michelle Stern!" I bellowed.

"Don't know her. Hey, let me go! My Dad's a lawyer."

What was it with kids these days?

"Where's Daphne?" I shouted.

"I dunno. How should I know?"

One of the girls nearby – all bright-red lipstick and eye-shadow, in a fluffed out pink, tutu dress – popped her gum at me and said: "Hey, leave him alone. Daphne's over there." She pointed with a mesh-gloved hand and bright purple nail polish. What *was* it with kids these days?

I weaved my way through the throng toward a confection of bouffant hair, red and blue ribbons, and black skin-tight leggings that bore a resemblance to my target.

"Daphne. Daphne!" Finally she turned to me.

"Well, Hello," she said, and, I swear, she actually batted her eyelashes. "Daphne, have you seen Mishi?"

"Who?"

"Mishi! Mishi Stern! Have you seen her? Where is she?"

"Mishi? Mishi Stern?"

"Yes, Mishi Stern!"

"No. I mean yes," she giggled. "She was here, but she left."

"When?"

"When what?"

"When did she leave?" This was exhausting.

I grabbed Daphne's wrist and looked around. I headed for what I hoped was the kitchen with Daphne in tow. I glanced back at her. She was smiling coquettishly at an admiring audience.

When we got to the kitchen the decibel level was reduced to merely deafening.

"Where is Mishi? When did she leave? Where did she go?"

"You're her brother right?" said Daphne, blinking up at me.

"Yes, I am, I am her brother. Now please, tell me, where did she go?"

"I don't know where she went. She was pissed and she left. With that friend of hers, Embecile, Embolism."

"Emma?"

"Oh, yes," holding her hand up palm out, fingers splayed, looking at her nails. "That's right, Emma."

Wow, I thought, this girl is everything Mishi said. "How long ago did they leave?"

"I dunno, ten minutes, half an hour, an hour. Like I said, she was pissed. She didn't, like, stop and say goodbye or thanks or anything like that." She had one hand on her hip, and she wiggled and eye-rolled like she was imitating some extra-rude guest, insufficiently gracious to the hard working hostess.

I left before I did do something to her that I would regret. Half the kids at that party were probably lawyered up, and they would be on the cell to Daddy, or post the clip on YouTube.

3.

I headed out the way I'd come and got back in the car. I did a K turn and roared down the drive to the street. I had no idea where Mishi was, or what direction she had taken, or if she was walking, or got a ride with someone.

So I began quartering the area. My sphere of operations widened as the minutes ticked by, and I could feel my heart sinking with every yard that I covered.

No Mishi anywhere.

My heart fell even further when I thought about telling Mom and Dad.

Ponte a Moriano, Tuscany

Dawn, July 22nd, 1161

Leonardo Da Silva was trapped in a nightmare. Wild beasts with red-hot claws and razor-sharp teeth were tracking him, driving him through a dense forest of black leafless trees. He came to a steep slope and began scrabbling upwards, but the vicious monsters followed his every move. The grass turned to sharp needles tearing his feet, which were now bleeding and raw. He fell painfully to his hands and knees, climbing desperately, and still he could not get away. He felt the hot breath of his pursuers on the back of his neck.

Now they were on him! They had him! His arm was gripped, they were shaking him, their ravenous maws were opening wide, they were going to eat him alive. He was going to die!

He screamed in terror. "Master, Master! Wake up!"

Leonardo felt himself shaken again as he slowly returned to this world. He opened his eyes to see Geminio, his faithful servant, kneeling over him and shaking his arm. He was lying on the floor of his study, surrounded by wax candles, ink, parchment, a cow's pelvic bone and the splintered wreckage of a chair. His desk was lying on its side against the far wall and two braziers had been knocked over spilling their red-hot contents across the floor and over his hands and feet.

Geminio began rubbing salve into the burns and wrapping bandages around his injured limbs.

"Thank you, Geminio," Da Silva gasped. His voice was a croak, his throat felt like it had been shredded by knives. "Thank you. What happened?"

"Ah Master," said Geminio, unfolding another length of cloth. "The mysteries into which your Lordship delves are not for the likes of a humble peasant such as myself."

"Geminio," Leonardo croaked. "Enough. Tell me what you saw and heard."

"Master," said Geminio, "I saw you sitting at your desk writing. It was most strange, your eyes were lifted heavenward and they turned from left to right as if following a lazy bird in flight. But your hand had a will of its own. It wrote, dipping the quill and covering the vellum with words and diagrams, and each finished page was thrown aside onto the floor. Here, Master, see, the floor is covered in pages."

Leonardo grunted and raised himself onto one elbow. He surveyed the room. It was, indeed, carpeted with wrecked and toppled furniture, stationery and books. And dozens of sheets of vellum with closely written words and diagrams and pictures.

Geminio reached for Leonardo's right hand, covered with welts and burns. He rubbed ointment into the wounds, but when he was about to swathe it in bandages Leonardo stopped him.

"No Geminio," he said, "not yet. Perhaps later. Now I have need of this hand."

Gingerly, with Geminio's help, he stood up. Each step on his burnt feet was agony, but he took a pace or two to the nearest sheet of parchment and picked it up.

"*The Maleficium et Maledictiones Arcanum: Secret Crimes and Curses*," he said slowly, scanning a few more lines. "The coming together of the Four Signs will herald the opening of the Gate. Destiny will turn back, the protection of the righteous will be no more." He turned to Geminio. "This will make interesting reading. Gather the pages my lad. But I tell you this, it is lucky for you that I never taught you to read. A single word of this text would turn your eyes to molten lead and burn through to your brains. Now, there's a good chap, pick up the pages and stack them on my desk. Oh, I see, well yes, set the desk upright first."

CHAPTER EIGHT

28TH SEPTEMBER

CONTINUED

RANDOLPH LASSITER

1.

Lassiter settled back in his office chair. He was at home and, even at two in the morning, he was sitting upright at his glass desk turning the pages of the *Intergovernmental Panel on Climate Change: Report Number 10E/47Z239: African Pygmy Population Statistics in the Ituri Rainforest Region.*

Earlier that evening he had reported on the progress of the Da Silva Project to his superiors, a terse update on Svensson's research, and Singh's activities.

"We need results."

"Yes, Sir, and..."

"Three days, Mr. Lassiter. The stakes could not be higher and failure will not be tolerated. If you need additional incentive may we remind you that the addresses of your children's schools are known to us? Another Columbine. So messy."

Lassiter had held the phone to his ear. He couldn't speak.

"Three days."

The connection had broken.

Lassiter turned another page, apparently the pygmies of the rainforest were showing precisely no ill-effects from climate change whatsoever. He made a note in the margin: 'Unacceptable, reorganize statistics?'

The cell on the desk vibrated.

He picked up on the second ring.

"We have the girl in the warehouse," said Singh. "The Poisoner is going to start working on her."

"Good, excellent," said Lassiter. "She has an impressive track record. And the girl didn't get to use her powers on you?"

"No, it was as Miss Portland advised, the fear blocked her. And Miss Portland was on hand in case of mishap. We will text the mother."

"We have to be ready in," he hesitated, "two days. Pressure from on high, which I am passing on to you. The mother, she eluded us in Iowa. She must know where this scroll is. One of them must, all of Svensson's researches point in this direction. Get the Poisoner to squeeze the girl. Find out what she knows about them."

"With pleasure," said Singh. "But she is fourteen. She may not know very much."

"Do it anyway. Every piece of information will help us put the whole puzzle together. And if we record her screaming we can send that to the family."

"Consider it done."

"The main thrust of the questioning must be about the Four Signs. The plans are in place for an earth-shattering coup. We already know the Time and the Location. This scroll, this Moses Revelation as Svensson calls it, is the third sign, the Word. Svensson is sure of that."

"And the last Sign?"

"The Twins. Svensson and his team are working through the manuscripts to get a line on these Twins. I'll contact him."

2.

The phone next to Professor Svensson's bed began chirping. It rang three times while Svensson turned, fumbling for the light switch and his eyeglasses.

"Hello?" he said, and yawned.

"There is pressure for quick results," said Lassiter, without preliminaries. "We are working from our end to find and question as many Adepts as possible about this Scroll. But they are slippery. We only have one girl, a fourteen year old."

"So young?" said Svensson, he was rubbing his eyes. "Is this someone who knows much? Or is it just for the pleasure of getting the information out of her?"

"Her mother is known to us. Having the daughter will have added impact there."

"Ah, well, yes, this is good," said Svensson, thoughtfully. "It is a beautiful art, the infliction of pain, and on a young girl, who may not have anything to tell, especially delightful."

Ex-Nazis, thought Lassiter, so great to work with.

"As for this scroll," Svensson continued, "I am sure this Moses Revelation is Da Silva's third sign. But it is the last of the four signs, The Twins which is most intriguing. I believe that it will turn out to be a brother and sister with Adept powers that we are looking for."

"Well, that is most interesting," said Lassiter. "We may well have had some luck there. Let me check a few things and I'll get back to you."

Lassiter rang off and immediately placed another call.

3.

"This girl, she has a brother. Find out more about him."

"Yes, Sir," said Singh, "the brother."

"Get him, get the brother. And keep the girl alive. At least for now. We can use her as a lever."

Lassiter placed the cell back onto his desk. He saw a fingerprint on the glass desk top, curled his lip, and rubbed it away with a white handkerchief. His children were asleep upstairs. He had an image of his daughter playing at school, and his son on the Little League pitcher's mound. He forced the pictures out of his head and returned to the Iturian Pygmies.

AARON STERN

I was circling and circling, moving slowly out from Daphne Bernstein's house. No sign of Mishi.

I left a hundred more messages on her phone, and sent about the same number of texts, with more and more exclamation marks.

I had run out of options. I had no idea what to do next.

So I quartered the swanky suburban streets and houses of upper-middle class America, viz Bel Air LA, home to many of the nicer, or at least wealthier, families of California.

One simple fact was pounding in my skull. I had been late getting back to pick up Mishi, I took too long to respond to her text. I should have turned around straight away. I'd been too fixated on getting to my date with Katie.

Stupid, stupid, stupid. I banged my fist against the steering wheel. Punishing myself for my idiocy. I showered God, whom I believed in but generally felt it safer not to bother, with extravagant promises of future good behavior if only my sister was OK.

No, I said to myself, this is crazy talk.

Mishi was fine. This was all a big mistake. She was somewhere safe, and we'd all laugh about it (after she, and Mom, had hauled my ass over hot coals, of course).

And then I had a brainwave. Relief washed through me. I practically shouted with joy.

Emma! Emma Schwartz. I was an idiot! I should have remembered her! Mishi's party pal.

Emma. One of Mishi's giggling, non-stop talking, hair tossing, cell-phone addicted friends. All yakking at once like a flock of birds.

Mishi and Emma had been at the party together. Mishi had said so. Daphne had said so. Mishi must have gone to Emma's house.

I had taken Mishi there once or twice.

At the time, ferrying Mishi and her friends around with a car load of teenage girls, I had thought: 'Why Me, God?' (See? prayers are reserved for real emergencies.) And now I offered fervent thanks to that same God, because I remembered where Emma lived.

At least I thought I did.

It had to be round here somewhere.

The car kept nosing its way up and down identical dark suburban streets.

As Mr. Worry started whistling for his friends Panic and Terror to come and join him, I let out a squeak of delight.

There it was! I recognized the house. I accelerated toward it. Mishi was there for sure. She would have enough ammunition to make my life a misery for weeks. Her capacity to wheedle and cajole and remind me of all the many crimes I had committed, and for which I therefore needed to do penance, was legendary. But I didn't care.

I skidded to a halt, jumped out and double-timed it to the front door. It was late but what did I care? I leaned on the bell.

After a geological age Emma opened the door. I could have sobbed with relief. "Oh, uh, hi," she said.

"Hi. Is Mishi here? You know, like after Daphne's party?" My voice trailed away. I looked past Emma into the brightly lit hall with polished floorboards and spindly fake French pieces. At least I thought they were fake. Emma's Dad was some big wheel in the Democratic Party so I assumed he was able to lay his hands on sacks of cash. Maybe the furniture was real.

But no Mishi.

"Gee, no, she's not here." Emma, her blond ringlets waved, looked up at me. Ball in my court.

"See, like, I was meant to pick her up. And..."

"And, she rang you to get her but, let me guess, you were late. Yeah, that bit I know.

Like, you're always late. Anyway, then she left."

"Left?"

"Yeah some guy, his name was Justin, and he was dressed in a totally terrible way, like one of those old-fashioned people, like out of history, you know, a hippie or something, with a headband and old tuxedo coat, like out of a gloom movie. And he grabbed my wrist, can you believe that? I said it was, like, assault, but he kept holding on saying I was, like, a goddess, and he totally wanted a date or something, which was kind of cute of him so I didn't struggle, you know, like, really hard."

"And Mishi left with this guy?" I said.

"No," said Emma, packing that single syllable with all the contempt the young have for terminally dense oldsters like me.

"But you said she left the party," struggling to keep up.

"Yeah, she left. I saw her. While hippie boy was trying to get my phone number. I gave it to him, just to get rid of him. Mishi was down the drive on the street. Waiting for you. Then she went."

"Went? Where did she go? With whom? What did she say?"

"With the big guy," she said. "Yeah, she went off. In a white van." Warming to her theme now, "some Asian looking dude. It was under a street light and Daphne's got all these like security lights so it's like, I dunno, all

'Stop, who goes there?'"

I felt the ground dissolving under my feet. What was going on here? I forced my voice to sound normal.

"Gee, uh, Emma. That sounds screwy. Not like Mishi to go off with a stranger."

"Really? You don't know this guy? I thought she must've known the guy coz, you know, she looked cool about it. I called to her but she said she was OK, and seeya later and like that. Not like she was being kidnapped or anything. Ha, ha." The ringlets skipped back and forth, while a dark lump of lead took up residence in the pit of my stomach.

"Look," I said, walking a tightrope now. I was attempting rational speech with an alien being. God, was I like this at her age? "No, I don't know this Asian guy."

I was hoping against hope that that was true. That I didn't, in fact, know him. After all, there are a lot of Asian guys in LA, aren't there? It couldn't be Snell's pal. Could it? "Can you give me more of a description of him? Maybe it'll jog my memory."

"Oh, OK, um, let's see. Ah, Asian, of course, you know kinda ... Oh, I don't know, what are we allowed to say these days? I don't want to be you know racist or anything."

I assured her that I wouldn't report her to the PC police. I urged her to go on.

"And the eyes, uh, you know..."

"Chinese looking?"

"Yeah, that's it", relieved that it was me who had entered the minefield.

"And, and..." she said excitedly, on safer ground now, "he was wearing a suit." My heart sank. This must be the guy from home, and with Snell. "I noticed that because I thought. 'Gee, if this guy had dark glasses he'd look like the Secret Service.' You know, tough, and no smiling and looking around like someone was going to assassinate the President or, ha ha, Mishi. You know he was kind of helping her along into the van, like with his arm behind her."

Emma was on a roll now. I didn't dare to break the flow.

"For an old guy this Asian dude, he was... Well, you know... Cute." Emma looked up at me coyly.

"Cute?" I said.

"Yeah!" said Emma, enjoying the memory. "Handsome. A looker."

"And when you say old..."

"Oh, I dunno, thirty, maybe."

I was too weirded out to take it all in. Some Asian dude, my night stalker, wearing a suit, who looked like a secret service agent shepherding Mishi into a white van.

"Emma! Who's at the door?" a shout from somewhere back in the house.

"Oh, gosh, I have to go! No one Mom, just Mishi's brother.

"Does he want something to eat? We've got plenty. Tell him we got cake. It's fresh. Imaculata made it this morning."

Emma rolled her eyes. "No Mom, he's just leaving."

"Tell him we got chicken soup too. Your grandma dropped it round. There's lots. And knaidlach."

"Thanks Mrs. Schwartz," I called back. "I gotta find my sister Mishi. Thanks Emma. You've been a great help. Bye Mrs. Schwartz!"

"Ok, hope you find her," Emma's face showed a fleeting sign of worry, but her mother called again and she closed the door.

I made my bewildered way back to the car.

Mishi had gotten into a white van, apparently willingly, with the creepy Asian guy who looked like he was protecting the President. But who also looked like my guy talking to Snell.

None of this added up, no matter which way I looked at it. And I couldn't shake the feeling that all this was my fault. Just this once, why couldn't I have turned around when I got her message, why couldn't I have been there earlier?

I had to get home.

I unlocked the car door, got in, and started the engine.

It was not that far. The streets sped past, but I didn't see any of them. I knew the route blindfold so I let the car find its own way while I batted my thoughts back and forth. The car took Sunset to North Carmelina then, just before the corner of Cliffwood Ave, turned into our driveway.

My final pathetic hope was that Mishi would be home, mad as hell, tapping her toe impatiently and waiting to drag me through a level of hell purpose-built by Angry-Little-Sisters-R-Us.

Mom's silver Lexus and Dad's racing green Jaguar XJ were side by side in the garage. I pulled in next to Mom, got out, locked the car and went in to face the music.

MISHI STERN

I sat still. I kind of had to because I was cabled-tied by the wrists and ankles to a metal chair bolted to a concrete floor in a large warehouse.

I could see steel girders holding up a roof soaring above me in the gloom. Grimy windows high up in the walls filtered the streetlights.

There were bright lights on stands with cables snaking away into the dark, fully illuminating my little area of the warehouse.

In front of me, a few yards away, was a metal table laid out with medical looking stuff – small glass containers of colored liquids, hypodermics, rubber gloves, small metal dishes – why weren't they round, or square, not shaped like Dimity Berkovitz's stupid swimming pool?

When we'd arrived in the van they had picked me up by the ankles and shoulders and carried me like a sack to this chair. They'd cut my traveling cable ties and used fresh ones on my wrists and ankles. Then they'd pulled the bag off my head.

I hadn't been there long when I heard hard footsteps approaching from behind. The woman from the van walked around the chair and stood in front of me. She'd put on a white lab coat. She raised an eyebrow and tilted her head, and smiled. Like she was trying to put a guest, me I supposed, at ease.

Except most houseguests aren't cable-tied to a chair. At least not at the dinner parties that Mom and Dad have, which I used to sneak half way down the stairs to watch through a slit in the double doors. Nope, no one tied to chairs there.

Her jet-black, ruler-straight hair was like a gleaming helmet. Very pretty, green eyes, clear skin, bright smile. It was the smile that really scared me.

She looked at me while the seconds ticked by. Sizing me up. Finally she spoke.

"Well, Mishi," she said, "I think we are going to have some fun today. If you cooperate. If you don't cooperate one of us will still be having fun, but it won't be you."

She had a tinkly laugh.

Crap, I thought, another sicko.

Double crap. My heart rate, clenched fists, and knotted stomach were playing merry hell with my thought powers.

Any attempt bounced off that black helmet hair.

I waited for my heart to stop trying to jump out of my throat.

"So, Mishi," her hair waved back and forth like a curtain, "tell me everything you know about these people with the special powers. The ones you hang out with."

Oh Christ, she knows about the Elders, I thought. I stared back at her.

The woman spoke again. "All right, how about this one? Tell me everything you know about a powerful ancient scroll."

I didn't think my heart could sink any further, but it did.

Even if I had been able to speak there was no helpful contribution I could make to this conversation.

Part of me was watching the scene unfold, but another part was frozen with terror. And the speaking part was definitely in the frozen camp.

Whatever this nut-job had planned for me I needed as much time as I could get. I had to hope that whoever was coming to rescue me would do it quickly.

So I stared back, my eyes round, and hoped that the 'fun' wouldn't begin anytime soon.

AARON STERN

I stood at the front door with my keys in my hand. I was in a private hell. Emma had really spooked me. A strange man had taken Mishi. The Asian guy, who I was sure was the Joe talking to Snell.

And I had to tell Mom and Dad something.

I opened the front door and went down the hall to the living room. Mom and Dad looked up.

"Hi, Ronnie," said Mom. "How was your date. Where's Mishi?"

"I don't know. The date never happened. And I gotta tell you something.

Mishi called me and I went to get her from the party, but she wasn't there. I spent time circling around looking for her then I went to Emma's. She said something crazy about Mishi going off with an Asian guy in a van."

Mom and Dad looked bewildered. But before they could say anything Mom's cell pinged with a message. She looked at it and her face changed color.

"Oh my God," said Mom, her hand to her mouth. "Oh my God, Oh my God, Oh my God!"

"Miriam, Honey, calm down," said Dad. "What is it? Is that from Mish? She'll be home soon. Or she'll call. Someone offered her a lift home, or she's at a friend's house."

"No, Reuben, you don't understand." She held out her phone and Dad took it. His face went white too.

"What?" I said. "Show me."

Dad handed over Mom's cell. There was a text message: 'We have the girl. We want the Scroll. Santa Monica Pier. Midnight. Send the boy.'

"Miriam," said Dad, "what's this all about?"

Mom was proud of being able to keep her cool under all circumstances. Well, I can tell you, she wasn't keeping her cool now. Her face went through a range of emotions and finally settled on despair. She led us into the kitchen.

"Sit," she said. Dad and I sat.

"I know this will sound crazy but I have to tell you a few things. About Mishi, and me."

And then she explained about the Elders, and Adepts, people with mind powers, and finding influential people, and persuading them to do the right thing. Dad had the sense not to interrupt. Me too.

I don't know what I would have thought a few days before, but now Mom filled in some blanks for me.

See, it turned out that since Mom was a kid she had always had a power over machines and physical objects, and anything electrical. Even as a little girl apparently she could turn out the lights without getting out of bed. People were starting to worry about her, so she learned pretty quickly to hide the power. (Sound familiar?)

Then, also similar to me, at college she was approached by someone, who knew someone, and before long she was studying all that quantum stuff during the day, and working with the Elders at night.

She had an assigned group of people she was meant to influence, scientists and policy makers mostly. She hinted that there was a Middle Eastern thing about to go down a few years ago, something nuclear and nasty, which she had nudged out of harm's way.

She told us how she'd kept an eye on us, Mishi and I, to see if we were, you know, developing along the same lines. Me? Nothing she could detect, but Mishi showed signs as a baby. She had developed some pretty awesome mind control powers, which she used on her unsuspecting older brother.

Mom kind of confessed to Dad that Mishi is involved with these Elder people.

And then she started crying.

"And you're only getting around to telling me this now?" Dad sounded pissed, very unusual, and, I must say, just as disturbing as Mom crying. "Now that our daughter has gone missing? Miriam..."

Mom took both his hands, "I know, I know, I should have told you earlier but I wanted to protect you." She turned to me, "and you."

Suddenly I knew how Dad felt.

Mom had been one of these Adepts for, like, ever and she hadn't told us? I had only just found out from Dr. C and his happy band. My life to date flashed in front of me. All the hiding, all the times I'd been zapped by someone with a sniffle or suicidal thoughts. All the anxiety that no one find out that I was a freak. A few words from Mom and everything would have been different.

And, yeah, I felt jealous too. She had known about Mishi, and had drawn her into the Elders' web. Well, what about me? Was I just Grandma's gefilte fish?

But the picture of Mishi made the flash of anger deconstruct itself. This wasn't about me.

Mom hadn't mentioned my involvement with the Elders. Either she didn't know yet about Ronnie in Wonderland, or she didn't want to add to Dad's worries that I'd been swept up into Dr. C's world as well. So I figured I'd keep that one in reserve also. Enough on his plate at the moment.

"So, look, Miriam," Dad was saying, "I always knew there was something. Something more than just Science Conferences."

"Really?" said Mom.

"Yes, really," said Dad. "But I trusted you. I still do. You're the smartest person I've ever met, except for marrying me that is, but that one mistake I'll let you have. Now the question is how can we get Mishi back. I'll ring the police, and you get these special friends of yours to help."

See, that's Dad. Quick recovery. No theatrics, no jumping around wasting time. And no long back and forth with 'Whaddya mean you can turn the lights off, and Mishi can read minds?'

Just, let's get our daughter back.

"What about the Pier?" I asked.

"I'm going," said Mom in her 'And that's final' voice.

"No, you're not," I said. Or at least I think it was me. It certainly came out of my mouth, but I hadn't heard that voice before. Whatever had taken over my body kept speaking. "I'm going. I was late, I lost her. I'll get her back. They're asking for me anyway. I'll find out what these guys want with this Scrolly whatsit and, and... I'm not sure what, but I'll get her back."

And, right then and there, I knew, no matter what it took, I would.

Mom and Dad tried to talk me out of it of course but I wouldn't budge. Finally they gave in to the New Ronnie.

Of course I had no way of knowing then what I would have to go through to get Mishi back safe and sound. My fancy powers didn't include foretelling the future, which, on the whole, was a good thing cause if they had, I might've told New Ronnie to shove it.

MISHI STERN

1.

"Look Mishi," said the helmet-head lady. "We're not getting anywhere with gentle persuasion, and, to tell you the truth," she bent closer, "I'm glad. Because I enjoy my work. And you," straightening up and snapping one cheerful yellow latex glove on, "have given me the perfect excuse," snap went the other glove, "to party. But what a silly I am, I haven't introduced myself. Sally Portland at your service. They call me 'The Poisoner', did you know that? Of course you didn't. Well, you do now."

This 'Poisoner' hottie had been asking me all sorts of questions for a whole bunch of time. I hadn't been able to speak and now she was getting crabby. Those gloves were definitely a sign that she was going to take our relationship to the next level.

She turned back to the steel table, picked up some syringes, one after the other, and looked at them with a critical eye. She was humming 'I get no Kick from Champagne' to herself.

Who were these people?

They knew about the Elders, but not a lot. They knew about the Moses Revelation but, again, not much. And they were willing to do anything to find out more. Including kidnapping and, gulp, torturing a fourteen-year-old girl.

So far, so incredibly bad.

I decided on a new tactic.

"Um, excuse me, ah, Miss? Um, Sally?" I said tentatively.

"Yes, Mishi," she said, keeping her eyes on her work.

"Um, can we talk about this?"

The lady put down her things on the table. She walked over and leaned over and showed me her cleavage. Who was she trying to impress?

"Now Mishi," she stroked my hair with a gloved hand. I tried not to shudder. "We had time to talk, and you didn't want to. Now you do. Are you trying to delay things?" She waggled a playful finger in that 'Mother can't be fooled' way.

That was exactly my plan.

"No, no, not at all," I said, "I was scared before, and couldn't speak. I was too frightened. But I've calmed down and I can talk now. What was it you wanted to know?"

"OK, I'll play," steel crept into her voice. "Tell us about your Power-Ranger Playmates, and that manuscript. Do it now. And do it truthfully."

I was about to start spinning the lies I had been carefully constructing over the past hour or two. Before I could begin, the lady held up a hand.

"Before you begin can I say this: Miriam Stern, 17 Acacia Drive Brentwood, Reuben Stern of the same address and of course, Aaron Stern, known as Ronnie to his friends. I could go on. We have a list of your friends and relatives. We know where they live, and some of my colleagues aren't nearly as nice as me." She flashed her teeth at me again, "so, let's start, shall we?"

2.

When I first met Dr. Califario he had said: "This work is not for everyone, Mishi." We had been sitting opposite each other in his office. My legs were swinging back and forth. "We won't knowingly involve you with anything dangerous. But there are bad people out there and if worse comes to the worst you mustn't try to be clever or brave. It's like being mugged. Just give them the wallet."

"What do you mean?" I remembered asking him.

"I mean, if you are in any danger, give them what they want, stay alive and safe, as long as it doesn't directly endanger others. There is a higher power at work here, Mishi, and it means that in the long run evil cannot prevail."

"What does *that* mean?" I'd said.

"Well, those who do evil are mean-spirited, cowardly, weak, cruel, mistrustful of others and untrustworthy themselves. They fear their enemies, but they fear their friends more. Stalin, he was a horrible murderous tyrant in Russia who killed his comrades and ended by causing the death of his son and his wife. Hitler had many of his early comrades murdered. It's a pattern."

"I still don't get how this works if something dangerous happens," I had persisted.

"What I'm saying is don't worry that you're giving something important away, some secret. It may sound a bit corny, but the good and the true always win in the end. That's the lesson of human history from the caves till now."

This conversation came back to me as I looked up into the smiling face of Helmet-Head. So I spilled the beans: "These 'Power Rangers' are people who can do stuff."

"Like what, Mishi? What kind of stuff?"

"Spooky stuff like read minds and, I dunno. Stuff."

"Names, please."

"I know a few of them. There's a guy called Califario. He says he's a Doctor. I don't know his first name." (A girl has to have a few secrets.) "And another guy called Mordecai, and there's Wolfgang. I think Mordecai is Israeli and Wolfgang is German. Dr. Califario is American. But he sounds and dresses like he'd like to be English."

"See, now that wasn't so hard was it. Anyone else?" she asked politely, her hands resting on my wrists, right where I was strapped to the chair, her face a few inches from mine.

"Well," I swallowed, "there's Mom."

"Sorry," she said, "a little louder please."

"I said, there's my Mom, she's one as well."

"Wow!" Portland said in mock horror. "Your Mommy. And she has all these powers, and yet here you are with me, alone, abandoned."

Then she laughed.

"Now, next question, where do all these guys hang out?"

"I don't know."

"Now, now Mishi, let's not play games. I asked you nicely." She took hold of one of my fingers and started bending it back.

"No, no, don't. I don't know. They have a place near Longbeach, it's called The Migdal, it means Tower in Hebrew. But they drive me, and it's all, like, you know, streets, and empty lots, and thrift stores and pawn shops. And they go a different way each time. I don't know the address. They want it that way, I think, so no one can tell where it is." I was squirming against the straps.

She let my finger go. I listened to my heart pounding.

"OK, I'll believe you. For the moment. I have other ways of getting you to talk anyway. Do you know Mishi," she said conversationally, "they have done studies. Torture makes people say anything. Apparently the intel is very suspect. So they have to either do it to lots of people, and check that the stories are consistent, or they have to use other methods." She swept her hand toward the steel table like a game show barrel-girl revealing the prizes. "We don't have lots of people, just you, so I won't hurt you to get information."

I felt a wave of relief. I hadn't liked that finger bending thing one bit.

"No," she said, "I'll hurt you, to have fun." The lady let me have another look at her teeth. I think she thought she was smiling. I tested the strength of the cable ties for the umpteenth time.

Then the Asian guy Singh came out of the shadows. There was a short man trailing along behind taking two steps to his one. The light fell on their faces.

"Mr. Snell?" I said, recognizing one of Ronnie's teachers. "What the heck are you doing here?"

"Good evening, Miss Stern, that is, ah, Mishi," Snell ran a hand over his bald scalp. "Apologies, most sincere apologies for this treatment, it is just that we, that is, they, need some inf..."

"Be quiet, Snell," Singh said. Snell shut up like someone had pulled his plug out from the wall. His eyes went round, and he looked like he was getting ready to barf.

Wow, I thought, he's really scared of these guys. Me too, but I'm the one tied to a chair talking to a bitch who thinks it's spectacular to be called 'The Poisoner'.

"Any progress?" said Singh.

"Yes, Mishi and I have been having a nice girl talk. I think we've made progress. I have a few names and an approximate location."

"What of the Moses Revelation?" He sounded impatient.

"We were getting to that." She turned back to me. "Next question Mishi. Have you heard of an ancient scroll called the Moses Revelation?"

"They've got a lot of old stuff," I said. "In some kind of basement. All dusty and depressing, I don't go down there if I can help it. Only sometimes they send me to give something to the guy down there."

"What guy, Mishi? You didn't tell me about the guy who looks after the old stuff." She stroked one of my fingers. I tried to curl it out of her reach.

She grabbed it and twisted. I squawked. It hadn't really hurt but that twist was full of the promise of things to come.

"Doctor Dunkeldorfer. That's his name. Little guy. My height, like one of Snow White's dwarfs, you know, Doc. I forgot, I don't see him much." I was gabbling, she still had my finger.

"OK Mishi." She let go, took a step back, put her hands on her hips and gave me the eye.

This was turning into one of those cheesy horror movies that Ronnie and I used to watch together. I'd hug a pillow tight until the scary stuff started. Then I'd bury my head in it, squealing to Ronnie to describe what was happening on screen. In one of them a snake was able to turn itself into a woman. Or was it the other way around? I forget.

But now that snake-woman was standing in front of me. This thought did not, I can tell you, improve my mood.

"So, Mishi, tell me about that old stuff. The Moses Revelation, an ancient scroll, it might be called the Scroll of Wisdom or Power, or some other 'mysterious name'."

She actually used those curly-fingered air quotes. What a loser, I thought. I felt a bit of courage beginning to return.

"Yeah, they've got something like that. Or at least I've heard them mention it. I've never seen it. It's a big secret. It's not like they get any of this junk out and carry it around. It's all, like, you know kind of locked up in boxes, and glass show cabinets and stuff. You know, junk. Like old pots and bits of wood and that Egyptian picture writing and little clay things, and some small statues. It's like a museum without the lights and crowds and guards."

"Go on," said Singh.

"Well, I haven't seen it, the scroll, and the way they talk I don't think many of them have. I think it's kind of hidden somewhere else. Not at the Migdal. I think only a few of them know where it is. That's how they talk. Once someone said something about it being close by. So I guess it's in Longbeach, or LA somewhere."

It sounded lame even to me, but the funny thing was, now that I said it I realized it was true. I hadn't thought about it before. Who cares about some dumb scroll? But now I knew it must be important because the location was a secret even from most of the other Elders.

"And do you think Mommy knows where it is?"

The color drained from my face. "Uh, I don't... No, I don't think so. She would have..."

"She would have what, Mishi?" Sally Portland's brow crinkled, "told you? Given you that dangerous knowledge? When, according to you, lots of these power guys are in the dark themselves. I don't think so. But I will tell you what I do think. I think either Mommy knows, or Mommy knows who knows. And I think Mommy will tell us, if Mommy thinks she's going to start getting little bits of Mishi in the mail."

The lady looked happy at the prospect, then she and Singh walked away into the shadows, with Snell skittering along behind. Leaving me with my bouncing heart and machine gun breathing.

A few minutes later I heard car doors opening and closing and the SUV engine start up. Someone was off on a field trip.

AARON STERN

1.

OK, OK, I know. Driving out to Santa Monica Pier at night to meet some guys who have shown how very, very bad they are by abducting a fourteen-year-old was right up there with the stupidest thing I could have done. Having no idea where this scroll thingy was, or how to get it for them, made it a gajillion times stupider.

I get that.

But 'stupid' is kind of what I do. I think of it as a feature, not a bug. Others, Katie comes to mind, Mishi as well, have expressed their disagreement.

And if anyone knows what else I should have done I'm all ears. Monday morning quarterbacking is fine when it's football. But Mishi's life was at stake.

What was my plan, you ask? Let's just say my plan was to drive to Santa Monica Pier, and get Mishi back. Great plan, huh?

I got down there in record time. I parked and walked down the concrete path toward the sound of waves hitting the beach and sucking back out. When Melvin, Katie and I had been there just the other day there were lots of people, families, girls, kids, all there to be out in the sun, and to enjoy the food and the fun fair. During the day this is a great place.

At night, when everyone has gone home, not so much. It was unnerving.

I was about to step onto the wooden platform leading out over the water, repressing the voice in my head that was telling me to turn around and get the heck out of there, when a guy loomed out of the darkness.

"G'Day Aaron," he said in an Aussie accent. How did these people recruit their gang? E-Henchman? "Step right this way."

I didn't step anywhere. "Where's Mishi? I want to see her."

"And I want to retire to the French Riviera with hot and cold running chicks and beer. Not necessarily in that order. But we don't always get what we want do we, eh?"

He laughed at his own hilariousness. I didn't join in.

"Where's Mishi?" I asked again, my voice was squeaky and querulous.

"All in good time, Ronnie. Come this way, and we'll get this whole mess sorted, shall we?"

I hesitated and he stepped toward me. He took my arm in an iron grip and pulled me along with him, down the pier, past the carousel.

We approached a small cluster of people. One of them turned to me. It was the big Asian guy I'd seen talking to Mr. Smell. This was a smack in the face. How were all these people connected, and what did they want with Mishi? And me.

The Asian guy looked me over for a second or two then he said, “We want the Moses Revelation. Get it, give it to us, and your sister goes home. Refuse and she will also go home, but in pieces, over time.”

He could have been reading a weather report. This was scarier than if he’d swirled a black cape, and thrown his head back and gone “Mwa Hahaha!”

“You do not have a lot of time to respond, Mr. Stern.”

I continued to gape. I couldn’t have spoken if I’d wanted to. The Asian dude nodded to Crocodile Dundee. I felt a rush of air, a head splitting pain, and I began to fall into darkness.

2.

I came to slowly, lying on my back. I had an excruciating headache, and my mind was filled with cotton wool. I couldn’t remember what had happened. Where was I? How had I got here? Where *was* here?

I opened my eyes. It made no difference. I was in pitch-blackness, I couldn’t see a thing. I panicked.

I was blind!

My heart was pounding. I couldn’t suck in enough air. My lungs were too small, I was breathing faster and faster.

And then the horror really began.

I moved my elbow and hit a hard surface a few inches to my right. It was the same on the left. Instinctively I tried to sit up and cracked my head on another hard surface only inches above me. My head exploded with new pain and I collapsed back half dazed.

I felt the enclosed space smothering me. Terror gripped my throat.

I screamed, and thrashed about. I shouted and cried, and thumped and kicked and scratched at the surface above me until my nails split and my fingers bled.

No escape.

I had been buried alive.

I was going to run out of air. I was going to suffocate.

I felt the dread of death press down on my chest. My head throbbed and I began to lose consciousness, I thought of Mom and Dad, and Mishi, and Katie, and I heard someone crying and wailing.

It was me.

CHAPTER NINE

29TH SEPTEMBER

MIRIAM STERN AND DR. AMADEUS CALIFARIO

The phone on Dr. Califario's desk rang.

"Amadeus?" said Miriam Stern.

"Yes, Miriam," said Dr. Califario.

"Something terrible has happened and I think I've made a huge mistake."

"Tell me from the beginning," said Dr. Califario.

"The Organization has taken Mishi."

"What?" said Dr. Califario. "How did this happen?"

"She was at a party. Ronnie was on his way to pick her up and she was gone when he arrived. Then we got a message telling Ronnie to go to Santa Monica Pier."

"And he went?" said Dr. Califario.

"Over two hours ago. I tried to talk him out of it but he was determined."

"I don't know how this will turn out, Miriam, but I do know these monsters have made a serious blunder."

"Oh my God, Amadeus, what do you mean, what are we going to do?"

"We will do everything we can. But Miriam, I want to say that your children are extraordinary, I know you know that. But I suspect you don't know quite how extraordinary they are. In fact, Mishi and Aaron don't know either. When their full potential is realized they will be formidable, and when they work together, well, they will beoverwhelming."

"But how does this help get Mishi back, and keep Ronnie safe?"

"I honestly don't know," said Dr. Califario. "We will do everything we can from this end, but what I do know is that The Organization has grabbed a tiger by the tail, two tigers. And they had better hold on tight because they are in for a rough ride."

AARON STERN

I had no idea how long I was down there. I drifted in and out of consciousness. I had moments of blind panic, thrashing around, sweating, hitting the sides and top of the coffin, scratching at the wood with my bleeding fingers.

At other times I lay in a stupor.

I even tried the meditation techniques that Katie had taught me, but here's a bulletin: being buried alive, slowly suffocating, with no chance of rescue, is not the greatest time to practice mind control.

After a while it began to occur to my dim brain that I had been there too long. If I was going to suffocate I should have done it by now. There couldn't be that much air in this box, and I had been sucking in lungfulls of the stuff.

There had to be a source of air. I lay there in the darkness and listened and felt. Where was the air coming in?

It gave me something to do and took my mind off the terrifying claustrophobia.

I thought I could detect a minor temperature change near my chest, and then I went into another paroxysm of panic when I struggled to move my hands in the confines of the box.

But now I was sure there was air coming in. And a glimmer of hope lit up in my head. There must be a reason these crazies let me have air. Someone, whoever had put me here – Mr. Asia? Crocodile Dundee? – was making sure I stayed alive.

Then I blacked out again.

RANDOLPH LASSITER

Lassiter knew how to wait. He had turned his chair so he could see out the window, across the East River and the southern tip of Roosevelt Island to the sun rising over Brooklyn. He sat with his elbows on the arms of his chair and his hands clasped, poised, attentive, and ready.

He settled back, the aged diamond-buttoned upholstery gave another gentle creak. It was restful and soothing, the mantra of his patient meditation.

The cell vibrated. He turned to his mahogany desk and scooped it up.

"Did the boy come? How is he taking things?"

"Yes, he came, the brother. We asked him about the Moses Revelation. He had nothing to say, so we are in the process of persuading him."

"We need him alive and well. You haven't damaged him?"

"He is buried."

"Buried?" Lassiter laughed. "You excel yourself. He has enough air? Of course he does, otherwise you would be telling me of his untimely death. How long has he been down there?"

"About half an hour. He was unconscious when he went into the coffin. Then the mike picked up kicking and screaming and scratching. It's gone quiet again. He's still alive."

"And you say he has air."

"A little. A small tube. He won't suffocate but it isn't pleasant."

"Better and better." The fingers drummed on the desk. "You've got Severin with you? I want him to confirm that the brother is an Adept."

"Severin is with us."

"Good, good. Get him on to it. Dig up the Stern boy, find out what he knows, and tell him to get that scroll. We need it. But we need him as well, so make sure he is compliant. Threaten the sister. Something horrible. A finger or an eye should do the trick. These Jews are very family oriented. Then send him off looking for that scroll. He should be able to persuade his mother to hand it over."

"Understood."

He broke the connection. And settled back for more waiting. The Scroll and, perhaps, the Twins. Better and better.

AARON STERN

"Find out what he knows ... get that scroll ... threaten the sister ... a finger or an eye ..." As if the coffin wasn't enough, now that listening device thing in my head was kicking in. And the voice. Smooth and classy. I knew it from the Vision. The guy in the wood-paneled room with the hunting pictures.

Talking about cutting my sister up.

I went into a another frenzy. I did more damage to my fingers and feet and head. My voice was reduced to a rasping croak. I had no more tears.

I must have had another black out. When I came around I heard a sound, like scratching and sifting. Oh God, I thought, some animal is coming for me!

I listened some more, no it was sand being shoveled.

You'd think that I'd be elated by this imminent rescue. But as the minutes crept by the anticipation was almost worse. Then I began to think of who was 'rescuing' me, and that big Asian lug and the Aussie maniac loomed larger and larger in my mind.

The shoveling got closer and louder.

There was a thump on the top of my box. Then there was rocking and shifting and grunting, and the box and I were lifted up, moved a bit to the side, and dropped.

When the lid was prized off they were looking down at me. The Asian guy was modeling for the fifth face at Mount Rushmore, the Aussie grinning like a game show host opening door number two. Next to them was a short man with an Olympic Medal comb-over. He was dressed in a crumpled suit and he didn't look happy.

"Come on, Sport. Up we get." The Aussie reached down, grabbed my collar and hoisted me up one-handed like I was a feather.

I tripped and staggered getting out of the cheap pinewood box complete with metal handles for the pallbearers. Did these psychos carry these things around, in case they needed to torture someone?

We were standing under Santa Monica Pier. Nearby was a depression in the sand, its sides collapsed and softened. Two other guys stood next to a couple of shovels leaning against the wooden supports. The water was fifty yards away, and I felt sick all over again at the thought of the incoming tide.

"Well?" said Mr. Asia.

He was speaking to Comb Over Guy, who was leaning toward me. He looked like he was walking into a high wind, struggling to stay upright.

"Yes." Rumpled Stiltskin was gasping. "Yes. Jesus, you guys, Singh can't you feel it? No, I guess not. Christ it's like a hurricane, coming off this guy."

"So that is a yes?"

"You bet your yellow Asian fanny it's a yes," he said, not Mr. Politically Correct. The Asian guy, Singh, was unperturbed. Almost, what's that word, inscrutable? Maybe I missed PC classes as well.

"Mr. Stern," said Singh. "Time is not on your side. We require your cooperation or you will be returned to the coffin. For good."

I started crying. I couldn't help it. Tears flowed down my face like a river and I choked and sobbed uncontrollably. I hated myself but I couldn't stop.

That Singh bastard just watched me. The guy in the wrinkled suit looked worried. And the Aussie creep looked like he was enjoying the show immensely.

I think that's what changed things for me.

Previously I was terrified and a victim, at the mercy of these nutjobs. But looking at that Aussie guy's face made me mad. The tears dried up as quickly as they had begun.

But I didn't want to die buried alive under Santa Monica Pier. Or anywhere else, come to that. So I let the anger smolder away, biding my time.

"What do you want me to do?"

"That's better," said Singh. "There is a document, an ancient scroll, called the Moses Revelation. You will acquire this scroll and deliver it to us. Or you will die slowly and uncomfortably."

I was in the unusual position of knowing more about that scroll than anyone living, after all I'd seen Moses himself writing it.

Except for one tiny detail. I had no idea where it was now.

One thing I did know, however, there was no way I could go back into that box and remain sane.

So I did what I did best, I played dumb.

"What?" I said. "What scroll, where is it? What does it look like?"

"All these questions," said Singh, shaking his head sadly and tisk-tisking at me. "I'm afraid, you will have to find the answers yourself. You might start by asking your mother."

"My mother?"

"Yes, Mr. Stern, your mother will, no doubt, be eager to help you."

"Eager?" I said. See, what I mean about acting dumb? "What do you mean?"

"Mr. Stern," he gave me hard eyes, "we are wasting time. We want the scroll, and we will give you two days to get it for us. Ask your mother about it, that will be a good start for you."

"Yeah Sport," said the Aussie, "go ask Mummy. Coz things are going to get a lot worse for that pretty little sister of yours if you don't."

I could feel my blood beginning to boil. My head was throbbing and I was finding it hard to see these apes through the red mist.

"What my colleague is saying is your mother will not want to receive small pieces of her daughter by parcel post."

It was the way they were smiling that did it at last.

Before I knew what was happening, a bomb went off inside my head. The big Asian guy was closest to me. I leapt at him punching, scratching and kicking.

"What have you done to her!" I was shouting, roaring. Sounds were coming out of my throat which I had never heard, even on the Animal Planet channel. "What have you done to my sister!"

The Aussie and two other heavies finally pulled me off. Singh had blood running down his face.

Then Santa's three little helpers got to work on me. All fists and boots. Wolfgang would've admired their technique. I went down quickly and curled up in a ball, and they spent a few happy minutes, for them, kicking and punching.

When they stopped I lay in the sand groaning.

Singh stood over me and gave me one last kick in the stomach. He wiped his face with a bloody handkerchief.

"That was very foolish," he said. "You have made an enemy of me, and I do not forget my enemies."

What, I thought, like we were friends before?

"Your sister is alive Mr. Stern, and unharmed. At present. That will not remain the case should you refuse to cooperate. Choose quickly."

This guy was very persuasive.

"All right," I panted, from the ground. "I'll get you your scroll."

RANDOLPH LASSITER

"Svensson?"

"Yes."

"We think we have found the Twins. A brother and sister."

"Excellent, and do you actually have them?"

"Yes. We have the sister, and we are sending the brother to get the scroll, this Moses Revelation."

"Ach so," said Svensson. "Das ist gut, This is good. And both of them have these gifts?"

"Yes, the girl we have known about for years. A lucky find by Severin. The boy was not on our radar but Severin confirmed he is an Adept as well."

"And he has strong powers?"

"Yes. Quite strong according to our man on the spot. We are not sure what his particular area of talent is, but strong, yes. It is curious he wasn't detected earlier."

"Did either of them try to use their powers on your men? This mind control can be very, disruptive."

"We were ready for the girl. We sent Portland. Having our own Adept is most useful. She was on hand to block the girl if necessary, but apparently the fear did the job for us. So when we got the boy we instituted a little terror campaign."

"All this is most interesting. I must tell you, according to our friend Da Silva, when The Twins are actually related as siblings, then it presages some major catastrophe or crisis. Something, in any case, which the Twins are born to oppose or correct."

"Interesting," said Lassiter. "From the point of view of our opponents, what we are planning will be completely catastrophic. From our point of view, of course, it is a wonderful advance. Stability, clarity, world peace, environmental regulations and rational central planning as far as the eye can see. But sadly, no democracy, no free speech, property rights only when we allow them. Perfect order."

"And the scroll, does this fellow know where it is?"

"He knows some people who know. And he will need to persuade them to reveal its location."

"And he can do this?"

"For his sister's sake he'd better do it."

"Ah," said Svensson with scholarly satisfaction. "It is good. We can move forward with our plans."

"To victory, my friend," said Lassiter, allowing himself a small note of triumph.

AARON STERN

1.

I limped up to my car along the illuminated path through the grassed area that runs along the Santa Monica beachfront. I got the door open. I sat picking the worst of the splinters out of my hands. My head was spinning and I couldn't string two coherent thoughts together. I was in shock. I needed some time to recover.

I don't know how long I sat there with my hands on the wheel. I certainly slept for some of the time. I finally turned the key in the ignition and headed for home.

Parts of a plan were beginning to hobble toward each other in my mind. First, I had to ask Mom about the scroll. And then maybe nose around Elders' HQ.

There was a faint glow of dawn when I arrived home and looked into the living room. Dad was asleep on the sofa, still wearing his work clothes. A white short-sleeved shirt, a brown tie, navy-blue pants, and his black leather lace-up business shoes lying on the carpet where he'd kicked them off. He had never left for work wearing anything different. In winter, such as it is in Southern California, he threw an old suit coat in the back of the car, but seldom wore it.

Dad snorted and looked up when I came in. He got up and shuffled over in his socks. We went down the hallway together to the kitchen.

Mom was there sitting at the table, cradling a cold cup of coffee. She was in her professional clothes, black skirt suit with cream blouse and black pumps. She was a broken-hearted statue. Dad sat down next to her and took one of her hands in both of his.

"Oh my God, Ronnie," said Mom, looking up as I sat opposite them, "you look terrible. What happened to you?"

Dilemma. Tell them and I turn two distraught parents from panic to hysteria. Don't tell them and I've got a big secret which can blow up in my face.

"I spoke to the guys who've got Mishi."

"How is she, have they hurt her? Is she OK?" said Mom, wringing her hands. They were so focused on Mishi that they skipped over the cuts and bruises from my coffin-time. I kept my bloodied hands out of sight.

"I didn't get to see her or speak to her. But they said she was fine." What else could I say? Lying to my parents did not sit well with me. But what was the alternative? 'Homicidal gangsters have your daughter, and are threatening to chop her up if I don't find a million year old scroll which no one knows where it is, and I've got two days to do it or else they'll green-light the dismemberment'.

"You didn't ask to see her?" said Dad.

"I did ask, but they weren't in the mood for Q & A. Like they said in the text to Mom, they told me I had to get some sort of scroll thingy for them and then they'd let her go."

Mom's face went blank.

"They were pretty clear. Mishi for the scroll."

"What is this ferkakte scroll?" said Dad. (Ferkakte: crappy, literally. Yiddish is Dad's refuge in time of trouble.)

"Look Dad they gave me a few leads which I'll follow up on. They want it in two days."

"Two days? They keep Mishi for two days! And you can get this thing?" said Dad.

"I'll have to. Mishi needs me to. Have the police been?" I got this in quickly, before they could start asking me for more details.

"Ronnie, we rang the police," said Dad. "They gave me the run around."

"Run around?"

"Yeah, you know, How long has she been gone? How do you know she's not at a party?" said Dad.

"She just left a party."

"I told them. But they think every girl in California is hopping from one party to the next."

"Did you tell them about the text. Did they trace it?"

"They said it was probably a fake," said Mom, "from a secret boyfriend trying to cover her tracks. They said they'd seen this kind of thing a thousand times before."

"A thousand times?" I was incredulous. "Like, a thousand fourteen-year-old girls are wandering the streets, getting their secret boyfriends to text kidnap demands to their parents?"

"Yes," said Dad, "can you believe it?"

"So the cops aren't going to do anything?"

"Ronnie," said Dad in disgust, "any confidence I may have had in the forces of law and order, I am beginning to lose, at least as far they are constituted in our corner of the world."

"So that's a no," I said.

"That's a no," said Dad.

2.

Dad was exhausted and Mom knew I needed to speak to her alone. So she talked him into going up to bed. You know: You'll be fresher tomorrow to deal with all of this. I'm coming soon. See you up there.

Dad went and we heard teeth cleaning, throat clearing, toilet flushing.

We sat at the table in the kitchen. She looked dog-tired, her skin was gray and her eyes were red. We were a great pair.

She saw my hands and flinched.

"Oh, Ronnie, what did they do to you? I knew it wasn't as easy as you said."

"They were a bit rough. But can we get to that later? First, can I assume you know I've been out to the Migdal and I've met Dr Califario and his crew?"

Mom nodded, "Yes, Amadeus has kept me up to date."

"OK, that's good," I said. "So, I need to know about that scroll. Where is it now? I assume it's not at the bottom of Dad's sock drawer."

"No, not there," said Mom, "but Ronnie you need to know why these people want the Revelation so badly."

"I don't care why they want it," I said. "I don't know what it does, except turn the Sterns into freaks. What's it matter what they're going to do with it? They're not going to raise a race of Supermen to rule the world. Or chant some crazy incantation and turn everyone into zombies."

Mom just looked at me.

"They're not are they?" I shook myself. "Look Mom, it doesn't matter why they want it. They've got Mishi."

Mom let go of my hand and reached for tissues from a box on the table. She dabbed her eyes.

"Sorry, Ronnie. But both of my children are in danger."

"So let's get one of them out of danger. Do you know where the Moses Revelation is kept?"

"No," she said. "No Aaron, don't even think about it. That scroll is too powerful, it contains too many secrets. Not merely the text, which only a very few people have been able to read and survive, but the actual parchment has to be handled extremely carefully."

"Like it's radioactive or something?"

"Something like that. I haven't been directly involved, but Mortimer and Mordecai, who have, say it has to be handled, literally, with special leather gloves. Like you saw in your vision of King David and Solomon."

"Or?"

"Or I don't know. But what I do know is we can't give these evil people that scroll."

"Even if it means we lose Mishi?" I was beginning to heat up.

"Yes, even then," she reached out for my hand again, but I pulled back.

"Mom, it's Mishi! I don't care about some old scroll that glows in the dark. If it's so powerful and dangerous let these meshugenas have it, and let them get zapped to kingdom come. Look, Mishi is all I care about. And I would've thought you'd agree with me. Mishi being your daughter. I assume you remember her, curly hair, freckles, bad attitude, you know the one. She used to live here. Until a bunch of psychopaths grabbed her off the street!"

I was on a roll here. What a great guy, yelling at my mother, trying to hurt her. I couldn't stop myself. I just couldn't get that we were arguing about whether to trade some crappy archaeological artifact, for the life of my sister.

Suddenly I had had enough. I got up, ignoring my mother's shattered expression.

I slammed the door on the way out. I was going get that stupid Moses Revelation any way I could.

3.

I went to my car and drove out into the street. I felt the need to do something, to move. After about twenty minutes of this it occurred to me that Mordecai was my best bet. He was friendly, helpful and was part of Dr. C's inner circle. I had to start somewhere, so I rang him on the special number.

"Yes, my friend," Mordecai picked up on the first ring. At six in the morning. "Hi, Mordecai, I think I need your help."

"Wonderful, if there is one commodity which I have in abundance it is the desire to help. Speak."

"Look, have you heard, Mishi has gone missing, she's been taken by these guys, you know, that Organization. So it's somehow all mixed up with what you, I mean, we are doing."

"Yes," said Mordecai, all seriousness now. "I have been informed. This is very terrible, and believe me we, and I mean myself, Dr. Califario, Wolfgang, all of us are using all our resources to locate her."

"That's great, that's good to know. But..."

"And," said Mordecai, "I know she is your little sister and looks like an ordinary fourteen-year old, but you should not be deceived, she herself has very formidable powers."

"Look, yeah, great, but these kidnappers. They contacted my Mom and told me to go to Santa Monica pier."

"This we found out too late. A pity, we could have done something. Did you go to this ambush?"

"How did you know...?"

"This is the way they work. They are, how do you say, simple to read. Sometimes we feel they steal their plots and plans from the latest Hollywood action film, hoping that this time the lone knight in the armor that shines will not in fact save the day and prevent them from achieving world domination."

"Yeah I went, it didn't turn out so good."

"Of course, you were this knight shining in your armor. But I think you do not yet know how strong your armor is, and how to buckle it on most effectively."

"Look Mordecai, that's nice, yeah, I don't know my own strength. Sure, sorry, but these guys, they want me to get something for them."

"Yes?" I could hear a note of caution in his voice now. But I plowed on.

"All they want is that Moses Revelation thing. You know that scroll."

"Ah yes, they do not want very much these people," heavy sarcasm now. "All they want is the most formidable artifact in our possession, the key to our strength and whatever successes we have against the evil that these people try to propagate. No, Aaron, my boy, they must not get the Moses Revelation. We must find another way to get your Mishi, our Mishi back."

I felt myself getting mad again. Was I the only sane person in this asylum? These people, my Mom included, saw more value in a piece of old junk than Mishi. I kept my voice level, playing along. For now.

"Well, OK so no scroll for Mishi. What are we going to do?"

"We will locate her and effect a rescue."

"As simple as that, eh?"

"Yes, as simple as that."

"And this Moses Revelation. This powerful doodad, which everybody wants. We've got it and it's safe somewhere?"

"Yes, Aaron, we've got it and it is very safe. Not many of us know its location, we keep the knowledge in a tight little circle. And it is moved occasionally, not often, but when it begins to show itself."

"Show itself?"

"Yes, it begins to reveal itself with strange occurrences. Power outages. Its display case begins to heat up. People receive electric shocks when they get close. Even the flights of birds begin to alter. If we don't move the scroll these poor birds will fly in circles until they drop from the skies."

"But no swap for Mishi," I said bitterly.

"No, Aaron, I am truly sorry but no swap for Mishi."

I rang off. My plan was beginning to get itself organized.

MISHI STERN

This was getting totally boring. I'd been through fear and desperation and lots of anger, but now I began to wonder how much longer I had to sit in this cold, gloomy warehouse, tied to this chair while these idiots walked back and forth in the shadows talking on cell phones, and packing and unpacking things from crates and boxes. At one point the warehouse door slid aside and the SUV returned with the Chinese guy and the Aussie and a couple of others who'd been along for the ride.

Catching their eye, however, wasn't an attractive alternative to being ignored. So I just sat, dozing sometimes, asking to go to the bathroom as infrequently as I could manage, but mostly trying over and over to get inside their heads.

That was totally the worst bit. I had been able to manipulate people for fun and profit for as long as I could remember. But Dr. Califario had shown me that fooling with my power would suck me dry and lead to a bitter old age. And under his guidance I had started using my powers for niceness, not evil. It went against the grain I can tell you. Cause, like, let's be honest here, I had well-honed instincts for mischief and spite. Still do. It's just that now I've got it under control. Mostly.

Even *I* could tell how ironic this situation was. I could use my gift to get Ronnie to help with my homework or drive me to the mall, but when I needed these powers most, to foil genuine evil, and for self-preservation, my efforts to curl my way into the subconsciousness of these knuckle-dragging morons were just bouncing off.

But I kept trying. Hour after hour.

Every now and again Sally Portland, pretty Miss Poison, came over, leered at me, and threatened me with agonizing death. I told her everything I knew 'cause, one, I didn't know much, and two, they would probably find out anyway, and three, Dr. Califario was pretty clear that we weren't to be heroic unless there was an opportunity (cable-tied to a metal chair? Nope), or our death was inevitable (Gulp! not yet).

I think the boredom did it. It replaced the panic and anger.

The frat boys had been at it for hours. I heard them do a quick eeney meeney miney moe for guard duty. A thin piece of work called Gantz was to take first sentry shift and the others including the Aussie would grab the first nap. I heard the creak of camp beds in a dark corner and then stillness.

I got my heart rate down, centered my energy, and concentrated. I let my mind wander over to the Aussie, and started to probe his consciousness.

Eureka!

I could feel him on the edge of sleep. As he tipped over into dreamland, I was in.

Now, another word on this mind power thingummy. I can get into someone's head, and I can wander around inside. I can't hear their actual thoughts, like in English, in words, or like that. But I can 'feel' them, the thoughts that is. I can intuit their intentions, their fears, their hopes. And I can nudge some things along, and restrain other things, so that they do what I want. Correction (Dr. Califario are you listening), so they do what they ought to do.

Until now my panic had locked me out of their heads. Now I was getting my mojo back.

Trouble was he was asleep. And that was totally no good, if I wanted him to do something, or think something, he had to be awake.

Info-wise, he was no help, but mind-wise, I was back in business.

Goody.

AARON STERN

1.

Mordecai and I decided to meet at the coffee shop on the corner of 5th and Santa Ana. I drove through the LA dawn watching the sun light up the streets, the houses, the shops, feeling the warmth seep back into the city. I parked and left my car and walked around a corner. Mordecai was at one of the street tables just finishing a black coffee and stubbing out his cigarette. There were a few people at the other tables, a guy in a suit reading *The Power of Now,* and a trim couple in running gear with monitors strapped to their arms drinking something green and sludgy from tall glasses.

Mordecai looked up when I approached. He gave me a wave, left money on the table and we walked to his car. We didn't have much to say to each other.

He drove me to the Migdal, the Elder Fortress of Solitude. Same dingy neighborhood, same roller-shutter entrance, same steep downward drive to the parking lot.

And same cramped coffin-lift. I had a different view on that now, and it wasn't a nicer one. My nerves were just beginning to scream when the elevator shuddered to a halt and Mordecai worked the metal grid doors aside.

We walked in silence down the hallways. Same dim lighting, same faded wallpaper, same threadbare carpet.

2.

Dr. Califario was sitting behind his desk as we entered. Mordecai and I sat down.

Dr. C already had the outline of events, but he wanted me to fill in the gaps. It went on for a while.

For most of this he let me talk, at other times he questioned me in detail. And I mean real detail. What color was the van (white), its license plate (don't know), who told me what had happened (Emma Schwartz), was she reliable (seemed so to me), what was she wearing (are you kidding me?), insistent repeat of previous question. (Uh, I dunno, kind of girl's clothes, I guess.)

My anxiety grew with every passing minute.

"Why do you want to know all of this junk?" I finally asked.

"This junk, as you call it, can, and often is, the vital clue. An anthrax attack in Oklahoma City, for example, was recently thwarted because Beethoven's 'Eroica Symphony' was heard coming from a place where one would not, to say the least, expect to hear it. Hence my concern for the details. Believe me when I say that we are pulling out all the stops to get your sister back. This is how we will do it successfully. Please go on."

When we finished I asked what I'd been itching to say the whole time.

"They want the Moses Revelation, and then they'll let Mishi go."

"Aaron, my boy," Mordecai piped up, "they say they'll let Mishi go. But I do not think these are men who are worthy of your trust."

"So, what are you saying, we should leave her there? Abandon her?" I was getting louder. "Shouldn't we try anyway? Give them the damn thing and get Mishi away from them."

"Your moral clarity does you credit," said Dr. Califario.

"Credit, schmedit!" I said, "let's give them the stupid scroll and get her back!"

"It is *not* so simple as you imagine," said Mordecai.

What was it with these guys? It was that simple. One teenage girl in exchange for one dusty old thingummy, which no one has probably read for like a bajillion years. I got that it was valuable and, Yes, yes, they'd told me that its mystery was only exceeded by its power, but place it in the balance with the life of my sister and I would have traded the original Declaration of Independence, and thrown in the Hope Diamond as a bonus.

I couldn't see why they couldn't see it.

"Mr. Stern," Dr. Califario interrupted my thoughts. "It is not going to happen."

"What?"

"You heard. We are not going to trade The Hidden Teachings of Moshe Rabbenu, Moses our Teacher, for your sister's life. I am being blunt here so there is no possibility of misunderstanding. Neither you nor I, nor anyone else, is going to take this artifact and place it in the hands of men who would use it to do incalculable harm to an untold number of Mishis."

"So, what? We're going to let them kill Mishi?" Bluntness was all the rage.

He gave me a withering look. "No, Mr. Stern, we are not fiends. We are using all our contacts, all our resources, to locate your sister and to effect a rescue."

I looked at Dr. Califario sitting back on the other side of his desk. And Mordecai, all concerned and fatherly, and I realized this wasn't getting anywhere. I was alone. These guys who I had come to trust and depend on were not going to help. I had to do this on my own.

You'd think that that idea would be a bit of a downer. You know, a high school kid, cut loose by these smart experienced guys, has to depend on himself alone.

But it was funny. I knew I could do it. I had no idea where the Moses Revelation was, how to find out, how to get it when I did find it, or how to handle the bad guys when I had it. But, I was totally confident that I would do all these things, and figure out the details as I went along.

I nodded at them and asked Mordecai to take me back to my car.

3.

I was lost in these thoughts as we walked back down the dimly lit corridors to the elevator. Just before we got there a plain wooden door on the right opened and a girl came out, her head was down and she was reading some papers. Her blonde hair hung in front of her face. In the gloom we collided and then we did that corridor two-step trying to let the other pass while stepping into each other's path. Real comical. Until we both realized it was us!

"Katie!" I said, full marks to me for acute powers of observation.

"Ronnie," I guess she was runner up.

"Aaron," at this point Mordecai chimed in, "I've got to get a few things. I'll see you downstairs at the car. Katie would you be so kind as to show him the way when your business together is done?" And he walked off.

"What are you doing here?" she asked. "Did you get Mishi? Was she OK?"

Obviously she hadn't heard the news.

"I've just been talking to Dr. C. About Mishi. You were right it was bad. She's been kidnapped."

"Oh Ronnie," she took my hand. I winced. "What are we going to do? How are we going to get her back?"

So we went into the Sitting Room and sat down. I told her about the kidnappers' demand for the Moses Revelation, and my fruitless conversation with Dr. Califario.

"Dr. C doesn't want to hand over the Moses Revelation."

"Of course not! That would be crazy."

"Crazy! Everyone's saying that. No one cares about Mishi. You don't care about her!"

Katie recoiled, her eyes wide.

"Dr. Damn Califario sitting behind his idiot desk in that stupid study saying 'We're doing all we can'. And Mordecai giving me doe eyes like he's really concerned. And you. You. You're all 'Of course we can't hand over the Moses Thingy'. I mean some lame piece of garbage is more important than my sister. Well, I'm not convinced that sacrificing a fourteen-year-old girl so you guys can keep your moronic Moses Hoozamie is such a neat idea. And I'm going to do something about it."

Katie's eyes narrowed and her lips tightened. She looked at me while my heart rate slowed to near normal and my hands unclenched.

"And what, Aaron Stern," she said quietly, "may I ask, exactly is it that you intend to do about it? Am I allowed to ask that?"

Red alert, Mount Katie was about to blow her stack. But, you know what? I didn't care any more.

"Well, if you must know, I'm going to find out where this thing is. Then I'm going to get it. And I'm going to trade it for Mishi."

Katie stared at me, her arms folded across her chest. "That's your brilliant plan?"

"If you were to help me the brilliance of the plan might go up a notch."

"So 'we' includes me now. I mean in a good way. Not, like, 'we want to abandon Mishi', and 'we want to keep our stupid scroll'. More like 'we' are going to rescue her, and 'we' are going to steal an ancient, powerful, and irreplaceable artifact, and put it in the hands of the worst people possible, so they can use it to destroy all that is good and kind and peaceful in the world. That's *our* plan is it?"

"Yeah, more or less. Except for the destroying the world bit."

"And may I also ask exactly how 'we' are going to do all this, except for the destroying the world bit, that is?"

"I don't know. But I need to try."

"Look Aaron," her voice softer now, "I get it. I really do. Mishi is in the hands of these people and who knows what is happening to her. Although I know her in ways you don't. Like Elders' ways. And she is a lot more powerful and resourceful than I think you appreciate. She will be doing everything she can from her end to keep herself safe and look for any opportunity to get away, or get word to us."

"But..."

"Let me finish. I want to help you. I'll do anything I can."

"Except?"

"Except I won't help you locate the Moses Revelation. I don't know where it is anyway. And if you or I do find out where it is kept, I won't help you steal it. And I certainly won't help you hand it over."

See how she sugarcoats things, just to spare my feelings, you know, let me down easily.

I got up and left the room without another word and decided to find my own way to the elevator.

4.

The Seventh Vision

But I didn't get far. I'd only taken a few steps in what I hoped was the right direction when I staggered and put a hand out to steady myself. But my hand started sliding down the wall, the rest of my body followed.

Everything started to go twisty and stretchy and nauseous and dark. My final thought was, 'Oh Crap, here we go again'.

When the head twisting stopped I was standing in a dark room. Some people were talking and at first I couldn't see much or get what they were saying. Then my sight cleared and it was like a translator in my head switched on and I could follow the conversation.

"It is too powerful, and without the Temple apparatus, the fortified treasure house, the priests, the levites, the guards, it is in danger of being discovered and stolen. I got it out of Jerusalem by the skin of my teeth and with the strong right hand of the Lord's protection. And, with the Most High supplying my words, the General of the Romans gave me safe passage here."

"But Rabbi, copying The Hidden Teachings of Moshe Rabbenu? This is a thing which has never been done."

"Yes, and not one copy but several."

"How many copies do you propose?"

I was looking at a small room filled with men in robes with their heads covered in long shawls. I recognized Yohanan Ben Zakkai and there were seven other guys. It was like a synagogue on one of the main Jewish holidays, except the synagogue our family went to was considerably larger and swankier than this.

Ben Zakkai looked older than the last time I saw him. Better fed though.

"Seven copies," he said. "One for each of the Blessed Families. The families who have been chosen by the scroll itself."

"What do you mean? Who are these families?" asked a younger man.

"Ah," said Ben Zakkai, "have you not heard the legend, that there are men of power in Israel? Men who are mighty and touched by the Lord, and who protect his people."

"Yes, I have heard of this legend," said the young man.

"Like many legends it is based on a truth," said Ben Zakkai. He had a knowing smile, like he was in on some secret. "There are such men and they have special powers. Some have been written about in the Holy Bible. Men such as King David for his power to charm, King Solomon for wisdom, but also humbler men, Samson for his strength, Amos for his gift of prophesy. And many others whose names are unknown to us, with similar powers.

"Not only men, but women also. Again some whose names have come down to us, Deborah, Judith, Ruth. Wise women, women of courage, with powers to heal, to influence, to read the minds of men. The Rabbis tell us of seven families from among the priests and levites, who were tasked with caring for the Scroll of Revelation, protecting it and ensuring its safety in the Temple Treasury. These families began centuries ago to exhibit strange gifts. In every generation one child from each family showed the signs. The gifts varied but, so the ancient men of wisdom said, it was the scroll of the Teachings of Moshe Rabbenu, Moses our Teacher, that passed its power to these families. Some displayed their powers, but most remained hidden."

The young man looked around at the others in the room. "But Rabbi, what of this? Where are these people to be found?"

Ben Zakkai smiled. "Ovadyah, son of Ahaz, son of Joash, time to reveal yourself."

"Me?" said Ovadyah Ben Ahaz.

The other men began to murmur to each other.

"Yes you Ovadyah son of Ahaz, and you Nadav son of Amos, and you Adayah son of Nathan, and all of you who have been called here by me. The Lord has revealed it to me. The scroll is too precious, it is too powerful to fall into the hands of the unrighteous. Each one of you here in this room is the patriarch of one of the Blessed Families. Each one of you is possessed of special powers. You Azariah Ben Yosef, you heal with a touch. You, Tzadok Ben Nun, have power over men's minds. You, Micah son of Levi, you can move objects with a wave of your hand. You Hosea Ben Elihu, you have the power of life and death. You, all of you have power. I know you have worked all your life to keep this a secret."

"But, Rabbi, even if what you say is true," said Tzadok Ben Nun, "and even if these seven copies of the Teachings are made, what then? How can they be protected?"

"Hear the word of the Lord," said Ben Zakkai, he stretched out his hands and looked up. His eyes rolled up in his head and only his whites were visible. This was getting seriously creepy.

Ben Zakkai's voice changed, it deepened and reverberated. The room shook. "Each of you will make a perfect copy of the Scroll of Power, the Hidden Teachings of Moshe Rabbenu. Then you will take that copy, even the copy which you have made with your own hand, and you will depart from this place. And you, each of you, will travel in the direction that the Lord your God will show to you, each to his own path. You will take your families and your boon companions with you, and all the possessions you can carry on your backs. Your destination will be revealed to you. Even the Lord Most High will reveal it. And there you will settle and live guarding the Hidden Teaching, and passing on the secret from generation to generation."

And, that was me done. The voices faded and I woke up back in what I was coming to think of as The Migdal Recovery Room. My home away from home.

RANDOLPH LASSITER

Randolph Lassiter found himself seated in a darkened room with bright lights shining in his eyes. He could not have identified the other occupants even if he had wanted to. The journey had been tortuous, for some of it he had been blindfolded.

He had reported crisply, without interruption. Now the silence was stretching out. He knew better than to be the one to break it.

Lassiter felt his confidence seeping away.

"Let me summarize," the voice was icy. "We know the Time and the Place. And we think we know what the Word is and who the Twins are. But we don't have the scroll, and I assume we don't know where it is. Otherwise you would have retrieved it yourself. And we have sent out one of these invaluable Twins to get this scroll."

"We have his sister. We have threatened to kill her if he doesn't return."

"Well, all I can say is I hope, for your sake, he is fond of his sister. Now, let us discuss the disposal of any other witnesses."

THE SEARCH

Landon McAllister stood looking out his window at the central courtyard of the Pentagon. He had called in every favor he could think of, and more besides. Looking for news of any unusual Organization activity in LA, any whispers on the wind about rogue groups doing their own thing.

So far he had very little of any use in finding the Stern girl.

He did pick up snippets about Washington DC and the Washington Monument. The Organization dogs were sniffing around. And he got a line on some guy at the UN, but it wasn't much to go on, his focus was on the girl.

He passed everything on to LA.

Jamalia Brookes was distraught. She sat at her kitchen table with a glass of hot tea in front of her. It was getting colder by the minute. A little girl in the hands of these brutes. She shuddered.

No point sitting around. She thought of her mother and that bus ride from Chicago to Dallas.

Her Momma didn't sit around drinking hot tea. When her little girl was in trouble she had packed up all the Brookes children and got them out of there.

Jamalia Brookes got up and got dressed and headed off for the Barrios.

Francois Pierrot was not as young as he used to be. And his run in with Sally Portland hadn't helped matters.

He hunched over the clock with a fine sable paintbrush in one hand and a pair of tweezers in the other. On his workbench was a particularly beautiful double-movement carriage clock, with a hand painted ceramic case.

At least it had been beautiful until that fiendish woman had smashed it.

Francois was searching for the little girl the best way he knew. His hands worked on the timepiece while his mind went into the 'reading room'.

As the repairs to the carriage clock began to take shape a picture formed in Francois' head. He waited for it to crystalize and clarify, then he put down his tools and stretched.

He picked up the phone.

"Bon jour, Amadeus," he said, "she is in a chair, tied down, but otherwise she has not been harmed, in a large warehouse. She is tired and she is scared, but she is, how do you say, one with a great deal of courage. And she is, I think, to the south of where you are. But her exact location? It is not in my power to say. I regret I cannot be of greater assistance."

RANDOLPH LASSITER AND PROFESSOR OLAF SVENSSON

Olaf Svensson followed the waitress threading her way to the rear of The Tablespoon, a café in Brooklyn near Cardozo College. He held his briefcase against his chest with both arms. The lunchtime crowd had thinned and only a few booths were occupied.

The waitress deposited him near the kitchen. He selected the bench seat facing the glass entrance door, and placed his briefcase safely next to him near the wall. The high-backed over-padded benches, covered in red faux leather edged with unbroken strings of large shiny brass nails promised more comfort than they delivered. He perched on the end of the bench so he could see around the booth divider.

A few minutes passed and a trim, handsome man opened the glass door of the café. He was taller than average, dressed in a gray suit with a rose-colored tie. After a brief interchange with the waitress, she led the newcomer straight to Svensson. Svensson slid out of his seat and stood to meet him

They shook hands, and seated themselves on either side of the table.

The waitress took their lunch orders and retreated.

"I understand that this meeting is unusual," said Lassiter. "However, our plans are now at a point where electronic communication is no longer safe enough for certain matters."

"Matters, like..."

"Well," said Lassiter, "your experience in Argentina in the 70s, and with the Castros in Cuba, and with the Mullahs in Iran. The, ah, skills which made you so valuable to such discerning employers, are now required again."

"Come Mr. Lassiter, let us not be coy," said Svensson smiling like a favorite uncle, "you know, honesty is one of the most underutilized of virtues. Let us say what we mean to say, and then there will be no possibility of misunderstanding. I am now playing the part of the kindly old professor of arcane and irrelevant ancient manuscripts at a second tier University. Much liked by my students, but gently mocked behind my back for my eccentric mannerisms and my quaint Swedish phrasing."

Lassiter waited.

"But you, Mr. Lassiter, as you say, you value me for my other talents. Will you be so kind, Herr Lassiter, as to tell me what it is that you came to tell me?"

"We believe," said Lassiter, "that the Moses Revelation will be in our possession soon. We need you to be ready to use it, at the appointed Time and in the appointed Place, the Washington Monument in DC."

"Very good. I am ready to perform my part. And may I ask about these siblings. They are the Twins? You believe so?"

"Yes. Not only are they siblings, as Da Silva predicted, but they both have powers. These two young people are the Twins."

"Excellent. So, when we have the scroll, we will be ready to proceed."

"Indeed," said Lassiter.

"But now, Mr. Lassiter, what of my other skills? You wish to discuss these as well, nicht wahr? Is it not so? You have me on tenterhooks," said Svensson.

It felt good to let his guard down occasionally, speak a few phrases of his father's native German. Svensson had wonderful boyhood memories. Growing up in Sweden hearing his father's glorious wartime reminiscences, going with his father to the secret meetings of former SS officers, the singing of Nazi songs. Great days indeed.

The meals were placed before them, drinks poured, and their napkins laid across their laps.

"Yes, these tenterhooks," Svensson prattled for the waitress's benefit, "I noticed English speakers would occasionally speak of them. They sounded most uncomfortable, so I looked them up. Do you know, they are the little hooks on a wooden frame that was used to hang out bleached cloth to dry?"

The waitress disappeared.

"But," said Svensson when she had gone, "the hooks we used for the enemies of the Junta in Argentina, and which the Castro brothers still use on their opponents in Cuba, these were hooks of a different nature. And not only hooks. The Mullahs were, as you say, most appreciative of my refinements. The Shah's secret police were amateurs. But the Ayatollah's men? Artistes. This, at any rate, is what I witnessed at the Evin Prison in Teheran. I believe the inmates would have agreed, if any of them survived." Svensson sighed. "Ach yes, I rather liked those fellows at Evin, very conscientious. Very thorough."

Svensson returned from these reminiscences.

"And these other talents, how do you wish me to use them?"

"Well, there will be a tidying up process..."

"Come, come, Herr Lassiter. Honesty, remember?"

"All right. We want you to kill any unnecessary witnesses, starting with your team." Svensson grinned even more broadly.

"There now, Herr Lassiter. That wasn't so hard was it?"

The Vatican Dungeons, Rome, 1168

The prisoner groaned and stirred, his movements hampered by the heavy chains on his neck, wrists and ankles. His filthy rags barely covered his skeletal frame. His hair was white and wispy, his beard reached to his waist. His windowless prison stank. Rusty iron rings were embedded in the dark rock walls every few feet, the floor, covered with rotting straw, was home to warring tribes of rats that fought viciously for the scraps of food flung at the prisoner by the guards.

The cell, thirty feet long and twelve feet deep, had one heavy oak door. Its iron grill opened occasionally and a priest would look in at the prisoner. The chamber was designed to take a dozen inmates, it often held two or even three times as many when the Holy Father was feeling particularly zealous.

But now this prisoner, a heretic handed over to the Papal inquisitors by the local Tuscan Bishop, was alone. His reputation had preceded him. He had been detained several times in the past but had either eluded his captors or talked his way past his guards. That smooth tongue was scheduled to be torn out, just as soon as he had confessed his sins and, an important detail, revealed to the eternally cash-strapped Pontiff the hiding place of his hoard of gold.

After all wasn't this heretic a secret Jew from the land of the demon Musulmen? Hiding in plain sight, pretending to be a true son of the church, changing his infidel name to Leonardo Da Silva? The impertinence!

He would pay dearly, but first his gold had to be handed over so the Lord's work could proceed apace.

The prisoner lifted his head at the sound of heavy boots approaching his cell door.

"Well, Leonardo, old boy," he said to himself, "time, I think, to see if you can talk your way out of this one."

He opened his eyes. The right one a deep brown, the left a milky white with a misshapen cat-slit pupil.

CHAPTER TEN

30TH SEPTEMBER & 1ST OCTOBER

AARON STERN

1.

Oomph!" I said. "Aieee!" I added. These cries were accompanied by whistling and rushing as I flew through the air. Again.

Wolfgang was having a field day. It was another episode in the Wolfgang Holst Comedy Hour, with Special Guest Victim Aaron Stern. My mind was all over the place, not on the business at hand – or head, or feet or fists. And I was paying the price.

All I could think about was Mishi.

I didn't care about Wolfgang, and my growing collection of bruises.

"Come on, Krimm Puff," said Wolfgang, doing his bad imitation of Arnold Schwarzenegger. "I kenn do ziss oll day!"

"Zo kenn I, mein freund," Ronnie Stern what a laugh! I was on all fours. "Had enough?" I panted. "Fists sore yet?"

He picked me up by my collar and pants, and threw me like a pillow across the room.

"It is simple, Herr Stern. You are not getting out of here until you fight back. You will not take your pretty Katie for a soda. Until you fight back. Or talk with your friends and family. Until you fight back. Or bathe your wounds and recover from your injuries…"

"OK, OK, I get it. Until I fight back," I panted. I was sitting back on my ankles, my arms hanging loosely by my sides.

"And you will not be in a position to rescue your precious sister, if you are lying in a bed groaning and complaining that the Horrible Wolfgang was mean to you. You know, I think you don't care for Mishi at all. A real man would be desperate to get out of here and go and find her. But what does the Cream Puff do? He makes with the jokes, and lets the Big Bad Wolfgang huff and puff, and throw him around, without lifting a finger to defend himself."

Maybe this was not the oldest trick in the book but close enough. And you know what? It worked.

Because he was right. Assuming I lived, I would stay here, sailing through the air and crashing into the walls and floor for hours. Hours that Mishi was in the hands of her captors. The picture of Mishi, scared and vulnerable, drove the fatigue and pain away.

Wolfgang was a few feet away and sauntering in for another attack. I came up like a rocket, threw my arms around his waist and had him on the floor.

He twisted to one side, loosening my grip. He was up in an instant, leaving me on the floor holding nothing. His arm snaked around my neck and he hoisted me right off the floor. I used the momentum to keep my legs swinging up and out, and, at the top of my arc, my feet touched the ceiling and my head was pointing toward the floor, I straightened my body.

Wolfgang was tipped backward with the force of my swing. His grip on my neck loosened, I clamped a hand on each of his shoulders and I pushed straight down off the ceiling with my feet. That and my body weight drove him to the floor.

I broke my own impact with a forward roll. Wolfgang was not so lucky. He was lying prone, his arms and legs spread-eagled.

I was on my feet immediately ready for him to come at me again, but he wasn't going anywhere.

"Vell done, Mr. Stern," he wheezed. "I did not zee zet vun komink."

"Yeah, well neither did I. Can I go now."

"Yes, you can," he said. I helped him up. Carefully.

2.

Next stop was the meditation room. Katie and I sat opposite each other cross-legged on the bamboo floor mat, counting long slow breaths, and letting our minds settle. Well, her mind might have been settling fit to bust, but mine was dancing around, refusing to do any settling at all.

The mind stilling stuff was generally pretty good. And, with a bit of practice, I could go to places inside myself that were calm and invigorating, and come out refreshed and energized. (As long as no one had buried me alive, that is.)

But that was before my sister went missing.

And before the beating Wolfgang had just handed to me, on top of all the other beatings I'd been getting lately.

The fact that Katie was the guru was also a distraction.

After a time I cracked open one eye. Katie was sitting, calm and beautiful. Her blonde hair tied back in the usual ponytail, a few stray strands framing her oval face. Her mouth was closed and she breathed easily through that perfect straight nose.

Suddenly I couldn't take it any more.

My skin began to burn and my scalp prickled and I could feel my heart speed up. What was I doing here? I couldn't sit around while Mishi was who knows where, in the hands of who knows who.

I had a plan to devise, a manuscript to steal, and a sister to rescue; and this wasn't getting me any closer to any of that.

"Katie, pssst, Katie!" I didn't know why I was whispering. There was no one to overhear me, except Katie, and I *wanted* her to hear me. That was, you know, the reason I was speaking.

She slowly opened her eyes, and took a moment to focus.

"Katie," I said, "this isn't working. Not today anyway. I can't concentrate, or find inner peace, or become one with the universe, or whatever, not today. Not with Mishi, you know."

When I ran out of steam she said: "Ronnie, this is the exact time to try. It's always easy when it's easy. When it's hard, that's when the real work is done."

"That didn't come out of a fortune cookie did it?"

"No, Ronnie, it came out of personal experience. Things only stick if you practice them when they're hard. It's hard for you now, and, believe me or don't, it's hard for me as well. I hate that Mishi is in danger, and I hate that it's tearing you apart, and that I can't just mount my trusty steed and go and get her for you. But believe me, this will help when the time comes to tear those bastards limb from limb."

So much for becoming one with the Universe.

"OK I believe you but I can't sit here and do nothing. I have to..."

"You have to go and find Melvin, and together you're going to cook up a hare-brained scheme to find Mishi and rescue her."

"Katie Liebovitz, how could you possibly..."

"Because I know you. And I know Melvin. You'll think about it for a while on your own. You'll get nowhere, tying yourself in knots. And finally you'll go to him and together you'll come up with something insane, or rather he will, and you'll be swept along.

"All I can say," she continued, "is don't. This isn't like putting frogs in the school swimming pool, or adding glue to Madison Strasser's hair mousse, or pretending to be Ron Williams' long lost uncle to get him out of a Math test, or forging Street O'Hare's grandfather's Will so he'd think he'd inherited the old house on 13th Street or..."

"All right, OK, there's a pattern here isn't there?"

"A pattern? This isn't a pattern, this is the pants, jacket and waistcoat, with a tie and handkerchief thrown in, and the shoes polished. Look, Aaron, seriously, these guys, who have Mishi, aren't high school students, they occupy a different universe. They're very bad guys, and you need to let Dr. Califario, and Mordecai, and Wolfgang..."

"And you?"

"Yes, Ronnie, and me. Let us deal with them, and get Mishi back. We're actually quite good at this sort of thing."

"This sort of thing? You mean this has happened before?"

"More often that you'd believe. This battle has been going on for a very long time.

For millennia actually."

"So, no one ever wins?"

"Oh, we win, and then they do. That's why it goes on for so long. You should read more history. Evil can never defeat the Good, and the Good can never quite eradicate Evil."

"Why not? Wouldn't the eradication of Evil be, you know, cool?"

"Realistically? It's not going to happen. And, besides, without the temptation to evil, people wouldn't know how to be good."

"You mean 'when it's hard, that's when the real work is done'?"

"I couldn't have put it better myself."

"And just so I'm clear," I said, "the Elders under the leadership of the good Dr. Califario, and his golden knights of justice, including one Katie Liebovitz of Beverly Hills, California, will ride off to rescue Mishi and do battle for Truth, Justice and the American Way. And Aaron Stern and Melvin Shnayvise can rest easy in the comforting knowledge that we don't have to lift a finger?"

"More or less."

"I don't like it Katie, I really don't."

She reached forward, took my hand, and looked at me with a warmth that turned me inside out. I loved her more then, I think, than I ever had. She was beautiful, calm, wise, and confident that I could sit on the sidelines while she and Dr. Califario and the others, found and rescued Mishi and stopped whatever hijinks The Organization was cooking up.

She went back to meditating.

While I replayed over and over my plan to go get Melvin.

MISHI STERN

I must have nodded off again because I woke up with Sappy Portland grabbing a fist full of my hair and yanking my head up. She held her face about an inch from mine. Her smirk was getting really old.

"Mishi, we are getting close to the witching hour. Your precious brother has his orders and he's jumping."

"Is he asking how high on the way up?" I said. "I thought I'd join in the California All Stars Cliché Competition. Any minute you'll be wearing a black hat and twirling your moustache. Hey, I know, what about tying me to a railroad track?"

She spat in my face. Can you believe that! The spit ran down my cheek and curled under my chin. I tucked my chin in to wipe it off on my shirt. Look, no hands!

"Wow," I said, "I didn't see that coming. I was trying to get under your skin a little. But I kinda struck gold."

"You, Miss Stern," I wondered how she could speak with her teeth gritted like that, "are going to... It will be my greatest pleasure to..."

See, we were getting on so well. Building rapport. Any minute we'd be plaiting each other's hair.

"Miss Portland," Singh called her over before we could start our comfy girl chat, you know, like how she'd flay me alive, or inject me with something to melt my brain, "we are leaving for the east coast soon."

Good, I thought, fewer scumbags to watch Mishi.

There was more to needling Her Highness than being an annoying brat. My mind powers had been coming back.

But the signals I was getting were hazy. I picked up excitement and a sense of anticipation that whatever they were planning was going to happen soon.

And I got some pictures of Ronnie. This was very not good! Somehow Ronnie and all his jumping when they said to was a key part of the plot. I just hoped that the big idiot had enough sense to stay the hell away and let Dr. Califario and Mordecai do their thing.

Them I had confidence in. Ronnie? Not so much.

So I was trying to make la femme Portland angry, to put her off guard. I could get into the other guys' heads better, Snell especially, if I stayed calm.

So I was giving her the full Mishi treatment. If I could get her angry, and, let's face it, needling people was my super power, she'd let down her guard. I hoped.

AARON STERN

1.

It was the birds that did it for me in the end.

Mordecai dropped me at home after training. It was dark and as we approached the house I could see a police cruiser parked in the drive. Maybe the police were finally sitting up and taking an interest. I went inside. There were two boys in blue with Mom and Dad in the sitting room.

They called me in and I sat on the couch next to Dad. They asked me question after question about Mishi and the party and where I was going and what time this was and where this and that had happened. And then they asked the same questions, in different order and with different wording. And then they did it all over again.

My head began to hurt, and my voice sounded flat and bored even to me. Then I remembered what we were talking about, Mishi, and I refocused.

It was good that the cops were taking it seriously. And it was also frightening that they were taking it seriously.

Finally they finished with me, and went back to Mom and Dad, and spoke into their crackling radios, and dealt with different officers that were coming and going, doing the things we've all seen on TV in cop dramas every night for years. If only they could find and rescue Mishi in the forty-seven minutes, plus ad breaks, that it takes Castle and Bones and NCIS to figure it all out and dispense justice.

I slipped out and went upstairs to my room and lay down. I wanted to sleep but every time I closed my eyes I could see a picture of Mishi, terrified and alone.

So I switched to thinking about the scroll. Where was it? Mordecai had been talking about moving it about. That didn't seem promising. I might figure out the location, and find it was gone when I got there. Wherever the heck 'there' was.

After a while even Mishi's face couldn't keep me awake, and I was just dropping off, when I remembered the birds. I sat bolt upright.

I leapt from the bed and went straight to the computer and googled up strange bird behavior in LA. There were 3,142,891 hits, but the third one down was the *LA Times* reporting on birds circling over the Griffith Park Observatory. Bingo. I looked at the date of the article. It was five years ago. Not Bingo.

I went to the next entry. Same story but at LACMA, the LA County Museum of Art. This was three years ago. Better.

The next reference was to the phenomenon at the Hammer Museum in Westwood. (Not actually museum of hammers. Apparently it was a museum of art and design and stuff founded by a guy called Armand Hammer.) But that was a year ago.

The final entry was from the *Malibu Times*, from a week ago. Some resident in the Malibu area had written in that they had seen birds circling the Getty Villa. Perhaps it was time to get up close and personal with the Getty Villa, thinks I. Who doesn't need to expand their cultural horizons?

I ran downstairs past Mom and Dad and a cop who was still there. I shouted that I had to go out somewhere to do some stuff. I grabbed my keys and scooted out the front door. I jumped in the car and pulled up a map of the route and drove off toward Malibu. It was about twenty miles and took me nearly an hour even in light evening traffic.

I got there about 11 pm and turned off the Pacific Coast Highway onto Getty Villa Drive.

I drove as far as I could before I got to locked gates. There wasn't anyone around. I got out of the car and went to the gates. I could see illuminated paths and gardens that stretched away up the hill toward a large building with columns and balconies. It was dark and I couldn't see it very well from where I was.

I stood still, holding the cool metal of the gates. And then I heard it. Or rather, them. Birds, lots of them, flying, calling out to each other, roosting in the tall pencil pines. Just birds, right? But somehow I knew, I could feel it, without a doubt, that the Moses Revelation was in that building. And I was going to get it.

There was only one more thing to do now.

2.

I got on the phone to Melvin.

"Ah, amigo mio," said Melvin, "mein freund, mon ami, to what do I owe the limitless pleasure of this late night phone call? Especially since I've hardly seen you for the past few days. Now, I'll readily admit that I do not, like the comely Miss Liebovitz, curve in and out in all the right places, but we are supposed to be best friends."

"Look Melvin," I said, "I'm sorry, but there's a lot that's been going on."

"So now you ring, after all the excitement is over? Or are we still in the middle of this 'a lot that's going on'? Could it be that Ronnie wants something from his pal?"

"When you put it that way..."

"I may be dumb," said Melvin, "but I'm not an idiot. I can tell there's something up. You and Katie all cuddly-wuddly one minute, then the next a little piece of Antarctica blows in to LA. And not a word from either of you to me, Melvin Shnayvise, by all repute a friend to both of you." He went all sing-song, "you're keeping secrets from me."

"I'm hurt that you would think so."

"Great! My job is done! Now tell me what you want."

"Melv..."

"Aaron Stern, I can read you like a book. And by this time you should have a fair idea about me too. If it's a plot, a plan, a scheme, then Melvin's your man. Spill."

"OK, since you put it like that."

"I do."

"It isn't such a huge deal. I just need you to help me break into the Getty Villa at Malibu, locate an ancient scroll of immense power and value, and having located it, to steal it."

"Oh good. I thought you were going to ask something tough. Are you nuts!"

"Melvin," I dropped the banter, "I really, really need this, and I really, really need you to help. Cause you're the El Supremo of computer and electronics whizzerie, and this place is bound to have a ton of security."

"You think?"

"And first I need you to help me make a couple of copies of this thing and smuggle one into the Villa with us."

"While we make off with the original?"

"Kind of. At this point you're going to have to trust me and not ask too many questions. Believe it or not, lives are at stake. One in particular. But I can't tell you any more. Are you in?"

"Silly boy. You had me at 'Hi Melvin, will you commit several felonies with no real explanation beyond helping out a pal'."

"You're the best."

"You only just figured this out?" he said. "OK, so first I'll do one of those secret internet searchie thingies and come up with a way into the Villa, and how to bypass the security on the scroll. I'll get back to you."

MISHI STERN

Got it! A head picture from Charlie Chan. He was over near the SUV, out of earshot, speaking in low tones to Miss Personality. I let my mind drift over to them. I got a clearish picture of the tête-à-tête between Sally the Homicidal Nurse, and Fu Manchu, the Emperor ofEvil.

Her mind was like steel, no getting in there. But his was another story. I found cracks and edges I could slide between.

I felt a mix of words and images. And I could read them. Years of practice, and some very focused training from Dr. Califario.

They were using me to threaten Mom and Ronnie, and to get Ronnie to get the scroll for them. This scroll was incredibly important to them. There was more. Ronnie was important as well. No killing Ronnie when they got what they wanted. That was a hugerelief.

They needed Ronnie for more dirty work. And me too! I was a piece of their puzzle too. Ronnie and I were to be kept safe. Phew!

But I couldn't get why. That bit wasn't clear.

At least we had some time up our sleeves.

But then I realized, my mouth-breather brother Ronnie, who couldn't pour piss from a boot if the instructions were printed on the heel, was meant to keep these freaks happy by pulling off the theft of the millennium. He had to find, acquire and deliver this scroll.

My breathing got a lot tighter.

AARON STERN

1.

Melvin and I parked at the Villa and made our way to the entrance. It was about 10 in the morning, right on opening time. I noticed the birds flying around and around above us, settling in the trees and then flying off again to join the swirling mass over the museum.

We paid for a ticket each, and began a slow wander around the exhibits. They were quite impressive. Or would have been if I hadn't been anxious to find one exhibit in particular.

"It's nice to see how billionaires use their well-gotten gains," said Melvin. "All that lovely Getty oil, warming the houses of the poor, and the cars of the rich, and fueling the prosperity of a grateful nation."

He was walking like the Duke of Edinburgh, you know, Mr. Queen Elizabeth, his hands behind him, peering at one exhibit, stopping to examine another.

I was in a sweat to find the Moses Revelation, but Melvin was all, 'Hey, look at this', and 'Wow, look at that'. Like we had all the time in the world.

We went through a maze of rooms full of old sculptures with missing bits and pieces, arms and noses and, some, well, you know, I think the Missus would be a little disappointed on the wedding night.

And we finally came to a special exhibits area. Next to the entrance was a pull-up cloth sign swaying gently as people walked by with 'Manuscripts of the Ancient World' emblazoned across it. It had an image of a scroll wrapped in purple cloth embroidered in gold, like the torah scrolls that are carried around in synagogue.

When you read a Torah scroll you have to run your finger along as you read, so you don't skip a word or line. But you're not allowed to touch the parchment, so you use a pointer that has a small carved hand at one end, with an extended index finger.

When I thought of the things I'd seen in my visions I wondered if this synagogue tradition was more than just respect for the Torah. Was it a holdover from the real deal, when touching the scroll would get you zapped into the next world? If you weren't the anointed king of Israel, that is.

I grabbed Melvin's arm and propelled him past the sign and into the exhibition.

The room was large with wood paneled walls and a high, ornately carved ceiling. Display cabinets and information posters stretched over frames were spaced around the walls. In the exact center of the room was a long waist-high display case.

A dozen people were in there, including two bored guards, one seated at the entrance, and the other at a far doorway. They didn't look like they were expecting to foil an insanely stupid, but thrilling, heist of a valuable artifact.

A few people were leaning over the glass top of the central display, looking down at a partly unrolled parchment with columns of writing covering its surface. An ornate blue velvet cloth with gold embroidery was carefully arranged next to it.

A young woman with straight brown hair and glasses was examining a cardboard information note. I sidled up next to her, and started reading.

Ancient Judaea; 1st Century AD; ink on parchment.

This unique scroll is written in a mix of demotic Egyptian script of the Early New Kingdom (circa 1600–1400 BC); Hebrew of the 1st century AD; and a yet undeciphered script thought to be a pre-hieroglyphic Egyptian.

It appears to be a copy made in Palestine/Judaea at the time of the rebellion against Rome in 70 AD. The contents are a mix of incantations, prayers, and exhortations, as well as arcane instruction in the mysteries of the God referred to as El Elyon, God the Most High.

On loan to the Getty Villa, through the generosity of the Ben Zvi Foundation for Antiquarian Studies, of Rehovot, Israel.

I was looking at the Hidden Teachings of Moshe Rabbenu. The Secret Revelation of Moses. Or at least, if my vision was to be believed, one of the seven copies made by those dudes sitting around the table in Yavneh with

Yohanan Ben Zakkai.

The Ben Zvi Foundation? Mordecai! (Sherlock Stern, that's me.) Mordecai must be using this Foundation to move the scroll around from this Museum to that Art Gallery. Using the security measures of the gallery to protect it. And the fact that they were hidden in plain sight would allay the unwanted curiosity of prying eyes. Clever.

I stood there, looking down at the scroll, lost in thought, when the familiar blackness and stretched out feeling began to sweep over me.

Oh for God's sake, I thought, not again.

2.

The Eighth Vision

I was getting sick of this, but at least I was getting some interesting insights into the life of the Moses Revelation. Like it was trying to tell someone its story, and I was elected.

I was on a boat on a flat wide ocean, I could see a coast a few miles away and we were moving pretty fast with the wind filling a large sail rigged crosswise to the length of the ship. The deck was covered in coiled ropes, barrels, stacked crates with live chickens and goats, and lots of other sailory stuff which this landlubber didn't understand.

There were men moving back and forth like they knew what they were doing, moving cargo, climbing rope ladders up the mast, and calling out to the helmsman, who was at the back of the ship on a raised platform.

Sitting between two piles of crates was a small man with dark skin and a sharp narrow nose. He was dressed in a long brown robe, gathered at the waist with a threadbare cloth belt. A white shawl covered his head and he was rocking back and forth with his eyes closed and his hands held out palms upwards in front of him. He was, I realized, praying.

The guy looked familiar. And, I recognized the words of his prayer from my Hebrew School days. Same phrases I remembered from synagogue. Thanks, Rabbi Elbaz. Interesting, the consistency, and the fact that a bored teenager in twenty-first century LA used the same liturgy as this scruffy dude in... Now when was this?

I couldn't tell from what I was looking at, and I certainly didn't know enough naval history to place the design of the ship.

Then one of the sailors turned to the man.

"Hey Jew! Add a prayer for me while you're at it."

The Jew broke off from his prayers. "Most assuredly, my friend. You are Caius Legatus, are you not? A native of Neapolis?"

"You have a good memory, Jew. And you are Ovadyah Ben Ahaz, traveling with your wife, your children, and your kin. You are like an entire tribe on the move."

Both men laughed.

"Yes, we are on the move," said the Jew. "I fear that it is not a good time to be in Judaea. The recent rebellion is over, but the authorities keep a watchful eye, and a heavy hand, on the people. Those that survived the slaughter and the slave markets."

The sailor looked sober now. "Yes, a bad business. I had friends in Judaea. Some, God rest their souls, were trapped in Jerusalem." He shuddered. "They were followers of the teacher Iesus Christos, as am I. Some were caught up in the fighting. A very bad business. Still I'm glad you were able to get away, with your family."

"Yes, a miracle," said the Jew, looking thoughtful. "And now we journey to a strange land, to start a new life. Rome first, then further north. After that?" he shrugged his shoulders. "Who knows. It is the Lord of All who guides our steps."

"Well, I wish you all the best of good fortune. And, I meant it, say a prayer for Caius Legatus of Neapolis, and his family and comrades."

"I will my friend," said Ovadyah Ben Ahaz.

The sailor nodded and moved off.

Ben Ahaz reached for a leather satchel that was by his side. He opened it. Inside was a cylindrical bundle wrapped in cloth. He held his hand an inch or so away from it. I heard a snap and crackle and felt the metallic taste of charged air on my tongue. Ben Ahaz withdrew his hand and retied the cords around the satchel.

And everything went black.

3.

When I came to I was being hustled out of the Getty Villa by Melvin who was waving and shooing concerned guards and fellow visitors away.

"No, no," he was saying, "happens all the time, ha ha." He mimed drinking with his free hand, and rolled his eyes meaningfully. "A bit of fresh air, a walk around the block. He'll be right as rain. No, no, he's OK, really, thanks, you're too kind."

We made it out into the sunshine, and we walked up and down the colonnaded porch. I began to feel better and Melvin shepherded me to the car.

We got in and he drove me home.

When we got to my room I lay down on the bed. Melvin drew up a chair.

"OK, buddy boy," he said, "what was that all about? This isn't some strange tropical disease you've picked up in the day or two you've been off the radar, is it? Ebola? No, your innards would be liquefying by now. Malaria? Possible, but its more fevers and sweats than dead faints. A stroke? You're a bit young for that. So, my money is on this Mystery, which, in a mysteriously mysterious way, you have shrouded in such mysteriosity. Am I making myself clear? Or am I being too mysterious?"

"No, I get it," I said. "My brain has not, in fact, liquefied. I do get it. And yes, this is part of the secret wrapped in an enigma, shrouded in, as you say, a mystery."

"OK Mr. Wizard, time, I think, to draw back the green curtain and reveal all."

He sat back and crossed his legs, clasped his hands over one knee, and raised one eyebrow.

"Well, that scroll we saw in the Villa," I started. "You remember the one. The one I was looking at when I blacked out."

"Yes, I remember the one, it's the scroll that's in the locked glass cabinet. In the middle of the room, that's in the middle of the Villa. The Villa with lots of gates and doors, all with big locks. The scroll that you have to pass through other rooms to get to, all with security cameras, in that glass cabinet you'd have to open, or smash, no doubt setting off alarms from here to Bratislava, in that room, have I said this bit already, which has security cameras. Oh, yes, in the Villa which has armed guards in attendance. Yes, I saw that scroll. What about it?"

"That's the one we're going to take."

"Waddya mean 'we', Paleface?" he said. "Just kidding, Ronster, I'm in. You are the Lone Ranger, and I, Kemosabe, am your Tonto. After all, what could possibly go wrong? Two high school seniors with no prior knowledge of burglary waltz in, take the scroll, and waltz right out. Simple!"

"You forgot the bit where we copy it."

"Twice."

"Yeah, twice. And put one copy back."

"Yes. What was I thinking? That makes it so much easier."

"I don't mean to rush you. And don't think I'm not thoroughly enjoying this hilarious banter, but do you have any actual, you know, constructive suggestions?"

"I thought you'd never ask."

And then Melvin did what Melvin does. He outlined in detail the steps to be taken over the next few hours to get the job done, including him looking after the electronics and computing, while I bought velvet and gold thread and a glue gun from a local fabric store. How'd he even know such stores existed?

We headed off on our separate errands to get the supplies and two hours later we rendezvoused back at my house with a whole slew of electronics and other high tech doodads (Melvin), and cloth and thread, and parchmenty paper, scissors and specialist ink for the printer (me).

After another hour or two, and lots of false starts, with Melvin tootling away at my desk with wire, a soldering iron, pliers and snips, and me searching the internet for ancient Hebrew and Egyptian fonts and drawing programs and printing options, and measuring and cutting velvet and using the glue gun on the gold thread, we had what we wanted: two copies of the artifact that one of us (Melvin) thought were just peachy and would do the trick to perfection; and the other one (me) thought would not fool a blind three-year-old in a dark room for more than three seconds. But the copies were the best we could do in the time we had, and after a while they started to grow on me too.

While I had been busy with my fourth grade craft project, Melvin had produced an astonishing array of technical wizardry, suitable for today's gentleman cat-burglar, or at least a desperate teenager trying his hand at high tech theft for the first time.

"OK," said Melvin, "so follow me closely, Amigo Mio. This," he said, pointing to a computer screen full of codes and lines and colored boxes, "is the security array of the Getty Villa. Sophisticated, yes, but not state of the art. Which is a bit of a lucky break for us, no?" Seeing my blank face, he went on, "we will use our access to this code to jam the cameras before we go in. The system is designed with a back up in case of power failure or some other glitch so then we do this." Melvin played with the keyboard and another similar page of meaningless (to me) computer stuff popped up. "This is to override the override. They have no third back up. Careless of them, so we'll have until a technician is called out to fix the problem. If they're quick and have someone on speed dial, who lives close and jumps in his car immediately, we'll have about half an hour. So we should plan for that amount of time."

I nodded, finally something I understood.

"Now," Melvin continued, "once we've disabled the electronic security we'll have to get past locked doors, make our way unerringly down several corridors which we walked down today."

"In broad daylight," I said, "with helpful guards to point the way, and with a map. And we still got lost."

Melvin was smiling and nodding like I'd rolled over on command. I felt like a good boy.

"Precisely. So I've got these," and he pointed to two baseball caps with lights fixed to the peak, and to two pairs of sunglasses with wiring dangling from them. "These are laser lights connected to night vision goggles with a little extra something that I've added, a link to a GPS system to give us instant information on our position, giving us second by second lateral spatial and locational feedback."

He looked at me grinning, eyebrows raised expectantly. I just stared back.

"They'll tell us how to get to the scroll."

"Oh, good," I said, keen to join in somewhere, "and the locks? You know, on the doors, and the glass cabinet?"

"Ronnie, Ronnie, Ronnie, Ronnie, have a little faith in Wise Old Uncle Melvin, genetic product of generations of shifty, shyster Shnayvises. We've spent the last thousand years successfully fleeing Goyim who decided they hated their Jews more than they loved the prosperity, scholarship, and intellectual brilliance that we brought with us. And you think a lock or two will stymie us? Silly boy!"

He then pointed to the desk. On it was what looked like an oversized cell phone with wires, a keypad and a screen. Next to it was a set of lock picks. "The plans for the Villa are available to the conscientious hacker from the City Building Code archives, and the records of the lock supplier I got after a little squirreling around, and this is the result."

"Melvin you are..."

"The greatest loss to high end theft the world has ever known?"

"I couldn't have put it better myself."

"Aaron Isaac Stern, let's go steal a priceless artifact from its impregnable location!"

"Melvin David Shnayvise, from your mouth toGod's ear."

The Vatican Dungeons, Rome, 1168

"Israel ibn Ibrahim, falsely known as Leonardo Da Silva," the inquisitor read from a sheet of parchment. He was a sallow-skinned, pale man in his early thirties, his eyes sunk into darkened sockets, his head half in the shadow of the black cowl of his monk's robe. He sat at an ornate oak desk, its legs shaped into spirals, its panels carved with scenes from the journey of Joseph into Egyptian slavery, its surface completely clear of any object, except the pages from which he read.

"You are hereby indicted on the following charges: Item, consorting with forces of darkness, to whit, one incarnation of the Prince of Darkness known by his satanic name, Baphomet; Item, summoning up from the depths of Hell demonic forces to whit..." The Inquisitor droned through the charges. If he were reading out his washerwoman's laundry lists he couldn't have shown less interest.

Da Silva sat on a low three-legged stool, his hands and legs chained, his stringy beard falling to his knees. The small room, its windows shuttered against the Roman sun, was stiflingly hot. It was, Da Silva could not help thinking, doing a good job of imitating the antechamber of Hell, and it held a foretaste of his ultimate punishment.

Two meaty soldiers, standing a few feet behind Da Silva, guarded the only exit, their faces set like stone. Their swords and halberds gleamed, the edges honed razor sharp.

The reading of the charges went on for an eternity. Da Silva nodded off several times and woke with a snort as he was about to tumble from his perch.

"...Item, seducing several young virgins of the village of Ponte a Moriano, to whit, one Francesca Diveroli, one Laura Angelica, one Lizabetta..."

Da Silva perked up at this. How had they found all this out? Perhaps it was one of the members of his coven. The fat Baptista Ranieri, or the local butcher, Frederico di Maggio, that sly rat.

Or his servant Geminio. He had fled from the approaching inquisitors at Da Silva's insistence, carrying off his greatest treasures, in hopeful anticipation of his master's triumphant return.

His reverie was interrupted.

"How do you plead?" said the Inquisitor, still looking down at his notes.

"Oh," he said, "Your Worship, these charges are the trumped up ravings of jealous..."

"Silence!" shouted the Inquisitor. "How dare you question the integrity of the Holy Office of the Faith!"

"No, your Worship, of course, I would never..."

"Excellent," said the Inquisitor, he picked up a quill and dipped it in ink. "I hereby record that the prisoner has of his own free will pleaded guilty to all charges."

CHAPTER ELEVEN

1ST OCTOBER

PROFESSOR OLAF SVENSSON

1.

Olaf Svensson, warmly admired Professor of Medieval History at Cardozo College, generous supporter of murderous regimes, and Organization operative, was in a good mood.

The Da Silva manuscript was yielding long-hidden secrets about when and how to bring about an apocalypse. And the plans to bring this apocalypse about were well advanced. Svensson felt a glow of satisfaction.

"Mr. Plensk," he called out from his small private office, "come here please, I should like a word with you."

Jeremy Plensk sidled past Singleton and Blakely, and sat down on the other side of Svensson's desk. It was, he noticed, clear of the usual papers, pens, paper clips and the other accumulations of a working office.

"Shut the door please," said Svensson.

Plensk reached over and gave the door a push. It swung into position and the latch clicked shut.

"Our project is nearing completion, Mr. Plensk, and it is time to wrap things up."

Plensk nodded.

"But I would like to talk of the future, rather than the past."

Plensk remained silent.

"You have certain qualities which I admire, and feel would be useful on a continuing basis for other collaborations."

"What other collaborations?"

"We can discuss them in detail in due course, but there is one that is going to happen in the next half hour or so."

"And what does it entail?"

"There is going to be a tragic fire at the Benjamin Cardozo College buildings. Specifically in the Medieval Research Center. Unfortunately all the recent research on the Da Silva manuscript will disappear in the conflagration. And even worse two promising young research assistants will be unable to make their way to safety and will succumb to the flames."

"And this is the first 'collaboration'?"

"Mr. Plensk, it is. Are you in, or are you out?"

Plensk laughed. He looked through the clear glass divider into the main room. Sean Singleton and Mary Blakely, on the last day of their lives, were intent on their computer screens. "I'm in. I never liked those two anyway."

He looked back at Svensson. "When do we start?"

Svensson smiled. He released his grip on the silenced pistol strapped under his desk.

"Immediately."

2.

About thirty minutes later Svensson and Plensk walked down the ornate stairs of Cardozo College and out into the Brooklyn streets. They carried a suitcase each, filled with papers, computer disks and a printed copy of Da Silva's *Maleficium.*

Plensk couldn't resist a glance up over his shoulder to see the first tendrils of smoke beginning to curl out of the second floor window. Soon the alarms would kick in, and the sprinkler system, and the fire brigades would race through the streets. But it would be too late for Singleton and Blakely.

Svensson and Plensk made their way to a parking garage and deposited the cases in the trunk of Svensson's car, driven into Brooklyn today just for this purpose.

They went to a nearby café and Svensson made a fuss over the waitress's pretty eyes.

She would remember the nice old man with the angry looking student.

"In my experience of these things," said Svensson, "the television police dramas are far too flattering to the actual day-to-day workings of the authorities. The timeline of poor Blakely and Singleton's demise will be muddy and unclear. And also the drugs which they ingested with their coffee are almost undetectable."

"Almost?"

"You have to know what to look for. And you have to have a reason to look. In other words, you have to suspect the kindly old Swedish Professor, whom everybody speaks well of, and his efficient but brittle research assistant, with no prior criminal record, neither of whom have a discernible motive, and who happened to be discussing their research over coffee away from the bustle of the college."

"And if all of these unlikely events actually happened," said Plensk.

"Well, our final option is to disappear. As Svensson and Plensk, and reappear somewhere, less inquisitive."

"You've done this before?"

Svensson's eyes hardened.

"Mr. Plensk, you will learn quickly that there are some topics it is much safer for you to avoid. The fire brigade will discover two bodies in that awful fire. But it is not too late for a third."

Plensk swallowed.

"OK, got it. No trips down memory lane."

"No, indeed, Mr. Plensk." Svensson was all smiles again. "Looking forward into a bright future is a much healthier option. After we have dealt with the college and fire authorities our future involves a drive to Washington DC to get the next phase of things underway."

They heard the rapid approach of a fire engine. Svensson crumpled his napkin and pushed back his chair. "That, I believe, is our cue."

KATIE LIEBOVITZ

Katie sat in an armchair, her hands resting gently in her lap. Her eyes were closed. Her head moved slowly from side to side and up and down, like she was searching for something, or for someone.

Mordecai sat nearby, watching her. They were in the Migdal sitting room. Mordecai had a glass of hot tea on a side table. An unlit cigarette twirled in his fingers.

After about half an hour Katie opened her eyes.

"Anything?" he asked.

"Something," she said, "not much, but something. A direction. South. Definitely South. And not far. We're not talking Mexico here. Or even San Diego. Definitely in or near LA."

"This is good progress. Yes?"

"Yes, absolutely. Much more than yesterday. It's like something has cleared, a fog or a mist. Like Mishi was hidden by something, and now there are a few cracks of light."

"So Mishi is somewhere south of us, but not so far as San Diego. San Clemente? Newport Beach?"

Katie thought for a while. Then she closed her eyes again and relaxed.

Mordecai watched.

The hands on the clock crept around. The tea, untouched next to Mordecai's right elbow, continued to cool.

Katie opened her eyes. "Not San Clemente, or Newport. If I were forced to decide I'd say here, in Longbeach."

"Longbeach? That is close. If we shout she might hear us. And this power to locate people, this is getting stronger for you?"

"Yes," she sounded doubtful. "In a way."

"In a way? What does this mean, 'in a way'?"

"Mishi is sharper, that fog or blanket that was over her is clearing. But I'm getting interference from another direction."

"I'm afraid Katie you will have to take pity on a dull-witted old man. I have my own gifts, but they do not include locational sensitivity. What is it that is happening? What is this source of interference?"

"I'm sorry, Mordecai," said Katie, rubbing her face with both hands, "this is new for me as well. I'm getting Ronnie, instead of Mishi. As well as Mishi.

I don't know."

"The intriguing Mr. Stern? Your quarry for all these years."

"Yeah, him," she sounded glum. "I don't know how, but when I try to focus on Mishi, and it's hard enough with this blocking cloud, but when I get close, then Ronnie appears. And he's somewhere else altogether. I have Mishi and Ronnie, both in my head, it makes it hard to focus on either."

"You are saying that he is appearing on your radar? Without you consciously turning your attention to him?"

"Yes, it's like punching in the address on your GPS, and you only get about a third of the directions to where you want to go, and you get other directions to somewhere else as well."

"This, it sounds disconcerting."

"'Frustrating' is the word I'd pick. Totally annoying actually, and it's draining my energy as well. I don't know how to handle it. It's new. Up to now, today, I could put my mind on someone. Someone I loved, or hated. It didn't matter which, I just had to have strong feelings about them."

Mordecai nodded.

"And I would know immediately and clearly where they were. And how they were feeling. Sometimes I even see what they are seeing. That part can be very disorienting, that's why I usually do it sitting in a chair somewhere safe. Not moving about, you know."

"Perhaps... How can I put this tactfully? Perhaps, you care more for the brother than the sister? This is perhaps why she is not so clear? And he jumps in uninvited."

"Oh, don't worry, I have feelings for Mishi. And she has feelings about me. She can't stand me. I'm the spoilt Jewish Princess who has stolen her precious brother from her. She wouldn't admit it in a thousand years, but she worships the ground Ronnie walks on. And she'd rather die than show that anyone has any power over her. That's why she's always so rude to him. But Ronnie, in his dumb, wonderful way, if he lifts his little finger, looks at her, calls her name, she can hardly think straight. Then it's all 'Hey, dumbass' and 'Get lost, Loser,' just to cover up."

"And you?"

"Me, she hates. I'm the evil witch that has charmed her precious brother." She couldn't keep the bitterness out of her voice.

"Yes, but what do *you* think of *her*? What do you think of this little minx of a sister, who thinks these oh so hurtful thoughts about you?"

"Let's just say," Katie smiled to herself, "that I shouldn't be having any trouble locating Michelle Stern. And it's not because I love her. Is that honest enough?"

"Yes," said Mordecai, "you paint a picture which is clarity itself."

"But," Katie sighed, "she's *not* clear. And Ronnie keeps jumping into my head uninvited."

"And this, as you say, is new."

"And this, as I say, is new."

"Well, we must roll with the punches, is this the saying? We must accept this and not fight it. If I were to be asked, I would say that your Ronnie, and his spirited little sister are linked somehow. You try to locate one, and the other appears. Locating one locates the other, no? We must keep trying to locate the young girl. She is our focus here. But Mr. Stern, your Ronnie, is the special bonus, is he not? So tell me Katie, where is Mr. Stern now?"

"Well that's the funny thing. He seems to be on his way to Malibu. What's in Malibu?"

"What indeed," said Mordecai. "Katie will you excuse me for the briefest of moments? I have to have a word with the esteemed Dr. Califario."

AARON STERN

1.

Melvin perched forward in the driver's seat. He gripped the steering wheel like it was going to make a break for it. The car jerked and swerved, mostly in the direction of Malibu. For a techno-geek genius, he drove like he'd just arrived from Patagonia – do they have cars there? – anyway from somewhere where they've read about cars, but have never, you know, actually driven one.

Navigating? That was my job. Down to the Palisades Beach Road, follow that for a few miles, hang a right past the Fleishman Theater, and up another road to the Villa.

Except we sailed right passed the Fleischman, 'cause by then Melvin and I were arguing about when to put on our balaclavas. I was worried if we put them on too early, and someone saw us, and we looked like burglars, they'd call the cops; he worried about putting them on too late, and our faces would be picked up by the security cameras before he could disable them.

So, slick and professional, we missed the turn off.

Then we had to find somewhere to turn around, and when we did we were so nervous about missing the turn off again we turned too early, into Coastline Drive, and then it took more time to figure that out, turn around again, and get onto the right street for the Villa.

And then my phone vibrated.

It was a text from the wack jobs who'd taken Mishi. It said: '3 hrs left. Union Station 1 am.' I just stared at the screen.

The car wove its way up the hill toward the Villa.

We arrived. Melvin braked. And the phone flew out of my hand, bounced off the dash, and landed in Melvin's lap.

"Who's this from?" he said, reading the text, "the guys we're giving our ill-gotten gains to?"

"Yes, except for the 'we' part, Tonto."

"Ah, so, 'we' do all this dirty work together. And then 'we' get ready to go to meet the bad guys. And one of us, me, all fresh-faced and innocent, thinks this is still a team effort, 'cause, like, we're partners, or so he, that's me, thinks. But the other partner, you, is already planning to give him, and by him, I mean me, the slip, and go alone to meet the danger, in whose face he laughs, or at least smirks. And this is because he, you, thinks his eager partner, me, needs to be protected, and can't be trusted to deal with the villains. Is that about the size of it?"

"Ah yep," I said, "that's about the size of it."

"OK," said Melvin.

"OK?" I said.

"Yes, OK."

"Is that 'OK, we now understand each other, and, like in the movies, you'll try to talk me into letting you come along'? Or 'OK, I get what you're planning, and I totally agree with your wisdom and concern for my safety, and I, Melvin, also totally agree to leave it to you, Ronnie, to deal with the bad guys on your own.'"

"Yep," said Melvin, "the second one, the one where I jump ship, and leave you in the lurch. To go it alone. Without me. That one."

"You do?" I said. This definitely wasn't how it went in the movies. He was supposed to protest and beg to come along. I was, I confess, a bit miffed. What sort of friend was this, who wouldn't try to talk me out of talking him out of tagging along into the jaws of death?

"But," Melvin continued, "it's not as bad as it sounds. I will be with you in spirit.

And technologically."

"Explain."

"I will wire you up the wazoo, and will track your every move, and will have the cops, the FBI, the Bilderberg Group, the Illuminati, and the Girl Guides on speed dial, in case of emergency. I believe this to be a much better deployment of my mind-blowing skills than wandering into the hands of dangerous kidnappers, who might decide to work their mischief on the heir to the Shnayvise fortune."

"Good plan," I said, I was impressed. It was a good plan. "Now let's go and commit that felony."

"You got it, Buddy!"

2.

Melvin and I were parked on a tree-lined drive. We couldn't see the Villa behind a gentle curve in the road, but its lights and the birds gave it away.

We got out of the car and went around to the trunk together. We gathered up all our paraphernalia. Realized we had no free hands to put on our balaclavas. Put everything back in the trunk. Got our balaclavas on. Then tried to find the eyeholes so we could pick up all our gear again. With the eyeholes, like, in front of our eyes, we bent into the trunk simultaneously. After saying 'Ouch' and rubbing our heads we adjusted our co-ordination.

Incredibly I had thought to create a checklist, and even more incredibly, we had everything on it.

Then we staggered through the dark, lugging the electronic equipment between us, to our first port of call, a junction box, half way up the slope to the Villa.

This was where the Melvin Magic was to begin. He got the junction box door open, peeled back some of the insulation on the wires, and connected the thing that looked like a big cell phone with some alligator clips.

Then he tapped away for a while at the keypad.

"There," he said, with an air of triumph.

"Where?" I said.

"We've turned off the power to the security system."

"Wow," I said, "I didn't know we could do that."

"When I said 'we'," he said, in his worship-me-now-and-avoid-the-Christmas-rush voice, "it was a rhetorical flourish. What I meant was *I* have turned off the power to the security system. Ooh! There's the back up generator. Right on cue."

I could hear the faint purr of an engine coming to life. It sounded like it was a long way off, coming from the other side of the Villa.

"OK," said Melvin. "Round Two."

He bent over the gizmo again and started typing. It was very impressive. His thumbs flew over the keys and he swiped the screen left and right, up and down until, after a few minutes, the noise of the generator died away.

"How did you do that? I mean, isn't the whole point of a generator that it's off the grid?"

"Fuel pump," he said.

"That's a little terse. I get each individual word, but I'll need a few more sprinkled around to derive some meaning."

"The generator needs fuel. The fuel flows from a tank through a pipe to the generator. And it does this because the hamsters running around in that wheelie thingy on the side of their cage are powered by electricity."

Melvin's condescension could be a one-man cause of worldwide anti-Semitism.

"So you turned the power off to the fuel pump?"

"Yes, I did," warm friendly grin. Pogrom averted. "And we have about half an hour to get the goods."

"OK," I said, "let's go."

Melvin put away his contraption, and a pile of other equipment, zipped it into a duffel, and we trotted back to the car and put it back in the trunk. This made going back up to the Villa a lot quicker.

We arrived at a side door to the Villa, which Melvin had marked out as our entry point. He got to work with the lock picks and more electronic thingummies and silently eased the door open.

We padded in carefully. The museum was in total darkness, so we slipped on our laser hats and night vision glasses.

In the distance we could hear someone speaking. It was one end of an angry phone call.

"That's our guard rousing the emergency electrician," I whispered.

"Brilliant, Miss Marple," Melvin just couldn't help himself.

We made our way through a few hallways and up a flight of stairs. It was definitely easier with the glasses, the map and GPS, but we still made a few wrong turns and came to the manuscript display room with about twenty minutes left on the clock.

We switched on LED pencil flashlights.

I went straight over to the display case housing the scroll. And it wasn't there.

I stood looking at the empty case for what seemed a century when Melvin who had been putting our gizmos and museum maps away, came up next to me.

"Bummer," he said.

"Yes, as you point out with your usual pinpoint accuracy and grasp of the obvious: 'Bummer'."

"OK, let's see..." Melvin fiddled with his smart phone, "I'll search the Villa security procedures and see what they do with this farshtunkeneh thing at night."

I was only half listening. Melvin had his computers and smart phones.

I had me.

And the Moses Revelation. Over the last few weeks I had a growing sense that it had been calling me. Those visions, they can't have been random. If that scroll wanted me to find it then it had better get busy and tell me where it was. And quickly.

I closed my eyes and held my hands down by my sides away from my body, palms turned forward like receiving antennae. Feeling the energy flow in the room. I turned slowly in a full circle.

There! My hands and fingers tingled. I could feel a pulse of power washing over me. I stopped and opened my eyes. In the light of the pencil flashlight I was looking at a large information panel, attached to the wall, detailing the techniques scribes used to select goose feathers, trim them and how they mixed lamp soot with gum Arabic to make the ink. I'd read it on our day visit.

I walked forward, still feeling the tingling and the energy flow.

"Melvin?"

"Just a sec, nearly there."

"Melvin."

"What?"

"It's here."

"It's where. What do you mean?" He came up to me.

"It's behind that panel."

"OK Svengali. How do you know this? A little birdie told you when my back was turned?"

"I'll explain later." I was already working my fingers around the edge of the panel. "Can we get on with this?"

The panel was about three feet high and two feet wide. And it was about an inch deep. It was hinged to the wall down its left hand side. It took me a few moments to find a small circular catch on the bottom of the frame. It yielded to pressure. There was a click and the panel swung out. I let the flashlight play over the paneled wall.

There was a door set flush to the wall with an old-fashioned brass outlined keyhole. It was about the same size as the panel, about a yard high by two feet wide.

"Can you..." I started to say.

Melvin patted my cheek. "Uncle Melvin is here to take care of all your safe cracking needs." He sorted through his lock picks, held his own flashlight in his mouth, and got to work.

I rummaged in my bag and took out one of my copies of the Revelation. I also took out some heavy leather gloves and a foil-lined chiller bag. Everything I knew about this scroll shouted 'Handle With Care!'

After an agonizing minute or two Melvin got the wall door open, revealing a space a eighteen inches deep with three wooden shelves. There were various items on the top and bottom but on the center shelf, alone, was the Moses Revelation, lying on its blue and gold velvet wrapping, in a glass box.

Of course, Museum staff had to be able to move the scroll without being blown to smithereens.

There was no time to waste now. I had the gloves on and the chiller bag open. I took the glass box off the shelf, and put it on the floor. I lifted the lid and scooped the real scroll out of the box with my gloved hand, put it in the chiller bag, and replaced it with our copy. Then I closed the lid, hoisted the box and put it back on the shelf.

Melvin closed and locked the door, and we clicked the information panel into place.

And that's when the lights came back on.

"Oops," said Melvin.

"Oops is right, Melvo," I said. "Let's get out of here."

3.

We did a last eyeball of the room. No evidence of any crime. Except for two balaclava-clad miscreants fully laden with break-in equipment, carrying off a priceless manuscript. Exiting stage left seemed on the whole to be the smart move.

"Security cameras?" I asked.

"We've got about five minutes. The lights come on first, the cameras have to be reactivated manually," said Melvin.

"OK," I said, "this way," and we moved at a fast trot down one corridor after another, toward the flight of stairs leading down to our side door.

When we got near the stairs we heard footsteps coming up. We looked at each other, then we did that comical left and right search for somewhere to hide. We ducked into the closest display room.

The footsteps came to the top of the stairs and stopped. I peeked out and saw a guard with his back to me looking into the room opposite. He was making his way down the corridor doing a security check. I supposed he wasn't expecting to find anything so his search wasn't exactly thorough. We retreated further into our hidey-hole and crouched behind a display cabinet. We remained frozen. The footsteps approached the entrance, stopped for a moment, then they moved on.

We were out from behind the cabinet and at the doorway in seconds. We stopped and checked each way. The guard was rounding a corner to our left. We headed to the right, to the stairs.

We were half way down when Melvin kicked his equipment bag. The clang sounded to us like the Getty Villa Big Brass Marching Band was tuning up.

We froze, listening. Nothing.

We moved again, as fast as we could go with Melvin holding his bag awkwardly away from his body. We'd already used three precious minutes until camera time.

We made it to the side entrance, and slipped out. The grounds were illuminated now. And those cameras were stretching and yawning, swinging their feet out of their little camera beds, and getting ready to get back to work.

A hedge lined the side path of the Villa. We crouched and ran with the foliage to our right and the Villa to our left. Anyone looking would see us against the hedge. I spotted a gap, turned and grabbed Melvin, took his bag in one hand and shoved him through the opening with the other. I tossed both bags over the hedge to him. He caught the first one, and the second one flattened him.

I pushed through, disentangled Melvin and the bags, and helped him to his feet.

Then we moved fast, now with the low bushes between us and the building. We got most of the way down the slope to the street where we had parked, when we heard an approaching car. The headlights began to play on the hedge next to us as it came up the drive.

We ducked down and played Ronnie and Melvin statues.

I peeked out through a thinner part of the foliage.

No way! It was Mordecai's car. He wasn't exactly speeding, but he wasn't out for a leisurely evening drive either.

"Mordecai," I whispered to myself.

"Who's Mordecai?" said Melvin.

In books and films the hero draws all sorts of plot advancing conclusions from these events.

Aha! Thinks our hero, 'So Mordecai has somehow discovered our cunning plan to steal the scroll, and he has jumped into his car to thwart us, but he is seconds too late! Let's get out of here.'

Me? Not so much. I looked at the rear of the car heading up the hill, and thought: What's Mordecai doing here? It was only later I found out. And by then a lot more had happened that moved it down my list of priorities.

"Add that to the growing list of things I'll tell you later," I said.

We headed away from the Villa to our car.

KATIE LIEBOVITZ AND MORDECAI BEN ZVI

1.

"We are here," said Mordecai to Katie. They parked at the front entrance. Not a place where cars were usually allowed. But this was not a usual night.

Earlier that evening, when Katie had detected Aaron's movement toward the Villa, Mordecai, as the fictional hero of Aaron's imagination would no doubt have inferred, understood that the Moses Revelation was the target.

There was no other reason for Aaron to be heading that way, at that time of night. Time to get out there and see what was what.

After a brief word with Dr. Califario, Mordecai had roused Katie from her meditative state, collected his car from the basement, and had driven as fast as LA traffic would allow.

At the Villa Mordecai flipped up the cover on a concealed keypad beside the entrance door. He punched in a number and the door clicked open.

"After you, my dear," said Mordecai.

Katie went in and found herself in a lighted entrance hall. It was large and beautifully proportioned as befitted the former home of one of the wealthiest men in the world. The walls were a rich dark wood, and the floor a geometric pattern of colored marble. The information counter, shut now, was on the left. Tastefully designed signage pointed down different corridors toward a range of permanent and temporary exhibitions. In other circumstances Katie would have been interested.

Mordecai led the way toward a broad staircase. They climbed to the next level, walked swiftly down another corridor and through several more rooms. Katie glimpsed masses of beautiful and intriguing items.

They came to yet another display room and Katie saw the banner announcing ancient manuscripts. The penny was beginning to drop, but she said nothing. Mordecai would tell her what they were doing here when he was ready.

The display cabinets were empty and a guard was standing self-consciously in the center of the room.

"Good evening, Mr. Ben Zvi," he said.

"Good evening Roger," said Mordecai. He indicated Katie, "this is my assistant Miss Delgado."

"Pleased to meet you Miss Delgado," said Roger. Katie nodded politely.

"Anything to report?"

"Just an electrical glitch," said Roger. "We had everything back up in about half an hour. We've done a search. No one here who shouldn't be, and nothing missing. This is the last room to be checked, we were waiting for you."

"Shall we?" Mordecai asked.

Roger hesitated, he looked meaningfully at Katie.

"Oh, don't worry about Miss Delgado, she is privy to all my little secrets. Well, ha ha, perhaps I exaggerate. Not *all* my secrets, but this one, about the manuscripts, yes, she knows."

Katie arranged her face to look competent and knowing and secretarial.

Roger moved to one of the information panels, pressed a catch on the bottom edge and it swung out. He then took a large ring of keys from his belt, selected a small one and inserted it into a keyhole in the wood paneling. A part of the wall swung open, and Roger stood aside.

Katie could see shelves covered in wrapped bundles. By itself on the middle shelf, in a clear glass container, lay one scroll lying on a blue velvet cloth embroidered in gold.

Mordecai approached the wall cabinet.

He sorted through the objects on the top and the bottom shelf, unwrapping a small corner of each one. Then he looked at the scroll on the center shelf. He pulled a pair of thick gloves from the inner pocket of his jacket and slipped them on. He took hold of the glass box, carried it to the central display case and put it down carefully. He opened the lid and touched the scroll lying on its cloth with a gloved finger. Then he removed the glove and touched the scroll with a bare finger. And he laughed.

"Something wrong?" said the guard.

"No, Roger, not at all," Mordecai sounded vastly amused. "No indeed. Everything is exactly as it should be."

He slipped off the other glove, closed the glass box, and indicated to Roger to put the box back and lock everything up.

"Come, Miss Delgado, we are no longer needed here."

2.

They were silent on the first half of the drive back to the Migdal. Finally Katie had to ask.

"What were we doing there? What has the Getty Villa got to do with anything?"

"You must understand Miss Liebovitz, Katie, that there are some things I cannot divulge to you. But what I can say is that tonight your young man staged a daring heist of a priceless ancient treasure."

"A heist? Ronnie?"

"Yes, your Ronnie has shown a talent for grand theft, a flair for getting in and out of a secure building, and making off with one of its most valuable exhibits."

"Is that why we went to the Villa?" she said, "to try and stop him?"

"Yes," said Mordecai, "and no."

"Look, sorry, I don't get any of this. Tell me the yes bit and then the no bit. Start at the beginning and tell me what's going on. And why aren't you upset or something? How come you're smiling? If Ronnie has committed a crime, that's serious."

"I apologize Katie for my levity, but without, as I say, being able to explain everything I can assure you that your young man has not taken to a life of crime. What he took tonight is important. Important in itself, and important in the greater scheme with which Dr. Califario is concerned. Your Ronnie certainly caught me by surprise."

"But not Dr. Califario."

"Not, as you surmise, Dr. Califario."

"He didn't want us to stop Ronnie?"

"Correct. He merely wanted us to confirm the scroll had gone and to make sure the museum didn't institute a search."

"And this thing that Ronnie stole, this scroll. Look, I know about the Moses Revelation, we all do, but you and Dr. Califario, you keep pretty close about it."

"You know it is powerful," said Mordecai, "written by Moses himself prior to the flight from Egypt, in an ancient demotic Egyptian and Hebrew and some of it, so I am told, in languages yet to be deciphered."

"So you are told?"

"Yes, it is a work vastly beyond the poor abilities of your humble driver."

"But I don't understand why you and Dr. Califario aren't upset about this."

Mordecai was silent for a few moments as he made a left turn across traffic at a set of lights.

"Perhaps, at this point I can ask you to defer your questions. We are nearly there and Dr. Califario is without doubt the best person to fill in these blanks."

Katie's self-calming techniques were working overtime tonight.

3.

"You were right," said Mordecai, when they were ushered into Dr. Califario's study. "Congratulations. I did not, I must confess, see this one coming."

"Yes, well, now that he has the scroll we need to keep an even sharper eye on developments," said Dr. Califario, who was in his chair behind his desk. "Miss Liebovitz have you got any clarity on the location of the Sterns?"

"A general sense of direction," Katie replied. She had seated herself on the old sofa. "Mishi is somewhere near Longbeach. I think. Not far from here, but the signals are patchy and weak. Ronnie is also somewhere nearby but now it's like... It's hard to describe. Like looking at someone standing between you and a bright light. You can see the outline but the details are obscured."

"Interesting," said Dr. Califario, "that will, without doubt be the work of the Moses Revelation. It shows he still has it. Which is good."

"Can you tell me," Katie said tentatively, "is he safe? Will he be OK?"

"Miss Liebovitz, I will not sugar coat this. I do not know whether your Aaron is safe, nor do I know whether he will emerge from this event unscathed. I also do not know whether his sister Mishi, who is in the hands of ruthless and pitiless people, will come through unharmed."

Katie clasped her hands tightly.

"But, what I can say is that the Sterns have gifts, powers, that even they do not understand. Already we have seen Aaron grow and develop in a remarkable way, and at a remarkable speed. You have seen this for yourself. His ability to access inner energy."

"Yes," said Katie in a small voice.

"In addition, and this is important, there is a universal confluence coming, a gathering of cosmic forces. These forces are moving us, and it would be foolish in the extreme to attempt to resist that flow. Harnessing the energies and running with them is the only way to win through."

"And the Sterns?" Mordecai prompted. He was standing behind Katie, his hands on the back of the sofa. "What of them? How do they fit in with all of this?"

"Our information, not unlike your signals Miss Liebovitz, has been patchy. What we can deduce is that the Organization is planning a dramatic coup. It will happen in the next few days. We believe it will be somewhere in DC. We know that they wanted the Moses Revelation to complete whatever it is they are doing. The Sterns' role? This is not clear yet. They have certainly been used to acquire the scroll."

"And when they have got it in their hands?" Mordecai interrupted. "What then for the Sterns?"

"Well, there you have me," said Dr. Califario, rocking back on his chair, "I don't know. The possibilities range from bad to disastrous. Either their usefulness will beat an end."

"Or?" said Katie.

"Or they are needed for some element of the final event."

"So they will keep them safe?" there was a hopeful note in Katie's voice.

"For the time being. After they have fulfilled their role I fear the worst."

"Well," said Mordecai, "I'm glad you warned us about the sugar coating."

"Unrealistic optimism is not at this stage helpful," said Califario crisply. "You can see Miss Liebovitz why we would be very much in your debt, if you could bend your will to locating them. This would render our task of keeping them safe so much the easier."

AARON STERN AND MELVIN SHNAYVISE

"OK, Ronnie my boy, that should just about do it." Melvin checked the micro-wires taped to my back, and made a few adjustments to his computer.

We were at Melvin's house, in his room. The Shnayvise clan were in bed. On arrival we had opened the front door carefully and tip-toed along the hallway in the dark.

"OK, will you tell me what it does," I said. "I feel I have a right to know. I mean these are seriously bad guys and I don't want them to find this on me and, you know, get testy."

On the drive I had told Melvin about Mishi's abduction. A look had flashed across his face that scared the crap out of me. Melvin had two younger sisters, Hannah and Sadie, and he would have cut off his right arm, and every other appendage, for them. He got back to his normal bantery self, but I could tell he was mad.

"My brilliance," he was now saying, between clicks of the computer, and checks of the gizmo stuck to my back, "will once again save the day, and you as well my friend. And Mishi. This stuff can't be seen. Molds to your body. Very hi-tech. And the wires are only a few microns thick. It can't carry a very strong signal, but if I'm within a few hundred yards of you I can locate your exact position."

"And this helps how exactly?"

"Well, Oh You of Moderate Intelligence, *you* go with your copy of the scroll, whose mystery is only exceeded by its power. You hand it to the bad men. They hand over Mishi. You leave, they leave. Birds sing, ribbons unfurl, flowers sway in the breeze, unicorns gallop away, and pigs fly."

"And your point is?"

"If," he said, "and I repeat, if. You heard me say 'if'?"

"Yes, I heard you say 'if'."

"So, right, if these evil, untrustworthy, child-abducting ne'er-do-wells, decide – are you sitting down for this? – to act dishonestly and not deliver Mishi, or not to let you go, or break faith in a hundred other ways. If, as I say this happens, then..."

"Then you can follow me from a safe distance?"

"You know, you're smarter than you look."

"Yeah, I get that a lot."

"Really? People say that?"

"No, actually they don't. Come on, buddy, let's do this thing."

Melvin snagged his Mom's car keys. We padded back down the hallway, went out the front door. I got into my car, Melvin jumped in his Mom's beige Volvo station wagon and we headed in convoy to Union Station.

CHAPTER TWELVE

2ND OCTOBER

MISHI STERN

I'd spent the last hour battling with the image of a whole bunch of FedEx guys lined up on the path to our front door delivering bloody pieces of me to Mom and Dad. This definitely did not help me get my mind-reading power back under control.

But now, with the breathing, stillness, and presence exercises, I settled down again and I was able to gently send out feelers. I was too weak, at the moment, to do much with the Aussie guy, the Asian man and the battle-ax Poisoner. So I decided to concentrate on Mr. Snell. He was a total wuss. He was over in a corner sitting at a foldout card table, drinking coffee and jumping every time someone walked by.

I concentrated, and worked on getting him to stand up and offer coffee to the others.

They told him to sit down and shut up, and not interrupt them again.

I could feel his fear. I won't pretend I didn't gloat.

Now that I could get him to do stuff, what exactly did I want him to do? Short answer was fight off the baddies, cut me free, throw me over his saddle and ride off into the sunset. Something like that.

But somehow my imagination didn't run to a picture of a dumpy, hairy, nervous high school teacher doing all that hero stuff.

What about a cell phone? Maybe he had one, and I could send a message. I got down to business.

JEREMY PLENSK

Plensk and Svensson arrived in DC in the early hours of the evening and drove to a three-story house in Georgetown. It was dark by the time they arrived but the streetlights illuminated red brick walls and black and white painted shutters and woodwork, with an iron railing painted glossy black. It was an old colonial. Thomas Jefferson would have looked right at home walking out of the front door for an evening stroll with Sally Hemmings on his arm.

Svensson knocked. A stocky man with thick black curly hair, and eyebrows to match opened the door. His eyes were dark and his mouth set. Plensk was not tall but he had a couple of inches on this guy. He was dressed as an undertaker, black suit, black shoes, white shirt, black tie. If someone hadn't died yet he looked like he'd be happy to correct the error.

Svensson entered carrying his battered leather briefcase. Plensk followed wrestling with two overnight bags.

In Brooklyn Plensk had accepted Svensson's offer, and had become an accessory to murder. Since then Svensson had used him as a messenger boy. Plensk's duties ran to buying toiletries and other supplies for a getaway.

Then they had set off for DC in Svensson's car.

"Good evening, good evening, Georgiakis," said Svensson to the doorman. "How goes it with you and all our fine friends?"

A brief grunt and Georgiakis resumed his cigar store Indian routine. Svensson sailed past smiling while Plensk struggled after him into the high narrow hallway.

Svensson led the way up a set of wooden stairs, which squeaked and cracked as they climbed up. Plensk was breathing hard when they reached the next floor. They turned along a corridor leading toward curtained windows at the front of the house overlooking the entrance. On the right were two doors.

"This is your room," said Svensson, indicating the first door. "And I will be right next to you. Here give me my bag, thank you my dear boy. Drop your bag, settle in, then we will meet downstairs in a few minutes in the living room."

Plensk opened his door. He stepped into the room and looked around. There was a four-poster bed, covered by a white quilt with frilly lace trimmings. Five or six pillows were artfully arranged against a polished oak headboard.

In one corner was an armchair with a flower-printed cloth covering. It had a low round matching footstool. And against one wall was a tall freestanding wooden closet with mirrored doors.

Plensk had no idea how long he was going to be here. And he only had the clothes he was standing in, and the new set in his bag. No need to unpack then.

He dumped his bag turned and left the room.

He went back along the landing, down the creaking stairs and found himself back in the entrance hallway alone. No Georgiakis, no Svensson, no nobody. And no idea where the living room was. He stood looking one way then the other for a moment, then he headed down the hall to the door closest to the front entrance. He'd try each one until he got lucky.

The first room overlooked the street. It was illuminated by the streetlights and it was full of period furniture and display cabinets but no people.

He opened the next door as Svensson let out a chuckle. Plensk went in. He saw Svensson and Georgiakis and two other men. Svensson was seated in a comfortable armchair in his tweed jacket and plaid woolen tie. Seated next to him was a handsome man in his late thirties, neatly dressed in a gray suit. He was wearing a yellow floral patterned tie. Georgiakis was sitting in a deep armchair in a corner by himself, and another man, tall and Asian, dressed in a pale dove gray suit, was standing near a glass-fronted bookcase.

Plensk, in his faded jeans and army coat, for possibly the first time in his life, felt underdressed.

"Come in my dear boy," said Svensson waving a genial arm. He had a drink in one hand. "This is the young man I was telling you about. May I introduce Mr. Jeremy Plensk. A young fellow who, I believe, will go a long way in our humble fraternity."

The men nodded at him.

"Jeremy, may I present to you Mr. Kim Park Singh," he indicated the Asian man near the bookcase. "Nikos Georgiakis you have already met, and here beside me is the brains of the outfit, Mr. Randolph Lassiter."

Plensk nodded to each man in turn. No one offered his hand.

Svensson kept talking, "I have invited Mr. Plensk along because he has shown remarkable insight in deciphering our friend Da Silva's manuscript, and I detected in him a certain lack of commitment to the normal human weaknesses of compassion and rule-following."

"Excellent," said Lassiter, "welcome aboard Mr. Plensk. We have a world-shaking mission before us. It has taken months of meticulous preparation and will reach its apogee in a few days. You will not be allowed to contact anyone under any circumstances until we say so, and you will not be allowed to leave this house until we say so. Do I make myself clear?"

Plensk looked into the cold blue eyes, and knew that his life hung by a thread.

"Understood, Mr. Lassiter."

"Excellent," said Lassiter, all joviality again. "So far Professor Svensson's assessment of you appears to have been accurate. Let's hope it continues. Take a seat please Mr. Plensk."

Plensk looked around. There was a hard wooden upright chair in a corner. It turned out to be as uncomfortable as it looked. He began to wonder if he had made the right choice back in Brooklyn. But then he thought of Singleton and Blakely. Whatever was happening here was better than that.

MISHI STERN

Snell put down his coffee cup, stood up, yawned and stretched. He looked at his watch and took a few steps in my direction.

I'd been waiting hours for this. Singh had disappeared yesterday. Portland had questioned me again, going over the same stuff. The Aussie and another weasely looking dude had just driven off in the SUV. A few of the others were taking a break, sleeping in corners on camp beds.

Now or never.

Easy does it Mr. Snell, just stretching your legs, nice and casual, not heading anywhere in particular, don't catch anyone's eye.

That Stern girl, Mishi, her parents must be worried, should let them know she's OK, she'll be home soon, a quick call or a message, set everyone's minds at ease.

Snell was coming toward me, he reached into his coat pocket for his cell.

"Um," he said, standing in front of my chair, "Ms. Stern, ah, Mishi, your parents."

"Yes Mr. Snell?" I asked.

"They're probably worried."

"I'm sure they are. Do you think we could let them know I'm OK, and I'll be home soon?"

"Ah, yes, yes, that's a good idea. We could use my cell."

"Gee, Mr. Snell, that's very nice of you, my hands are tied up here, could you hold it so I can dial the number?"

"Dial the number, Oh yes, yes, I see, of course, yes, of course."

He got up the message app, and held the cell under my index finger. I dialed Dr. Califario: 'Mishi alive longbeach? moses revela...'

"What the hell do you think you're doing," Portland screamed from the other side of the warehouse.

I pressed 'Send'.

AARON STERN

I arrived at Union Station at about 11.15. It's a big Art Deco pile with a long waiting room, like a large concert hall, lined with armchairs. I was early for the exchange, the Moses Revelation for Mishi.

My stomach was doing a polka and my hands were clammy.

I'd wrapped the genuine scroll in its velvet and gold cover in a beach towel, and I'd put the whole bundle in a plastic Safeways shopping bag. The fake scroll was next to it in my backpack.

I went straight to the checked baggage desk. I took out the Safeways bag with the real manuscript and handed it to the clerk. I took the reclaim ticket, shouldered my backpack with the fake scroll and wandered over to wait in one of the armchairs.

The minutes crept by. I was just thinking of reporting the clock to the maintenance section when a train pulled in and a million travelers from somewhere far away came streaming through, wheeling brightly colored hard-shell suitcases, carrying tired children clutching soft toys, and everyone talking on their cell phones. The noise was tremendous.

My mind had drifted off so I nearly sprained my neck when a voice in front of me said: "Aaron Stern. We meet again. This is a real pleasure, for me at least."

The Krazy Killer from Kangarooland was back in my life. I stood and looked at the stocky man with the craggy face and thick brown hair and cold eyes.

"Now where are my manners?" he was still talking, "we weren't properly introduced last time. You can call me McInnes."

There, in front of me, large as life and twice as ugly was the Aussie mental case. But no Mishi as far as the eye could see.

I knew everything had gone wrong.

DR. AMADEUS CALIFARIO AND MIRIAM STERN

Miriam Stern sat opposite Dr. Califario in his study. She looked down at her hands clasped in her lap. The evening sun had set long before. The corner lamp was on. Califario, dressed in his tweed suit, placed his cell phone on the desk.

"Miriam," he said, "you know we will find her. Katie is working on it unceasingly. She is our best hope. Her powers of location are extraordinary. She and Mordecai are even now working on a strong lead."

"Amadeus, I know," said Miriam, "but I can't just sit here and treat this like another riddle to be solved, or a plan to be devised. I'm not a machine."

"I know that," said Dr. Califario, "and that's why I asked you to come. I received a text from Mishi a few hours ago."

"Oh God," said Miriam, "what did she say? How did she get a phone?"

Dr. Califario showed Miriam the text.

"'Longbeach'?" said Miriam. "She's nearby. 'Moses revela', she was cut off mid-word."

"Yes, we know that she is alive, she was capable of sending a message. She somehow got her hands on a phone. She is in Longbeach, and the Revelation is a key element of the situation. These are the things we now know."

"Can we tell where the cell is?" Miriam said. "Does it have a GPS device?"

"We will see," said Dr. Califario. "It will take a little time, but we have people trying to track down the location now. Triangulating the cell towers. I wanted you to see that action is being taken. And also I wanted to keep an eye on you."

"So I don't do anything foolish? Like attempting to rescue my daughter?"

"Precisely."

"And Ronnie?"

"He is another kettle of fish entirely. He is a surprising young man Miriam. You know that already. But as one who has observed his progress over the past few weeks, I can honestly say that I've never seen anything like it. Do you know that he defeated Wolfgang several times? Wolfgang is most impressed. Not wholly happy, but deeply impressed."

"Aaron didn't tell me."

"Well, no, and that's another thing. He's a typical young fellow. Full of bounce and push, but he keeps certain of his cards very close to his chest. He can keep a secret. After all he kept his healing power from us for years. Now he has begun to develop more powers."

"Yes," said Miriam, "his visions. Mortimer told me a little."

"Precisely. Mostly they concern the Moses Revelation and its history. Dunkeldorfer has been debriefing him. What he has been able to relate has filled in a lot of gaps in our knowledge of the manuscript, its creation, and its power, and the journey across the world of the copies made in Yavneh."

"How does this relate to Mishi?"

"Miriam, your son's training has built his confidence in himself and his powers. Now he has plans to rescue her."

Miriam sat back in her chair, her eyes wide, her hands gripping the armrests.

Dr. Califario continued before she could speak. "During their last session he told Katie he was planning something. She is as anxious as you, of course, and she had some clear pictures of Aaron and a friend. Melvin?"

Miriam Stern nodded.

"And they are devising something. We are not clear what."

"We have to stop them. He can't. He'll get hurt."

"Miriam, now is the time for you to trust in everything we have been talking about for years, everything we have worked for, everything that we know, everything our predecessors carefully passed down to us. 'There is a tide in the affairs of men...' And this is one of those. All the signs are here. And I tell you, this scheme of your son's, this apparently foolhardy venture. It is part of a larger plan. Trust me on this. You know this is my 'talent'. This is why I sit on this side of the desk."

"But, he is just a boy."

"No," Dr. Califario's voice was gentle, "he is a man. If you, we, let him do this, he may grow into quite a formidable one. If we stop him you will be proved correct. He will be a boy. That tide I spoke of. It isn't just for the world, and for peace and truth, and all the grand things. It is also for us, for him, for the players in the drama. He has to do this. Perhaps it sounds pompous, but you might say it is his destiny. Believe me, Miriam, both Mishi and Aaron have a role here that is presently beyond our scope, beyond our means, to know precisely, but I can assure you, all the signs point to a major cataclysm which only they can prevent."

"And, what am I, their mother, supposed to do?" she said bitterly, "just sit and wait?"

"Now why would you suppose that? You do have a role, and it is an active one. Do you have black clothing?"

KATIE LIEBOVITZ

Katie and Mordecai raced north along the One Ten. They sailed past the Walt Disney Concert Hall, which was lit up turning the silver metal finish to bronze.

"Turn right at the Hollywood Freeway," she said.

Mordecai took the off ramp and passed under North Grande, then jinked left up another on-ramp.

"Here, here!" Katie shouted. "Take this one!"

Horns blared as Mordecai veered across toward the West Aliso exit.

"You do not make it easy for an old man," Mordecai grunted.

"Sorry," said Katie. She was in two worlds. She was surrounded by late evening LA traffic. And she could see Ronnie in her mind's eye, feel his presence in her heart.

When her sixth sense was clear it told her the direction to go to find him. All afternoon that clarity had faded out, then come back, then faded again.

The chaotic car ride reflected Katie's struggle to maintain the connection.

She knew they were close. She was looking at a world Mordecai could not enter.

They were coming up to North Los Angeles. "Left here!"

Mordecai ran the lights.

"Right! Turn right here!"

They crossed North Alameida. More angry cars dodged and weaved around them. They looked forward through the windscreen, then at each other and said simultaneously: "Union Station!"

MELVIN SHNAYVISE

A few hundred yards away Melvin sat in his mother's Volvo. He was in the passenger seat so he could flip his laptop open comfortably. A can of soda nestled in one of the many cup holders, and a box of Krispy Kreme donuts sat on the driver's seat.

Melvin was determined to settle once and for all the important philosophical divide between him and Aaron: Was the chocolate custard-filled glazed donut far and away Krispy Kreme's best product? Aaron was a traditionalist and adhered, blindly in Melvin's view, loyally in Aaron's, to the original iced donut.

"Melvin," Aaron would say, donut in hand, "I have simple tastes and simple loyalties."

"No," Melvin had replied, "you are just simple. I, on the other hand, like to live life at the cutting edge of excitement, pushing the boundaries of knowledge. I do my research. I regularly scan the Krispy Kreme website, and make a dash for a handy franchise store when a new flavor comes out."

Aaron had shaken his head sadly. The last such conversation had come to a happy halt (as they all did) when they could no longer speak, their mouths full of their respective favorites.

Melvin made a few more adjustments to the laptop and bit into the baked goodie. He was reaching for a cloth to wipe custard from his keyboard, when the red dot on the screen stopped moving.

OK, he said to himself, Big Dog is in position. He dabbed at the computer. Another spritz of custard landed on his shirt. He took a sip of cola, and waited.

AARON STERN

1.

I couldn't take in what I was seeing.

McInnes, yes; Mishi, no.

I was totally out of my depth. I felt like a stupid naïve kid.

I'd risen from the armchair and now I stood flapping my mouth like a landed fish, waiting for McInnes to say something.

He came right up close. I backed away until my legs hit the chair behind me. He reached out a meaty hand and gripped my shoulder.

I could smell his sweat. Hadn't they heard of deodorant in the Southern Hemisphere?

"Now mate," he said smiling, "let me explain a few things. We don't want to invite attention, do we? So your job is to look happy and relaxed, like we're two old mates talking over old times. And you'll keep looking happy and relaxed no matter what happens. Because if you don't keep looking happy and relaxed, I'll make sure you never look happy and relaxed again as long as you live. Are we clear?"

The power of coherent speech had deserted me. I nodded.

"Smile," he said. There were people milling about, checking their tickets, unzipping side pockets of their bags, shoving things in, pulling things out.

My mouth made a kind of ghoulish rictus. McInnes beamed at me.

"There you go! That wasn't so hard was it?"

"What happens now?" I managed to say. "Where is Mishi?"

"Ronnie, Ronnie, can I call you Ronnie?" He smacked my cheek with his free hand. My cheek stung. "Are you trying to make me angry with stupid questions? Cause I'd strongly advise against it.

"See, what's going to happen now is you're going to hand over that thing you promised to bring, and then we'll take a ride together to see your bitch sister, and the whole time you're going to look...?" He raised his eyebrows and waggled them at me.

"Happy and relaxed?" I said.

He laughed and gave my shoulder a bone-crushing squeeze. "Top marks, Mate. Got it in one. Now the big question is, have you got that thing on you, or do we have to go and get it?"

When I didn't say anything, he gave me a pitying look. "Ronnie, if you try to pull a fast one, I will slit your belly open, pull your guts out with my bare hands, wave them in front of your face, and then strangle you with them. And I'll do the same to your little sister. Hey Ronnie! How come you're not looking happy and relaxed?"

I gave him more of my landed fish look.

"So, where's the scroll?"

I was about to answer when Mordecai walked up to us.

2.

"Aaron my boy, who is your friend?" said Mordecai. He was wearing the cream linen suit, with his panama at a jaunty angle. His brown wingtips gleamed.

Now, if there was a proper etiquette for introducing Mordecai – an eccentric member of a giant conspiracy to guide the world past the rocky shoals of economic and political dangers – to McInnes, a crazed killer from a far off land, then I didn't know it.

The gaping fish act was getting a pretty heavy workout in Union Station that night. The three of us were frozen for a nanosecond. Mordecai stood waiting. McInnes, his hand still gripping my shoulder, was twisted around to see who had interrupted our little tête-à-tête.

Then in one fluid movement McInnes let go of my shoulder, reached under his jacket, and turned. I saw the glint of a metal blade as his hand whipped out toward Mordecai. McInnes pulled his hand back, the blade vanished and a red stain began to spread out over Mordecai's shirtfront.

Mordecai stood still for an instant, the color drained from his face, then he looked down at his bloody chest and staggered. It happened so quickly none of the commuters in the hall seemed to notice anything amiss.

Before Mordecai could fall, McInnes scooped an arm around him, and guided him to an empty armchair.

"There we go, mate," he said loudly, "you've had one too many. Ha, ha. Sleep it off for a bit, eh?"

I took a step forward and reached out to Mordecai. McInnes tried to bat my hand away, but Mordecai's dead weight made the move awkward. My hand came to rest on Mordecai's cheek.

All the pain of the chest wound ran into my fingers, up my hand and along my arm to my heart. Which stopped beating. I sucked in air. My mouth was pulled back and my teeth were bared. I was paralyzed. I saw the whole of Union Station through a blood-red haze.

The last thing I remember was Mordecai looking up at me, his face gray, his eyes calm. And then I fell down a black hole, my body was stretched and twisted, and I lost consciousness.

Vatican Apartments, Rome 1168

Leonardo Da Silva groaned in agony, his body had been burnt, beaten and wracked, and his fingers crushed.

Now he lay on the rotting straw of his cell, awaiting the next bout of torture. There was no real purpose to all of this, except to amuse the inquisitors and entertain the torturers. They had his confession and the location of as much gold as he thought prudent to give up. Now a fiery end, chained to a stake in the central square in front of St Peter's basilica, was the best he could expect.

The sallow-skinned inquisitor had asked about his associates and co-conspirators and Da Silva had named everybody he could think of, starting with Pope Alexander III and Frederick I Barbarossa, the Holy Roman Emperor, and ending with Roberto the Lame who sat at the gates of Lucca begging for a few spare coppers. He was going to add Bobolino, Roberto's one-eyed dog with the yellow teeth and the missing tail, but that might have been going too far.

Now he lay on the filthy straw trying to think of anyone else he could denounce. The Khan of the Mongols? The Emperor of Cathay?

He heard approaching footsteps. A moment later a key was inserted into the lock and the door of his cell opened. Two guards entered and the prisoner flinched as they unchained him from the iron ring embedded in the wall and looped a hand under each armpit. They dragged him out of the cell into the hallway. Da Silva, his head lolling, tried to take in their route but the dark stone corridors, flights of steps up and down, and the final curling ascent to a high tower toward a small iron bound door, defeated him.

One of the guards knocked and opened the door.

They had arrived at a solarium, an airy space at the top of the tower, with views of the Holy City of Rome, the Tiber, and in the far distance, the sun glinting off the sea.

There were two chairs in the hexagonal room, and a small writing desk against one wall between two arched windows framed by carved stone columns. The morning sun illuminated and warmed the room.

The inquisitor stood, looking out of one of the windows, his hands clasped behind his back.

"Leave us," he said turning to face the guards. "Wait outside. I believe I will be safe with this prisoner." It was the first time Da Silva had seen anything resembling a smile crease the monk's lips.

The inquisitor went to one of the chairs next to the writing desk and sat. He indicated the other to Da Silva.

When they were both settled the monk lifted the lid of the desk and withdrew a leather-bound volume with a dark cover tooled with symbols and letters.

He opened the book and read the title: *"Maleficium et Maledictiones Arcanum, Secret Crimes and Curses."*

More symbols, suns, moons and planets, and a detailed etching of a goat-headed man surrounded the title. Hieroglyphs, Hebrew words, Latin, Greek and Arabic incantations and the Lord's Prayer in Aramaic accompanied these symbols.

"You have been busy," said the Inquisitor, the thin smile was back.

"Me?" said Da Silva, all innocence. "I'm sure I don't know what you mean."

"Come, come," said the Inquisitor, "we have the tools of your devilish experiments, we have your servant Geminio, we have your papers, we have your confession, and we have this book. We have enough to roast you in the flames of salvation a hundred times over. If you had a hundred tongues to be torn out of your heretical head it would hardly be enough to expiate the black sins which stain your soul."

"And yet," said Da Silva, "I can't help noticing that the stake and the bundles of wood, the iron calipers and knives are nowhere to be seen. Can I begin to hope that the evil hour has been temporarily delayed?"

"As a true son of the Church I cannot, of course, confirm the outrageous suggestion that the punishment of unbelievers is anything but swift and severe."

"Of course," Da Silva agreed.

"However," the monk continued, "there are one or two minor matters which, for the sake of completeness, it would be good to have cleared up."

"Such as?"

The monk turned a few pages of the *Maleficium*. They were covered with neat lines of text, the margins were full of small but beautifully rendered drawings of dragons, fiery balls, diagrams of strange devices, runes and symbols.

"This book of yours," the monk began.

"Alleged book of mine," said Da Silva.

"Oh it is yours, that at least we know."

"We?"

"Aha, yes, well, let us for the moment assume that this book has been examined by myself only. It is a dangerous work of necromancy. Not to be trusted to those of weaker will."

"Heaven forbid," said Da Silva, "I shudder to think what would happen if less robust souls examined it."

"As you say," the monk nodded, "I have examined this nefarious work, and it is full of the most profound mischief and idolatry. But of course you already know this."

Da Silva fixed the monk with his one good eye, the other milky eye with the cat's slit seemed to look at a world not visible to the common cast of men.

"While we are playing with assumptions," said Da Silva cautiously, "let us say, purely for the sake of discussion, that I had some minor part in the preparation of this innocent volume of children's party tricks and old wives' recipes for country cures, what is it that a 'true son of the church' could possibly want with it? And," Da Silva held up a hand, his voice became firm, "if it so happened that I could be of some small service to this son of the church, what insignificant recompense could I expect to receive?"

A dark shadow passed over the monk's face before it returned to a studied calm.

"You dare to bargain with the Holy Church, Christ's Kingdom on earth, a renegade, a Jew, a magician, a heretic? Oh yes, don't bother to pretend Leonardo Da Silva, or should I say Israel ibn Abraham ibn Yosef, and, what was it you called yourself in Constantinople? Brother Clement of Aleppo. That alone would be enough to condemn you to the cleansing fires of holy retribution."

Da Silva shrugged. Silence appeared to be the best option.

"Let us just say," said the monk, "that some form of collaboration might prove mutually beneficial, to you, and to the Holy Mother Church, of course."

"Of course," said Da Silva, "I am all eagerness to be of assistance to Holy Mother Church."

"Excellent," said the monk placing the *Maleficium* on the angled wooden lectern attached to the desk, and pointing at the first lines of text, "let us begin at the beginning. This passage, 'invoking the powers of darkness and the powers of light', with references to the 'Mountains of Despair west of the City of Incessant Upheaval'. To what does this refer?"

Food was brought and, at one point, a surgeon and an apothecary who ministered to Da Silva's injuries.

Their discussions lasted long into the night.

CHAPTER THIRTEEN

2ND OCTOBER

CONTINUED

KATIE LIEBOVITZ

Twenty minutes before Mordecai had encountered McInnes's knife, he and Katie had slid into a parking spot, jumped out of the car and raced into Union Station's main waiting hall. Their plan had been to locate and observe Ronnie, see whom he met, and then follow them wherever they went.

They had come through the main doors at a fast walk. And had nearly collided with Ronnie, who had his back to them. Katie and Mordecai had both skidded to a halt, spun around in unison, and ducked behind a concession stand selling souvenirs.

Ronnie had made his way over to the big armchairs and had sat down. Katie was pretending to examine a "Kiss Me! I'm from Los Angeles" T-shirt, when a stocky tough guy in a cheap suit had walked up to Ronnie, put his hand on Ronnie's shoulder, and began to talk to him. They were both smiling, but, to Katie, peering around an 'I Heart the Lakers' tote bag, Ronnie didn't look comfortable.

Then Mordecai had said: "Wait here, my dear. I will go to put a stick in the snake hole and jiggle it a little."

"And this is a good idea?" said Katie.

"Good, bad," Mordecai had shrugged his shoulders, his hand rocking this way and that. "Who can say, but I fear your young man is in over his head. This fellow, the one who squeezes Aaron's shoulder so affably, I do not believe him really to be so affable. Please, Katie, stay here and keep watch, and call Dr. Califario on your cell. Keep him informed of what we are doing."

Mordecai had sauntered off. Katie put through the call.

"Yes, Miss Liebovitz."

"We're at Union Station, Ronnie is here, and he's talking to a man. Mordecai has gone over to speak to them."

"Describe this man, please."

"Medium height, about five nine, stocky, powerful looking. Like a prize fighter. Craggy face, nose looks kind of squished."

"Did Mr. Stern know this man?"

"Ronnie looked like he was expecting someone, and yes he seemed to know him. Oh wait, Mordecai has just walked up behind the guy. Ronnie hasn't seen him yet. Oh, now he has. Ronnie looks surprised. Mordecai is saying something. And the other guy has turned around. And, hang on, I can't see... What? Oh no, Mordecai! Oh my God!"

"What is it Miss Liebovitz? Please tell me what has happened."

"I don't know. I can't tell from here. But Mordecai... He's covered in blood. He's hurt! The guy is lowering him into a chair. Ronnie is trying to help. The guy's trying to stop him. I can't see it all, but Mordecai's down, in one of the armchairs, Ronnie's reaching out to Mordecai. Oh no!"

"Miss Liebovitz, tell me what is happening."

"I think Ronnie must have touched Mordecai. He went rigid, like he'd been tasered, and now Ronnie has collapsed as well. There's another dude running in. They're talking."

"Who is talking?"

"The goon who hurt Mordecai and another one, looks like a little rat, pointy nose, thin moustache, they're talking. They slipped Mordecai's hat off and dropped it on the blood, on his chest. Now they're picking Ronnie up. He looks bad, he's unconscious. They're walking him away. What should I do? They've got Ronnie, but Mordecai..."

"Ring 911 immediately. Avoid those men. But go to Mordecai. He is the chief concern here. You must see to him. Ring 911 and stay with him. Do it now. Help Mordecai."

MELVIN SHNAYVISE

Melvin was receiving Aaron's transmitter signal loud and clear. He was watching the red dot on his screen.

He was also wishing he hadn't drunk so much soda. How come TV cops never needed to pee? He was weighing up his chances of running into the station to find a bathroom when the red dot disappeared.

That's funny, he said to himself. What's happened to Big Dog?

He tapped some keys, adjusted the connections, checked the Wi-Fi strength.

He decided he'd kill two birds with one stone. Go in and find Ronnie. And take a leak. But not in that order.

AARON STERN

The Ninth Vision

I was watching a dockside scene. Lots of ships with masts and sails, and a monkeys' playground of ropes. They were like floating spiders' webs. I'd never realized how much rope these old sailing ships needed. The buildings surrounding the docks were tall and skinny, mostly three or four stories high with ornate, curved roofs, and each one had a kind of crane thing poking out from a big door on the top floor. Guess that's the only way to get the grand piano up there.

The wharf was crowded and everyone was dressed for a Thanksgiving re-enactment. Minus the Indians, and the turkey. It was like the pictures you see of the Pilgrim Fathers, and Pilgrim Mothers, and Pilgrim kids. You know, the men in black and white clothes with tall tapering hats; and the women in floor-length skirts, and bonnets, and tight head coverings. Little boys in knee breeches and coats ran between wooden barrels, stacks of hessian sacks, and wagons and horses. The little girls held each others' hands and stood close to their mothers, nervous at all the noise and bustle.

Men were talking with each other, sailors were yelling, mothers were calling their kids, workmen were hefting sacks on their backs, and operating pulleys and winches, and big nets filled with tightly packed bales were rising into the air and swinging out over the narrow water to the ships.

I could see the name on the side of one of the ships, *The Abigail.*

A new family came into the dock area. They were dressed like everyone else, but they were a bit shorter and their skin was swarthy. They looked Spanish or Arabic, while everyone else looked like extras in a film about Norway.

There were about a dozen people, men, women and children, in this new group. The oldest man consulted a notebook, and then he looked around.

He spotted a guy in the middle of a noisy circle of men shouting questions at him.

The dark guy, the head Spaniard I guessed, went over to the circle of shouting men.

I thought he was going to have to wait his turn, but he stopped for a moment and got a look of concentration on his face. The crowd acted like the Red Sea on the day Moses got down to business.

"Good morning," the dark dude said. "You are Mynheer Kapitein Van Houten, the Master of *The Abigail*?" The guy in the center of the circle nodded. "May I introduce myself," he made a little bow, "I am Reuben Ben Solomon, and I and my family are embarking with you today for the Massachusetts Bay Colony. Can you please tell us where to put our baggage?"

Van Houten pointed to a pile of crates and bales and bundles which the sailors were hoisting up and over onto the ship.

"Thank you Mynheer Kapitein," said Ben Solomon politely. "And can you tell me please at what hour we are scheduled to sail?"

The Captain told him.

Ben Solomon turned to the men grouped around them. "Gentlemen, Mynheer Van Houten, I thank you."

He walked back to his family. Had a short confab with some of the younger men in his party. Then he pointed to the bustling dockworkers, and the younger men began to carry and wheel and drag their baggage to the designated area.

He turned to one of the younger women, with a baby cradled on her hip. He said something to the woman and she beamed and nodded at him, then he held the baby's face close, and did that grandfather lip-blowing thing which made it gurgle and laugh.

Then he turned to one of the older women who was clutching a leather satchel to her chest.

"Thank you Sarah," said Ben Solomon, "I will look after that now."

She handed over the satchel.

"The scroll will be safe in a new land," said Ben Solomon. "It will help create that new land."

I could feel Ben Solomon's copy of the Moses Revelation pulsating and radiating energy.

KATIE LIEBOVITZ

Katie moved quickly through the evening crowd in the Hall. She dodged suitcases, and reunited lovers, and children glued to iPhones. She twisted and turned, apologizing and excusing herself.

She had her cell to her ear, listening to the 911-dispatch operator promising paramedics and police.

She looked around. She couldn't see Aaron or the men who had dragged him away.

Katie closed her cell and ran up to Mordecai. He sat slumped in the chair with his hat on his chest. She could see the edges of the red stain on his shirt.

She knelt down in front of him. She took his hand.

"Oh Mordecai. Oh, My God. It's OK, help is on the way."

She slid off her scarf, bunched it in her hand, and removed Mordecai's hat. She recoiled at the sight of the hole in his shirt, oozing thick blood. She pressed the scarf to the wound and held it in place.

Mordecai's face was the color of oatmeal. His eyelids fluttered open.

"Katie my dear," he said softly, "I am most sorry to have put you to this inconvenience. Talking to this man, it was, I now see, not a good idea."

Katie started crying. She couldn't help herself. Mordecai was bleeding out from a chest wound, and he was apologizing like he'd used the wrong fork for his appetizer.

"You do not have to worry. I will be fine," said Mordecai.

"Yes, Mordecai," said Katie, "of course you will." Tears rolled down her cheeks. "Of course, you'll be fine. Don't speak now, save your strength."

"No, Motek, Sweetie, you don't understand, I am going to be OK."

"Mordecai, sshh, don't speak. The ambulance is coming."

"No, I have to say this. Tell Califario. Your young man, he saved me."

"Ronnie, how?"

But she knew the answer. She had seen it. Ronnie had touched Mordecai.

He had healed him.

Then her blood ran cold. Ronnie had collapsed. He had taken on the pain and hurt of a dying man, and he had been dragged away. Who knew what condition he was in now?

"Yes," said Mordecai, "me, I will now recover. He saved my life, that Ronnie of yours. But it will cost him, it is costing him. He will be in shock."

Then without warning, Melvin Shnayvise was standing next to her, shaking water from his hands.

"Katie, hi!" he said. "What's going on? Where's Ronnie? Who's this guy? Wow! What happened to him?"

"Melvin, where did you come from? What are you doing here? Is that chocolate custard on your shirt?"

"I..."

"Shut up, Melvin. I can't explain. This is Mordecai. He's been stabbed. An ambulance is on the way. Put your hand on this scarf and keep the pressure up. No, not that way. Here. Good, that's it. No, shut up Melvin, no questions. I've got to look for Ronnie."

AARON STERN

1.

I was lifted up under each arm and half carried, half frog-marched away from Mordecai. My backpack was over my shoulder banging into my side.

We must have ended up in some kind of alcove because it went quiet and no one else was around. A lot of what happened next is hazy. My skin burned, my heart was leaping around in my chest.

And something was wrong with my eyes. When I prized them open everything was blurred and swimming and tinged with red.

I was sitting on something hard. A wooden bench I guessed. The pressure against my skin was agony. My eyes had closed again, I'd need a forklift to open them.

"Minnelli, look in the bag," said McInnes. I felt the backpack pulled from my shoulder. I must have groaned because McInnes told me to shut up, or he'd give me something to groan about. What happened to all that stuff about being happy and relaxed? Must raise that with him later, when my head got back to a normal size. Meanwhile I sat there with every individual inch of my skin screaming for my undivided attention.

"Here it is," said the guy named Minnelli. He had an American accent. Good, I was getting sick of Australians.

"OK," said McInnes, "get it out of that blue crap. Hurry, someone's going to trip over the dead Kike and raise the alarm. Good, now take your glove off and touch the parchment. Don't ask why, just do it."

I squinted and saw a short sharp-faced guy unwrapping the fake Moses Revelation. He hesitated, then he touched the parchment. He looked up at

McInnes and shrugged.

"Bloody Hell," said McInnes. Then he said a few more unrepeatable things. I'd heard Aussies were world-class swearers, but this was something else. It was quite an education. Lots of encouragement to do things with one's near relatives, which were almost certainly illegal in every state of the union, at least I hoped they were.

He was mad. And I could tell someone was going to be in big trouble. When I was yanked up from the bench I knew that someone was me. McInnes held me by my shirtfront with one hand. The other hand held a knife close to my face.

"Where the bloody hell is it?" he said.

I got a blast of his breath. Hadn't this guy heard of breath mints?

McInnes shook me until I thought my teeth would fall out.

"I warned you about playing games, Shithead! Tell me, you freak, where is the real scroll? That crap you gave us is a pile of dog's turds!"

You get the idea. Limited vocabulary. But he was excellent at getting the point across.

Then, without warning, he sliced his knife across my cheek. It stung like I'd been bullwhipped. Warm sticky blood flowed down to my chin. I cried out.

"Shut the bloody hell up! Stop squealing and start talking, or I'm going to take you apart, piece by tiny piece. And, then I'll get to work on that precious little sister of yours. In exactly five seconds I'm going to cut your left eye out of your head. One..."

In my defense, I was still disoriented by the dockside vision.

"Two..."

And half dead from the shock of healing Mordecai.

"Three..."

And did I mention that a homicidal maniac had just sliced my face open?

"Four..."

But most important Mishi was now in his cross-hairs.

"Fi..."

"It's at the checked bag desk," I croaked. "In a Safeways bag. Over there, past the concession stand. The ticket is in my pocket."

"Get it Minnelli," said McInnes.

The point of the knife hovered half an inch from my left eye. Hands went through my pockets.

"Got it."

"Go," said McInnes. I heard receding footsteps.

The knife withdrew from my face, and I was shoved back onto the bench. I struggled to get my handkerchief out of my pocket to staunch my bleeding cheek.

McInnes's cell rang. He pulled it out.

"Yeah, we're here. We've got the kid," he said. "That Israeli arsehole turned up, and now there's one less Jew Boy to worry about. Nah, nobody saw. We'll be out of here before anyone finds him. The kid tried to be cute.

He had a copy on him. Minnelli touched it but nothing happened. Smartarse kid. I persuaded him to share the location of the real one. Minnelli's getting it now. I'm here making sure the kid doesn't have an attack of heroics. OK, here's Minnelli, he's got it. Call you back."

2.

I was drifting in and out of a pain-wracked world. My cheek burned, and my head ached. I was covered in bruises.

But when the other guy, Minnelli, came back, carrying the shopping bag my head cleared. I could feel the Moses Revelation, like it was calling to me.

"OK Minnelli, time to earn your money. Do it again with this one. Glove off, scroll uncovered. Give it a touch."

The rat faced man looked up at McInnes.

He wasn't happy, but McInnes was doing a kind a magician's trick with his knife, rolling it back and forth between the fingers of one hand. And then he held it steady, pointing it at Minnelli.

Minnelli had his glove off in double time. He pulled out the scroll wrapped in the beach towel, and put the bundle on the wooden bench next to me. He carefully unwrapped the towel revealing the blue velvet and gold thread. He undid the golden cord and widened the mouth of the velvet bag. He picked up the bag with his left hand and reached his ungloved right hand into the bag.

"No," I said. "Don't..."

But it was too late.

Minnelli touched the scroll. And he just dropped to the floor. No scream, no dramatics, no clutch of the throat. His face didn't melt off, a la Raiders of the Lost Ark.

He was a puppet and someone had cut his strings.

"Screw a roo!" said McInnes. Aussies must like poetry. Lucky he wasn't into ducks. "That was bloody impressive."

He gave Minnelli's inert body a nudge with his foot. He knelt down and touched his neck.

"Bloody hell," he said to himself, "he's dead. What in Christ's name is this thing?" He turned to me. "Ah well, ours not to reason why, eh Ronnie? Put on the gloves and pack it up. We're getting out of here."

I put on the gloves, groaned again and knelt down. I used a corner of the towel to pick up the scroll from the floor. Then I jiggled it further back into its velvet cover, tied the thread, and rewrapped it in the towel. Then the whole bundle went back into the carryall, and into my backpack.

"OK Champ, let's go," said McInnes. He laughed. "We'll leave Mr. Minnelli for the cleaners to find. Should give them something to talk about at their next tea break. Come on, time to go."

He pulled me to my feet, grabbed my elbow and we headed for the exit.

"Let's go join that bloody sister of yours."

The Vatican, Rome, 1168

When other duties finally called the monk away Da Silva was escorted by his guards back through a labyrinth of hallways, passages and stairs. This time instead of his malodorous cell, the journey ended at an oak paneled door half way down a corridor at the end of which was a tall arched window. The hallway flagstones were covered in long intricately woven carpets. Torches were set into niches in the walls.

One of the guards selected a heavy iron key from a ring on his belt and he unlocked the door.

Da Silva was ushered into a windowless room, furnished with a low cot, a simple wooden chair and a plain table made of walnut wood. The door was closed and locked behind him.

On the table was a lit candle, a bowl of pears and apples, and a bottle of wine, cheap but, Da Silva soon discovered, drinkable. A loaf of bread and some hard cheese completed the banquet. His bandaged and damaged fingers made it awkward, in the absence of a knife or any other 'weapon', to tear at the bread and crumble the cheese. But he persevered.

Taking life as it came was one of Da Silva's chief philosophies. Taking the gold of any fool that trusted him was another. No gold, it appeared, was on offer, but a simple meal and a humble bed to Da Silva's way of thinking signified a vast improvement on his previous sleeping and catering arrangements.

He thought about the monk. There was a lot more to this austere inquisitor than met the eye. Da Silva wondered how long it would take him to figure out the real inner meaning of the *Maleficium.*

Oh well, Da Silva sighed, until then he would enjoy the comforts. And afterwards?

That was a bridge that could only be crossed when he came to it.

CHAPTER FOURTEEN

2ND OCTOBER

CONTINUED

KATIE LIEBOVITZ

1.

Katie walked through the Hall looking left and right for Aaron. The crowd from the last train was thinning and she stood in the concourse turning around, scanning faces.

Then suddenly Aaron and one of the tough guys, the thickset one, were nearly on top of her. They came from nowhere and she only had seconds to duck behind a pillar.

Aaron's head was down and he shuffled along with his backpack over his shoulder. He looked shell-shocked, his eyes were glazed and his arms hung down by his sides. She gasped when she saw the blood on his left cheek.

The thug had him by the elbow steering him toward the exit.

Katie stood still. What to do? Melvin was looking after Mordecai, and the ambulance and police were on the way. There was not much she could do here. How could she help Aaron and Mishi?

She put a call through to Dr. Califario.

"It's Katie," she said. "Mordecai seems OK. Ronnie did his healing thing. He's hurt. He's being led away by one of the goons. And Melvin turned up. He's a school friend, he's looking after Mordecai. No it's OK he knows what to do. So, what should I do? Go after Ronnie, or stay with Mordecai?"

She listened for a few moments.

"OK, will do."

2.

Katie and Melvin stayed with Mordecai. Katie explained to Melvin that they had to tell the paramedics and the police as much of the truth as they could, but they had to agree on a few embellishments.

Katie told him that it was in Ronnie's interest. Melvin wasn't persuaded.

Lying to the police after all. But when she threatened a repeat performance of his circumcision using a rusty chainsaw Melvin discovered that her reasoning was much more compelling.

The ambulance and the paramedics showed up first. Katie and Melvin answered a whole gaggle of questions about the injury as best they could.

Then the police turned up and they answered a thousand more questions. Katie Liebovitz. Yes, that's right, with a 'v'.

Mordecai Ben Zvi. M-O-R-D-E-C-A-I. No, two words. B-E-N, new word Z-V-I.

He's my, ah, uncle. We were out for a drive. Seeing the sights of LA.

Well it wasn't late when we set out.

Uncle Mordecai likes trains so we came to see Union Station.

No, we didn't know the attacker.

No, the attacker didn't speak to him.

No, he didn't take anything. He just stabbed Mordecai and fled.

Yes, that's right, I mean 'Uncle' Mordecai.

Well, officer, it was over so quickly, let me think, short, stocky, Caucasian, wearing a suit, yes, that's what I said, a suit.

No I don't know why someone in a suit should attack my Uncle.

No, I'm sure he didn't say anything.

No, there was no argument or anything like that.

Yes, I'm sure.

Yes, that's right, completely unprovoked.

Well, I don't care if it sounds unlikely, that's what happened.

Me? My name? Oh, you want my name. Melvin Shnayvise. S-H-N-A-Y-V-I-S-E. It means 'Snow White'. In Yiddish. Why aren't you writing that down?

Oh, OK. Let's see, I was out driving around and decided to come into the station to use the bathroom.

Why? Why does anyone need to use the bathroom? Because I needed to pee.

Oh, you mean why was I out driving around. Good question. Why? Why does anyone do anything? I mean do we really understand our own...

What? Oh well, like I said, I came in to take a leak. And I saw Katie. We're at high school together – Calvin Coolidge High – she was with her Israeli uncle Mordecai and I went up to say Hi.

No, I hadn't met Uncle Mordecai before tonight.

How did I know his name? Katie introduced us. No, after he was attacked. I wasn't here before he was attacked.

No I don't think that's strange. It's good manners. Didn't your mother ever tell you...

What? Oh. No, I didn't get that Uncle Mordecai had been mugged until I got up close.

And on and on it went until, well after midnight, Melvin and Katie were finally allowed to go. In the middle of proceedings some excitement started up over by a far wall near the telephones. Katie overheard the paramedics talking about finding a heart attack victim.

Katie also heard snatches of the paramedics talking to Mordecai.

"Very lucky. Missed vital organs. Lot of blood but the wound isn't deep. It's closing up already." The paramedic sounded mystified.

They lifted Mordecai onto a gurney and began to wheel him away.

"Wait. Wait," Katie called out. "Where is he going?"

"Mt Sinai."

"Uncle Mordecai! We'll follow. We'll come as soon as we can."

Mordecai smiled weakly, and waved a hand as he disappeared out the exit.

3.

At the hospital Katie and Melvin were allowed to see 'Uncle' Mordecai, on account of Katie being a relative, but only for five minutes. Although the wound was healing rapidly, it was still serious.

Mordecai was sedated, and Katie had squeezed his hand and told him everything was going to be OK.

Now they were waiting in a small area for visitors around the corner from Mordecai's room. They sat on hard gray plastic seats. There was a sink and a hot water heater. A cupboard above the sink had polystyrene cups, instant coffee, tea bags and sugar. There was milk in a small bar fridge under the sink.

"This is great," Melvin said in a whisper that could be heard in San Francisco. "This is like in the movies. Only in the movies someone is about to sneak in and kill..."

"Shut up, Melvin," Katie waved an imaginary chainsaw at him just below waist height. Melvin shut up.

About half an hour later a tall slender man with dark hair and dark penetrating eyes walked into the room. He was wearing a brown plaid tweed suit with a brown tie. He walked straight up to them. Katie stood, Melvin followed.

"Miss Liebovitz, Katie, my dear," he said, "you have had a difficult night. I'm so sorry. And this I presume is the redoubtable Melvin?" He held out his hand. "My name is Califario, Dr. Amadeus Califario."

Melvin took the proffered hand and shook it. "Shnayvise, Melvin Shnayvise, Sir.

"Are you a friend of Mordecai?"

"I have that privilege, yes."

"Dr. Califario is here to visit Mordecai," said Katie, "and to hear from us what happened at the station."

"Oh," said Melvin, addressing Dr. Califario. "Are you in charge? 'Cause you look like someone who's in charge. You have that 'I'm in charge, so don't piss me off' look about you." Melvin regarded Dr. Califario closely, then he nodded to himself, "definitely in charge."

"Yes, Melvin," said Katie, "Dr. Califario is in charge. Sir," she turned to Dr. Califario. "Melvin is Ronnie's best friend. And he and I get along OK on the rare occasions when he is not being extremely annoying."

She turned back to Melvin, "Dr. Califario needs to hear everything that happened tonight. Including," she said menacingly, "the part before you and Ronnie got to the station."

"Oh," said Melvin, "that part. You mean before the station. That earlier part. Like, what Ronnie and I did previous to the later part."

Katie glared at him.

Dr. Califario looked calm and expectant. Melvin took a deep breath.

MELVIN'S REPORT

"Well, it was like this," Melvin began. "Ronnie said he needed my help. And I said, 'like, how?' And he said, 'well, see, I need to steal a thing from a Museum'. And I said, 'well, that sounds weird. How come?' And he said, 'cause see, I have to hand it over to some bad guys, and, like, I can't go into details, but you have to help'. So I said, 'what museum?' And he said, 'the Getty Villa'. And I said, 'Oh OK, sounds intriguing, let's do it'. So we went there during the day to case the joint. And we saw this display cabinet with an old scroll in it with a blue cloth with gold threads sewn on it. Like a Torah. Do you know what a Torah is? You do? Good, OK, where was I? Oh yes. Then Ronnie took one look at the scroll and kind of collapsed, so we hotfooted it out of there and we went back to his place, and I downloaded plans and schematics for the Getty Villa, and Ronnie got busy with making a couple of copies. Of the scroll. 'Cause, see, he wanted to leave a copy so they wouldn't know it was gone. At the museum, you know, the guards. So then we drove back to the Getty Villa, but we got a bit lost, 'cause it was night now, and we were talking about when to put on our balaclavas, and we had to turn around and then we took another wrong turn. Anyway we finally got there, and I switched off the cameras and the power feed to the emergency generator, and then I picked the lock on a side door, and then we got to the room with this scroll thingy. And, it was totally gone. Vanished. Go figure. But Ronnie figured out where it was stashed behind a wall, I don't know how he did that, do you? Anyway we got a door in the wall open, and found the scroll and got it out, and put the copy back and then we left. But we had to hustle 'cause by now the guards were coming 'cause we had taken too long and the lights came back on. So, we got out and ran alongside a hedge to the car. And then we saw another car coming toward the Villa, and Ronnie recognized it. He said it was Mordecai's car, only I didn't know who Mordecai was then. But I do now 'cause I met him tonight at the station. But I think 'met' isn't the right word 'cause, like, he'd been stabbed and all, and wasn't, you know, talkative. So anyway, we drove away from the museum, and we went to my place and I wired Ronnie up with a tracker so I could follow him. I drove my Mom's car and followed Ronnie. But, like, I already knew we were going to Union Station, 'cause Ronnie had told me that. He got a text from the bad guys telling him where to meet up. So I thought it wouldn't hurt to stop at a Krispy Kreme and get a box of donuts and a few cans of soda, you know, so I could do a real stake out. But then I needed to pee, and I was just deciding whether to go into the station when the tracker went dead, and then I did go in, and I found the bathroom, and then I went looking for Ronnie and I saw Katie so I went over to say 'Hi, what are you doing here, have you seen Ronnie?' And I saw Mordecai covered in blood. It was totally gross. But it got grosser 'cause Katie was, like, 'you stay here and hold this scarf on his wound, I'm going to look for Ronnie'."

"Thank you, Melvin," Dr. Califario interrupted the flow, "that was most informative."

"It was?" said Melvin and Katie simultaneously.

"Yes," said Dr. Califario, "I believe I was able to sift the essentials from the narrative. You appear to have useful skills when it comes to burglary."

"Thank you," said Melvin. "I think."

KATIE AND MORDECAI AND MELVIN

1.

Dr. Califario 'convinced' the night nurse to let him in to see Mordecai and he spent about ten minutes in the room. When he emerged he said his farewells to Katie and Melvin and went to do whatever it was that Dr. Califario did.

Both Melvin and Katie were growing anxious about their parents. They needed to tell them they were OK, and that they had witnessed an attack on a friend in Union Station, and they were going to stay at the hospital overnight in the waiting room.

Melvin's mother, with four other children at home, was cool about the whole thing.

When Katie rang home Melvin could hear Mrs. Liebovitz squawking down the phone from across the room. Katie was like, "Yes Mom, No Mom, I'm OK Mom, Really Mom, No I can't come home yet, Mom. Yes, I'll call if anything else happens Mom. No, Mom, Uncle Lenny doesn't need to ring the Chief of Police."

They told their parents they had met some friends – true – and had been driving around – also true – and that Melvin had to stop to use the bathroom and Union Station had been the closest one – sort of true – and they didn't know anything about the attack and the attacker – getting a lot less true – or the victim – not true at all.

Melvin and Katie had squirmed inwardly at having to sail close to the line, and then cross it, with their parents. They both knew it was a slippery slope, which they didn't want to skate down.

They settled into the molded plastic chairs.

"We'll tell them the truth when we can, when it's all over," said Katie.

"Sure we will," agreed Melvin. "When we put it all behind us. Whatever 'it' is, and wherever 'behind us' is, and whenever 'when' is. Sure we will."

"Melvin," said Katie.

"Yes, Katie," said Melvin.

"Has anyone ever told you that you are a total putz?"

"You mean in so many words? Like, using that exact term? Given my winning ways, and clever turn of phrase, not as many as you'd think. But then again how many people know Yiddish? If you mean in general, using terms that could, at a stretch, have the same meaning as 'putz'. Well..." he spread his hands in an expansive gesture. "How high is the sky? How deep is the ocean? How long is..."

"Melvin," said Katie, folding her arms and closing her eyes, "you are a total putz."

2.

At 8 am the next morning they stirred in their plastic seats. They washed their faces in the bathroom, and bought soda and candy from the vending machine for breakfast.

Then they went to see Mordecai.

He was sitting up in bed reading the *LA Times.* When he saw them he put the paper down and peered at them.

"This is indeed a pleasant surprise," he said. "Welcome to my humble temporary abode. Pull up a chair. Pull up two."

"Thanks Mordecai," said Katie. "How are you feeling?"

"I am feeling very well, thank you for asking," said Mordecai. "In fact I feel better than I did before I was attacked."

"Sorry," said Melvin, "how is that even possible? I mean, you were stabbed in the chest. I saw it. Not the actual stabbing, but I saw enough blood to supply a Halloween Costume store several times over."

Mordecai looked at Katie and raised an enquiring eyebrow.

"He's already involved," she said. "He's met Dr. Califario. He helped Ronnie get the Moses Revelation from the Getty Villa. And despite appearances to the contrary, he is not a complete numbskull. He already has an idea of what this is about. Not all of it, neither do I, but Melvin's going to add two and two and come up with four a lot quicker than most would. He's actually a genius and he can be a lot of help. And," she said, turning to Melvin, "if you tell anyone I said that I will personally staple your tongue to the roof of your mouth."

"Katie..." said Melvin.

"Don't!" she said holding up a palm to his face, "don't start with the blather. Don't say a word. Ronnie and Mishi are in incredible danger and we need you. I need you. Let's just leave it at that."

And then she grabbed him and hugged him tight. His glasses skewed off his face, and his neck cricked up painfully. It was one of the nicest moments he had ever experienced. When she finally let him go, he was lost for words.

Katie sniffed, and brushed tears from her eyes.

"OK," she said, "back to business."

3.

Katie explained Aaron's healing power to Melvin as briefly as possible and then turned to Mordecai: "What's our plan?" she asked.

"My plan," said Mordecai, "is to convince the medical fraternity, or at least the small part of it concerned with my welfare, that, like that Lazarus fellow, I can come forth from the tomb to which they were so ready to confine me."

"Sounds like a good plan," said Melvin. "What should we do?"

"You need to track Aaron and Mishi, report your findings to Dr. Califario and take your instructions from him."

"Yeah," said Melvin, "and that sounds like a good plan too, except the tracker I placed on Ronnie only had a range of a few hundred yards at best, and it got fried somehow."

"Ah, yes, well, about that," said Mordecai. He looked at Katie, "shall I tell him or will you?"

Katie looked at Melvin. "There's a bit more background you need."

Melvin looked expectant.

"See the group Mordecai and I and Dr. Califario are part of..." Katie hesitated, looking for the right words.

"Yes," said Melvin encouragingly. "This group?"

"Well, all of us have powers, abilities. Unusual abilities."

"Like what?" said Melvin. "Can you leap over tall buildings? Bend steel with your bare hands? Are you faster than a speeding bullet? More powerful than a locomotive? Do you fight for Truth, Justice and the American Way?"

Katie laughed, she couldn't help herself. It was the first time in a while, and it felt good.

"No, none of those, well except the last. We do fight for Truth and Justice and, Yes, the American Way. It's a bit corny these days, but I don't know of any other way which is better."

"Right," said Melvin, "imagine fighting for Untruth, Injustice and, say, the Russian Way, or the Chinese Way, or the Cuban Way. Hey those Commies have still got a lot to answer for. And as for those crazies in the Middle East..."

"Melvin!"

"Oh, right, you were saying."

"What she was saying," said Mordecai, "is that this group has existed for centuries, millennia, and for that reason is called The Elders. For reasons a little too long to go into, but involving that scroll you and Aaron stole, we,

The Elders, have developed powers."

"Yes," Katie said, "like mind control, manipulating electronics, insight into the future, and healing, like Ronnie. And distance location, that's me."

"That's you?" said Melvin.

"Yep, that's me, I can locate people. I know where they are."

"Like everyone? How do you filter?"

Katie turned to Mordecai. "You see."

"Yes." Said Mordecai, "I see, he talks interminably when it is not important. But goes straight to the essentials, when it is, and doesn't waste his words, when such a waste would obscure understanding. He is, as you say, good."

"You know I can hear you from here?" said Melvin.

"Shut up, wiseass, we're complimenting you."

"This I get, and I will encourage you at some future time to develop this theme to your heart's content, but like Mordecai said, at this point brevity is important. Ronnie and Mishi are important. So, how does your power work? 'Cause I'm guessing that's how we find them."

Katie and Mordecai gave each other another look.

"I can only find people I have strong feelings for, love, hate, compassion."

"Respect? Admiration? Adoration?" said Melvin smiling. "So you always know where I am, every minute of the day?"

"Remember the 'Shut up, Wiseass' thing?"

"Oh yeah, continue, please."

"OK, I have to focus my attention on them in a special way, to bring them into sharp focus. I was doing some of it last night in the waiting room."

"And this is how you and Mordecai found Ronnie at Union Station."

"Exactly."

"And Mishi? You and her don't get along all that well."

"Same deal," said Katie, a bit awkwardly, "I can still track her."

"Whoa," said Melvin. "Strong feelings for Mishi. But not good ones. Wow, you girls."

"Well, yes," said Katie, and Melvin was interested to see her blush. "OK, so Mishi and I are not BFFs, but it's handy now because I can track both of them, Ronnie and Mishi."

"So, $64,000 question. Where are they?"

"Longbeach," said Katie. "About an hour away in today's traffic."

MISHI STERN

"What are you doing!" The Wicked Witch came flying across the warehouse, her heels clacking on the concrete. "How did she get that phone?"

Snell looked stunned. I would've felt sorry for him, but I couldn't muster any sympathy for a stupid doofus who'd signed up with a bunch of homicidal maniacs, who had kidnapped and threatened to torture my family and me.

"I... I..." he stammered.

"You what?" Portland hissed. Snell was sweating, his face was white as a ghost. She grabbed a fistful of his shirtfront and lifted him. She must've been pretty strong 'cause he was up on his tiptoes.

"I don't know. I thought her mother..."

Portland flung the little man away. Snell staggered backward. She turned her fury on me.

"You did this," she screamed, snatching up the cell and hurling it down. It shattered, pieces flying in all directions. "Your freaking mind control, you used it on this... this... this worm. Didn't you?"

There wasn't a lot I could do to help this conversation along. Her face was an inch from mine so I leaned back as far as I could, the spittle showering my face.

She was all red and blotchy. Not so pretty now, I thought.

Abruptly Portland stopped and turned.

"Gantz! Mulligan! Get your asses over here. Now!"

Two hoods hotfooted over.

"This little bitch has used a cell to send a message."

"What was the message?" said one of the scumbags, Gantz or Mulligan, I didn't know which was which.

"I don't know, you idiot." Then she said, in a singsong voice: "'Poor little me trapped by big bad Sally in a warehouse, please come and rescue me.' How should I know what she sent? What does it matter? They'll be able to trace the call. We have to get out of here. Start packing up."

The guys just stood there.

"Now!" She screamed at the top of her voice. Snell turned to go with the others.

"Not you," she said softly. Snell froze in his tracks. He turned back toward her. "Mr. Snell, if you ever do anything like that again I will kill you. Do you understand?"

Snell nodded.

"The only reason you are still alive is we need to get this place packed up. Now go!" I thought Snell would drop dead on the spot. When he'd recovered he scurried over to join the others who were already hefting boxes and packing away equipment. "And as for you," she said, turning to me, "you're dead anyway."

She stalked off to shed sunshine and light in some other corner of this gloomy world.

AARON STERN

My head lolled left and right as the black SUV moved through the dark streets. I had the vague idea of trying to remember the route but gave up after the first few twists and turns. McInnes kept glancing at his rear-view mirror, turning into side streets without signaling, occasionally stopping, turning off the engine, and waiting and listening. Then he would start up again and head off. Once he did a quick U-turn to a chorus of angry horn blasts.

McInnes didn't say a word the whole trip.

We finally turned into a drive, past a chain-link fence, and drove a short way to a large warehouse. There was a heavy metal door across a wide high entrance.

McInnes pointed a remote at the door and it began to slide sideways.

Inside I could see a cavernous space. We rolled forward. The edges of the warehouse were in darkness except for high windows lit by the surrounding streetlights. In the center of the space was a floodlit area with some chairs and tables with electronic equipment, monitors, computers, lots of wires. There were a few people scurrying around, talking to each other, and packing things into boxes.

And in the center of all of this was a single chair. Next to the chair was a woman with straight black hair, cut like a pageboy. She had her hand on the back of the chair in a kind of proprietorial way. Like she was a hostess welcoming another guest to her home.

And strapped to the chair by her wrists and ankles, looking straight at me was Mishi.

MISHI STERN

When the SUV pulled in through the warehouse door Sally the Sadist came over and grinned at me. She'd gotten over her anger management issues I noted. She stood behind the chair.

I was so sick of this freaky creep. I wanted to rip that stupid smirk off her face. And peel her face off her skull. I knew my rage wouldn't melt the cable ties but I gave it my best shot.

That's me. Milk of human kindness.

With these happy thoughts in my head I didn't give the SUV my full attention. But then it pulled up about twenty yards away and the headlights went out. And my heart jumped into my mouth. Ronnie was in the front seat.

The night had just got a lot, lot worse.

The driver was the Aussie. He got out, went around to the passenger door, and opened it. He grabbed Ronnie by the collar and yanked him out.

I could see Ronnie clearly. He looked awful, exhausted, he had bruises on his face and a horrible gash on his cheek. His hands were bloody and raw.

The She-Devil walked over and said a few words to Crocodile Dundee. McInnes handed Ronnie's backpack to her. Then they both looked my way and laughed. Sally Shitface put the backpack into an aluminum case and snapped the lid shut. One of those other guys took the case away into the shadows.

McInnes half carried, half dragged Ronnie toward me.

"Get out your hankies, boys and girls," he said when they got close, "time for a touching family reunion."

"Well, I finally get to meet the cool older brother," said Portland. Then she looked at me, "he doesn't look so cool, Mishi. In fact he looks like a bunch of crap. Now that I see you two together I can see the family resemblance." She laughed.

Ronnie stood swaying, his head down, held up by McInnes' grip on his elbow.

Gantz, or was it Mulligan, came out of the shadows. He nodded at McInnes and Portland.

"It's genuine."

"So," said McInnes. "Rat Face Minnelli didn't die in vain."

He turned to Ronnie, lifted his head by his hair and looked into his glazed eyes. He let go and Ronnie's head fell forward.

"Ronnie Boy appears to be a bit under the weather," he said, smiling.

Portland looked at her watch. "We're on the clock here, McInnes," she said. "The brat sent a text message using Snell's phone. They'll have the location in about an hour. Put them both into the container. Give him half an hour to recover. It'll take that long to finish packing up. Then we can put the proposition to him."

"What proposition?" I said.

Portland turned to me.

"To cooperate, or to die," she said, cutting the cable ties on my wrists and ankles. She dragged me to my feet and hustled me toward an open shipping container, half hidden in the gloom at the back of the warehouse.

I could hear McInnes dragging Ronnie along behind.

When we got to the container Sally gave me a shove. I tried to do a little dance to get up over the lip of the entrance, but I caught my foot and went sprawling.

McInnes did the same for Ronnie and he fell heavily beside me.

The steel doors, Portland on one and McInnes on the other, swung shut and we were plunged into darkness.

The Vatican Dungeons, Rome, 1171

It had all been going so well, he thought, feeling the needle-sharp claws of the rats making their tentative way up his chest toward his straggly beard. Seeking hidden crumbs, no doubt.

He made the effort to rock from side to side as far, at least, as his chains would allow. The rats skittered off.

The cell was dark and damp. The floor cold and hard, and the only sound to be heard, aside from the scratching of claws on stone, was the regular drip, drip, drip of brackish water that had seeped and oozed its way down to the dungeons from the sewers and gutters of the capital ofChristendom.

Da Silva allowed himself the unaccustomed luxury of letting his mind wander back to images of his previous living arrangements, the comfortable bed, the candles, the fruit and the wine.

But not for long. If he had learnt only one thing in his long and inglorious life it was that the Wheel of Fortune never stood still. The Great Magician of the Universe always had another card up his sleeve, ever ready to drop it onto the Gaming Table of Life.

Da Silva himself stood as the very epitome of this truth.

His comfortable sojourn had ended abruptly with the crash of the door, the appearance of a white-robed priest, his lips curling with contempt, the light of triumph in his eyes, the blazing torches of the Papal Guards, the outraged protests of the monk. All this played across the screen of Da Silva's mind.

And after that?

Ah well, in the twinkling of an eye he had been whisked back to the fetid straw and the thin gruel and kitchen scraps. To rejoin the rats.

The nice thing about Down, thought Da Silva, was that Up was sure to follow.

Unfortunately, the traitorous thought crept in, the only Up presently on offer was to the top of a wooden stake, to await the purging flames of Christian justice.

Da Silva sighed, shifted position as far as his manacles permitted, kicked weakly at another venturesome rat and fell asleep.

CHAPTER FIFTEEN

2ND OCTOBER

CONTINUED

AARON STERN

I lay still on a cold metal floor. It was kind of agreeable. Maybe they could call me in a year or two and then I'd be fine to talk, or play racket ball, or go surfing. But not now. Not n...

"Wake up, Meathead. What have they done to you?"

I knew that voice. It sounded like Mishi. But it couldn't be Mishi, someone had taken Mishi, and I'd let them do it. I should have gone back for her straight away, but I didn't and now she's gone, and I...

"Hey Lamebrain! Get up. We have a situation here. I know you're a dollar short for the bus ride home, but even you can figure that lying down right now is totally stupid."

This sounded exactly like Mishi.

I decided to take a chance and open one eye. A face was pressed up against mine; freckled nose, curly brown hair, brown eyes. It *looked* exactly like Mishi. It took my brain, you know, the lame one, a few more seconds to catch up to my lyin' eyes.

"Mishi?" someone moaned, me I guess.

"Who else, Bonehead?" said Freckle Face. "You think these guys go around kidnapping every fourteen-year old in LA?"

This was very convincing.

And my brain was beginning to fire on a couple of cylinders, putting two and two together, and coming up only just short of four.

Memories started wandering into my head to see if it was worth their while.

I remembered the Getty Villa and Melvin and the Moses Revelation.

Then Mishi kicked me. The memories vanished.

"Ow!" I said. "Quit it, Mish. That hurt."

"What do you think these guys are going to do if we don't figure out how to get out of here, manicure your nails? Take your breakfast order? These bozos are totally loco and we are definitely not going to like anything they are planning. And whatever it is they are cooking up is going to be a whole lot worse than a gentle tap on the ribs from your loving sister. So get up now!"

I rolled onto my side and got up on all fours. My head hung low, it took a moment for the world to stop spinning.

"Up, doofus," said Mishi. "Keep it coming. You've got to get up and walk whatever it is off. And what happened to your face?"

She sounded concerned.

"That Aussie guy, McInnes," I panted, still on hands and knees, "he was trying out a new knife. Works pretty good, don't you think?"

She was kneeling next to me with a cloth. She licked it and dabbed at the dried blood. Mom used to do that when I was, like, six. Is this a female thing?

Suddenly I remembered Mordecai, and McInnes, and Union Station. And the blood.

So much blood.

"Mordecai!" I said.

The shock of the memory drove the fatigue from my body. I struggled to my feet.

"What about him?" said Mishi.

"Mishi!" I said, gripping her shoulders, thoughts of Mordecai driven from my mind. "Mishi!"

"Yes, Mishi," said Mishi, "are you going to shout out every name you know that begins with 'M'?"

"Yes, no," I said, "Mishi, what have they done to you? Are you OK? What do these people want?"

"I'm OK," she said. "They took me from the party at Daphne's and drove me here, and had me in a chair, and asked a whole lot of idiot questions. And threatened to chop me up and to poison me. And then you arrived. What are you doing here? How could you be so dumb and let them catch you?"

"Well, in my defen..."

"There's four or five of them. A couple come and go. A big Asian guy, called Singh, who was the one who first grabbed me, but he's gone now. And an Australian..."

"Him I've met. Like I said, this is a present from Downunder," I said, pointing at my bloody cheek.

"Bastard," said Mishi with, to me, unusual sororal feeling. "And that dumbass Social Studies teacher from your school, Snell, he's here too. But the worst of them is this capital 'H' Hag, called 'Sally'," she made a face and did air quotes. "Can you believe that name? Like she's stepped out of a Shirley Temple movie. She's got this sick smile and black hair, and a bag of tricks..."

"Tricks?"

"Yeah she's a scientist or doctor or nurse or something and she's got poisons and hypodermics. She kept threatening me if I didn't talk. So, I talked."

I didn't say anything.

"Don't look at me like that. What? Am I as big an idiot as you? I suppose you would have gone all Bruce Willis on them and held out while they beat you up and injected you with every chemical under the sun. I suppose you would have done that."

Looking back, at the station, and the knife cutting into my face, and the threat to Mishi, and me giving up the Moses Revelation, I didn't think. I knew.

"C'm 'ere." I held my arms out and gathered Mishi in and we hugged each other for the longest time.

"And there's another thing," said Mishi, her voice muffled in my chest. "I kind of know what they are thinking and feeling."

"Oh, yes," I said. "Yes, that's your power. Mom told me."

"Mom?" said Mishi, "she told you?"

"Yeah, we had a little family confab, real Ozzie and Harriet stuff. You know, did you catch last night's game, how's your oatmeal, and by the way, your sister and I are part of a shadowy cabal saving the world from itself with the use of our super powers. You know, same old, same old."

"What did Dad say?"

"Dad? Oh, he sort of knew already what was going on. Apparently he's even smarter than we thought, and he figured out that Mom was into something, and he also figured he'd be told when the time was right. He's completely insane that you're in danger and going nuts cause he can't rescue you, and the police can't find you. But he and Mom held hands and did that gooey eye thing. It seems only good ol' stupid Ronnie can't be trusted with the family secrets."

"Yeah, well, probably a good call. We wouldn't want to interfere with you and Miss Perfect and your social calendar would we?"

"Hey, that's not fair, what has Katie ever done to you?"

"Forget it," she said pulling away from me. "I don't want to talk about the Princess."

Suddenly I had a thought. I put a finger to my lips.

"Yeah, Katie, you and her have never got on have you?" I raised my eyebrows and pointed around the dimly lit shipping container.

"Bugs?" I mouthed.

Mishi looked around as well.

"Cameras?" she mimed like she was winding an old-fashioned movie camera. I shrugged.

"Are you feeling OK? After your ordeal I mean?"

"Oh yes, fine thanks," she said. "After my ordeal. Thank you for asking." Smooth, that was us. We had them fooled.

Or maybe not, because just then the container door opened. Standing silhouetted by the floodlights were my old mate McInnes, Mr. Smell, and the pretty woman with jet-black pageboy hair. The Hag, I presumed.

"Come, Mr. Stern," said the woman. "Time to talk."

JEREMY PLENSK

Lassiter sat in the living room of the Georgetown house. He was in a comfortable office chair pulled up to a small table which had been brought in by Georgiakis.

Plensk, the sole survivor of Professor Olaf Svensson's medieval manuscript research team, watched Georgiakis set up a laptop computer on the table. When all the cabling was done Georgiakis dialed a Skype call.

Lassiter straightened his perfect tie and brushed back his immaculate hair. Plensk watched him take a pen from an inner pocket of his suit coat and a small leather-bound notebook from another and placed them on the table next to the laptop. Just before the connection was made Lassiter moved the pen an eighth of an inch.

The screen came to life. From where Plensk was standing he could see on the screen a large warehouse. A tall slender man was standing in front of several people.

"Good evening, Mr. Gantz," said Lassiter. "I hope you and your team are well."

"Yes," said Gantz, "we're fine. We have the scroll and the two kids. They're here now."

"Excellent. May I have a word with young Mr. Stern?"

Plensk saw a tough looking prize fighter push a young man with curly dark hair and dark rings under his eyes forward toward the screen. He had a fresh cut on his cheek.

"Good evening, Mr. Stern," said Lassiter.

"Look," said the young man, "I don't know who you are or what you're planning but I got you what you asked for. Let my sister go. I'll stay, if that's what you want, but you don't need her any more. Let her go."

Plensk heard an angry girl's voice begin to say something off screen, but it was cut short with a painful squeal.

The young man turned and shouted, "Leave her alone!" He made to move but the tough looking dude held him in place.

"You're staying here, Mate," said the prize fighter, he had an Australian accent.

The young man struggled but Plensk could see that he was no match for the Aussie.

"Thank you, Mr. McInnes," said Lassiter. McInnes the prize fighter nodded a mock bow. "But I believe we can secure Mr. Stern's cooperation by more peaceful means. Mr. Stern, if you would be so kind as to give me four and a half minutes of your valuable time, I will attempt to interest you in a proposition."

The young man, Mr. Stern, was sagging with fatigue. He waved a submissive hand at the screen.

"I will take that as consent to continue," said Lassiter, smiling broadly. "I sincerely regret that we found it necessary to offer violence to you and your sister, but time was pressing and we needed to bring matters to a head."

"You're wasting some of your four and a half minutes," said Stern.

"Indeed, indeed, well, then, to business. My name is Randolph Lassiter and I have the honor to be the Canadian representative on the United Nations Committee for Environmental Sustainability and Climate Change. In fact I hold the position of Under Secretary on that very committee. But it is not in that capacity that I speak to you now. I am also a senior operative in a society which does not have any official name and is simply referred to as The Organization. Some time ago we, that is my colleagues in The Organization and I, were made aware of a thrilling opportunity, which will open up very shortly. To take full advantage of this we needed certain, ah, ingredients, shall we say. The first was a certain Time, which is very soon. The second was the Location, which I will, for now, keep to myself. The scroll, which you so kindly provided, was the third of these ingredients, and your sister and you together constitute the fourth and final piece."

The young man lifted his head at this. His eyes blazed, and he made a move at the screen. McInnes held him back.

"Hear me out, Mr. Stern," said Lassiter. "Time enough later for outrage, and brotherly loyalty. We want you to join us in this great enterprise. And so much the better if you do so willingly. And a lot easier for all concerned. The Organization could make use of your talents going forward."

The young man turned to McInnes and said: "Does this guy ever shut up?"

Lassiter smirked: "Your involvement, Mr. Stern, and your sister's, willing or not, is,

I'm afraid, a given. So, the only question for you, and you have," Lassiter consulted his watch, "forty-eight seconds to decide, is whether you will join us voluntarily, or whether we will be required to coopt you by force. Forty-one seconds, Mr. Stern."

"No."

"No?"

"No, neither I nor my sister will join in whatever scheme you psychos are planning, in fact you can take your plans and your forty-one seconds and shove them forty-one feet up your collective ass!"

Lassiter laughed. "You have a commendably colorful turn of phrase. No room for ambiguity at all. Miss Portland, over to you."

Lassiter nodded to Georgiakis who broke the Skype connection.

AARON STERN

1.

I stood transfixed by the empty screen, slumped in McInnes's iron grip. I heard a metallic clatter behind me.

"No, no!" said Mishi. "Leave me alone. Get your hands off me you assholes!"

I heard struggling and more metal on metal noise. Mishi was shouting and screaming. I began to struggle too but McInnes smacked me on the side of the head, my ears rang and my vision blurred. I sagged but he held me up by one arm.

"Leave me alone, let me go." I could hear Mishi, but her voice was a long way off and I couldn't get to her.

"Oh Mishi," said a syrupy woman's voice, "no need to carry on so. This is going to be over before you know it. Such a big girl, you're not afraid of needles are you?"

"Let. Me. Go!" There was more struggling then the sound of a hard slap. Mishi whimpered, and was silent.

"That's better," said the woman. "Now I'm not going to lie to you. I rather enjoyed that. And if there's any more from you I'm going to enjoy doing it again. Strap her down in the chair, Mulligan."

McInnes turned me around.

I could see a couple of rent-a-henchmen holding Mishi down in the metal chair. Mishi was white with fear and a red mark was spreading on her left cheek. Snell was standing a few feet away, wide-eyed.

Sally Portland, with rubber surgical gloves on her hands, was busy at a metal medical trolley, sorting through hypodermics, vials of liquid, kidney dishes and gauze swabs.

Mishi looked at me imploringly.

Now, OK, I'm the big brother and I get it, my number one job in life, above all others, is to protect my little sister from harm. No one, as far as I can remember, ever needed to tell me this. It was, like, etched into my DNA. And now I was lolling in McInnes' arms, watching all of this going down. I urged my body to respond to what was happening in front of me. But I had nothing left.

Then I did something that, in retrospect, I should've done a lot earlier. The Stern family is God-fearing, but we don't set the pace at our synagogue for orthodox observance. We're regular attendees and follow a lot of Jewish practices, but we're not right up there with our most conscientious co-religionists, or any religionists for that matter.

But, up until now, I suddenly realized, I had been trying to do all of this myself. Now I had nothing left, and my sister was in real danger.

So I prayed.

I asked for one last ounce of strength to do what I had to do, then, I said, anything can happen to me after that. Just let me save Mishi.

Now, you may or may not believe what happened next. But I can only report what I experienced, and it was this: A presence entered the warehouse via one of the cracked upper windows. I could feel it head straight for me and enter my body. I felt the fatigue and lassitude leave and a strength and fire and clarity I had not suspected, soak into every cell.

I heard a roar fill the warehouse, and it was coming out of my mouth. I flung McInnes aside like he was made of paper and I flew at the henchman on Mishi's left.

Before he could react I caught him under the chin with an uppercut which sent him flying backward. He missed Sally Portland by an inch, as she stood frozen.

I grabbed Mishi by the wrist and hauled her out of the chair. And I was turning to look for the way out when I was hit from behind by a freight train.

I went down like a sack of potatoes. My body convulsed. Then I felt the stretching and twisting and I fell into that familiar black hole.

2.

The Tenth Vision

I was floating in an ocean of golden light. I felt a peace that I had never known before. It was completely wonderful. I had absolutely zero desire to be anywhere else. In fact I had absolutely zero desires.

I had no idea how long I floated there, feeling the caressing waves of golden light.

Time was non-existent.

Then a shape created itself out of the light. It is hard now to describe, but it was like a man, but so unlike any man you're likely ever to see that the word 'man' is too poor a description. 'He' was like everything a man should be, could be, but a thousand times a thousand times more than that.

And behind him, like golden light streaming through golden light, was a pair of wings. But, again, 'wings' doesn't do it either. It was like a flow of the purest energetic power and force. This Being was the boiled-down essence of all the power that ever was, is, or will be.

Then He spoke to me. Not in words, but in Speech. Everything in that Golden Place was like the Real version of everything. The man wasn't a man but a Man. His speech was not mere words but real Speech, of which every language on earth is a limitlessly small copy, bearing the same resemblance to True Speech, as a child's drawing of a smiling yellow face with wiggly lines does to the sun.

And He spoke to me, and He called me by name.

"Aaron Stern, son of Reuben Stern, son of ..." This went on for a while, listing, apparently, my ancestors going back generations of Sterns and Solomons, Mom's family name.

One name stood out, not because I knew it but because it glowed in the air "...son of Haym Solomon son of..."

Finally, the list ended.

With a courage I didn't know I possessed I said: "Who are you? What is your name?" I thought I felt laughter.

"I have a thousand names. And I have none. Today, at this time, you may know me as Michael, Archangel to the Lord of Hosts, General of the Armies of the Lord Most High, Smiter of those who would do evil in the sight of the Lord God of Israel."

These words filled me with terror, and sublime exhilaration. Every atom of my being trembled.

I had the chutzpah to try again. "What do you want me to do?"

The Voice spoke again: "You will be shown. You have been chosen. I am with you. I will always be with you."

"Will I succeed?" I asked.

But there was no answer. The Golden Light began to fade, and I was falling into blackness again.

MISHI STERN

1.

Well, that was something you don't see every day. My brother Ronnie showing unsuspected fighting skills. He caught Mulligan, or was it Gantz, a fantastic uppercut. The guy actually lifted off the floor. Ronnie grabbed me and I was up and out of the chair like a shot, and, who knows, we might have got away. But that Queen B of Bitchdom, the Portland Pig was too fast. Quickdraw Sally had a taser out and into Ronnie before he got a yard. He went down like a rock and lay on the floor twitching and groaning. It was horrible.

But it's the next bit that still has me waking up screaming.

They got me back in the chair. The cable ties went back on, especially tight.

Then Sally's eyes sparkled. She took a syringe, and filled it with a colorless fluid. She gave it a squirt so a tiny spritz shot up into the air. She stood in front of me with one hand stroking my hair and the other holding the syringe up.

"Darling, Mishi, that was very exciting. Who knew Big Brave Ronnie had it in him. I'm seeing him in a whole new light I can tell you. Yummy!"

I nearly threw up.

"What are you going to do to me?" I said, disgusted by my mousy pathetic voice. I tried to see into her mind, but the terror blocked me.

"Ah well, that is the best part. We are going to make sure Ronnie plays ball. And you are going to help."

"That's where you're wrong. I'm never going to help you. I'm not going to say a thing to Ronnie."

Sally Portland stood back and put her free hand on her hip and sighed.

"Mishi, Mishi, Mishi, you still don't get it." Holding the syringe in one hand, she went to the metal tray and fussed for a bit. She came over to me and rubbed my arm with a cool, wet cotton ball, which gave off that hospital smell. Then before I knew it she plunged the syringe into my arm and emptied it. Fire coursed up my arm, through my shoulder and neck, up into my head, which exploded with pain.

I writhed and struggled against the cable ties but I couldn't get away. My throat was closing, my fists clenched and unclenched, and my heels began to drum against the floor.

Then it was over. I was covered in sweat and my head was hanging down. The fierce pain had subsided to a dull whole-body ache.

"What... What did you do... to me?"

Sally Portland had been watching me calmly. Rats in a lab stare up from their cages and see that look.

"I injected you with a radioactive isotope," she said thoughtfully. "In its pure form it kills in a few, very, very uncomfortable minutes. Internal organs and tissues liquefy and you dissolve from the inside. A bit like Ebola. But we thought Ronnie might find that a bit extreme. Kill his dear little sister, and who knows? He might cooperate, he might not. So *I* came up with a plan."

"So," I managed to say, "what was your brilliant plan."

"Well, I must confess, you're a bit of a guinea-pig Mishi," she said. She was back to girly girl Sally. "It will make you feel sick, nauseous certainly, but I diluted the isotope to a point where it is essentially harmless."

"Harmless? That doesn't sound scary enough for you, Bitchface."

"Sticks and stones, Mishi," she said. "Yes, harmless, for about forty-eight hours, if I've calculated the dose correctly. For the next twelve hours after that your organs begin to breakdown until the process is irreversible. And you die in screaming agony."

She laughed and laughed. I wasn't getting the joke.

"So it's reversible?" I wheezed, every inch of skin ached. "How?"

"Clever Mishi. You've spotted the really ingenious part of my plan." She turned to the medical table and picked up a vial of light-pink fluid. She waggled it back and forth playfully. "This is the antidote. Inject this any time in the next two days, give or take, and you'll be good as new. And if you and your scrummy Ronnie do what is required, I'll do the deed and you can go free."

Even kidnapped, tied up, smacked around, and poisoned I wasn't stupid enough to believe a single word of that last bit. I knew she was lying, because her lips were moving and sounds were coming out of her mouth.

But I knew Ronnie. If there was a one per cent chance of saving me, there was a one hundred per cent chance of him agreeing to anything they asked.

Crap.

2.

Ronnie was still out cold when they cut the cable ties and pulled me up from the chair. They got him under the arms and dragged us both across the warehouse to a black SUV. It had a caged rear section and we were dumped in there. I landed on Ronnie. Better than the other way around I guess.

"All set?" called McInnes cheerily, as Portland and two other bozos, Mulligan and Gantz, buckled up. I could see the others, including Snell, packing away everything in the warehouse and taking boxes to two other waiting cars. "Off we go then."

The SUV roared to life and we rolled out of the warehouse into the night. I felt like throwing up. A gnawing pain in my stomach and a throbbing ache in my head were making it hard to think. But I knew I should at least try to see where we were going. I struggled against the pain and the movement of the SUV to get my head up to window level.

The streets and buildings sped by. This was an unfamiliar part of Longbeach, lit by the occasional unbroken streetlamp. It was all pawn shops and vacant lots with a few bunches of equally vacant kids hanging out, smoking and wearing their baseball caps backward.

After about half an hour of this we turned into a drive and up to a gate with a security booth. A chain link fence stretched away into the darkness in both directions. McInnes showed the guard a card and we passed through.

I peeked forward through the windshield. We were at an airfield, driving around the perimeter with the fence on our right. We made a ninety-degree left turn and headed toward some brightly lit low buildings in the distance. Lined up neatly in front of the buildings were three small jets. The kind mega-rich people use to get to the ski-slopes or polo tournaments or wherever it is those guys go.

We pulled up next to one of the jets, which up close didn't look so small. On its tail it had that light blue UN symbol of the world surrounded by leaves.

Ronnie groaned and rolled onto his side.

The Gang of Four got out, and Mulligan and Gantz came around the back, opened the tailgate and dragged Ronnie and me out. The sky was just turning that purple, orange pre-dawn color.

They hustled Ronnie and me over to the UN plane. The side door was open and we were pushed and prodded up a short set of stairs, through the small doorway into the plane. They shoved us down an aisle with single padded leather seats on either side. There was not much headroom. It was not easy going. I felt like throwing up every step, and Ronnie was still like a doll with the stuffing removed. We jigged and jagged down the narrow aisle using the seats to steady ourselves.

At the back of the plane was a walled-off area with a door marked 'Toilet'. They shoved me down onto the floor in the narrow space between this wall and the last seat on one side of the aisle. Ronnie was dumped across the way.

"Now you two lie there nicely," said McInnes. "Any fancy stuff and we'll tie you up, gag you, and ignore your pleas for mercy."

Say what you like about that Aussie guy, but he sure got the message across.

I managed to maneuver myself around into a sitting position with my back against the toilet wall and my legs stretched under the seat. I was staring at a leather seat-back about a foot away from my face.

I looked across at Ronnie who was curled awkwardly in his space. He was rocking his head back and forth, trying to clear his brain I guessed. I wanted him to come around quickly. My arm throbbed where Sally had injected me and my body ached and, was it my imagination? I felt a creeping gray sickness in my body.

Ronnie and I definitely had things to discuss.

The jet came to life, the engines screamed up to full power and then we jumped forward.

No 'here's how you put on the life vest' talk, and no pointing out the exits in case of a crash.

Boy, did these guys ever live dangerously.

WOLFGANG HOLST, KATIE LIEBOVITZ AND MELVIN SHNAYVISE

"Gone I'm afraid, Dottore," said Wolfgang, holding his cell to his ear and slowly turning to take in the whole warehouse. "In a hurry, and not long ago."

Katie stood next to him, Melvin at her side. Morning sunlight was streaming through the high windows leaving rectangles of light on the floor and walls of the warehouse.

Katie looked shattered. She and Melvin had waited in a second car down the street for Wolfgang and several other Elder operatives to give the all clear. They were expecting a knock down, drag 'em out fight, so when the call came almost immediately Katie had feared the worst.

And she was looking at it now. An abandoned warehouse. They were standing next to a metal chair bolted to the concrete floor. There were a few broken packing cases lying in dark corners. They could see an empty shipping container in the half-light against the far wall.

But no Ronnie or Mishi.

"He wants to speak to you," said Wolfgang. He handed over the cell.

"Yes," said Katie.

"Go home, and wait," said Dr. Califario. "That goes for Mr. Shnayvise as well. It is the best place for you. Your families will be extremely anxious. Go home and keep trying to locate Aaron and Mishi. Now they are together it may be easier. Keep me informed."

Katie felt like arguing, so did Melvin, but Dr. Califario was right, there was nothing more for them to do, and they both knew that their families would be increasingly frantic if they didn't go home.

Wolfgang arranged transport and they headed off north, away from Longbeach toward LA.

AARON STERN

I was only partly conscious during the car ride, bouncing and rocking from side to side, spending what little energy I had trying not to add to my rich collection of cuts and bruises. The same for the hustle into the jet and down to the cubby-hole at the back. It was a relief to curl up on the floor and breathe in the dust, and feel that nice polyester carpet scratching the non-sliced side my face. Then I was pressed against the back partition by the force of the take off. The floor tilted upwards and I was wedged until we leveled out.

I slowly got my bearings. I opened my eyes and looked around and saw Mishi sitting across the aisle with her back to the cabin partition. She was looking at me. She didn't say anything. She looked drained. I guessed we were a match, because this business had totally knocked me sideways.

I mean, one minute I was breaking into a museum to steal an irreplaceable artifact to give to some bad actors in exchange for my kidnapped sister, and the next, I was making a break for freedom, and being sandbagged in the process. Now we were on a jet heading who knew where.

Time to take stock.

"Hey, Mish," I said, "where are we? What's happening? Where are we going?"

"Hey Doofus," said Mishi, "we're flying. On a plane. I don't know where, they didn't get me to check over their flight plans for spelling mistakes."

"Are you OK?" I asked.

Sunlight was spilling in from the little round windows. She looked stricken. All that bravado vanished and her face scrunched up. She started crying and shaking. She turned away from me and buried her head in her arms.

"Mish, Mish," I said, "come on, we'll get out of this. I don't know how but we will."

She looked at me and said, "they poisoned me. I'm going to die."

"What?" I said, a lead weight crashed into my chest and crushed the air out of me. "That shitface woman injected me with poison, some radioactive thing, and I'll melt from the inside if she doesn't give me the antidote in two days."

"What?" I said.

"Don't keep saying 'What?,' it makes you sound even more stupid than usual."

"Why did they do that to you?"

"To get you to do what they want. And when you do, then they said they'd give me the stuff to cure me."

"Oh Mishi," I said.

Then I had a brilliant thought.

"If I can get over to you I'll touch you and I can heal you. That's my power. I can heal people. Not all the time. I've got to feel a build up inside, a kind of pressure. But you have to let me try."

"OK," she said, in the tiniest voice that broke my heart. My smart-mouthed, 'take the world by the lapels and head butt her way through' sister had turned into a scared little girl before my eyes.

I shuffled over a little and beckoned her to do the same.

The aisle wasn't wide and I could reach her easily, but I peeked out quickly. The gang was sitting in the forward seats. I could see their legs, and their arms on the arm rests. No one was watching us.

I reached out to Mishi, my hand inching across the aisle along the carpeted floor.

Her hand crawled toward mine.

Our fingers were half an inch apart when Sally Portland stood on them. We both yanked our hands back, waving and blowing on them.

"Naughty, naughty," she sang. "No playing handies or we'll have to tie up the bad little boy and girl." Then her voice turned cold and businesslike. "Get some sleep, you're going to need it."

"Where are we going?" I asked.

"My, my aren't we inquisitive. You'll find out soon enough. Just rest, and no talking or touching or we will make you wish you hadn't."

"And what if I refuse to cooperate?"

Sally Portland let out short laugh. She looked at Mishi, then she looked back at me. "I assume she told you. She's already dead, unless I give her this," she fished out a glass vial of pink fluid from her pocket. "Cooperate, she lives; don't, she dies." She looked at her watch, "in about two or three days, plus or minus. Me, I could care less if the brat croaks, no offence Mishi dear. But the people who hired me want you, Ronnie, to cooperate. I would if I were you."

PROFESSOR OLAF SVENSSON AND JEREMY PLENSK

"Not long to go now, Plensk," said Svensson, settling into the overstuffed floral armchair in the corner next to the window. He put a sheaf of papers onto a side table and looked around the room. Plensk was seated at the end of a three-seater sofa next to the tall bookcase that held gold-embossed leather bound volumes. Svensson looked uncharacteristically energized.

"Tomorrow night, my boy, we are going to change history," Svensson said leaning forward. "We are going to make straight the way upon which humanity is walking. The forces of order, strength, efficiency, racial purity and cleanliness, scientific rationalism, will finally overcome chaos, weakness, and individual freedom."

Plensk wondered how come the strong forces of order and scientific rationalism took such a long time to defeat weak chaos. But Svensson was talking again, his hands clenched into tight fists.

"The power that has protected our enemies for centuries, perhaps millennia, will be turned against them. Da Silva has given us a golden opportunity for greatness, for victory!"

Svensson was getting worked up. Red face, beads of sweat on his brow, his eyes blazing. Plensk had never seen him like this.

"What's the plan, Professor," said Plensk, trying to steer the conversation back to the here and now.

"Yes, of course, the plan. Well, as you know, when Da Silva's four signs come together a portal in the Universe opens and great power floods in, or, in this case out."

"Out?" said Plensk.

"Yes, out," Svensson said. "The protections embedded in DC were not of course the only legacy of the Founding Fathers. The Declaration of Independence with its references to Nature's God, and the iconography and traditions of the new Republic, the Constitution," Svensson spat the last word. "The dollar bill is covered in their symbols. I can barely bring myself to touch one. These are not accidental and they retain innate power regardless of today's pygmies who have custodianship of the nation."

"But I'm guessing that we are not going to change the Constitution or reissue a new dollar bill," said Plensk.

"No, no, indeed. We have another plan altogether. As you know, one of the most powerful protections the Fathers put in place was right here in Washington DC. The site was very carefully located on a powerful ley line. The city was the lynch pin for many years, which bound the Northern and Southern States. Without it the Civil War would have come about much earlier. But the location of DC we cannot change," Svensson smiled, back to his avuncular self. "But L'Enfant, Washington, Franklin and above all that Jew, Haym Solomon, made sure that the city layout, the buildings, the iconography wove an impenetrable web of protection over this country. That web has been working its mischief for over two hundred years. It is obvious, is it not, that something must be afoot, given the fools and weaklings elected to Congress and sent to the White House?"

"Well, now that you mention it..." said Plensk.

"And tonight we have the opportunity to dissolve that web of protection."

"With the four signs," said Plensk.

"Yes, my dear boy, The Twins, a gifted brother and sister; and The Word, an ancient scroll of such power that its mere touch can kill. These last two Signs will be here from Los Angeles," Svensson consulted his watch, "in about an hour."

KATIE LIEBOVITZ

Katie unlocked the door and walked into her home. Her mother stood in the hall, her hands on her hips. Her father, his face mournful, stood behind her.

"Young Lady, where have you been?"

"Mom, I told you we were at a hosp..."

"Don't say a word! I don't want to hear. You're grounded, and you'll stay grounded until your father and I say so. I have never, do you hear, never experienced such behavior. Tell her, Donny, tell her what we think of her behavior. What were you thinking young lady, going gallivanting around the city late at night, worrying your parents sick? I could have died you know, I was so worried about you, I could have had a heart attack. But would you have cared? Tell her Donny, tell her how worried we were. This friend in hospital means more to you than your own parents. *We* would have been in hospital in another second. And would you have cared? Would you have come to visit us? I should say not. You are not leaving this house until your father and I say so, don't even think about asking because do you know what the answer will be? Well, do you? Tell her what the answer will be, Donny. The answer will be No. N. O. And that is final. Well, young lady, are you just going to stand there, or have you got something to say for yourself? Donny, ask her if she has something to say for herself."

Katie stood with her head bowed. When her mother paused for breath she whispered: "Sorry Mom, sorry Dad."

"Sorry! *You're* Sorry! *Now* you're sorry, well you weren't sorry when you were out at all hours of the night in God knows what part of town, with God knows who. With that Stern boy, that's who you were with I suppose. Sorry? Well, you're certainly going to be sorry now."

After a century of this, Katie was allowed up to her room. She was e-grounded. She had to turn over her cell, and she was forbidden to contact anyone on her computer.

MELVIN SHNAYVISE

"Mom, I'm home," Melvin shouted over the slamming of the front door. "I've been out, with Ronnie and Katie."

"That's nice dear, did you have a nice time?"

"Yeah Mom it was nice." No need to worry his Mom with tales of violent criminals, and knives, and blood, and ambulances, and police.

His sister Sadie came running bare foot from the kitchen. She was wearing a pink T-shirt and denim overalls. "Melbin, Melbin!" she shouted. Melvin lifted her up and swung her around and around, careful to miss the old hat stand and mirror with piles of shoes tossed in cheerful disregard of all rules about trip hazards. The paintwork on the walls and skirting boards and high ceiling needed work, but everything, the bare floorboards, the threadbare rugs, was scrubbed as clean as a hospital.

"Ooh, Lady Sadie," Melvin said. "You're getting big. Soon I won't be able to do this. You'll have to pick me up and swing me around."

Sadie was laughing too much to reply.

They were joined by Myron and Mendel his twin brothers. Five years old, andjust started school.

"Hey it's the Shmendrick Twins!" Melvin cried. "C'm 'ere you." Melvin, Sadie, Mendel and Myron did a Shnayvise family hug.

"You want something for breakfast? Food, we got." Sarah Shnayvise shouted from the kitchen, "there's chicken soup, your favorite."

"Really Mom? Chicken soup, for breakfast?" Melvin shouted back.

"But it's your favorite!" Mom shouted back.

"Yeah, Mom," Melvin called, realizing how hungry he was and how chicken soup was exactly what he felt like. How did Mom do that? "I'll have some of your special breakfast soup."

"Hannah, pour your brother a bowl of chicken soup," said Mom to Melvin's other sister.

Melvin heard bowls and ladles and the sound of pouring. He disentangled himself from the family scrimmage.

"Come on Team Shnayvise, race you to the kitchen. There's some soup that's not going to drink itself!"

They all scampered down the hallway, everyone shouting and speaking at once.

Hannah put the bowl down at the head of the table. It had been Melvin's father's place until two years ago.

"Thanks Hannah," said Melvin. "That's a nice dress you're wearing. It suits you."

Hannah, fifteen, blushed to the roots of her dark hair. She turned away quickly and helped her mother with the dishes.

Melvin spooned in the soup. Around him the kitchen was filled with talking and shouting, the clatter of dishes, toast popping and eggs frying. Myron showed Mom something he'd painted at school that week. Hannah was rocking Sadie to sleep on her lap.

Melvin looked at Sadie. She had given their father the greatest gift ever.

Mom had been pregnant when Dad was diagnosed.

"Sarah, I'm gonna hold my kid in my arms if it's the last thing I do," he kept saying from his hospital bed.

And it was.

Melvin remembered the happiness on his Dad's face, looking down at his three-week-old daughter, in his arms, when he took his last breath.

But Melvin was only half listening to the Shnayvise family chaos.

He was worried about Ronnie, and Mishi. Where were they? Katie had promised to call him. His cell was in front of him on the table. He kept one and a half ears open for any messages.

KATIE LIEBOVITZ

Katie flopped onto her bed, exhausted. She stared up at the white ceiling and lay still. Her inner vision of Aaron and Mishi was crystal clear. They were in the air, flying. They were over Missouri.

Now, she thought harshly, when she couldn't do a thing about it, her power came back stronger than ever!

She rolled over, buried her face in her pillow and started to cry.

A few minutes later she heard a light tap at her door. Not Mom then.

"Yes," she sighed. Her mother must have thought up a few more things for her Dad to tell her. "Come in. It's not locked."

The door opened slowly and her brother Sam, two years younger, and in

Katie's opinion an uncommunicative nerd, came in.

"Uh, hi," he said. "I heard Mom. You OK?"

Katie was surprised. She and Sam were not close. They inhabited different planetary systems. Katie lived in the top student, most popular girl in High School world; Sam was from a galaxy far far away, a strange visitor from the Planet Dweeb.

His clothes never fitted, he sat with his fellow dorks in the school lunchroom. They never went out into, like, the sunshine or anything, they watched *Star Trek* reruns, and they argued forever about whether Jar-Jar Binks or the cancellation of *Firefly* was, like, *the* worst thing to happen, ever.

"Yeah, fine, excellent, what do you think? After a cozy Mom and daughter chat like that. We'll be planning a trip to the Mall before you know it."

"She was way harsh."

"You think?"

"And you're, like, not allowed to use your computer?"

"No, Sam," Katie sighed. "That's right. I'm not allowed to use my computer."

"To contact your friends. The ones you do secret stuff with."

Katie gave her brother a closer look. She sat up.

"Yes," she said carefully. "That's right. I'm not allowed to use my computer, to contact my friends, the ones I do secret stuff with."

"But it's important."

"It's more important than you can imagine."

"And you can't use your computer."

Katie was getting tired of this. She lay back down on her bed. "No, Sam, I'm can't."

"But you could use mine?"

Katie sat up again, and saw the laptop under his arm. She leapt from the bed and hugged him.

"Sam, you're the best!"

"Hrnnh," said Sam.

Katie let go and they set up the laptop on her desk.

She thought for a moment and, to her surprise, it was Melvin she emailed.

I know where A and M are. Have to get word to Dr. C. I'm grounded. Get me out of here. Get me on a plane. Have to follow A and M. Please, K.

CHAPTER SIXTEEN

2ND OCTOBER

CONTINUED

AARON STERN

The flight took hours, and Mishi and I dozed and woke and dozed and woke until the jolt of the landing brought us round to what passed for consciousness.

We were pulled out of our cramped places behind the seats, hustled down the narrow aisle and out of the plane. It was daylight. We were at another airfield. I had no idea where. As far as I could see the plane stood on a tarmac in an empty flat expanse. There were two black SUVs nearby, their engines running. We could have been anywhere a few hours flying time from LA.

The guys named Gantz and Mulligan kept watch over us while Portland and McInnes conferred, and Snell hovered nervously nearby.

Sally Portland came over and pointed at the cars.

"Him in that one, the girl in the other."

"No, wait, we need to go tog..."

Sally Portland landed a slap on my face that made my head ring. I felt the blood start again from the cut on my cheek.

"Shut up!" she said. "Just shut up. I am completely sick of this 'Ooh my sister this, my sister that'. No one believes you, Ronnie. No one does anything for anyone but themselves. So Cut. The. Crap."

I lunged at her but Gantz had me by the arms and held me back. Can I say at this point that I'd been punched, kicked, slapped, sliced, and, oh yes, buried alive. I was losing count. This, and especially the cruelty to Mishi, was making me angrier and angrier. But I was physically spent, I was being held tight from behind, so I just resolved to bide my time.

Mishi was taken to one SUV and I was thrown into the back of another, unable to see out the windows. I lay on the floor letting my blood boil, working up the rage. The red haze was making a return appearance.

After about half an hour the cars slowed, turned and started down a slope. They leveled out and came to a stop and the back door was opened. We were in an underground garage.

Mishi was standing next to the other SUV, held up by a dark, hard-faced man, with black curly hair.

"Which way, Nikos?" McInnes asked.

The dark guy pointed and we headed to an elevator bank.

We all went up together. Redness flickered at the corners of my peripheral vision. I could feel the sickness in Mishi and the build up of pressure inside telling me I had to heal her.

I didn't get a chance before we arrived at the third floor and stepped out into an empty corridor. Nikos and Snell, and the other guy, Mulligan, took Mishi down the hall one way. McInnes and Gantz took me in the other direction. Portland completed our happy band.

There were labels on the doors: 'Manager', 'Secretary' and so on.

Gantz knocked on a door marked 'Authorized Personnel Only'.

"Hey, is this OK?" I said to McInnes, who had my elbow in an iron grip. "Are you sure we're authorized? I wouldn't want anyone to get into, you know, trouble."

McInnes rolled his eyes and shook his head. He opened the door and we all marched in.

Behind a desk was Lassiter, the guy from the Skype session, the slick UN dude. Singh, his face blank, his gray suit immaculate, was standing in a corner. The room was snug, with filing cabinets down the wall to the left, and open shelving holding file boxes down the opposite wall. Behind Lassiter was a window with venetian blinds, angled so no could see in, and I couldn't see out. A clock on the wall said it was twelve after four in the afternoon.

"Welcome, welcome," said Lassiter, smiling at me like I'd turned up for canapés and cocktails. "Gentlemen, please get a chair for our guest."

There was a dragging of furniture across the navy-blue carpet, and I was pushed down into a chair. McInnes and Gantz stood behind me. Portland stood near Singh, leaning against the filing cabinets, her arms folded.

"Now Mr. Stern," said Lassiter, beaming at me. "So good to meet you in person. And, again, apologies for the, ah, vigorous treatment that has been meted out to you and your charming sister."

So he hadn't met Mishi yet.

"I wanted to have this little meeting, to clarify a few things."

I wasn't quite ready to become Facebook friends with this guy. So I sat and waited. "I've already explained some of what we are up to. It would make things so much more convenient if you undertook your role willingly. But if not, well..." he shrugged and spread his hands. "Your sister, for example, will die if you don't do what we want. And, of course, you will too. And, just so there is no possibility of misunderstanding, your deaths will be as lingering and painful as Miss Portland can devise. As I'm sure you are aware by now, Miss Portland is a dedicated professional who is passionate about her work." He nodded in Portland's direction. She smirked and gave me a bow. "No, Mr. Stern, it will definitely not be pleasant, for either of you."

I had heard a lot of this baloney before. It was just making me angrier.

"So," he clapped his hands together, all business. "We need you and your sister to attend a small ceremony using those components we discussed before. You constitute one piece, that scroll you so thoughtfully provided is another, and the Time, tonight, and the Location..."

"I've been meaning to ask about that," I interrupted. "Where the heck are we?"

"You are in our nation's capital, Washington DC," said Lassiter. "Not far from the White House. To say more, would be telling. But the ceremony will take place here in DC tonight with the Moses Revelation, and you and your sister, in starring roles. If you fail to cooperate you will die. And so will your sister. And we will keep killing your family and friends until there are none left. Am I making myself clear?"

"Yes," I said, yawning. "Yes, you have made yourself clear."

"So, Mr. Stern," Lassiter leaned forward in his chair, "can I count on you? Can I, Ronnie?"

"Yes," I said, leaning right back at him. "Yes, you can, Randy. You've been pretty persuasive. And since, as you say, we're gonna be dragged into this jamboree anyway, we might as well go willingly. With the added bonus of how we get to emerge with our skins intact if we play ball. Is that about the size of it?"

"Yes, Mr. Stern," said Lassiter beaming. "Yes it is. Excellent."

He nodded to his goons and McInnes stood me up and, with Gantz in tow, took me along the hallway back past the elevators to a room marked 'Storage'. Gantz shuffled through a set of keys. He unlocked the door and McInnes, with mock courtesy, indicated I should go in.

"We'll come and get you when it's time for you to do your stuff," he said.

I was crossing the threshold when I felt a shove in my back and I went flying into a stack of cardboard boxes, knocking them over and spilling papers and files all over the floor.

Curled up in the corner, gray-faced and trembling, was Mishi.

KATIE LIEBOVITZ AND MELVIN SHNAYVISE

Email, from Sam Liebovitz's laptop:

Katie to Dr. Califario

> *I'm at home, grounded. I've tracked A and M to DC. Our new friend MS is going to get me out, and on a plane. I hope. K*

Text from Sam Liebovitz's phone:
Melvin to Katie
Hang tight, hlp is on the way! 1 hr ☺
Email:
Dr. Califario to Wolfgang
Gather all operatives at The Migdal, immediate. Urgent. AC

Email:

Dr. Califario to Colonel Landon McAllister
Trouble in DC. Contact everyone. Weapons. AC

Text:
Katie to Melvin
Yr a life saver

Text:
Melvin to Katie

Text (one hour later):
Melvin to Katie
Am under yr window cn u clmb dwn?

Katie to Melvin, in person, through bedroom window, in a whisper:
Melvin. Melvin! Where are y... Oh, OK I can see you. Yes, I can. Climb down that is.

Melvin to Katie, in person, standing in flowerbed:
What? What did you say? I can't hear you.

Katie to Melvin, in person, from bedroom window, louder whisper:
I said, Yes I c... Oh, never mind.

Melvin to Katie, in flowerbed, underneath Katie:
Oomph!

Katie to Melvin, standing and brushing dirt from jeans:
Come on Melvin. Don't just lie there. We've gotta go.

AARON STERN

1.

I disentangled myself from the files and papers on the floor, slipping and sliding on invoices and inter-office memos. I made my way over to Mishi.

"How are you, Mish?" I said.

"Oh, you know, fine." She tried to smile. "I've got a few days before I die a horrible death, but, look on the bright side, we can help the nice people who own this building by alphabetizing their five year old correspondence."

"Yeah, that'll pass the time. But I've got a better idea." We were in a small storage room, a few feet wide and stretching back about twenty feet. It was fully lined with shelving and at the back were a broken swivel chair and a small table with a missing leg. "OK, so, like I said, I've got this healing power and I'm going to use it now. I suppose the bad guys don't know about it or they would've kept us apart."

"I guess," said Mishi, all her energy used up on her wisecracking. "Knock yourself out."

"Sit tight and I'm going to hold your hand. It doesn't take long."

"And you think it'll work?" she looked worried.

"Only one way to find out." I gave her my most reassuring smile.

I shucked over closer to her and reached for her hand. I braced myself, ready to be knocked over or zapped or something. That had always been the way with this thing.

But when we touched it wasn't like that at all.

I got the red mist, shimmering at the edge of my vision and slowly coloring the room, the furniture and Mishi.

But no jolt. Instead a greeny-gray oily feeling flowed from Mishi and oozed its way into me.

It moved slowly up my fingers. My hand began to throb and ache. The pain moved along my arm to the elbow, and was traveling up to my shoulder when my heart began to race and flutter and beat out of rhythm.

I was trying to suppress a moan, when Mishi snatched her hand away.

"What are you doing?" I said between gasps. "It was working."

"Yeah right!" said Mishi with her old fire. I looked at her and some color had returned to her cheeks. "I was tracking your mind, while we were playing hospitals and I was about to ask you the same thing. What the heck do you think you're doing?"

My head was pounding. I was finding it hard to concentrate.

"Think about it Doofus." That was the Mishi we all knew and loved. It was encouraging. "So you're some hero miracle healer, but you left out the teeny-weensiest, little-bitty detail. In the process you get a full blast of the bug. Do I look like an idiot! If you think I'm going to let you be the big brave Sir Galahad, who then collapses, or drops dead, well, there isn't room in this family for two people without a couple of neurons in their skull. One of us has to do the thinking."

Good ol' Mishi. And she was right about me collapsing. Already I could barely move.

"I can't let you die," I managed.

"Yes, Dingbat," she said. "I know that. And I don't want to die. And I get the whole older brother looking after the little sister routine. And, don't think I don't appreciate it, and love you to death for it. But think about it. *I* can't deal with these people. I'm a fourteen-year-old girl. My mind powers are only working on and off. So one of us has to be fighting fit, that's if you want to rescue the damsel in distress."

I just looked at her. "That'd be me, Moron."

Then the door opened and Katie came flying in. She landed at our feet.

"Katie!" I shouted.

"Oh great," said Mishi. "Just what we need. Another damsel."

2.

"Katie," I said. "What are you doing here?"

Katie fell into my arms. I gave a small yelp, what with all the cuts and bruises, and Mishi's poison. But judging by her tears, it was painful for Katie too. I held her tight. Mishi sat and watched us.

After a while we let go of each other. Katie sat back and looked at us. "God, Ronnie, Mishi, what's happened to you? You both look, awful, green, and gray, and awful. Are you OK? Ronnie what's happened to your face?"

"No, we're not OK," I said, holding her hand. "But it's a long story. Can we hear yours first?"

"Mine's simple. I located you both flying across America, and landing here in DC. Melvin got me on board a flight as, let me see, yep, here it is," she consulted a boarding pass, "as far as United Airlines is concerned I'm Brenda Tuttle of Wallah Wallah, Washington. Anyway I came to find you, and some gorillas guarding the building got suspicious. They grabbed me and they called an Asian guy, I guess he's the one who took Mishi. He had my photo. So, Brenda Tuttle didn't cut it. And here I am. The semi-good news is I got a text off to Dr. Califario before the gorillas got me. But I only got to say 'ymca', hope he can figure it out."

"YMCA?" I said.

"Yes," said Katie. "On 16th Street. Didn't you know?"

"No, we only got a few glimpses on the way here. I saw a Denny's sign a few blocks before we arrived, but that's about it. We were both kind of out of it," I said.

Mishi had been silent through Katie's recount. "You came to get us?" she said.

"Yep," said Katie. "I guess I messed up, huh?"

"That puts things in a whole new light," said Mishi thoughtfully.

Katie and Mishi were locked on each other. I had that familiar sinking feeling guys get when secret code is passing between the womenfolk in his life.

"What do you mean Mish?" I said with little hope of being allowed into the inner sanctum of female mysteries. But that poison must have done something to her. She turned to me slowly and I saw tears in her eyes.

"I always thought Katie was a spoilt ditz, who batted her eyelids at every man she saw, and made them all dance to her tune. You, of course."

"Of course," keeping up my end of the conversation.

"But Dad, and Mordecai, and Dr. Califario too," Mishi went on. Katie handed her a tissue to blow her nose.

"And now," said Mishi, "she's gone and ruined everything, coming here to rescue us, and put her life in danger, and, and..."

Katie moved over and put both arms around Mishi and began to rock her back and forth.

"It's OK," said Katie gently. "When this is over I'll try to go back to being a stuck up, Bel Air trust fund brat, who pops gum, and just soooo wants to be head cheerleader."

Mishi laughed. "Too late. I know your secret."

"Which is?"

"That you're really a super hero who loves my brother, and me."

"Well, that's true," said Katie. "About Ronnie I mean, but who said you're included?"

"You tracked us both. You can only do that if you loved us both. Mordecai told me

you had to have strong feelings."

"Hate also works. I might hate you," said Katie, smiling and continuing to rock Mishi gently.

"Yeah, right," said Mishi, and laughed.

And that's when I felt the blackness open up again. "Aw poop," I said, "not again, not now," before I fell, stretched and twisted, into another vision.

3.

The Eleventh Vision

I was in a dimly lit room, some kerosene lamps hung from hooks on the bare wood-plank walls. A single candle in a plain candlestick stood in the middle of a circular wooden table illuminating the three men who sat around it. They were leaning in toward each other talking in low tones. The room itself was free of any other decoration or furniture except for a few pegs upon which hung three coats. The coats looked thick and heavy and one of them had a lot of brass buttons and braid which glinted in the light. Another was plain black, and the third was a dull dark-brown with a wide collar and long tail.

My point of view moved in closer to the three guys and I began to pick out a few words.

"As we have discussed already..."

"Imperative that the plans are accurately carried out..."

"Protection for our new Republic..."

Then one dude leaned back and stretched. Even sitting I could tell he was pretty tall. I got a good look at his face. He had a commanding presence, a fine aquiline nose and an expression of calm authority.

And I thought, 'Holy crap, if that isn't George Washington, then someone else was staring at me from every one-dollar bill I'd ever handled.'

The man on his right was dressed plainly in a white shirt and old boots that came up to his knees. His eyes twinkled. He had a fringe of long hair framing his bald head, and a pair of half-moon spectacles perched on the end of his nose.

And I thought, 'Get out of town! That's Benjamin Franklin! He's on the hundred-dollar bill.' All I needed now was Hamilton, Grant and Jackson to complete the set.

"My dear Solomon," said the Father of Our Country to the third guy at the table, "I know that you have laid before us the details many times, but just for the sake of certainty and accuracy could I trouble you to tell us just once more before we part?"

"Yes, Solomon, my good fellow," said Franklin, "I concur with the General. You convinced us long ago, but perhaps just one more time?"

"I will my friends," the third guy, presumably Solomon, was small and dark, with curly black hair and a beaky nose. I was getting used to this, the guy on the Roman ship, the grandfather on the Dutch dock, this guy, there was a family resemblance to all of them. "But as I have emphasized before, I require a renewal of your promise of absolute discretion in this matter."

Washington and Franklin nodded.

"It is, as you know, a strange tale I have to tell but it is important that you are completely clear and in agreement with our plans."

Washington leaned back in as Solomon began.

"Centuries ago, in Ancient Egypt, a young scribe from an alien race, the Hebrews, sat and wrote down the secrets of the Universe. His name? We know him as Moses. And he had, as we know, a great destiny before him. It is this document, this scroll of limitless power, written in his own hand, called by those who know of it 'The Hidden Teaching of Moshe Rabbenu', or 'The Revelation of Moses our Teacher', which, through the centuries, passed closely guarded from father to son, the source of protection against those who would rise up in every generation to destroy the Children of Israel. It was kept in the Ark of the Covenant, in the Holy of Holies, in the Temple of Jerusalem, the Center of the World.

"When Jerusalem fell to the Romans in the 70th year of your Christian calendar, and the Temple was destroyed and the Jewish People dispersed, the scroll was rescued by a miracle. The Rabbis of Yavneh gathered to deliberate on how best to protect such a holy object from destruction, or worse, from having its power bent to the purposes of the unrighteous.

"Well, I could take a day, a week, a year to recount to you the vicissitudes which befell this wondrous scroll. Suffice it to say that the original scroll was hidden away by Rabbi Yohanan Ben Zakkai. To this day no one knows where. But legend has it that Ben Zakkai left hidden clues as to its hiding place. And, when the world is in greatest peril then the hidden original will be discovered.

"At Ben Zakkai's direction the seven patriarchs of the seven guardian families made seven copies of the scroll. They carried these copies away in seven different directions. One of those seven copies, only minutely less powerful than its original, found its way to these shores more than a century ago.

"It was my family that carried this copy of the scroll here to America, and we remain the custodians of that divine instrument. In ways too numerous to tell and too wonderful to recount, its power continues to work wonders. That power was, for example, a key factor in our recent miraculous survival against the might of our colonial overlords."

Washington shifted in his chair. "We are, I believe, in sore need of several more miracles if we are to finally defeat them."

"Indeed, General," said Solomon, "I believe such miracles will certainly occur and that is why I asked you here today to put the final seal on our post-bellum plans. For when the time comes, and the enemy is vanquished, the might of The Moses Revelation must be called on to raise walls of protection for our new nation, walls that are mysterious, and potent. And it is in our nation's new-minted capital city that these protective barriers against evil must be most carefully laid."

The scene in the room vanished and now I found myself in a carriage splashing and bouncing along a muddy road. Opposite me was a single passenger being jounced to and fro, holding on to a satin covered strap. It was the Solomon guy from the round table confab. But he looked a little different, like he was older. As if a few years had passed since that dark room and the round table. Interesting.

I heard a driver up front cracking a whip and calling encouragement to the straining horses. Out of the carriage window I could see a landscape of fields with a few stands of trees here and there. It was, I guessed, mid morning.

The carriage rolled past a large white plantation house with tall columns and balconies. Black people were working in the fields.

We came to a halt near a shady grove of trees where three men stood talking, sheltered from the sun. It was Washington and Franklin again, and they were with another guy, thin and dressed in a pale blue frock coat with red trimmings and white exercise pants, at least that's what they looked like to me, you know, real tight. They were all dressed as if they were going straight from there to sign the Declaration of Independence.

They turned to watch Solomon open the door of the carriage. He waited while the driver unhooked a small set of steps and put it in place for him. Then he got down carefully and took a nimble jump over the churned mud of the road. He landed on the tufted grass.

"Thank you my good fellow," he said to the driver from the safety of the roadside. He flipped the guy a coin. "Please see to the horses, and have the carriage ready in three hours."

Then he pulled a handkerchief from his sleeve, lifted his hat and mopped his brow. He turned to the group under the trees and made his way over a stile toward the other men.

"Good day to you all, gentlemen," he said. Solomon shook hands with Washington and Franklin.

"Good day to you Solomon," said the first President of the United States of America. "Thank you for making the journey. I trust it was not excessively burdensome to you?"

"No no, indeed not Your Excellency, no the journey was an easy one. Thank you for the use of your carriage."

"It is nothing. And please," said Washington smiling, "we have had enough of terms like 'Your Excellency' have we not? Has not our recent trial of arms been enough to rid us of these honorifics?"

"I believe, my dear Solomon," said Franklin, "that the term that was suggested is 'Mr. President'. Is that not so, George? I mean, Mr. President."

"Indeed, indeed," said Solomon. "Thank you Benjamin, and a very fitting term for the leader of our new-born Republic."

Franklin turned to the fourth man and said: "Solomon, my dear fellow, might I introduce Pierre Charles L'Enfant, engineer, draftsman, and civic planner." Then he turned to L'Enfant and said, "my dear L'Enfant, may I present our friend Mr. Haym Solomon, a man who, it might be said, with the stroke of a pen ensured the success of our armies over those of our former sovereign."

"Benjamin, please," said Solomon, "you flatter me."

"Not at all my friend," said Washington, turning to L'Enfant. "When we had General Cornwallis trapped at Yorktown, the Continental Army refused to move."

"Arrears of pay," Franklin explained.

"This man," Washington clapped his hand on Solomon's shoulder, "wrote a letter of credit guaranteeing sufficient funds, the army marched, and as a result we are here today, on the banks of the Potomac, at the site of the new capital for our new nation."

"It is a matter which to me is most pleasing," said L'Enfant in a French accent, "otherwise I would not have this opportunity to design a new city from nothing."

For some time the men stood on the small rise, under the trees, whisking gnats away, pointing out various landmarks and topographical features. They made suggestions and discussed possibilities, while L'Enfant scribbled down notes.

After an hour or so of this Franklin said, "my friends, we might let Pierre make some sketches and suggestions for the new city. Let us now turn to those protections against the inevitable dangers that will beset our new republic."

He turned to Haym Solomon and said, "my Friend, shall you tell him?"

Haym Solomon nodded and turned to L'Enfant. He recounted more or less the same story he'd told the other two round the wooden table.

When he'd finished L'Enfant's eyes were alight.

"Sacre Dieu," he whispered. "This is most wonderful. It is a strange story, yes? But I do believe, in my heart, that if it is true, what you say, then these walls, this protection, they will make my city, our city, a city of wonders, a city for the ages."

"Yes, indeed," said Solomon. "But I caution you. These are powerful forces with which we are dealing. Great care must be taken in the laying out of the city streets, the positioning of its main buildings, and even in the carving of its statues and monuments. All the details, if performed correctly, will weave a golden safeguard around the city, and will ensure the strength, power and success of these United States of America, against all foes, external and internal.

"We must build an obelisk on this very spot, on this hill upon which we stand, within sight of this river, reaching to the heavens and drawing power down to earth. That will be the Key.

"The Revelation of Moses came out of Egypt through the hands of the Hebrews. The copy of that very scroll came to these shores in Hebrew hands. Now an obelisk, a shape sacred to the Egyptians, must be placed here to form an anchor and a bridge to the wisdom and power of the Ancient Ones."

"The hour draws on," said Washington. "Perhaps the time has come to adjourn to Mount Vernon. Mrs. Washington will welcome us and we can take our supper and continue our discussions there."

And the scene vanished.

PROFESSOR OLAF SVENSSON AND JEREMY PLENSK

Plensk reached into this back pocket, pulled out his wallet, and paid for two tickets to see the Washington Monument. He and Svensson were booked for the 1 pm tour so they had some time to kill.

They walked a short way along a concrete path to a concession stand and bought pretzels and bottled water. The sun was shining, it was a beautiful day. They turned and looked at the fluttering flags that ringed the obelisk, the tourists milling around taking photos, talking to their kids.

"I came here on a school tour when I was, like, eleven," said Plensk. "All I remember is sticking gum in Becky Sullivan's hair, and Mrs. Chen sending me back to the bus, to 'think about what I had done'. I never got why that was a thing. 'Thinking about what I had done'."

Svensson chewed and sipped.

"When I first came to this country, it was many years ago, certainly many years before the young Miss Sullivan's hair succumbed to its fate at your hands. I made a point of visiting all the places that are revered by you Americans. So I went to the Statue of Liberty, and to Independence Hall in Boston. I went to Paul Revere's House. I suspect I saw the Holocaust Memorial on the Freedom Trail a little differently than most. Since it was one of my father's life ambitions to see the last Jew sent to his or her final resting place. It is a work in progress shall we say?"

Plensk didn't say anything. He had learned to keep quiet when Svensson got on one of his favourite topics.

"And, of course, I came to Washington DC. I went to Ford's Theater first. To pay homage to John Wilkes Booth, the assassin of the war criminal Lincoln."

Plensk noticed that Svensson's accent got stronger when he talked like this.

"I visited all the other sites, of course, the White House, you could still take tours in those days, Congress, the Lincoln Memorial, Arlington Cemetery, the Pentagon. And I came here and took the tour. No little girls with chewing gum in their hair on that day!"

He screwed up the brown paper bag and threw it in a nearby trash can.

"I must say," said Svensson, "I was most impressed. You Americans seem such a superficial people. Concerned with your iPhones, and your football teams, and your Hollywood celebrities. But if you look around a place like this, you have built your monuments, your Congress, your capital city as a home for giants. I have often counseled our people to proceed with caution when it comes to dealing with the Americans. One of your greatest strengths is that people always underestimate you."

Plensk wasn't sure how to feel. Proud of his country, or inspired in the presence of this strange man whose chief ambition was to destroy it.

"Come, Plensk," said Svensson, taking a last swig of water, "the time draws on. Let us take our tour and, what is the phrase, 'case the joint'."

RANDOLPH LASSITER

Lassiter was in a paneled room sitting at an ornate desk. It wasn't quite the same as his home office, or the rooms at the UN building, but it was adequate. The proportions were not exactly as he would have had them, the ceiling a little low, the window a little small, and the desk too big for the space. He was reading a report on the statistical anomalies of bushfire frequencies in North-Eastern New South Wales, Australia. Fascinating.

There was a knock at the door. "Come."

Georgiakis came in.

"There's word from the Y. A girl was snooping around. They have her locked up with the other two."

"A girl?"

"Yes, she's the girlfriend, according to the LA team. She must have tracked them here. Do you want them to search her for devices?"

"From my understanding of how these people work, no, she is able to track them without such devices."

"It's one of these powers?"

"Yes."

"So, get rid of her?"

"Well, my dear Nikos," said Lassiter his elbows on the desk. He interlaced his fingers, leaving the two index fingers free to tap against each other. "Let us consider, shall we? If we kill her it might upset our other young friends. But, on the other hand, who knows what other powers she has. She may be able to alert others to her whereabouts. We can't have that, can we?"

"So, kill her?" Said Georgiakis.

"Yes," said Lassiter returning to his papers, "kill her. But not yet."

St Peter's Square, Rome, 1174

The day was perfect. The late spring sky was cloudless. A light wind blowing in from the Mediterranean Sea cooled the vast crowd. Food and drink sellers plied their trade amongst the tens of thousands of spectators milling in St Peter's Square in front of the basilica and the palace, the home of His Holiness Pope Alexander III.

The hours passed, the sun rose higher and the heat grew. Children became fractious and babies cried. The tall stake, carefully fixed in the exact center of the Square adorned with chains, had long since ceased to hold the interest of the crowd. Some people at the edges of the throng were beginning to drift away.

Suddenly trumpets blared and kettledrums began a rhythmic tattoo.

The carved doors of the papal palace opened and a troop of soldiers marched out, jostling the spectators aside. They formed two lines facing each other, a human corridor stretching from the iron bars of the papal prison to the tall stake. Several tumbrils, pulled by mules, laden with firewood emerged and made their slow way between the lines of guards toward the wooden post. They were followed by chanting priests, four swinging smoking censers and four sprinkling holy water.

When the tumbrils reached the foot of the stake workmen unloaded the bundles of wood and stacked them so high they eventually needed to climb ladders laid against the pile. Finally the pile was twice the height of the tallest papal guard. One of the workmen took a hammer and long iron nails and fixed a small platform, big enough for a man to stand on, to the stake above the woodpile and just below the chains and manacles.

At last the moment all had come to see arrived. The iron bars of the papal prison swung open again and another tumbril, with high openwork wicker sides, came rolling out, slowly pulled by six ragged prisoners lashed to ropes.

In the tumbril a gray-haired old man stood defiantly, gazing out on the crowd with one good eye, the other milky-white with a cat-slit pupil. The crowd shrank back. The papal troops looked nervous.

When the tumbril reached the foot of the piled firewood two enormous guards hauled the prisoner down. While the eight priests chanted and prayed, the guards each took one of the prisoner's arms and carried him up the ladders to the top of the mountain of firewood. The prisoner was manhandled onto the small wooden platform. Chains were wrapped around his body and manacles were locked onto his hands.

The guards withdrew, the prayers swelled.

When all this was complete the trumpets and drums sounded a crescendo and fell silent. The shutters on one of the high windows of the papal apartments opened and a white-robed priest appeared and stepped out onto a balcony. He unrolled a scroll and began to read, the sound echoing around the square, his words repeated in excited whispers to the far corners where his voice didn't quite carry.

"Leonardo Da Silva, also known as Israel ibn Ibrahim, also known as Brother Clement of Aleppo, you are charged this day by the authority of the Holy Father and the Office of the Purity of the Faith, with the following heinous crimes..."

The reading of the charges took nearly an hour and was accompanied by gasps of dismay and howls of outrage from the crowd. Men crossed themselves, mothers covered their children's ears, and everyone made a variety of signs to ward off the evil eye.

When all the prisoner's many crimes had been proclaimed in loving detail the palace doors opened for a third time and a papal legate, carrying a burning torch, appeared and walked down the corridor of guards. A sallow-skinned, black-robed monk accompanied him.

A Vatican choirboy pulling a small replica of the prisoner's tumbril followed them. In the tumbril on a bed of straw lay a single large book. A guard carrying an unlit brazier filled with coals completed this final procession.

The legate stopped and the guard set down the brazier next to him.

The boy, wearing gloved hands, lifted the book from the straw and carried it to the legate. He stopped and held the book like a human lectern.

The legate lit the brazier and as the coals caught and the flames began to leap and dance, he opened the cover of the leather bound volume, took hold of the first page, and with a violent jerk he tore it from the book. He held the sheet aloft, turning and showing it to the crowd.

"Here is the profane book of devilry, written by this degenerate man." The crowd moaned. "See how the Holy Mother Church deals with those who dare to defy her sacred teachings!"

He threw the page into the brazier. For a moment it lay unaffected, then its edges began to curl and buckle and a dark brown stain began to spread inwards. The words and symbols, which covered the parchment, moved and danced. Then the vellum caught and flames engulfed it until all that remained was a shriveled blackened travesty.

The legate tore page after page from the book and threw each one onto the brazier to be consumed by the flames.

While this display was entertaining the crowd the sallow monk had walked to the foot of one of the long ladders leaning against the piled firewood. He began to climb and finally reached the prisoner. He inclined his head and whispered in the prisoner's ear, as if encouraging him to make a last confession.

What no one saw was the key passed into the prisoner's hands, and what no one heard were the final murmured words of the monk: "Best of luck my friend, do not fear, the book is safe."

The monk climbed down the ladder and took up his position next to the legate, who called up to the prisoner.

"Do you confess your sins, and will you seek the absolution of Holy Mother Church, before your body, like this book, is consigned to the flames of this world and your soul is condemned to the everlasting fires of Hell?"

"If my soul is going to Hell, Priest," the prisoner called down from his perch, "I will greet you warmly when you come to join me." Then the prisoner raised his head and surveyed the crowd. "I have a message for you all," he cried. "Cursed be the Pope, cursed be his priests, cursed be this land, may it be ravaged by fire and pestilence and war and famine. You may think that you see my body burned, but I promise you this, I will escape these flames by the power of the Lord I serve and will return to see this city destroyed!"

The legate, his face a mask of fury, snatched the flaming torch, took four strides to the massive woodpile and thrust it toward the nearest branches. He walked around the pyre igniting twigs and sticks as he went.

The flames began to lick at the pile of wood. Wisps of smoke curled upwards. The crowd could see the prisoner raise his head, his lips moving silently.

The flames made their stealthy way upwards toward the little platform and the small figure in filthy rags held upright by his chains. As the smoke swelled the mob's view of the prisoner was obscured.

The front ranks of the crowd retreated from the searing heat, but were pushed forward again by an excited surge when the smoke cleared briefly to reveal that the flames had reached the prisoner's feet. The mob roared its approval. Then the smoke, the flames and the flurries of sparks hid the prisoner from view.

POST SCRIPT

St Peter's Square, Rome, 1227

Fifty-three years after the burning of the Magus in the square of St Peter an old man sitting outside a tavern recounted for the ten thousandth time the story of how, as a boy, he had held a book while a priest tore out its pages and threw them into a burning brazier.

He told anyone who would buy him a drink of the curses and the shouting and the terror of the crowd. How he had stood transfixed while the priest set fire to the mountain of firewood. His audience would lean in as he described the flames growing and creeping upwards like a living thing. And they would recoil when he recounted how the prisoner had cursed everyone and had promised that his demon master would rescue him.

The old fellow ended his harrowing tale by swearing that at one point he had seen the smoke form itself into the shape of a man with a goat's head and curling horns. And how he had seen this Demon Lord strike the chains from the prisoner's wrists and ankles, and lift him up, and carry him away.

His audience invariably crossed themselves and made signs to ward off the evil eye.

And bought the fellow another round of drinks.

CHAPTER SEVENTEEN

2ND & 3RD OCTOBER

DR. AMADEUS CALIFARIO

Dr. Califario sat opposite Reuben and Miriam Stern at the kitchen table. The kettle was on the stove and the teacups were ready. Miriam sat perfectly still. Reuben kept turning a paper clip in his fingers. He looked older than his fifty-two years.

"Amadeus, you have news for us? About Ronnie and Mishi, do we know where they are? What are we doing about it?" said Miriam.

"Yes," said Dr. Califario. "I do have news, but I'm afraid it is not good news. They are both in the hands of The Organization. And they are in DC."

"DC?" Reuben spoke for the first time since Dr. Califario had rung their doorbell. "What for Christ's sake is in DC that my kids are there?"

"Why they are in DC?" Dr. Califario shrugged, "the key question is how to get them back from DC. We think we have the exact location, down to the building that is."

"And can we rescue them?" said Miriam.

"We are going to see. Above all no harm must come to them. If a rescue can be mounted safely then it will be."

"By whom," said Reuben. "Who exactly is going to 'rescue' my children? I'm guessing, from the way you're talking, it isn't the police or the army."

"Reuben, Honey, Amadeus has resources..." Miriam placed a hand on his arm.

"Resources?" said Reuben, "what resources? Look Miriam, and you Dr. Amadeus Califario, the way I see it my wife and my children are involved with some crazy thing that's got them into a world of danger. I don't know what is going on, and I don't want to know the details, but I want your absolute assurance that they will be safe."

Dr. Califario looked at Reuben Stern for a long moment.

"I cannot give you that assurance. What I can say is that every effort, and they are considerable, will be made to get your children home safely to you."

Reuben's shoulder's sagged.

"Fine," he said. "Just get my children out of this."

Miriam put her arm around him.

SAM LIEBOVITZ AND MORDECAI BEN ZVI

"I don't care what you say," Alice Liebovitz stood in the living room shouting at the phone. "My daughter is missing. Yes of course she is a runaway, that is exactly what I have been trying to tell you. She was grounded and she was in her room and now she isn't. She has run, and she is away. And you are going to find her."

Sam Liebovitz lay upstairs on his back on his bed listening. Every inch of space in his room was covered in posters of old sci-fi and horror movies. Bela Lugosi looked down from the ceiling, battling for space with Godzilla, Frankenstein and the Mummy. On the wall next to his souvenir Stars Wars Stormtrooper helmet was a *Serenity* poster signed by Nathan Filion and Adam Baldwin.

Sam's thumbs flew over the smart phone screen, texting his friends, playing a car-racing app, and checking his messages.

He listened with a quarter of an ear to his mother whose voice carried clearly up from the living room.

"Yes, she left a note," his mother shouted, "but her note did not say where she was. It was not a helpful note, which is typical of her, when I ask her something I never get a reply."

Sam's thumbs were a blur.

"What did the note say? It said. 'Sorry Mom, I have to go. I'll explain when I get back. And you can ground me for the rest of my life'. I suppose she thinks that's funny. Her father and I are worried sick. You have to find her."

Sam got loads more messages off and was approaching level eight of *Speedracer! VI*, when he heard the doorbell ring.

He was aware of his father shuffling down the hall.

"Hello," he heard Donny Liebovitz say, "may I help you?"

Sam heard a low, pleasant voice, but couldn't make out the words.

Then the door closed and footsteps approached.

"I don't care what the standard procedure is, young man. You can try to snow the next caller, but you won't get rid of me..."

"There's a man here wants to talk to us," said Sam's father.

"I'm on the phone. To The Police. About Katie. Don't you even care about your daughter? Who is this man? Tell him to go away. Yes, you there, go away, we don't want whatever you're selling."

"Madam," said a polite voice, lightly accented. Sam shifted more of his attention to the conversation. "I apologize most humbly for interrupting. But perhaps, just a few minutes of your time. It is about Katie."

Sam's thumbs stopped typing mid-text.

"Oh, well," said Mrs. Liebovitz, her voice much quieter, "I suppose. I'll ring you back Officer. What's your name? Officer McCleary. I'll ring you back. We are not done yet."

"Come into the kitchen," Sam heard Donny Liebovitz say.

The man said something Sam didn't catch then his father called out,

"Sam, come down, there's someone here."

Sam swung his legs onto the floor and went downstairs to the kitchen. He saw a dark man of medium height in a light tan suit with a pale blue tie standing next to the double-front brushed steel refrigerator. He was holding a panama hat in his right hand. His left arm was in a sling.

"Ah," said the man, "and this must be the young man of the house."

Sam was surprised to find himself offering the man a seat at the marble-topped table. The man nodded his thanks but waved his hat at Sam's father and mother, indicating that they should sit first. He had become the gracious host making the Liebovitzes feel at home in their own kitchen.

When everyone else was settled the man sat, placed his hat on the table, and introduced himself.

"My name is Mordecai Ben Zvi, and I am a friend of your daughter Katie."

Mrs. Liebovitz was about to speak but Ben Zvi held up his good hand. She subsided, her face relaxed, she looked younger. In fact, Sam thought, she looked like Katie. He'd never seen that before.

Sam turned back to the strange man at the head of the table.

"I am here to explain what is, I am sure, to you, a mystery. What it is that your daughter, the capable Katie, is up to."

"Thank you," said Mr. Liebovitz. "That would be nice."

Sam listened to Mordecai Ben Zvi speak for thirty minutes. He explained Katie's involvement with a charitable organization, funded by a secretive benefactor who insisted on anonymity. He told them how she worked tirelessly in her spare time for the unfortunate and the disadvantaged. That she was a tower of strength and an inspiration to all who met her. And that she had been put in the uncomfortable position of having to practice some minor but, to her, troubling deceptions to keep her work confidential. She was busy and she had asked Mordecai to come here on her behalf to explain, and he knew they would understand.

Occasionally, when his mother began to work herself up, Ben Zvi would raise his hand again and Sam would feel a calm settle over the group.

When it was all over the man placed his hat on his head, bowed courteously, and let himself out. The family remained around the kitchen table for some time, lost in their individual thoughts.

A couple of hours later, across town, Officer McCleary's day brightened considerably when it gradually dawned on him that he was not, in fact, going to get a return call from the crazy lady with the missing daughter.

COLONEL MCALLISTER

Landon McAllister pulled into a Government-Employees-Only space on 16th Street, two blocks north of the YMCA on the opposite side of the road. He locked his car and strode south in the direction of the White House.

He crossed M Street and saw Sumner Row ahead. Past that and across the street was the Y, a plain light-stone structure with two projecting wings. The main entrance was set back from the street and down a few steps.

Some parts of DC came alive as evening fell. Sixteenth Street, near Sumner Row, was not one of them. The DC rush hour was thinning. The early morning crush at the Y, with pre-work exercise fanatics, was long-gone, as was the smaller lunchtime crowd who squeezed in some laps of the pool or a session on the treadmill.

Landon McAllister crossed the street and walked to the YMCA entrance. He knew what he was looking for. When he saw the two men near the main door he knew he had hit the jackpot. The jackets in early Fall DC were a sign. The bulges under those jackets were the clincher.

He turned on his heel. When he was back on 16th and another block south of the Y he checked his flight tracker. Dr. Califario and his team would be landing in an hour.

JEREMY PLENSK

Plensk wasn't sure how Lassiter had wangled it but the Washington Monument had been exclusively theirs since the early evening.

Svensson had warned Plensk to wear a suit so that afternoon, after their tour ofthe Monument, he'd gone to a thrift store and picked one out. Now he knew why. The National Parks Service guide had been all solicitation for the UN Under Secretary's VIP party. Nothing was too much trouble.

Now they were back at the observation level, five hundred feet up. The guide had left them alone and Plensk had changed back into his jeans, T-shirt and army coat.

The space was small and the stone walls tapered in, each pierced with two windows looking out at the four compass points. Plensk and McInnes cleared space and set up a platform about five feet square on the eastern side of the area. In the center of the platform was a post, eight feet high and six inches in diameter. It was held in place with four guy-wires fixed to the corners of the platform.

Svensson spent what felt like ages in the alcove near one of the eastern windows with a compass and spirit level making minute adjustments to a reading stand that faced the platform.

"The alignment has to be exact, my dear Plensk," he said. "Sirius, the Dog Star, sacred to the Egyptians and Freemasons alike will be shining through there," he pointed at the eastern window, "onto the platform at the exact moment our ceremony begins."

After an hour or so of this he was finally happy, and under his directions Plensk weighted the feet of the lectern with heavy sandbags.

A woman with straight black hair, peaches-and-cream skin, and clear blue eyes appeared from the stairs leading up from the museum area.

"Everything is ready downstairs," she said to Svensson. "Care to check?"

"Yes, my dear, of course," said Svensson. "Miss Portland, have you met my associate Jeremy Plensk? Jeremy this is Sally Portland, a most accomplished young lady."

Jeremy recognized her from the Skype call. But she had been in the background and he had only glimpsed her. Now he stood mesmerized. She was simply the most beautiful creature he had ever seen.

Sally Portland smiled knowingly.

"Come on Champ," she said. "Close your mouth or something'll fly in."

She turned away, freeing Plensk from her spell.

"Come gentlemen, Miss Portland," said Svensson. "Let us do this last minute check, and then we can sit down to wait."

They moved toward the stairs together. Plensk looked around the room and felt an unfamiliar swelling in his chest. He was excited. Fate was at his elbow. History was looking on.

They went down to the museum level and threaded their way past glass-fronted exhibits.

A plain aluminum carry case was on a glass-topped display table. It had riveted sides and two clasps holding it shut.

They got closer and Plensk could hear humming. The case was vibrating, rattling against the glass.

"It is eager to fulfil its destiny," said Svensson. He laid a hand on the case. "Warm. Well, things will be considerably hotter before tonight is over," he consulted his watch. "In one hour and twenty-seven minutes it is the time of destiny. McInnes, I believe we can tell our friends to join us. Yes, I think we can have the Twins brought to us now."

McInnes made the call.

"Yeah, Mr. Lassiter," he said, "everything's ready. The Prof wants those two kids brought over."

Plensk heard a tinny response.

"Well, well, well," said McInnes, "that makes things more interesting. What do you want to do with her?"

More tinny talk.

"OK the more the merrier," said McInnes. "We'll make sure she's nice and comfy."

McInnes held the phone to his chest and turned to the group. "How about that," he said. "The girlfriend turned up looking for her Ronnie. They've got her locked up with the Sterns. They're bringing her over as well."

"No!" said the Professor. The easy charm had vanished. "No, she has tracked them. She has some sort of power. Give me the phone."

McInnes handed it over.

"Lassiter?" said Svensson, "you must get rid of her straight away. She may already have sent word to others in their group. The time is approaching and in a couple of hours they will not be able to do anything. But until that time the balance is delicate. The smallest thing might tip it. I do not like that the girl is here in DC."

Svensson listened for a moment.

"Ach so," he said. "Very good. Thank you. Yes, get it done immediately."

AARON STERN

I was gaining strength and Mishi was losing hers. Katie was trying to keep her comfortable but she was in a lot of pain. I was sitting with my back against an old desk facing the door. Katie and Mishi sat together a few feet away between me and the door leaning on some file boxes.

We were talking in low tones, discussing our lack of options, when I heard voices. In my head.

"Use a silencer."

"No point scaring the neighbors."

Laughter.

"Just the girl right?"

"Yeah, the blond."

"A little fun with her first?"

"Keep your mind on the job Gantz."

I could hear footsteps approaching down the hallway, and then the door burst open. The one they called Nikos, squat and dark with curly black hair and a six o'clock shadow, came in with the tall, thin one. They had guns. With silencers.

"OK," said Nikos to Katie. "Time to go."

"No!" I shouted.

He looked at me like I was a bug.

"Shut up, kid." He turned to the thin guy. "Grab her, Gantz."

Gantz came forward pointing his gun, he reached out with his other hand to grab Katie's wrist but she scrambled back out of reach.

Mishi crawled out of the way of Nikos's feet, and Katie jigged further backward away from the door toward where I was sitting.

The tall guy tried again. This time he got Katie's wrist, but she struggled and squirmed and he had trouble getting her to her feet.

"Get out of the way, Gantz," said Nikos. "She doesn't want to come. We'll do it here." He raised his gun as he spoke.

"No!" I screamed, and shot up from my sitting position. I took two steps and launched myself at the slime ball with the gun.

I heard that cough that a silenced gun makes and a sledgehammer hit me. I was knocked sideways in mid-flight. I crashed to the floor.

"Oh Jesus," I thought. "Not this, not now. I have to save Katie."

Her name, ringing in my head, was the last thing I remembered.

MISHI STERN

Ronnie was in mid-air when the guy shot him. I can't even say those words now without feeling sick. I mean I'm no expert but a bullet from that close, he was finished.

I was paralyzed. I couldn't even scream.

He hit the ground and lay still.

I don't know where Katie was or what she was doing. I thought I heard a whimper or a cry, but it was miles away, and it meant nothing to me.

My brother was dead.

The only thing I could think of was I wanted him to be alive so I could tell him over and over again how much I loved him.

The dark guy, his face like stone, turned the gun on Katie.

I could hear her crying hysterically. She was trying to crawl toward Ronnie's body but the tall guy, Gantz, had her by the wrist.

Then everything slowed right down. I remember the position of the furniture and the files and papers scattered over the floor, the paint peeling on the back of a metal chair.

The dark goon's finger was squeezing the trigger. It was all in slow motion.

And then Ronnie opened his eyes and lifted his head and rose up from the floor roaring. Blood was pouring down his left arm and side. His right hand came up and closed around the dark guy's wrist and drove it and the gun up toward the ceiling. The gun went off and bits of plaster rained down on us.

The roaring was deafening. My body shook, I put my hands over my ears but the sound was inside me. I couldn't get away and I couldn't look away.

The dark guy looked shocked and angry. He made a move to beat Ronnie off him, but Ronnie held on. He was made of steel. And all the time he was roaring and shouting and speaking in a strange language that sounded like it was old when God was in diapers. It was the language of violence, and death.

And it scared the hell out of me.

The dark guy's face turned from anger to fear as Ronnie one-handed forced him back and down to the floor. Blood was still streaming from Ronnie's left arm and side, but he didn't seem to notice. His face was contorted with rage and he drove the man to his knees. He wrenched the gun from his hand and hurled it out the door. Then he took the man's face in both his hands and raked his nails down his cheeks. The man screamed and clutched at his face. Ronnie grabbed the front of the guy's jacket and picked him up above his head like he was a feather. He jumped and twisted and threw the man down so hard the floor shook.

The guy lay still.

Ronnie was growling like an animal. He turned around glared at the other guy. He bared his teeth. His eyes were red. He held his hands out and his fingers curled like claws.

Gantz, the sleazoid who had grabbed Katie, was standing open-mouthed watching Ronnie close in on him. The gun was hanging by his side, like he'd forgotten it was there.

"Listen," the guy said, "don't. I didn't mean to..."

Ronnie leapt on him.

I don't want to describe the rest. It still gives me nightmares. Ronnie started with the throat, which meant the guy was already dead when Ronnie tore him to pieces with his bare hands. At least I hope he was.

Katie crawled over to me and we held each other tight, crying.

When he'd finished, Ronnie collapsed and lay still.

AARON STERN

1.

I came around as per usual. That stretchy, twisty feeling and the residual nausea. I felt sticky and wet and looked at my hands. And then I really felt sick. They were covered in blood and little pieces of squishy jelly.

I don't know how long I sat there, looking at my bloody hands and clothes, before I began to wonder whose blood it was. I did a quick inventory of my body. My cheek, and my left arm and ribs were sore and throbbing but everything else seemed OK.

Then I saw the body of what used to be the tall thin guy lying on the floor next to me. And I threw up.

He looked like he had been ripped to pieces by a wild animal.

I sat panting and exhausted. I went to wipe my mouth on my sleeve but it was torn and bloody. So I picked up a few sheets of paper from the spilled files and used them.

I became aware of sounds in the room. A low moaning and whimpering, like someone in distress. I looked around and saw Mishi and Katie huddled in a corner holding on to each other. They were staring at me.

I wanted to tell them that I was OK. That I wasn't hurt. I wanted to ask them what had happened. Who had killed this man. I didn't remember a fight.

What I did remember was a bright light. A glowing presence, and a feeling of heat and power. A sense of being invulnerable, and of being furious, angry and outraged. It was like being on fire. Like being made of fire. Like nothing could withstand that fire.

And I was that avenging fire.

Whoa!

Had I done this? I remembered the two men coming for Katie, and I remember leaping at one of them to protect her. Then darkness.

Then I panicked, where was the other guy?

I twisted around and saw him lying on the floor, between the open door and me. His eyes were closed but his chest was rising and falling.

"Ronnie?" Katie's voice was tiny and tentative. "Are you OK?"

I turned to her.

"Yeah, I guess," I said. "Yeah I'm OK. How about you? How are you? Mishi? Are you OK? What happened? I blacked out."

"You don't remember?" said Katie.

"No, not after I tried to stop that guy shooting you. I don't remember anything, except a feeling of being on fire. And really, really angry. And now I'm covered in blood and.... Oh God, what did I do?"

"Well," said Mishi, wiping her eyes. "You saved us. They shot you, and you still saved us. I was so scared. I thought you were dead. I thought they'd killed you. And I thought, I'm always so mean to you and I never got to tell you how much I love you, and I wanted you to be alive so bad. But I thought you were dead. And I thought, I'm dying too and then I thought about Mom and Dad..."

She was choking and sobbing and coughing.

Katie put her arms around her again, and kissed the top of her head and said, "It's OK. It's OK. We're all OK. Ronnie is OK."

Then Katie looked up at me.

"What does she mean she's dying?"

I told her about the poison, and the antidote, and my attempt to heal her.

Katie's face twisted with rage. If I'd looked half as scary as she did then those guys would've died of fright.

"I hate these people," she hissed, and she looked at me. "You were amazing, Aaron Stern. I mean literally amazing. You picked that one up over your head and slammed him into the floor. With a bullet in your arm. And then you, you... Well..."

She indicated the body lying on the floor behind me.

"He had me by the arm and he had a gun and he was going to shoot me, and, and you... Well, you... You did that." Pointing at the bloody mess on the floor.

She had to stop for a few moments. She tore her eyes away from the dead guy and turned back to me with that vintage Katie look, all square-jawed and flashing eyes. "And now you have to go out and you have be amazing all over again. Go and get that antidote and save your sister."

I couldn't speak, my throat was too tight.

"You killed him," said Katie, there was steel in her voice. "You tore him to pieces. You saved my life. Our lives. You were terrifying, and you were howling and roaring like an animal. You were magnificent. You saved my life and now you're going to save Mishi's. And, in case I don't get to say it later, I love you Aaron Stern."

I was filled with warmth. It dispelled the chill and the dread. Here were two of the people I treasured most. And I had saved them. Or at least the power that had entered me had done the dirty work. But I had been a vessel for that power, and that was good enough for me.

"I love you too, Katie Liebovitz."

Mishi looked up at me.

"You too, Michelle Rachel Stern, I love you too. And I will be very annoyed with you if you don't recover and start giving me a hard time again. I'll wonder if you've gone and got yourself kidnapped again, and substituted a cheap imitation."

"Deal, Loser," she said.

"Deal," I said.

2.

I got up and went to the man lying near the door, Nikos. He was still out cold. I looked around and found an old phone sitting on a desk. I yanked the cable from the wall and turned him over, took both his arms and tied his wrists and ankles as securely as I could. I'd never been a Boy Scout but a friend who had taken me sailing told me, "when you can't tie knots, tie lots." So that's what I did.

Then I peeked out the door. I saw the gun lying on the hallway floor, silencer still screwed into the barrel.

I picked it up. I had very little experience with guns but I was happy to learn on the job.

Then I saw a bathroom a few yards away and went in. I looked at myself in the mirror and nearly threw up again. It was like something out of a horror movie. My face was streaked with blood. My hair was matted and tacky, my clothing was torn and bloody, and pieces of flesh were sticking to me.

And my left arm and ribs were beginning to ache badly.

I washed myself down as best I could.

I couldn't see the wounds, so I tore my sleeve off and saw that the bullet had cut a furrow across the inside of my arm and had made a matching groove across my ribs as well. Both arm and ribs were painful, and leaking blood. I tied the torn sleeve of my shirt around my arm, and wadded up some left-over cloth for my ribs. The sticky blood held it in place.

There wasn't much I could do about the rest of my clothes. I rinsed as much blood out of them as I could, then tugged the damp clothing back on.

I had a coat which I'd taken off when Mishi and I were first locked in. So I put it on over my ensemble. It would have to do.

I went back to the room. Katie and Mishi were on their feet and Katie was holding Gantz's gun between her finger and thumb.

"So," she asked. "What do we do now, Superman?"

"Good question, Lois. How about you take Mishi, and one of the guns, and go find help. I'll take the other gun and go and get the antidote, and thwart whatever it is that these bad guys are cooking up."

"Sounds like a plan," said Katie. "How will you know where to go to do all that thwarting?"

"Well, I thought that our friend here would be willing to let us in on that secret. I'm going to get some cold water and throw it in his face to bring him around. It works in the movies."

"Well, let's hope it works in real life," said Katie. "I'm not sure we have a lot of time."

"Good point, I'll get the water. You get going with Mishi. Head for that Denny's sign two streets over. We'll meet there."

Mishi was leaning against Katie, her face ashen and haggard. Her shoulders drooped and her head was hanging forward.

"I've got to go and do this thing. That woman has the antidote and we need it as soon as possible. If I can't get it I'm going to use my healing power, I don't care what it does to me."

"OK, Sweetheart, you do your hero thing, again." She stood on her toes and kissed me.

Leaping tall buildings at a single bound? That'd be me.

"And Katie," I said.

"Yes?"

"Go. Get help. And, please, shoot anyone who tries to stop you."

"Will do."

3.

Katie helped Mishi out into the corridor and cradled her down to an elevator. She carried the gun awkwardly against her side. I didn't know if she would be willing to pull the trigger. I was just praying that if she waved it in the face of some bad actor it would give her precious seconds to get away.

I found a metal trashcan and went to the bathroom, filled it and returned to the storeroom. Nikos was beginning to stir but I threw the entire basket-full over his face anyway, just for the fun of it. He spluttered and coughed and choked in a most acceptable manner.

When he had finished his gasping and wheezing he tried to sit up but his tied hands stopped him from doing anything other than rolling back and forth. I had the gun trained on him.

"You're a dead man," was his conversation opener.

"Not yet," I said. "But your friend is. And you can join him if you don't give me what I want."

"You can go screw yourself!" A friend of McInnes I guessed.

"No thanks," I knelt down beside him. "What I am actually going to do is shoot you in the knee. Then your other knee. Then one elbow, then the other elbow. And if you're feelin' lucky, punk, 'cause you think a kid from California doesn't have the sand to pull the trigger, then let me tell you this. I just tore your friend limb from limb. My sister is dying because of you people, and you were going to kill my girlfriend. I am not in a merciful mood. But, against my better judgment, I am giving you this one chance to begin your redemption. Help me to stop whatever Lassiter is planning, and to rescue my sister, and I won't hurt you."

He sneered at me. "You don't have the..."

So I shot him.

He screamed, and writhed, and thrashed back and forth.

"Look, Nikos, is that your name? Whoever you are, surely these people are not worth what is going to happen to you. Tell me or I will shoot your other knee."

He looked at me with such hatred, it was almost physical. I took the gun and held it against his other knee.

"No, no, don't," he gasped. "I'll tell you."

"Tick tock," I said. "I'm in a bit of a hurry here."

"The Washington Monument," he gasped. "The top, the observation level. That's where they are."

"Now that wasn't so hard was it?" I tied more torn shirt around his knee to slow the bleeding. I riffled through his pockets and found two extra magazines for the gun. And a cell phone.

I jiggled the cell in front of his face.

"Password please."

He told me the PIN.

And then I left him. A man who came to murder Katie, and who assisted in the slow agonizing death of my sister, did not rate highly on my mercy list.

4.

The wounded arm and ribs, and the wet clothes, and my other injuries didn't make the walk to the Washington Monument an unalloyed joy. And I didn't think carrying a loaded weapon with a silencer was going to endear me to DC's finest. So I stowed the gun, silencer and two spare magazines about me in the pockets of my coat.

I had no plan except go to the Washington Monument and stop Lassiter, but more importantly to get the antidote from the Portland woman. Lucky the Washington Monument is hard to miss. I pressed on through the thin DC crowds, down 16th toward the White House, illuminated and stately, set in wide lawns with flags flying.

I reached Lafayette Square, cut diagonally left until I reached Pennsylvania Avenue, then I headed up 15th.

My arm was on fire. The blood leaking from my inexpert medical self-help was sticking the coat sleeve to the wound. At least the warm October night was drying my clothes.

I could see the Washington Monument ahead of me. A bit hard to miss actually. According to Mrs. Fricker, my fifth grade teacher, it is the tallest obelisk in the world. It was the tallest man-made structure in the world for a few months in the 1880s, until The Eiffel Tower took the title.

Those French.

I passed The Ellipse and crossed Constitution Avenue and took the path uphill past the ring of flags. I took out the killer's cell, keyed in the password and rang Mordecai. His voice message kicked in.

"It's Aaron Stern," I said. "We're in DC. Mishi and Katie are together and need help. They should be at the Denny's on 14th Street. I'm at the Washington Monument. I'm going to stop this thing and get some medicine for Mishi. I'll explain later. If there's anything you can organize I'm open to offers. Bye."

I got to the visitors' entrance, a charmless box completely out of character with the smooth soaring stone behind it. What were they thinking? Maybe the French deserved their Tallest Building title.

The door was locked. Natch. I was just screwing the silencer onto my all-purpose door unlocker when I heard footsteps behind me.

I turned around and saw a young man carrying a heavy box heading my way up the path. He was thin, with sharp features, and long unkempt college student hair. The army surplus jacket, skinny jeans, T-shirt and boots completed his ensemble. I put the gun away, and waited.

He looked up and saw me when he was a few feet from the door. He stopped.

"Who are you?" he said. He didn't seem to notice my disheveled state.

"I'm here to help with the box," I said.

"Great, it's heavy," he said.

"What's in it?" I asked.

He snorted. "You think they tell me anything? These guys are like, fetch Plensk, fetch, good boy Plensk. It's getting really old, Man."

"Yeah," I said. "Tell me about it." I was getting the hang of this. "Have you got the key to the door?"

"Yeah, sure, Man, it's in my coat."

I fished around in his coat pocket and found a ring of keys. I unlocked the door and we manhandled the box inside the entrance. There was another door. More sifting through the keys and then we were in the main foyer with the bronze statue of George Washington holding a cane and leaning on a column. His bronze eyes were eternally fixed on the elevator doors opposite.

I offered a silent prayer to the Father of our Country, suddenly conscious that I was trying to preserve what he had made. Awesome.

I turned and pressed the call button and Plensk wedged his box against the wall while we waited for the elevator to arrive.

When the doors slid open we stepped in and Plensk jostled the box down onto the floor. We began the seventy-second ascent.

"I haven't seen you around," said Plensk. He took a closer look, eyeing my torn damp clothes and scruffy hair. And, no doubt, my interesting array of cuts and bruises. "Don't I know you? Who are you exactly?"

"Exactly?" I said, "I'm Aaron Stern. My friends call me Ronnie."

Plensk's eyes widened. I guess the name was familiar.

"I'm here for the antidote to the poison that your friends injected into my sister. And I'm going to stop whatever it is you guys are doing to destroy my country. And you're going to help me. Or," I smiled at him, "I will kill you."

I had the gun out by now and I was pointing it at Plensk's chest.

He seemed lost for words.

"For instance," I said conversationally, "how many goons has Lassiter got up there?"

"Um, ah," Plensk was copying my landed fish look.

"Look, we don't have limitless time here. If you haven't told me what I want to know by the time the elevator arrives I will shoot you and take my chances. I wasn't expecting you anyway so, for me, you're a bit of a bonus."

I was still smiling.

"I've already beaten one man to death tonight, and shot another, who might also be dead by now. We can only hope. So one more?" I shrugged. "No biggie."

"There's five or six of them. Up there, on the viewing platform," he was stumbling over his words. "Lassiter and Svensson, he's an old Swedish Professor. And that Aussie psycho, and another guy called Singh, and a dweeb teacher called Snell, and there's that hot chick Portland. They're expecting a couple of others, A Greek guy."

"Dark, curly black hair, personality issues? Nikos?"

He nodded. "Georgiakis."

"He's not coming. Neither is a thin tall dude. Gantz. Ever."

The elevator came to a halt.

"Now that wasn't so hard was it?" I said, and I brought the butt of the gun down hard on his head. He dropped to the floor.

The doors opened and I stepped out into the viewing room. The doors closed behind me and I heard the elevator start its downward journey, taking Plensk and his box with it.

5.

It wasn't a large space but I loved what they'd done with it. There was a platform with a tall post held up by wires, and near one of the viewing windows was a lectern with an old man leaning on it reading something, peering over his eyeglasses.

Lassiter was there talking to my old pal Mr. Snell. And lounging against a wall, picking his teeth with his fingernail, was my new friend from Downunder, McInnes. We really had to stop meeting like this.

I couldn't see the snake Portland.

No one was looking my way so I fired the gun up toward the tapering inner stones of the pyramid. I had forgotten to put the silencer back on. Silly me.

That and a small shower of stone splinters got their attention. The four of them stood frozen in position. McInnes's hand was moving slowly to his side. I fired another shot at the wall just to his right. More pieces of stone ricocheted around and McInnes's hand flew to his face. Blood seeped out between his fingers. Good.

"Hi, Everyone," I said, stepping down into the well of the room. "This needn't take long. I only want two things. First I need the antidote for my sister. And second, I need you to stop whatever the heck you're planning with the Moses Revelation, and me and Mishi, and whatever. Oh, I suppose handing you all over to the police is sort of a third thing. My bad."

They weren't keeping their end of the conversation up, so I went on.

"OK, so first, the antidote. Hand it over now please."

No one moved.

"Now. Please." I pointed the gun at Lassiter and began to squeeze the trigger. I guess I would have shot him. It was that kind of night. But I never found out because the elevator doors opened behind me and Sally Portland said, "Drop the gun Ronnie, or I'll kill your girlfriend first, and your sister second."

Albi, Languedoc, Southern France, 1175

A sallow-skinned, dark-eyed monk dismounted from his horse and threw the reigns to his manservant.

"Find us a place to stay Geminio," he said. "I have business with the fathers of the Cathar church."

The priest hefted a satchel over his shoulder, checked that the leather-bound book, with intricately tooled symbols and letters on its cover, was safe and walked into the town.

CHAPTER EIGHTEEN

3RD & 4TH OCTOBER

AARON STERN

1.

I turned around and Sally Portland stood in the elevator smiling at me. Katie and Mishi were standing beside her. She had a gun and it was pointing at them. Behind her was Plensk rubbing his head and looking daggers at me. I wasn't adding to my circle of friends.

They all stepped out of the elevator. Katie looked at me and mouthed "Sorry."

Mishi didn't look at me at all. She was in another world, her skin was white and she shuffled forward, held up by Katie.

McInnes came over, grabbed my gun and frisked me. He found the silencer, the spare clips and Georgiakis's cell.

Lassiter spoke for the first time.

"You have shown admirable initiative Mr. Stern. My congratulations. But the time for children's games is over. Tie this one," he waved a hand at Katie, "over there. And these two," Mishi and me, "to the post."

Singh took Katie, and McInnes grabbed Mishi. I made a move to stop McInnes but Portland kicked my legs out from under me. She grabbed my wounded arm where the fresh blood was oozing through the sleeve, and squeezed. I yelled out in pain.

She laughed, withdrew her hand and slowly licked the blood from her fingers.

"Ooh you're such a bad boy!" she said, standing up. "I think you should be punished. Now let me see ..." She fished around in a pocket of her blazer and pulled out a small glass vial filled with a light pink fluid. "Was this what you were after? The antidote to that horrible poison that mean old Sally injected into sweet little Mishi?"

She held the vial out toward me. I tried to get up but before I could she let it drop from her fingers. It fell to the ground, bounced a couple of times and rolled. It came to a halt against the toe of her shoe. She lifted her foot and stamped down hard. The glass crunched and pink fluid oozed out like pale blood.

I was mesmerized by the crushed glass and the tiny trickle of antidote. I sagged back onto the floor. My last ounce of fight vanished. Whatever had come over me back at the YMCA didn't look like it was going to do an encore.

"Oops," said Sally Portland, "butter fingers." Then she gestured to the center of the room. "Get moving asshole, times a'wastin'."

I staggered up, robot-like, and I stepped onto the platform. McInnes had already secured Mishi's hands to the central post with plastic cable ties. He took another pair out of a back pocket and tied my hands above hers.

Out of the corner of my eye I could see Singh push Katie to the ground and tie her wrists to the bannister of the stairs that headed down to a lower level.

"Excellent," said Lassiter. "Time to get this show on the road. Professor Svensson, would you care to begin?"

2.

An old guy I assumed was Svensson was standing near the lectern. Next to him was a small table with notes and papers. He fussed over these for a few moments, then he nodded to himself and turned to Plensk and called his name. He had to repeat himself because Plensk had basset hound eyes on Sally Portland who sashayed across the room past the platform. Portland allowed her hand to brush my arm as she passed by, I looked at her and she blew me an air-kiss. Is it flattering that a black spider wants a date? I was definitely not in the mood.

She took up a position off to the side with McInnes and Singh.

Svensson cleared his throat again and Plensk got the hint. He bent down, opened a small suitcase and pulled out a bundle of cloth. He shook it out and, hey presto, it turned into a white robe shot through with red and green threads. A large gold pentacle covered the front of it. A goat's head with long curly horns was embroidered in the center of the pentacle. Plensk held it out and Svensson slipped his arms into the sleeves. Then he secured it with a red sash tied around Svensson's waist.

Plensk picked out another length of white cloth from the case, which Svensson wound around his head into a turban.

Were we all getting Halloween costumes?

Plensk then produced a pair of heavy leather gloves. Svensson held his arms out and Plensk pulled the gloves on right up to Svensson's elbows.

"The scroll please Mr. Plensk," said Svensson.

Plensk went over to a metal case. He reached down to grab its handle and recoiled, dancing about yelping and waving his fingers. After a few moments of this he took a corner of his flappy coat and grabbed the handle again. This time he got the case up onto the small side table and, tugging his coat sleeves down to protect his hands, he managed to flip the catches and lift the lid.

There was a sound of crackling and snapping like loose wires shorting in a storm. Plensk jumped backward. The air in the room tasted metallic.

Svensson went over to the case and lifted out a blue velvet bag with gold embroidery. The leather gloves slowed him down but he finally managed to open the bag and slip out the contents.

It was the Revelation of Moses, the Scroll of Destiny. Things were definitely not looking up.

Svensson held the scroll above his head and began chanting in a foreign language.

Outside there was a flash of lightning which lit up the room like a flash bulb, and a moment later an ear-splitting crash of thunder.

3.

There was a movement next to me. I tore my eyes from Svensson and his chanting and looked down at Mishi on her knees slumped against the post.

My heart felt like lead. My sister was dying in front of my eyes. I made up my mind. I didn't care what curing her did to me. Besides, keeping myself fighting fit so I could do the hero thing hadn't worked out so well. Time to go back to Plan A.

I wriggled the cable ties around the post and jigged myself down until I could reach her. Her head was resting against the post, I stretched down and touched her hair.

The flow of poison immediately started up into my fingers again.

I gritted my teeth and steadied myself. My head began to throb and ache. I could feel the sick gray fog of death curling its way into me, through my hand and along my arm, into my chest and stomach, down my body to my groin and legs. My wounded arm, ribs and cheek became shards of glass slicing into me.

Mishi stirred herself.

She tried to shake her head free of my fingers but I pressed them down onto her.

She leaned back, away from the post. The contact broke.

She looked at me. I have that look etched on my memory, I will treasure it, and dread it until I die.

She was calm, and brave, and implacable.

She was a little girl, and a goddess.

She was my little sister, and she was the Queen of the Universe.

Without words she was telling me, no, commanding me to stop. She was dying, and she knew it. And I was not to prevent it. I was to keep my strength and prevent these people from doing evil.

And if that meant she had to die, then so be it. The fate of one small girl wasn't to divert me from what I had to do.

I understood all of this, and I nodded, tears were streaming down my face.

Under her unwavering gaze, the poison in me began to dissipate, and the strength flowed back into my body. Mishi wilted, her head fell forward, and her hands were held high by the cable ties, she looked like she was praying.

4.

I used every calming technique that Katie had taught me. I waited for my heart rate to slow down. I looked over at Svensson.

He had laid the Moses Revelation down on the lectern. The leading end of the scroll was attached to a wooden rod about an inch in diameter. He carefully unrolled it until about two feet of parchment was visible. He turned the leading roller to take up the parchment so pages of the text passed across the lectern from one roller to the other.

He peered closely at the writing on the parchment as he transferred it from left to right. Occasionally he would hold the parchment steady with his gloved hand and look carefully at the words. He consulted some photocopied pages that Plensk handed to him. Then he continued searching through the document.

The crackling in the air grew in intensity and the hair on my arms stood on end. McInnes, Singh and Portland stood in a loose group over near one of the other viewing windows. Snell emerged from the shadows and hovered near them. Katie was sitting awkwardly down a stair or two, tied to the bannister.

Everyone's eyes were on Svensson. I turned back to him as well.

"I see you are interested in this process, Mr. Stern," said Lassiter. He was standing beside the platform looking up at us. "Professor Svensson is comparing the work of Leonardo Da Silva, a medieval savant, with passages in the Moses Revelation. At precisely the correct moment he will read out the relevant parts in the original language. This will open a passageway in the cosmos, or so Da Silva promises. And we have every reason to believe him."

"And will Peter Pan fly in and take you and your happy band away to Neverland?"

Lassiter chuckled. "Oh Mr. Stern, I think I can speak for all of us when I say that it will give us the greatest of pleasures to silence your smart mouth forever."

"So, all that, 'help us, and we'll let you go' crap was just, what, crap?"

"Yes, Mr. Stern, I'm sorry to say it was indeed a departure from strict truth."

"So what if I withdraw my generous offer to help you, because, like, the incentive, that we will survive, has kinda disappeared."

"Oh well, yes, in a way you're right. But of course we have you, and we have your sister, and we have the delectable Miss Liebovitz. And Miss Portland can be terribly creative when she wants to be. I feel sure that their screams of agony will secure your cooperation."

Sally Portland was leaning against a railing, smiling at me. McInnes and Singh had weapons drawn and held at their sides. Snell had a gun as well, but he looked like it would bite him. Plensk was still over with Svensson, helping him shuffle the pages of Da Silva's manuscript.

"You know, Lassie," Lassiter's cheek flinched fractionally, "you haven't actually shared what it is that we're meant to do. Look at us. We're all tied up. Surely it can't hurt to tell us."

"You're right," he said. "When the good Professor begins intoning, and the portal opens, then the occult protections, so carefully laid down over two centuries ago by L'Enfant, the designer of this great city, at the behest of Franklin and Washington, under the guidance of Haym Solomon, will begin to dissolve. Haym Solomon was, you will be interested to hear, an ancestor of yours."

I raised my eyebrows. "No kidding."

"In fact, Mr. Stern, as far as we can tell, he was one of the Guardians of your scroll. Perhaps *the* Guardian of the scroll. And he used its power to fix these protective measures in place. Measures, which I must say, have been astonishingly effective to date. Keeping the United States of America safe from harm and cataclysm and civil unrest that would have destroyed a less well-guarded nation. It has been infuriating to those on our side of the argument."

"And me, us, my sister and me?" I prompted.

"Tonight we will unlock these protections using the very key which Solomon used to fix them in place. The Moses Revelation itself. And his descendants, the Twins mentioned by Da Silva, a brother and sister of unusual power will be sacrificed to ensure the process is irreversible."

"Sacrificed? That doesn't sound good," I said.

Svensson lifted his head.

"My Dear Lassiter, I have found the passage. The Dog Star is in the ascendant. It is now time to begin in earnest."

Lassiter sneered at me. "Settle back and relax my friend, you have the best seats in the house."

5.

Svensson settled himself at the lectern, cleared his throat and began to read from the scroll. His gloved right index finger traced the words and his voice settled into a rhythmic throaty chant.

The spoken words had shape and substance, like they were living material things. As if Svensson were a doorway and each word was marching out, through him, from their world into this one. They were weighty, serious, and unstoppable. I felt a flutter in my guts rising to my chest. My skin was cold and tight, my breathing shallow and quick. I could see panic lurking around the edges of my mind. I worked to quell it, to take in slow lungfuls of air.

The chanting kept going and now my head began to pulsate to the rhythm. Each syllable Svensson spoke was like someone banging my head with a rubber mallet.

I stole a glance around the room. Everyone was watching Svensson. All of them, Lassiter, McInnes, Singh, Snell and Sally Portland, had an eager light in their eyes. The Plensk dude was behind Svensson ready to jump if he was asked. I should have hit him harder.

I twisted around slowly and saw Katie. She was trying to wedge her head down between her arms, to block out the noise.

The physical blow of each word was painful and hypnotic. I found myself wanting to let go, to dive in, to give in to the words. I fought to keep myself centered, alert.

Then the sounds began to change.

Svensson lifted his arms up and spread them out above his head. He was still chanting but the heavy thud of a marching army was replaced by the skittering of a thousand insects. The words had a glassy high-pitched edge that burrowed into my skin and brain.

My eyes were drawn to the scroll on the lectern. The letters on the pages, written in black ink, began to change color, from black to yellow and orange and red. They began to glow. The letters were catching fire.

Svensson's face was illuminated from below like something in a horror movie. His eyes were in shadow while his chin, nose, cheeks and forehead were brightly lit.

His mouth moved, the screech of words kept pouring out.

The fiery letters loosened their grip on the parchment and began to leap up from the page like sparks from a fire.

They spun and flew over Svensson's head, held between his upraised hands in a frenzied swarm. Svensson looked ecstatic, transported to another realm.

The glowing letters, hundreds, maybe thousands of them, began to twist into a burning vortex, which spread and filled the whole space, swirling around all of us. McInnes and Singh looked at each other, uncomfortable. Snell looked like he really, really wanted his Mommy.

Outside, lightning flashed and the rolling thunder was deafening.

Inside the spinning whirling sparks gathered speed.

Now I noticed tendrils of light were beginning to seep through the walls, flowing in from outside to join the sparks of golden light rolling around the room. The ribbons of light came through the small viewing windows, and through the stones of the walls and through the ceiling and up through the floor. The observation room was filled with this golden light, which curved and twisted and joined the vortex of glowing letters.

The noise was tremendous. Svensson's chanting, the rush of the vortex, the lightning and thunder.

"It's working!" Lassiter, standing beside our platform turned his head this way and that, his face aglow, he shouted. "It's happening. I can feel it."

He laughed louder and louder. It wasn't an attractive laugh. His hair was wild. He was turning and turning with the glowing vortex his arms spread wide.

6.

I could feel it too. The energy was filling the room but I could feel something else. Only a hint at first. But soon my body resonated with a sense of thinning and melting. Like something solid and rocklike was beginning to soften, and in a short time the softening would lead to a full thaw.

Lassiter was almost dancing with excitement.

The other bad guys, and one very bad girl, stood their ground. They were wary, they had weapons in their hands but this was not a weapon-friendly environment. How do you shoot at swirling fiery letters and streams of light?

Plensk was staring around wildly.

Svensson called his name, at least I guess he did. I couldn't hear over the roaring noise, but his lips moved and Plensk shook himself out of his daze.

Svensson rolled the scroll tight and took hold of the two protruding rods that held the parchment. He lifted the scroll up above his head. He stepped away from the lectern and began to walk around the perimeter of the room in the same counter-clockwise direction as the vortex. Plensk followed him carrying the pages of the Da Silva manuscript.

The light was moving around and through them. And ribbons of light started to peel off and flow into the scroll.

"Look, look!" Lassiter shouted and pointed. "The energy, the power is flowing into the scroll. It is being captured, drained from the city."

More laughter.

Lassiter turned to Mishi and me. His face was the stuff of ghastly dreams. Some force had taken possession of him. His eyes glowed with fire. His lips were pulled back, his perfect teeth glowed white.

"Now!" he screamed over the freight train roar. "Now Aaron Stern! Now Michelle Stern! Now it is time for you to fulfill your destiny."

I wasn't exactly sure what he meant, but I knew he didn't mean this to turn out well for us.

Svensson and Plensk had done a full circuit of the room and now they reached the platform. They turned to face us. Svensson began chanting again. And he took one slow measured step toward us, then another.

"Show time!" Lassiter screamed.

7.

Svensson held the scroll out toward me.

"Plensk," Svensson barked. "Release one of his hands and one of hers."

Plensk came forward with a knife. He took my right hand and bent it back. With a little too much force, I thought. Some guys sure hold a grudge.

He snicked through the plastic, leaving my left hand firmly tied to the post.

He bent down and was about do the same for Mishi, when I raised my fist.

"I wouldn't, Mate," McInnes bellowed above the noise. He had moved across the room and was now holding Katie by the hair. His gun was pointed at her head. I let my hand drop.

Svensson looked at me and yelled, "Grasp the scroll."

I didn't move.

"Grab the scroll you little turd," Lassiter screamed. "Grab it! You and that little bitch sister of yours. You have to hold the scroll simultaneously."

"And then what?" I shouted.

The noise in the room was increasing. We were all shouting at each other. The swirling light was dazzling and disorienting.

"Then the Circle of Power will be sealed," Svensson roared. "The Twins of Destiny must complete the Circle. And a Choice will be made, a Path will be taken! The Twins will choose a path!"

The Circle of Power, the Twins of Destiny. These guys needed a better scriptwriter.

"Grab the scroll Arsehole," McInnes' voice came over the noise. He was pulling Katie's head back exposing her neck and holding the gun against her temple. "Do it! Now!"

He shook Katie's head back and forth and she cried out.

I reached out with my bare hand and grabbed the scroll.

CHAPTER NINETEEN

4TH OCTOBER

MISHI STERN

I felt like weights were tied to every part of me including my mind and heart. I sat on the floor my hands held above me, my wrists tied to the post. The room filled with noise and light, and my ears hurt. My shoulders ached, but I couldn't move. I didn't want to.

My eyes were closed, and I wanted to sleep. For about a thousand years. Then I'd be ready. Yeah, that was it. Just let me sleep.

But my stupid eyes decided that now would be a good time to open. Ronnie and I were tied to a post stuck into a low platform in the middle of the room. Around us was a flying swirling tornado of fiery embers and ribbons of gold.

I was hypnotized.

Then a strange man in fancy dress came up to the platform and held out the scroll to Ronnie. Another guy, dressed as a college loser, cut one of Ronnie's hands free and then he did the same for me.

There was a lot of shouting and Ronnie reached out to touch the scroll.

I didn't think that was a good idea and I wanted to tell him to stop, but my voice wasn't working, and anyway I wasn't sure I'd be heard over all the noise.

Ronnie's right hand closed around the scroll. I felt him flinch. It was hard to see from where I was sitting, my hand tied, and my body twisted. So I humphed and bumphed myself up first into a kneeling position and then I pulled myself up with my free hand.

Black smoke was curling up from the scroll. Where Ronnie was holding it. Ronnie was rigid, and his back was arched. His face was all contorted.

The smoke smelled pungent, foul, I nearly gagged. It swirled and curved around his hand like a living thing. Then it was whisked away by the whirling vortex. When the smoke cleared and I got a glimpse of Ronnie's hand. It was smoldering, the skin turning black, his curled fingers unable to let go.

My left hand was free and I reached out to take hold of Ronnie's arm to pull his hand away from that horrible burning thing. But the creep in the army jacket grabbed my hand and shoved it onto the scroll just below Ronnie's.

I cringed when my fingers touched the parchment. I was waiting for my hand to go up in flames too.

But it didn't.

Instead the smoke around Ronnie's hand thinned out and disappeared. His face relaxed and his body drooped.

And something was happening to me too. I could feel the thick poisonous ache that had been killing me from inside loosen its grip. A healing flow, light and gentle, gathered strength and moved around me.

The feeling moved to every corner of my body, my legs and arms, my chest and head. My toes started to tingle. I wiggled them. How long had they been numb? I didn't know, but I could sure feel them now.

The dull, gray sickness melted and thinned and vanished. I could breathe, my heart was beating strongly.

I could have shouted with joy.

It was like being born again. Although, to be honest, I don't remember the first time too well. Must ask Mom.

Ronnie and I looked at each other. We knew what we had to do.

We had to complete the circle. Our free hands were linked via the scroll. So we stretched and strained the hands that were still tied to the pole. We touched fingers.

And the world exploded.

AARON STERN

1.

I was hardly aware when Plensk forced Mishi's hand onto the scroll. I would've tried to stop him but I was a little preoccupied at the time, what with my right hand being barbecued. The skin had peeled away from the nails, which were cracking, and taking on a blue-black glossiness. Fiery stabs of pain shot through my whole body, the smell of my own burning flesh seared itself into my nostrils.

But as soon as Mishi's hand closed around the scroll everything changed. Healing warmth flowed into my hand. The scorching pain subsided to a dull throb. The putrid smoke dissipated and blew away.

I tore my eyes away from the blackened ruin at the end of my arm, and turned to Mishi. My heart leapt when I saw her eyes clear of pain. We looked at each other. We were tied up, and held captive by murderous lunatics bent on destroying the world with an ancient artifact of unstoppable power. But we could have laughed for the sheer joy of beingalive.

We both knew what we had to do. I can't explain it. We weren't two people agreeing on something. We were one. With one thought process.

Our tied hands found their way to each other until our fingers could touch. A lot happened when they did. I can only describe what I saw and felt.

It was as if someone had sewn a nuclear device into my chest and hers. And when Mishi's fingers met mine, it detonated.

A wave of energy exploded from us in all directions. I saw the Plensk guy flying like a ragdoll across the room. He landed at Sally Portland's feet, where she stood flattened against a wall. Singh was thrown into McInnes and they were writhing on the floor. Snell seemed to be out cold. Lassiter was holding onto a handrail and had managed to stay upright. I couldn't see the Professor dude until a pile of clothes and robes groaned and moved. He disentangled himself and tried to sit up.

Lassiter and his crew began to collect themselves.

But they looked all distorted, like I was looking at them through badly made glass. Glass that kept moving and changing, and casting a golden light over them. I looked up and down and sideways, in each direction.

Mishi and I were enclosed in a sphere of coruscating golden light.

We looked at each other and this time we did laugh.

The swirling vortex had stopped. The golden letters of the Revelation, and the ribbons of energy and light, were drifting and hovering, as if they were waiting for someone to command them, to tell them what to do.

I knew what they should do. And I'd have told them if I knew what language they spoke. Get back to where you belong and make sure those occult protections are good and strong. And be snappy about it.

But I didn't have to give the command out loud because they read my mind. Or I guess they did because, as soon as that thought had crystalized, the letters and the golden threads began to spin and weave around the room again, but in the opposite direction.

Svensson was sitting up, his head turning left and right, looking at this gathering whirlwind of light, now flowing clockwise around the observation level.

His face was a mask of panic.

"Lassiter!" he shouted above the building roar. "Stop them! It is going into reverse. Stop them!"

The golden streams were now peeling off from the tornado in the room and flowing out the way they'd come, through roof and floor and walls. The fiery letters, first in ones and twos, then in swarms, flew toward Mishi and me, they passed through the golden sphere and through our hands into the scroll, and disappeared.

Lassiter looked around, his eyes wild and his hands waving.

"Shoot! Shoot them! McInnes, Portland, Singh shoot them!"

Lassiter's cronies were still collecting themselves. No one was reacting. They were dazed and disoriented.

McInnes picked up his pistol but he looked at it as if he didn't know what it was for. Singh also had a handgun. He was looking at Lassiter with his mouth open. But he wasn't moving.

Lassiter pushed himself away from the handrail. He staggered across to Singh, weaving like he was drunk.

He wrenched the gun from Singh's hand. He managed to work the slide then turned toward Mishi and me. He looked much too familiar with that weapon for comfort. And the look of murder in his eye didn't help either.

2.

Mishi and I stood side-by-side, the fingers of our tied hands were entwined. Our other hands were holding the Moses Revelation, the Scroll of Moses's Hidden Teaching. Healing energies were weaving in and around us, forming that protective shell of golden light. Filling us with joy and strength.

We watched Lassiter pick his way toward us, closing the gap.

He passed Plensk, who was sitting with his back against the wall. Plensk's left arm was twisted at a gruesome angle, his face was white with pain. He looked up at Lassiter and saw what he was going to do. He grabbed at Lassiter's ankle.

"No," Plensk gasped. "Don't. Don't hurt them."

Lassiter glanced down at Plensk, and shot him.

Plensk fell back against the wall. Lassiter watched the red stain spreading across the army jacket. He couldn't have looked at road kill with less emotion. All his fury and mania had gone, now he was a machine. And Mishi and I had moved right to the top of his to do list.

I watched him approach and felt a stirring in my chest. It was light and tentative at first, but it quickly gathered strength and power. That atom bomb was getting ready for another explosion. This time its entire focus was on the homicidal freak coming toward us, pointing a gun at my little sister.

Cold black hatred surged up from my gut.

A sense of delicious fierce joy filled my heart.

I knew I could unleash this cosmic force with the power of a single thought. I could destroy Lassiter in the blink of an eye.

In front of me, in the rippling golden light, a face began to appear, a man but distorted, like an animal face as well. The eyes were cat slits, and rising from the top of the head was a pair of goat's horns. The face was grinning, eager, hungry. Urging me on. The vicious joy was burning me up. And I saw a path shaping itself in front of me. A road to power and strength and might. The goat-horned man was laying out a path just for me, to riches and success. He promised me that I could have everything I had ever wanted, and things I didn't even know I wanted. All I had to do was bow down to him, to worship him.

Time stood still. Lassiter was frozen in position holding the gun, pointing it straight at us. Everyone else around the observation deck were statues.

Then I felt something tickle my left hand. And a voice in my head said, "No." It was Mishi's voice.

I stopped. Mishi tickled my hand again.

I looked down and saw her gazing up at me. I saw her friendly smile, and her freckled nose, and she gave a small shake of those brown curls.

They told me everything I needed to hear.

Stop. Don't do it, don't misuse this power. Even if the guy totally deserves it. Even if he is trying to destroy all that is good in the world. Even if he has tried to kill us. Even if he is trying again, right now.

Not out of anger and hatred.

I smiled down at Mishi and nodded. I felt the fury go. I looked back at Lassiter through the golden sphere of light. And right through the transparent image of the goat-man, which faded away with my anger.

I focused on Lassiter. I saw a tired, pathetic man. Puffed up by a pitiful sense of his own importance. Drawn by degrees into a world of conspiracy and evil that he didn't fully comprehend.

I understood him. I felt sorry for him. I even kind of liked him. And *that's* when I killed him.

3.

But first I said, "Don't shoot, Lassiter." I needed to give him a chance.

But he wasn't in the mood for a chat. He raised the gun and fired. And kept firing, over and over again straight at Mishi and me.

Each bullet ricocheted off the sphere of light, and sprayed around the room. Stone chips flew from the walls, one of the viewing windows shattered. McInnes and Singh dived for cover. Svensson was lying in a fetal position, tangled in his dress-up costume. Snell was on his knees, with his head down on the floor covered by his hands, his ass was in the air presenting a rather tempting target.

Plensk was in no condition to do anything.

Lassiter took another step toward us, changing clips when he ran out of bullets.

This evil had to be brought to an end. For Lassiter's sake. There was only one way that was going to happen. I closed my eyes and concentrated.

One more shot rang out, and the firing stopped.

When I opened my eyes Lassiter was on his back with a neat hole in the exact center of his forehead. His head was lying in a halo of blood spreading out over the floor around him.

"Wow!" said Mishi. "Did you do that?"

"Yep," I said. "At least I think I did. I saw it in my mind, I saw Lassiter lying there, while he was still shooting at us. It seemed the easiest thing in the world to let one of his own bullets find his forehead."

"Awesome," said Mishi, with that slow nod and turned-down mouth you make when a totally cool thing has just happened.

I felt quite gratified. My sister was not, as a rule, easily impressed.

4.

After that it was all a bit of a blur. We were still tied up, and holding the scroll. But the energy filling the room was dissipating. The golden sphere was fading. I looked over at Katie and she gave me a weak smile. She had been over in a corner out of the firing line.

McInnes, Singh and Svensson, after the initial shock of Lassiter's abrupt exit, were recovering. McInnes was fingering his gun in a way I didn't like. But blood was oozing from his cheek and shoulder in a way that I did.

Svensson was getting up and dusting himself off, and Singh was doing the same. Snell stayed in his tush-in-the-air yoga pose begging for mercy, until Singh hauled him to his feet.

It was only later that I realized Sally Portland wasn't there. We never did find out how she got away. Maybe she'd brought her broomstick with her.

Plensk moved and moaned. Good, I thought, the one guy who had come to his senses and had tried to help. He was alive.

Katie made a sudden move, which got my attention. She had turned at the sound of the elevator pinging and its doors opening.

My heart sank. More of Lassiter's goons.

Then my Mom came into the room, took one look at Mishi and me, and leapt over the sprawling bodies like a gazelle. A very worried, and ecstatic, gazelle. A gazelle dressed head to foot in black. Way to go Mom.

She was followed by Dr. Califario, Wolfgang and Mordecai, along with a guy in military camouflage. I found out later he was Colonel Landon McAllister. And all of them had guns drawn. Righteous.

Mom cut through our cable ties and grabbed Mishi and me in a bear hug. The scroll clattered to the floor. Mom wasn't capable of speech. Neither were we, come to that.

I could see Mordecai, his arm in a sling, cut through Katie's restraints, then he went over to look after Plensk. Katie rubbed her wrists, got up and scooted over to join Mishi and me and Mom.

The army guy disarmed McInnes and Singh, and Wolfgang grabbed Svensson and Snell to complete the set.

After that it was hugs and kisses and tears, until Katie saw my hand. In the excitement and relief I had forgotten about it. Can you believe that?

But when Katie cried out the pain returned, turned up to eleven. I grabbed my right wrist with my left hand and fell to my knees. The gash on my cheek and the bullet wound in my arm and ribs were nothing compared to this.

Mom put her arm around my shoulders. Katie was stroking my head and back, and Mishi was kneeling in front of me with tears streaming down her cheeks. I certainly didn't lack for female companionship. Too bad I was in a hot world of private torment, and in no condition to appreciate it.

Dr. Califario had been supervising the round-up of Lassiter's crew and the salvaging of the Moses scroll safely back into its pouch. Now he came over to our little family group.

I couldn't see his face but I felt his warmth and concern. Literally. The pain reduced a notch just because he was standing there. Who was this guy?

He asked the women to give him a little room. He knelt down and examined my hand. It was the first time I wondered if 'Doctor' meant, you know, *Doctor*. He called Mordecai over.

Mordecai had a backpack, which he placed on the floor. He unzipped it and pulled out a first aid kit. Dr. Califario took a hypodermic and injected me with something that made my head go woozy, and the pain go away. It sure got my vote.

Then everyone got to work with tubes of anaesthetic cream, rolls of gauze, and swathes of bandages. When all that was over, at the end of my right arm I had a white cloth club.

Then they did the same for the sundry cuts, bruises and bullet holes I'd collected on my holiday travels.

Finally they moved us down the stairs to the next level to catch the elevator and a bunch of us went down together. George Washington was still there to greet us when the elevator doors opened. I gave him a friendly nod and we walked through the lobby, out of the entrance, and across the Mall to some waiting cars. I was still groggy when I climbed into a black Ford Explorer with three rows of seats. Mishi was with Mom in the back. It didn't look like Mom was ever going to let her go again, ever.

Katie and I got into the middle seats together. Dr. Califario was in the front passenger seat next to Colonel McAllister.

Katie clipped my seatbelt in. I put my head on her shoulder, and fell asleep.

Next thing we were pulling into an airfield, climbing aboard another executive jet. I missed the take off. When I woke again Mishi and Katie were sitting in rear-facing seats opposite Mom and me. Mom was holding my good hand. She was crying again, but she looked a lot happier. Mishi had her arm through Katie's and her head on Katie's shoulder. They were smiling at me. But I think they were crying a little too. I tried to summon up the energy to ask where we were going, but I fell asleep before I could get the words out.

The Maleficium et MaledictionesArcanum

Secret Crimes and Curses

of

Baphomet, Lord of the Underworld, Prince of Darkness, Bringer of Pestilence and Purveyor of Plagues

As transcribed in a trance by
LeonardoDaSilva,
Magus and Initiate into the Mysteries of Demonic Wisdom

Extract 7: Canto VII, Verse 1

1. And when the Four become One, the Power of the Most High will shine on the Earth, the Word will catch Fire, the Gates of the Mighty will be thrown down, and Darkness and Light will struggle, and there will be a weeping and wailing and a gnashing of teeth. The Chosen of God will pass through the Fire. And the seals will be resealed, and the Gates re-barred...

EPILOGUE

AARON STERN

1.

The Twelfth Vision

I was in another one of those visions. This time I was following a young woman with a blond ponytail, keeping pace with her as she walked purposefully from the sidewalk up some stairs toward a set of revolving glass doors. She was dressed in a navy-blue pantsuit and was carrying a black leather briefcase. She entered the building and walked straight across the cavernous lobby, weaving smoothly past men and women wearing a mix of business suits and military uniforms. Her high heels, black and mirror polished, clacked sharply over the marble floor, inlaid with the great seal of the United States of America.

I could only see her from behind, but she seemed familiar. She walked like Katie and she had Katie's build, but she looked different, maybe a little older?

She showed a lanyard ID to a security guard, put her briefcase on the X-ray conveyer, and walked through the metal detector.

She picked up her briefcase and went to the long mahogany reception desk.

"General Landon McAllister, please. He's expecting me."

'General'? I thought. He was a Colonel, surely. Could there be two Landon McAllisters in the army?

"And your name Miss?"

"Rachel Stern."

That was another coincidence. Intriguing.

"Please proceed to the elevator six Ms. Stern."

Rachel Stern walked with Katie's walk and Katie's blond ponytail to the elevators. I hadn't seen her face, so when she got to the elevators and turned around to survey the entrance foyer I was taken aback. She could have been Katie's sister. Except Katie didn't have a sister and this girl's eyes weren't the clear blue that made my heart melt. They were a deep brown. They were more like my eyes. And my heart was melting anyway.

The elevator dinged and a man who could have been Landon McAllister's father stepped out. Same height, same ramrod back, but with more lines on his face, and salt and pepper in his hair.

What was going on here? A Katie look-alike, and now Colonel Landon McAllister, aged and promoted.

"Rachel, good to see you."

"You too, General." They shook hands.

"How was your flight?"

"Uneventful. I had time to go over the proposal."

"Great," said the General, turning to the elevator console and waving a key card in front of the panel. "Let's go upstairs and go over it. Your father's plans are always very creative, and your mother makes sure they'll actually work."

"Tell me about it," she said, rolling her eyes, "I grew up with them."

"And now you all work together. How's that working out?"

"It's actually totally great. But if you ever tell them I said so, you're off my Christmas and Hanukkah card list."

"I won't breathe a word. So tell me, how are Ron and Katie?"

"Oh Mom and Dad are fine. They send their love, of course."

"And your Aunt Mishi?"

The scene faded away.

2.

I woke up, desperate to see more of this... this what? A vision? A dream? A product of my fevered imagination and my recent adventures, and that nice stuff they kept pumping into my arm?

It took me a few moments to drag myself back to the here and now to take stock. I was in a room, lying in a bed looking up at a white painted ceiling. In my peripheral vision I could see hospital paraphernalia, machinery and clutter.

"Good, you're awake," said Dr. Califario.

I turned my head to the left. He was sitting in a visitor's chair, a book resting on his lap.

"Hello, Doctor," I said. "Where am I?"

"Mt Sinai Hospital," he replied. "You're home. In LA."

"That's nice," I said, my head felt light. "And how long have I been here?"

"Two days," he said.

"Wow, that's a long time. I don't remember any of it."

"We'll get to what you remember and what you don't in due course," he said. "For now we have something a bit more pressing and I needed you conscious for it to work."

"Work?" I said, slurring my words. "What do you mean? What are we going to do?"

Dr. Califario didn't answer directly. Instead he put his book down, stood up and walked around to the right-hand side of the bed.

He carefully lifted my hand, which was completely covered in clean bandages. The whole burning thing came flooding back, and my hand started aching and throbbing.

With practiced efficiency Dr. Califario unwrapped the bandages, exposing a blackened claw.

He held my wrist with his left hand, and gently stroked the damaged skin with his right forefinger.

I felt the healing flow straight away. So many times the pain and suffering and disease of others had flowed up that hand. This time the warm healing flowed into me, from Dr. Califario.

I looked at him. Was he absorbing the pain? He had his eyes closed, and he looked calm. He touched my hand for a long time. I think I even drifted off to sleep at one point.

When he was satisfied he re-bandaged my hand.

"You know," he said, conversationally. "The medical fraternity was unanimous. The hand was too far-gone. Your mother had to fight tooth and nail to stop them amputating it. So, let's hope a little magic will help things along, eh?"

Then he looked at me seriously. "Actually, I believe that what just happened here will restore much to your hand, but I think it will always bear some mark of your injury. And Aaron Stern, hear me when I say this, that injury, and the others you sustained, are a badge of honor. I wanted to say this to you before the others came in. What you did over the past few weeks was extraordinary. All of you, Katie, Mishi and even that friend of yours, Melvin. I was, I am, most impressed. And I thank you."

"Gee, that's very kind of you," I stammered, no marks for oratory. "Mishi and Katie?"

"They are both fine. Your sister is remarkable. She is back to her usual self."

"Uh oh, that bad?"

Dr. Califario laughed. "Yes, I'm afraid so. Medically she is as healthy as ever. You must tell me how that came about. But not now. When your strength has returned."

"And Katie?"

"She too is fine. Some bumps and bruises, but she is also a very resilient young woman."

That was a huge relief.

"Have you any more questions?" he asked.

I thought for a moment. "What happened to that Plensk guy?"

Dr. Califario laughed. "This is your first question? Why him?"

"He tried to stop Lassiter, and Lassiter shot him. He was trying to become one of the good guys."

"After all the excitement, Colonel McAllister called in the DC police and explained that some criminal dealings were taking place. McInnes, Singh and Svensson, and your friend Snell, were arrested. But Plensk was badly injured so he is presently under guard in a DC hospital. I will make enquiries for you. They will of course have questions for you and Mishi."

"Sure, happy to oblige," I said. "There was a woman. A real piece of work, Sally Portland. She poisoned Mishi."

"There was no trace of her. We still don't know how she managed to elude us. A very capable and dangerous woman. But the police are looking.

And we have resources as well. We will find her."

"What about the guys at the YMCA?" I said, the image of that bloody wreck on the floor made me shudder.

"Yes, it took a little while for McAllister to get back to check. The Organization must have been busy because the room you were held in was completely cleaned by the time he got there."

"What!" I tried to sit up, but that wasn't going to happen. "There was the guy with the knee. I shot him... And the other guy..."

"Perhaps it's a blessing," said Dr. Califario. "There is just so much the police can be told. If they don't ask about that episode, I feel there is no need to trouble them."

"I guess," I said. "And the Moses Revelation. I'm..."

"You're sorry for stealing it?"

"Yes," I looked up at him. "They wouldn't have got as far as they did without it."

"Can I tell you how I see it?"

"Sure, knock yourself out."

"A young girl is abducted by despicable brutes. Her brother drops everything and races down every possible avenue to rescue her. He even commits a felony, for which, may I say, he shows a surprising and troubling aptitude. Then, with a depth of courage we who were spectators can only wonder at, he attempts to outwit the kidnappers, and he enters the lions' den alone. He defeats several of his guards, takes their weapons, tries to send his sister and girlfriend out of harm's way, and goes back again into the firing line. Alone. That's what I see. What do you see?"

I was squirming with embarrassment at this retelling.

I wanted to tell him that wasn't how it happened. I wanted to tell him of the fear and the blunders and the missteps.

"Mishi needed the antidote," was all I could manage. I wanted to say more but he smiled at me and the words disappeared.

"And at each turn of events," he continued, "this astonishing young man stuck to his course. And won through. You say that they wouldn't have got as far as they did, but look what happened. Those mystic barriers protecting this great nation are now stronger than ever. Because of you, my friend. And the Moses Revelation? Back where it belongs. Think about that."

I was beginning to think about it when the door burst open and a crowd came pouring in.

3.

I got squeezed harder than I can remember in such a short time frame. Lucky I was up to the eyeballs in painkillers. Mom first, while Dad held my good hand and pumped it like he was trying to strike oil.

"Miriam," Dad said finally, "leave him. You want you should break his neck with your hugging? And I see there are some others who want a piece of the action."

I nodded gratefully at Dad. Mom sat back and held me by the shoulders and looked at me, her head tilted and tears streaming down her cheeks.

She sneaked in one more hug, and then it was Katie's turn. She didn't seem able to speak either, and my shoulder was getting soaked.

"Oh Ronnie," she managed a few times.

Then Mishi was standing next to the bed with her hands on her hips looking daggers at me.

"If you ever pull a stunt like that again," she said.

I missed the next bit because my cheek and arm and ribs and hand started skewering me with daggers of pain. I was laughing, and yelping, at the same time.

"Oh, you are so annoying," said Mishi, and then she came diving in and clamped on to me like she'd never let me go.

"OK," she said, finally. "If ever I'm in danger again, you have my permission to come and rescue me."

"Gee, Sis, thanks," I said. "That's the nicest thing you've ever said to me. Except, I seem to remember right after I got shot you said..."

"Don't you dare!" she shouted, and she was laughing too.

Then it was Mordecai, and Melvin who, for some reason, had brought a supersized cup of hot chocolate. "After all, doesn't everyone drink hot chocolate after saving the world and getting the girl." Nodding at Katie who was now sitting on the bed holding my left hand like she'd got the title deeds. I looked at her beautiful profile, her blond ponytail, and those gorgeous blue eyes, and I wondered if there really was a Rachel Stern in our future. I kind of hoped there would be.

Melvin wiggled his eyebrows and the Styrofoam cup at me.

"I don't know buddy," I said to him. "Do they? Drink hot chocolate? All I know is I'm glad it's over, I'm extremely happy to be home, and I hope I never have to do anything like that again."

Oh well, as events were to prove, two out of three ain't bad.

THE END

And now a preview of:

THE WARRIORS OF THE ELDERS

Book 2 in The Elders Series

THE WARRIORS OF THE ELDERS

Book 2 in the Elders Series

Xianyang, China, 215BC

Hong So the magician, bowed until his head touched the cold marble floor of the vast Audience Chamber in the Imperial Palace of His Serene Highness, The Son of Heaven, The Supreme Lord of the Middle Kingdom, the Great Emperor Qin Shi Huang.

Standing next to the Great Emperor his hands hidden in the sleeves of the red silk gown, decorated with dragons and occult symbols was His Excellency Xu Fu, Lord of the Spirit World, Summoner of Apparitions, Chief Necromancer to the Great Emperor.

At the many doors which led into the Audience Chamber were guards in polished armor. Around the walls stood ministers, courtiers and officials in an exact hierarchy governed by the detailed dictates of the court rules. These high court officials watched Hong So the magician, a tiny figure in the centre of the vast hall, make the required seven genuflections to the throne of the Great and Terrible Emperor. An observant watcher might have detected the tiniest shudder pass through body of the kneeling peasant.

Weeks before, when the summons to the court to display his prowess had reached Hong So's mud-streaked hands, he had been puffed up with pride. His fame had reached the ear of the highest in the land. He had boasted over distilled rice wine to the men of his village.

Hong So the magician had not been entirely clear which of his wonder cures, magic spells or elixirs had prompted this unprecedented honour. That shower of rain after the prolonged dry spell? The old lady who found she no longer needed her walking stick? Or was it the new village well, dug where Hong So had pointed with such confidence? Hong So the village magician did not know. But this he did know, his fortune was made.

When his wife had been caught gossiping to her friends about her husband's forthcoming journey to Xianyang, the great capital of the Middle Kingdom, he had given her only a mild scolding.

The day after the summons had arrived Hong So the magician made his preparations. He offered prayers to his ancestors. He carefully packed up boxes of powders and jars of potions. Then he loaded the cart and hitched the ox, and set off on the two-week journey to the capital.

When he finally arrived in Xianyang, Hong So the magician had worked hard to hide his dismay at the crowds of people, the smell and the filth of the streets, the lurking dangers in the back alleys. He had found few who could even understand him when he spoke.

But the precious written summons bearing the seal of Xu Fu himself, Lord High Necromancer to His Imperial Highness, had eventually opened doors and cleared paths.

Three days after his arrival in Xianyang, Hong So had put on his best robe, shouldered his travelling bag carefully packed with the powders and potions, and had stepped through a postern door set into a tall red lacquered gate separating the hurly-burly of the streets from the rarefied world of the court.

The first thing that Hong So the magician had noticed was the silence, broken only by the gentle splashing of fountains and the singing of tiny blue birds that chased each other through the shady trees.

He had been met at the postern by an unsmiling court official who scanned the invitation, ordered Hong So to follow, and had turned on his heel. The magician scurried after him, the regulation three paces behind. They walked along endless paths, past gardens, through arches, along porticos until they reached a set of external stairs that climbed the eastern wall of the palace to a small door.

They passed through the door out of the bright sunshine into the semi-gloom. Their feet whispered along miles of corridors until the magician's head spun. Hong So lost count of the paintings, suits of armor, swords, vases, tables and other imperial bric-a-brac. Nor could he number the stern guards standing at regular intervals along the way, their weapons sharpened to a gleaming edge.

And the mirrors! Hundreds, perhaps thousands of polished brass mirrors, fixed to the walls, hanging from silken cords, different shapes, different angles, all reflecting back to Hong So hundreds of images of a short stocky country magician with a thin beard and red cheeks hurrying to keep up with the courtier.

It was, after all, a well-known fact, settled science, that demons, sprites and imps were confused by their own reflections, disoriented by polished surfaces, beguiled by seeing themselves and others in shiny objects. This everyone knew. The more powerful overlords of the demon world, no, they needed to be kept at bay by stronger magic. But your every day goblins, pixies and such like? Polished brass, incense, the orientation of rooms, and the shape of the roof. These were just basic common sense.

The powders and potions in his bag grew heavier and heavier as they processed along hallways, through doors and up and down stairs.

With every step along these superb corridors past those magnificent ornaments, the confidence of Hong So the magician seeped away. He fought in vain to keep down the unease that traitorously climbed up from his bowels and made his heart knock at his chest.

"We are here," said his guide stopping so abruptly that the magician dug his toes into the polished wooden floor to prevent himself sliding into the man.

Hong So bowed as low as he could without toppling over.

"Oh, Your Excellency..."

The courtier cut him off with a wave of his hand.

"Be silent, Fool," he said, "That title is reserved for Level Twelve Court Officials and above. I have the immeasurable honour to serve his Serene Majesty as a Level Eight Scribe in the office of Xu Fu, Chief Necromancer to The Great Emperor, the Right Hand of His Serene Highness, Ruler of the World."

"Oh yes, yes," the magician was bowing again and again, breathing hard, and sweating profusely, "forgive my unpardonable stupidity. May I admit my inexcusable ignorance and beg you to tell me how I should address you."

"You may," said the Court Official thawing to a minute degree, "address me and those of the equivalent rank as 'Noble Sir'."

"Oh, Noble Sir," Hong So gushed, "You honour me beyond my insignificant worth."

"Yes, yes, that is all very well, here is your room," the courtier waved towards a plain wooden door. "You will prepare and be ready in one hour."

"Thank you, Noble Sir," said the magician, the panic beginning to peep around the corner of his consciousness again, "But what am I to prepare, and for whom?"

It was the next sentence that opened a bottomless abyss beneath his feet.

"Word has reached the ear of the court," said the Official pulling a slip of paper from his sleeve and consulting it, "that you have the knowledge of an elixir which grants all who drink it the power to rise from the dead. Prepare this elixir and be ready to demonstrate its potency. You have one hour."

"Oh Your Exc... Noble Sir," his mental wheels spinning, "to whom shall I make this demonstration?"

But he already knew the answer. The Great Emperor's fear of demonic spirits and terror of death was famous throughout the recently unified kingdoms of the Qin Empire.

Hong So the magician was now fully engulfed by the horror of his situation.

"You will demonstrate your elixir to His Serene Highness, Lord of the Middle Kingdom, the Great Emperor himself," said the courtier allowing the smallest hint of a smile to crease his lips. "How I envy you. You, a humble peasant have been raised from the filth of a country village to demonstrate the power of your elixir of eternal life to the Great Emperor Qin Shi Huang himself. At least I hope, for your sake, you do."

THE WARRIORS OF THE ELDERS

Book 2 in the Elders Series

Due out in early 2018

www.gilbertmane.com

ABOUT THE AUTHOR

Gilbert S Mane spends his days writing the sort of thrillers he wants to read. He is a writer, keynote speaker and educational consultant. He started his working life as a lawyer. After a decade of that he jumped at the offer of becoming Headmaster of John Colet School in Sydney. He did that for twenty-six years. He now enjoys writing and speaking, and helping other school principals and staff. He also gets in as much ballroom dancing as he can. About being a lawyer? Better you shouldn't ask! He lives (and dances) happily in Sydney, Australia with his wife.